SECRETS OF THE STARS

BY APRIL ADAMS

First eBook Edition: August 2025

ISBN: 979-8-218-67741-1

Cover design by Tracey Thompson

I have one sister by blood but many by bond. You are all my ride or dies. A special thanks to Shan and Em, you helped shape me into the woman I am.

TABLE OF CONTENTS

# PROLOGUE

- A secret is giving your word. And, brick by brick, your prison is made.

Faith pulled Gwendolyn into an embrace and held her. Held her tight. Their hair, thick and long and an equal mixture of gold and brown, fell together and was stirred by the breeze. The strands were momentarily indistinguishable to the human, or elfin, eye as to which locks of hair belonged to which sister.

Overhead, the night sky over the moon of Dione was a drape of black velvet, pierced with the shards of distant stars and the reflective glow from Saturn's other moons.

"I'm scared," Gwendolyn whispered into the ear of the woman who, though separated by five years, was her twin.

Faith held onto her biodentical sister and stroked her hair. "I know," she acknowledged gently before she pulled away, still gripping Gwendolyn firmly by the shoulders. "But you are going to be fine. Doctor de Rossi!" she added, a grin splitting her face.

For once, Gwendolyn's face was not a mirror of the woman in front of her.

"Ugh! Absolutely not!" she exclaimed. "I'll play your game," she agreed with a dour expression. "I'll masquerade around as you, wearing your ridiculously uncomfortable and even more ridiculously expensive shoes..." she said, fighting a smile while

Faith tipped her head back, laughing softly "...but I refuse to be called doctor. That's too much."

"Alright," Faith conceded. "But you absolutely have to be me. No wavering. No waffling."

Now it was Gwen's turn to laugh. "No waffling? Very well." She straightened her shoulders theatrically, placing her right hand over the left side of her chest as she held her left hand up, palm out. "I hereby promise not to waffle or waver until your imminent return to relieve me from duty." She lowered her hand and gave her sister a congenial but dubious smile. "Which will be...?"

Faith chuckled, the dry night breeze pushing her hair back from her face. "A few weeks." Gwen hoisted her eyebrows in suspicion, turning her twin's chuckle into laughter. "You got me," Faith confessed. "I'm going to squeeze in a trip to Earth so it will probably be two months, possibly three. I seriously doubt it will be longer. A few days more or less will be of no consequence. Appointments and reminders will pop up on the mainframe vanity. Just follow the notes attached to them, if you need to."

"Will I be able to talk to you?"

"Of course," Faith answered. "But only in absolute privacy. No one must know."

Gwen nodded in understanding then tilted her head to the side and smiled. She reached up and cupped Faith's face with her right hand, letting the ball of her thumb trace the bone of her sister's cheek. "Love," she said.

Faith reached up with her left hand and gently grasped Gwendolyn's wrist. "Love," she replied. She leaned forward and gave her twin a kiss on the cheek. "You are going to be just fine," she assured her.

"And you?" Gwen challenged.

Faith laughed lightly. "I'll always be fine if I have work to do...and if I know that you are alright." She gave her twin a look of love and admiration, and let her go.

The bioengineer who had earned her first doctorate at twenty-five, turned and walked away to the waiting transport. She felt she was embarking on one of the most challenging things she had ever done. Knowing that, however, made it better.

Gwendolyn watched her go, stealing herself against the loneliness that wanted to close over her heart.

I'm her now, I am Faith, she thought with a wave of responsibility, nostalgia and apprehension that was followed by a throaty chuckle. *And Faith would not waste time on any such emotion.* She sighed, clasping her hands in front of her body as she watched her twin stride up the ramp of the spacecraft. *What would Faith do?* Gwen thought and then laughed out loud. *She'd get to work, of course.*

With that in mind, she turned on her heel and walked back into the compound before the woman everyone knew as Faith de Rossi disappeared from sight.

Dr. Faith de Rossi boarded the craft via a ramp, carrying just a small satchel. It was a large and fairly luxurious vessel, but one she had chosen for other reasons entirely.

The Captain, dark-haired and blue-eyed, wore his most tight-fitting uniform and greeted her at the top of the ramp to welcome her aboard. It was not a common practice for him, but he was not above what he hoped might be a flirtatious encounter with a woman who was quickly becoming one of the wealthiest figures in the universe. One look into her eyes, however – which, like her hair, were a fetching combination of brown and gold – told him it would be a waste of time.

Still, he gave it a try.

"It is pleasure to be working for you this evening, Dr. de Rossi," he greeted formally. "I am Captain Arbiter." Faith bit the inside of her cheek to keep from smiling, wondering if kids in school used to call him Arse-biter. She acknowledged him with a nod as he escorted her into the vessel. "We should be at the first Thermopylae by morning, local time. There is a private bedroom if you would like to sleep or..."

"No thank you," Faith interrupted as she followed him through a metal entryway to where steel walls and floors gave way to softer, darker textiles. "I have work to do."

The Captain responded with a curt nod and led her through a door into a comfortably appointed lounge area. The floor was covered with a thick carpet and the walls were paneled with fabricated wood. There was a couch facing a low table and several straight-backed chairs with velvet padding.

"Thank you," Faith told him with a bit of a gracious smile. "This will work perfectly."

The Captain gave her another nod and motioned to a side table next to the couch. "The green sensor on the side there will summon a steward. The black one will give you direct communication with myself and the copilot. Your assistant had your things placed in the larger of the bedrooms so, whenever you wish to retire, your quarters will be ready for you."

"I doubt I will need them," she replied with a smile as cold as the waters on Europa. "But thank you."

The dark-haired Captain gave her a short bow. "Very well. Please secure your safety webbing until we are into orbit."

Faith sat herself on the couch as he left, unable to keep from shaking her head in exasperation. She found the safety webbing deep in the edge of the cushion and pulled it across her lap, securing it into the lock on the opposite edge of the cushion. She put her satchel down beside her and pulled her portable compute from it, placing it on the low table in front of her. She felt it drop suddenly at the last second, as if sucked down, and knew that the table was topped with magnetic glass to prevent such items from sliding around. Or worse, flying around.

Within a few moments the voice of the Captain came on

over the com, coming from unseen speakers, announcing their clearance for departure, but Faith was already deep into her work on the compute. She was unaware of their lift-off or at what moment they cleared the atmosphere. He gave another broadcast when they were clear of Dione and approaching Jupiter, and another a few minutes later letting her know to buzz him if there was anything to be done to make her more comfortable.

She did not respond to either announcement vocally but gave an enthusiastic and caustic mental reply of *thank you Captain Arse-biter* as she typed biothermic equations into her compute. She supposed she should be comforted that men and their behaviors held no surprises for her.

She was proved wrong in less than a minute.

Only seconds later her assistant, her *male* assistant, who was supposed to have remained at the compound to help Gwendolyn - walked into the room with a chill bucket and a champagne flute. Tall and slim and prim in an impeccable gray suit, his skin dark brown and his face completely without expression, Thomas set the chill bucket on its stand and removed the bottle inside.

His cool nonchalance was countered by Faith's shock, so great that for a moment she was rendered speechless.

"Thomas!" she finally exclaimed. The tone of her voice had the fervor of a woman coming home to see her puppy piddling on the floor.

"Yes, Dr. de Rossi?" he asked, relieving the bottle of a rubber stopper before filling the empty glass.

Faith could only gape at him for a spattering of seconds, something else she never did. "What...what are you doing?" she demanded.

Thomas looked at her as if she had gone mad as he handed her the glass. "You told me you wanted to finish this bottle on your trip."

Faith's lips pressed into a line at his innocence, unsure of whether it was feigned or real, while she regained her composure. But regain it, she did. When she spoke, her voice was firm and measured. "What are you doing here, Thomas?"

The PA frowned. "You instructed me to pack for a six-week trip."

"I told you to pack *my* things for a six-week trip."

"Which I did," Thomas assured her.

Faith frowned at him, her jaw set. "It was my intention that you stay with Gwendolyn."

"Ah!" Thomas exclaimed softly, bringing his hands together as his head tipped back momentarily. "I believe you told me that Miss Gwendolyn was to take your place for a while and to help her out, which I did. I did not realize you meant for me to physically stay behind."

"Mmhm," Faith intoned as she sipped her champagne, her tawny eyes fixed on him over the rim of her glass.

"Besides," Thomas added, "Miss Gwendolyn has gotten along fine without me for decades. I am sure she will continue to do so, especially for just a few weeks."

Faith lowered her glass quickly. "Are you suggesting that I could not?" she demanded.

Thomas sighed and set his face in an expression that portrayed he was about to give news that was regretful but true. "In all honesty, Dr. de Rossi, I think you would be dead within a month. Starvation the most likely cause."

Faith felt her breath hitch at his audacity yet, at that moment and as if to emphasize his words, a steward strode through the aft door with a small tray laden with greens and fruits along with half of a turkey sandwich. Thomas took the plates from the tray and placed them on the table next to her compute, also laying down utensils and a napkin.

Faith glared at him as her stomach rumbled and the steward left the room. "I'm sure I could scare up, and subsist upon, champagne if need be."

Thomas dipped his head in polite agreement. "Which is why I gave you a month, rather than a week."

Faith's lips drew down at the corners as she gathered the half sandwich in the napkin and returned her attention to her screen. "Send my grandfather a request for a holo-con," she instructed. Thomas bowed and turned to leave. "And Thomas..."

The PA paused and turned back, waiting.

"I'm glad you are here."

Thomas' lips pressed out at the corners. "It is my pleasure, Dr. de Rossi."

He took his leave and Faith dug into her...lunch? Dinner? She honestly could not remember the last time she had eaten. When the sandwich was mostly done, she left the remains on the plate and drained her glass. Thomas was back in the room by the time she had put down the glass, followed by a steward. The steward cleared away the plate and wiped down the table while Thomas plucked the champagne bottle from the chiller and poured the last of it into her empty flute.

"Your grandfather is at an event that prohibits his appearance," he informed her. She accepted the glass with a wry smile.

"Your timing, as you, is always impeccable," she remarked.

Thomas nodded as if his actions were only what could be expected. He snapped his wrist from the end of his jacket sleeve and glanced at his watch. "It is 2 a.m. our time, so to speak. It is 4 p.m. in London. Your grandfather will be occupied for the next six hours, possibly more. It might be an opportune time to get some rest."

"I'm not tired," Faith informed him as the steward returned with a pillow and a neatly folded blanket. "Besides," she continued with a glare as Thomas relieved the man of the items, "I have work to do."

Thomas gave a curt nod as he placed the pillow on one end of the couch and the folded blanket on the other. "We will be going through the first Thermopylae in roughly twenty minutes. Would you like the Captain to keep you updated on our progress?"

"Certainly not. I would like a little peace and quiet so I can get my work done."

Thomas gave her a curt bow and followed the steward from the room. When he returned thirty minutes later, Faith was fast asleep with her head on the pillow. The PA shook out the blanket and laid it carefully over his employer before quietly closing her compute.

Faith awoke four hours later, needing to use the restroom. She sat up and used her pinkie fingers to clear away the grains of sleep that had gathered at the corners of her eyes. Thomas came through the door carrying a tray with a pot, a mug, and a pastry.

"The closest lavatory is through the door and to the left," he informed her as he began placing the items from the tray on the table.

Faith gave him a murmured thanks and left to relieve and refresh herself. When she returned, he was just pouring her coffee. She opened her compute and burrowed into her work, unconsciously sipping her coffee and nibbling at the pastry. Thomas refilled her mug twice as she worked through the next few hours. She was just wrapping up one project when she noticed her PA standing near and waiting for her attention.

"Your grandfather is standing by," he announced quietly.

"Excellent," Faith said, giving her hands two brisk claps while sliding her palms in opposite directions to rid them of any crumbs, vaguely wondering what she had eaten.

"We are also approaching the second Thermopylae," Thomas informed her. "Do you wish to hold the call until we are through?"

Faith shook her head vigorously. She closed her compute and moved it aside as Thomas leaned down to deposit a fat silver disc on the table. There was a clunk as it attached to the magnetic surface. To Faith, holo transmitters looked like metal doughnuts.

Is that what I ate? Faith thought, absently. A doughnut? Or was it a Danish? She realized it could have been moldy bread and she hardly would have noticed.

Thomas gathered up the remnants of her breakfast, judging by the flakes Faith guessed it had probably been a croissant, and left silently. Faith reached out and adjusted the position of the round transmitter and depressed the pin on the side. She sat back in her chair, combing her hair out with her fingers.

A rectangular piece on the side of the device dropped, revealing a lens that looked like a dollhouse window. A beam of blue light shot from the window and fanned out over Faith's head and then moved, traveling down her body to her waist. Then the light turned red and traveled back up, blinking out once it was done. After a moment, a white light poured out, this one surrounding her body like a second skin. Faith leaned forward, her skin aglow with holo light, and pushed the thick disc as far away as the table would allow. She did not need to have her grandfather's face only inches from her own.

She pressed a round button on the other side of the transmitter and then leaned back into her seat, smoothing down the front of her blouse.

From the hole in the doughnut rose a spiral of light that coalesced into a cone before widening out into a column a meter wide and a meter tall. Colors began to separate and take shape until they took the form of Cronus from the waist up, his trim figure sitting in a high-backed chair in his sumptuously appointed suite at the London Waldorf.

Steely gray hair was swept back from his aging yet smooth and handsome face. A fitted coat of navy blue covered a dress shirt as pale blue as a robin's egg. A paisley ascot trimmed with lace was tied at his throat, pinned with a jeweled broach.

His head raised as he saw his granddaughter and a broad smile overcame his normally stoic expression.

"Faith!"

"Hello, Grandfather," she replied, returning the smile as she took in the details of his ensemble. "How is the Queen?"

The elf's head gave a slight jerk, startled that she knew – or had guessed - of the exceptionally private dinner he had just left, before he gave a low chuckle at her perspicacity. "Alive, thanks to us," he shared. "Though her children are none too pleased. She has held the crown for four hundred years and has no plans to relinquish the throne. A few of them are getting quite antsy, I must say."

"She will need to watch her back," Faith agreed. "Greater Britannia has absorbed enough of the Euro Bloc to warrant an attack from without or within. She could face a revolt from within the royal house. Or a bad accident."

"Quite a few things are tenuous on this planet. Are you sure this is where you want to begin? We could buy a small moon in the Outer Banks, or in the Flower, where you could set your next plan into motion. No one would even know you were there."

Faith shook her head. "No, this is better. Shaky governments are better still. And, even better, if Gwendolyn convinces the universe that she is me, and I know she can, then no one will suspect me of being involved in this. They will think I was on Mimas or Dione the whole time. Besides, if any planet could use a reboot, it's Earth."

Over the ship's com she could hear the Captain advise everyone that they were on approach to the second Thermopylae and she mentally gauged where they would be coming through.

"Did you tell Gwendolyn what you are planning?" Cronus asked. "Or how long you would be gone?'

Faith shook her head, her gold and brown tresses undulating across her back. "No. I only told her I was going after Hope and paying a short visit to Earth. It's better if she takes one step at a time, and I set enough wheels in motion for her to do that."

"And you gave her the rings?" Cronus asked, leaning forward just a bit.

"I did, though I daresay I will be back long before she has the need to dole them out. If she even has the need to do so."

"Trust me, I certainly hope that charlatan was wrong, or even toying with me. But, just like you, I prefer to be prepared for anything."

"Something I understand completely," Faith agreed with a smile.

Cronus leaned back in his chair, pleased, and a smile touched the corners of his mouth. "I have a surprise for you when you get here."

Faith's own smile slipped from her face.

"Now, now, now," her grandfather chided at the sight of her darkened expression. "I know how you are..."

Faith eyes flicked up as Thomas entered with an uncorked bottle of champagne, a fresh chill bucket, and a glass glistening with frost.

Not a moment too soon, Faith thought, her eyes going back to her grandfather as Thomas filled the glass. He was about to leave it on the table, out of sight of the transmitter, but Faith motioned at him to hand it over.

The image of Cronus flickered and the sound of his voice was lost and then picked back up again.

"Faith?" he called, leaning forward in his chair. "Are you there?"

"We are going through the Thermopylae," she informed him. "I might lose you for a few seconds, but the transmission should still hold. We will be through it in a moment and it should be fine."

Her grandfather nodded in understanding and leaned back into his chair as he waited, not wanting to raise his voice or be forced to repeat himself. It would be unseemly.

A heartbeat later, as Thomas settled the champagne bottle into the chiller, they were indeed through, but far from fine. Cronus disappeared in a blink as the transmission was lost. The ship skewed hard to starboard as if it had collided with another craft. Alarms began going off everywhere.

Thomas was thrown sideways and stumbled, catching himself by grabbing a lamp that, thankfully and along with all the other furniture, had been bolted to the floor. The chill bucket was one of the few things not secured and went crashing down, disgorging the champagne bottle which was gracious enough not to explode. Its contents, however, glugged out unceremoniously in a bubbling foam that soaked into the carpet.

"Sit down, Thomas," Faith ordered, scowling at the wasted champagne. "Secure your safety webbing."

Thomas did as he was instructed, falling into the closest chair as the room tilted, one side rising high before slamming back down. It had the feel of a small boat on a stormy sea.

Faith's first instinct was to open a com with the cockpit and ask the Captain what was happening. But she knew that he would inform her directly, as soon as he had things in hand and, until then, it might be better not to disturb him.

The ship gave another sickening lurch, settled, and then the Captain came on over the com.

"Dr. de Rossi?"

"Yes?"

"Are you secure?"

"I am. We both are."

"We appear to be having a bit of trouble."

"So it would seem. Have we hit something?"

"Nothing that we can see," the Captain answered. "It feels like turbulence, except..."

"Except there is no turbulence in space," she finished for him. "What do you think we might have encountered? A solar storm?"

"Perhaps, but they are caused by solar flares and I'm not getting any readings or reports of flares."

The room bucked as if riding an angry beast. Thomas bit down on his tongue to quell a scream, determined not to show how frightened he really was. He watched Faith's face as she thought, knowing that her mind was racing faster than his heart. The muscles around her eyes and mouth went tight and he saw her jaw clench.

"Could it be from a bomb?" Faith asked the Captain. "A nuclear bomb?"

Silence came from the com and then Thomas could hear a murmur as the idea was put to another, most likely the copilot, in the control room. "It's possible," the Captain answered. "But who? Why? How?"

The room canted and turned. It felt as if they were sliding on slick ice. The Captain turned into the slide and righted the ship. Faith was angry enough to spit. She knew the who, the how, and the why. It was undoubtedly Hope.

"Captain, see if you can find the source and then see if it intersects the course you had originally plotted on my request."

There was a short pause and then his voice came back, quiet and speculative. "It does. How did you..."

"Keep to the same course," Faith instructed even as the ship began to skew again.

A soft laugh came over the com. "I'm sorry, Dr. de Rossi, but I am afraid I cannot do that."

"Captain Arbiter, I specifically selected this ship because…"

"It's not that I will not, Dr. de Rossi," the Captain interrupted, "I cannot. The ship is being pulled, somehow. I am so far unable to change the course on which it is being drawn. It is all I can do to keep us level."

"What are we being drawn towards?"

"Earth, thankfully. I'm sorry, Dr. de Rossi, but I am going to have to pick up this conversation later. It looks like this is going to get worse before it gets better."

As if to emphasize his words, the nose of the craft rose up like a ship cresting a dangerously high wave before slamming back down hard enough to make Faith's teeth come together with a click. Thomas blanched.

"Of course," she agreed, but the Captain had already cut the com.

The ship settled somewhat and she looked at her glass which was still, mercifully, mostly full. She switched it over to her right hand, shaking off the champagne that had sloshed onto the left as her eyes of gold and brown went to her PA. His hands were fixed on the arms of his chair in a death-grip and his normally dark tan skin had an ashy cast. She purposefully set aside her annoyances, which seemed enough to burst a blood vessel, and refocused her attention.

"Do you know what a Jack-O-Saucer is, Thomas?" Faith asked. "The round toy with a crank that plays an awful tune until a certain note is hit and then a nasty little jester pops out?"

Thomas, surprised out of his terror for a moment, gave her a nod. "The humans have something similar, but it pops out of a box."

Faith smiled but there was no humor in it. "I had one, of the saucer variety. I was very young, not quite six. Gwendolyn had taken a fall while we were playing and was in bed for two days. I was reduced to entertaining myself with toys. The Jack-O-

Saucer was one. I hated it." She paused long enough to take a sip from her glass. "Do you know why I hated it, Thomas?"

The PA nodded slowly, his dark eyes somber. He had never heard this story, in fact had heard no stories at all of Dr. de Rossi's youth, but he had worked diligently for her for one hundred and twenty years. He knew her well.

"Because you do not like surprises."

Faith's humorless smile widened. "That is exactly right, Thomas. I do not like surprises. But I played with that toy quite a bit for those two days. I would turn the crank slowly, so slowly that there were long gaps between each and every note. I would pause before that one note, that special note, stealing myself against the inevitable, and then POP!"

She shouted the last word, making Thomas jump. The PA stifled nervous laughter. The room bucked again but he hardly noticed. His dark eyes were like those of a child listening to a ghost story. Faith took a sip from her glass.

"After that," she continued, "I tried playing it faster, over and over again, to make myself numb to it. That did not work either. No matter what I did, I could not keep myself from that horrible start I would get when that jester would spring from the saucer. Finally," she said with a shrug, "I borrowed a few tools from a set my father had and opened it up."

A soft burst of air came from her nose, a personal sign of amusement, and now her smile was nostalgic. Her PA watched her, mesmerized.

"My first surgery," she said softly with the realization. "Anyway, I opened it up and took out the spring. The Jack would pop no more. Then I put it back together. I turned the crank, expecting now to enjoy the toy, but I reached that note – that one damned note that came before the spring, and it set my teeth on edge. I knew the Jack would not pop, and I played it over and over just to show myself. But every time I reached that note, every muscle in my body would tense and my teeth would all but grind. Can you guess what I did next, Thomas?"

The PA marveled at her as he made a guess, one inspired by knowing her so well. "You opened it back up and changed the tune," he said softly.

Faith's smile became genuine. "That's right, Thomas. I changed the tune. And I learned a lesson that has guided me my entire life."

The ship dove sharply and this time it took a few seconds for the Captain to pull it level. The PA swallowed the undignified yelp that wanted to leap from his throat, keeping it down to a weak gurgle.

"Don't worry, Thomas," Faith assured him, moving her hand like a snake in an attempt to keep the golden liquid in her glass. "This craft can stand a nuclear blast, as long the hull is not pierced. One of the reasons I chose this ship instead of the other two you found that had earlier departures."

"You knew this would happen?" Thomas asked, dark eyes large.

Faith gave him half a smile.

"Not this exactly, but I was prepared. You see, Thomas, I wired my brain – so to speak – long ago. I trained it, I made it a habit, to seek out any possibilities. Knowing the possibilities, expecting them, makes the window for surprise very, very small. But that window is still there. You cannot wipe it out entirely."

"You knew Miss Hope would fall in love with Master Hahn?"

"I did. It took me a while, longer than it should have, but I did. I did not foresee the child, because the possibility was so very remote, but it was a pleasant surprise, for once. I even expected her to run off with him at some point. Hope has always been, and will always be, a hopeless romantic. No pun nor irony intended. But that she would go to Eris, to make a run for it – where she would possibly never see her family again – that surprised me. And not pleasantly."

Thomas searched for something to say. He could hardly

believe that after all these years, all these *decades*, he was actually having a conversation with Faith. Everything before had always been clipped commands or requests, not that he minded. He felt something he thought was much deeper than love for his employer. She was brilliant, beautiful, strong and fearless. He revered her. He felt it was an honor to work for her, and silently prayed that it wasn't all about to end.

The craft jerked and moved sideways, again as if sliding on ice, the slipping speed increasing until the Captain brought the thrust to bear more on that side, steadying their movement once again. Thomas closed his eyes and swallowed hard, gripping the arms of his chair even tighter.

"Where did I go wrong with the Pantheon, Thomas?" Faith asked, startling him out of his abysmal reverie. "And I don't mean just the First Seven, I mean the first seven thousand human constructs that GwenSeven produced."

"Wrong?" he queried back, thinking she could do no such thing. "Nothing. They were beautiful, cultured, caring, trained, intelligent and unique. The Pantheon, the first run and the second as well, were...why, they were perfect."

"Exactly!" she exclaimed, thrusting a triumphant finger at him, seemingly oblivious to the turbulence that was currently tossing their spacecraft. "They were perfect!" She tipped her head back and the small laugh that burbled from her throat was almost maniacal. She lowered her head until her gaze was level with his once again. "And how many humans, or even elves for that matter, are perfect?"

"None," Thomas breathed. His stomach was rolling as much as the ship, but his attention was held captive by the woman across from him.

"That's right," she affirmed. "None." She tipped back her head and once again came that sound from her throat, edged with hilarity. Her chin came down and her tawny eyes were dark, serious as a grave. "I failed, Thomas," she said as if giving her final confession. "And failure," she continued before he could object, "is a tremendous thing. It is almost always humiliating, sometimes terrifying, often crushing. But at that greatest point of disappointment, we have a choice. We can let failure squash us in defeat, or let it be our greatest teacher. We can slink off into the dark – or we can rise above and be even greater than we had ever imagined."

"You will choose the latter, of course."

"You know me so well, Thomas." She took a drink of what was left in her glass and eyed the dregs with disappointment. "Starting over is rarely easy and often discouraging, but usually necessary for greatness." Her eyes went from her glass to her PA. "Do you know how to eat an elephant, Thomas?"

Tall, even though sitting, and proper in his immaculate suit, he squared his broad shoulders. It was an analogy that he knew. "One bite at a time."

Faith let her breath out through her nose, a smile crinkling the corners of her eyes, but not her lips. "Exactly. And that is how I am going to change this universe. One world at a time. Earth is technologically advanced yet it is still plagued by racism, riots, even plague itself. We are going to Earth, and we are to set some wheels in motion."

Thomas, racked with fear as the ship yawed and swerved through space like an aircab dodging traffic, let out a small sigh of ecstasy.

Faith drained the remnant of liquid in her glass but held onto it, pinning Thomas to his seat with tiger-like eyes that glittered dangerously. "It might take me a few months, maybe even a whole year. But I am going to take it apart, and I am going to change the tune."

 ONE

"Nothing makes us so lonely as our secrets."
-Paul Tournier

Jasyn sat in a room at the GwenSeven medical center, reclining in a propped-up bed with white rails and wearing a white cotton shift printed with faded blue diamonds, a sad attempt at giving a medical gown some character.

Plastic tubes ran out of the inside of his left forearm and he could feel the tight pull of medical tape over his wound. Some sort of plastique clamp held tight to his ribcage. He blinked his eyes as if coming wide awake from a deep dream, trying to recall the events that led his to his current situation.

With him in the room were unarguably the two wealthiest and most influential women in the known universe. He had been shot by their sister, that much he remembered quite clearly. That damned one-eyed IGC Jordan had pulled something crazy from her flight boot and blasted him with it.

Many of his memories were clear but others, many others, were close to the surface of his mind and yet he could not grasp them. It was like looking at pictures under the moving water of a stream. Sometimes the water would calm and he could almost see what was underneath. Then it would start rushing again and become a blur.

He knew he had been a high-ranking officer in the

Chimeran military for nearly one hundred years. He was a close friend and confidante of JP, one of the top Commanders of the Chimeran Rebellion. He had been sent as a spy but was also under orders to kill either of the women in the room, both if he could. It turned out that they had known who he was all along.

Some spy, he chided inwardly.

Most of the pain was gone, at least the pain in his side. There was a strange, dull ache in the left side of his chest that he suspected had nothing to do with the Jordan's weapon. He guessed the sting he felt was his pride. It had been wounded as bad as the rest of him.

Sitting next to him was Gwendolyn, the woman he now knew was masquerading as Faith de Rossi. As her twin, it should not have been difficult and wouldn't be - under most circumstances where twins were concerned. But, at the time of her disappearance, Faith de Rossi held seven doctorates in medical fields ranging from bioengineering to pharmaceuticals. Gwen had been an artist, not a scientist.

Yet she had pulled it off, and not just barely. The company had expanded and bourgeoned. Despite growing governmental restrictions, immense pockets of public opposition throughout three galaxies, and a violent uprising by the very people she had created, here she was. The GwenSeven Corporation was the largest, wealthiest, and most powerful corporate body in the universe. Conceivably as efficacious as the reigning government, the InterGalactic Council.

He took a deep breath and looked up at the quiet room. Charity sat in a chair against the wall, taking a long draw from a steel cigarette. Her green eyes sparkled with mischief as he spotted her.

"I'm sure you are not supposed to smoke inside a hospital," Jasyn told her, smiling in spite of all that had happened. Charity returned his grin, her eyes glittering.

"One, it's my hospital. Two, it's a vapor cigarette. Three, even if one or two were not the case, do you think anyone would have the balls to tell me to put it out?"

"I wouldn't," Jasyn admitted and looked at Faith, who had been Gwendolyn all along. She had sat up during the brief exchange, blinking the sleep from her eyes. She saw Jasyn's smile and sighed with relief.

"How are you feeling?"

"Fine, I guess."

"You guess?"

"My side is okay," he explained, "if that's what you mean. I'm sure they are giving me something for the pain." The tone of his voice was monotone flat. Faith nodded and Jasyn's hazel eyes looked into her eyes of brown and gold. "Inside, I'm not sure how I feel."

She nodded, understanding. "I know. This hasn't been easy on me either."

Jasyn looked away. *Stop acting like a child,* he told himself. Yet he could not shake the feeling of anger that burned inside him. *No one likes to be played a fool,* he acknowledged silently.

"When did you know you loved me?" he asked, redirecting his thoughts.

Faith swallowed before she spoke. "A long time ago," she whispered.

From her chair against the wall, Charity gave a loud *Ahem!* - clearing her throat. Faith looked over and Charity nodded at her as if encouraging her to get moving. Faith nodded back, took a deep breath, and looked back at Jasyn.

"What do you remember?"

He started to shrug and then stopped as he felt the clamp on his side bite into him. "I remember walking in, and then the Jordan..."

Faith shook her head quickly. "No. What do you remember about us?"

Jasyn frowned, puzzled. Did she mean their life at the villa?

"I don't know what else to do," Faith said, her voice oddly desperate. "You need to try. Try to remember. Us. Before you came to the villa."

"Remember us?" he asked. "*Before* I came to the villa?" Faith's head dipped in the barest of nods and he felt something inside his head, something that felt like a dam. Something was in there, clogging up the works. He closed his eyes and concetrated, focusing on Faith.

But she's Gwen, isnt' she? he thought.

Then the water began to trickle through the dam. His breath came out in a soft rush and he turned his face away as pieces of the dam began to break away. "A train. I remember a train. And a bullfight." Faith's next breath came out in a choked sob. "I remember a house," Jasyn continued, "a house made of glass, near an ocean." Jasyn frowned and shook his head. "No, on a lake."

"It was both," Faith said, tears spilling down her checks.

The memories came pouring through the hole in the dam, sweeping away not all of the blockage, but some. His hazel eyes opened wider and wider as if watching the past on a holo screen.

"I remember," he said, his voice tinged with wonder. "I can tell it's not everything. But I remember us."

Faith laughed, wiping her tears away with the back of one hand.

"Enough!" Charity stood up, tucking the steel cigarette into a pocket on her sleeve as she came towards the bed. "You can stroll down the avenues of the past at another time," she told Faith, her smile never faltering and her eyes never leaving Jasyn's. "Right now, we have much more important things to start discussing."

"Charity..." Faith started but was cut off with a single look.

Charity's white-blonde hair was done up in a coif and she was dressed in a smart silk blazer over a ruffled shirt and short skirt, all black. The pale, slender fingers of her right hand wrapped around one of the metal rails. "It is time for the rebellion to come to an end. Actually, it should have come to an end ninety-nine years ago. But, sometimes things do not go as planned." A small chuckle escaped her red lips, but her knuckles turned white as they grasped the bar tighter. "So now," she told Jasyn, "we need to know what you know. We need to know what the Chimera have planned."

He glanced at Faith, her eyes the same color as her long brown and gold hair. Faith de Rossi was rumored to be a puppet master with unparalleled skills and unconceivable foresight. Gwen truly was her twin, or had become so.

It was a fact he could not argue. He had come to surreptitiously pry out her secrets and leave her for dead. Doing both would mark great triumph for the construct rebel group called the Chimera.

Instead, she had seen him coming, and seduced him in an air of innocence and cunning. He was so ensnared and the tables so turned that she knew *his* secrets. And he was willing to die for her.

Swallowing the bitterness that rose within him, he shifted his dark hazel eyes to Charity and nodded. "I know everything they have planned."

Charity threw back her head and laughed girlishly. "I certainly hope so," she told Jasyn when her laughter trailed off. "That was the plan."

Jasyn looked back at Faith, fighting against the lump that was expanding in his throat, wondering how long they had been using him. The whole time obviously, however long that was. Years. Decades. An entire century. He was filled with disgust.

"Your plan?" he asked Faith accusingly.

Charity laughed again, even though Faith's expression was one of misery.

"No silly," Charity answered. "It was *your* plan."

That was more than a surprise to him. It was a shock. He searched his memory but it was like looking through a house full of locked doors.

"You don't need to go into specifics," Charity told him, "not quite yet, anyway. But if you can give us an overall sketch right now, it would be greatly appreciated. There are moves that we need to start making, and we have dawdled far too long already."

The raven-haired construct paused, having a difficult time fighting the feeling that he was a pawn of these two women. But something in him believed Charity. It had been his plan. He just couldn't remember how or why.

"We..." he started and then saw Charity's blonde brows rise high above her green eyes. He pressed his chin to his chest and cleared his throat. "The Chimera," he corrected, receiving a small nod of satisfaction from Charity, "know that taking a Dragon by force is impossible, and drawing one out is albeit fruitless. So we... *they*, are going straight for the eggs. All the eggs. With the intent of hatching them and training them from birth. It has been known for some time that the Jordan does not need to be from the IGC, or from any other military or government for that matter, to control the Fledgling. The only thing that matters is the bond that is formed when they are hatched."

"We've surmised that much as well," Charity said, "and have speculated it is quite possible that the Jordan does not even have to be a pilot, although I am sure that it helps – immensely."

"We also managed to intercept the eggs from the Beryl Dragon," Faith added. "And without having to infiltrate the Chimeran ranks with one of our own."

Jasyn's dark brows drew together. Was that a reprimand?

Jasyn sighed. "Gwen," he started when she immediately shushed him.

"Don't ever call me that!" she hissed. Her tiger-like eyes darted about the near empty medical room and she continued, her voice low and hoarse. "Not when you think we are alone, not even when you are sure we are alone. Until you see my twin and I together in the same room, I am and forever will be, Faith de Rossi!"

Jasyn's lips pulled down at the corners and he turned his dark eyes back to Charity. "The plan has been set and unchanged for over a year. JP's directive is to go after the eggs, all of the eggs. Commander Van Zandt is to secure Jordans for them."

"Commander Van Zandt," Charity echoed softly, a small smile playing at the edge of her red lips. "Bjorn?"

Jasyn looked at her, his dark eyes wary. "That is his first name," he affirmed.

Charity's expression became as smooth as glass. "You don't remember everything, do you?"

Jasyn scowled. "You mean everything from a previous life I just now discovered that I had?" he asked and when Charity's blonde head dipped slightly in a nod his scowl deepened. "How am I supposed to know?"

Faith's own countenance fell and her sister shot her a look of sympathy so deep that it made Faith's features harden like water turning into ice. She turned her cold visage back to Jasyn.

"Go on with what you do know," she told him. The construct took a deep breath and pressed forward.

"The attack on the Copper Dragon will be next. The attack on the Silver Dragon will be almost simultaneous. It should be possible due to the proximity of the Dragons at the time."

"Proximity?" Faith repeated. "The IGC never lets the Dragons get close to one another. That exact risk is one of the reasons."

"JP's source assured him that it would happen," Jasyn told

them. "It's even possible that more than two will be there."

Faith looked dubious but Charity leaned closer, her green eyes gleaming. "When?"

"The date isn't fixed. It is dependent on an event, one that we are certain will happen. And happen soon."

Faith lips tightened. "You have someone on the inside," she said. Jasyn nodded.

"Who?" Charity asked.

"Commander Van Zandt's contact aboard the Opal Dragon."

The sister's glanced at each other in alarm. That was Noel's mother Dragon.

"What event is supposed to trigger the attack?" Faith asked.

Jasyn told them.

The sisters stared at him, wide-eyed and breathless for long moments. Then Charity's eyes went to Faith.

"You knew there would be another rainbow."

Faith lifted her chin. "But I did not know how. The Chimera are attempting to force one."

Jasyn nodded.

"Do you know when this will happen?" Charity finally asked.

Jasyn shook his head. "No. But it could be any day."

There was a rustle of expensive black silk as Charity was up and away. She paused with her hand on the door long enough to look back at the construct and give him half a smile. "It's good to have you back," she said, then was gone.

The door clicked shut behind her.

There was a whoosh that came from a machine behind the hospital bed, a sound that was repeated every twenty seconds, and a bleep from another that came every ten. Silence filled the spaces in between.

Faith knew that Charity was wrong. He was not back. Not all the way.

She wanted to fidget, wanted to wring her hands, wanted to lay her face against Jasyn's neck and bury her head in his chest.

He draws me back to my old self, she thought, feeling her old weaknesses crawling back, seeping into her. She hardened herself against it.

She wanted to talk to him but she felt that a wall had risen between them - and she could feel animosity emanating from him in hot, angry waves.

He's still Chimeran, she thought. Not much, but enough.

She made herself be still and wait.

The black-haired construct struggled mentally for long moments. He knew that he loved her – loved her so much that he would die to protect her. But, suddenly, he hated that he did.

"We were together," Jasyn finally said. "Before."

Faith did not know if he was asking a question or making a statement, but she answered anyway. "Yes."

There was another long silence broken only by the soft rhythmic sounds of the machines as Jasyn racked his brain for memories. He remembered much and some things were so clear. Watching Gwendolyn sculpt. Traveling. A medieval castle and a house of glass. The baking heat in a *plaza de toros* where he won her a rose. But he felt like they were old memories. The most recent, and even those were nearly a century old, seemed the hardest to access.

Worse, were memories that conflicted. Ones that did not deny one another as much as simply confuse the hell of him.

He looked at the woman next to him and remembered running his hand over the outside of her arm, only recently realizing that it was missing the scar that Faith de Rossi had worn since childhood.

How did I know of that scar? he queried inwardly.

Because you had stroked Faith's arm, in the same manner? And you had asked her?

He dredged at his memories, but they were dark.

"How did we get separated?" he asked instead, then shook his head, chuckling softly. "What was my big plan?"

Faith took a deep, even breath. "When it became imminent that the Chimera meant to go to war, your plan was to join both sides. It would better our chances, no matter who won."

Though Jasyn did not remember said plan, he nodded. "It makes sense."

"We decided that GwenSeven would openly back the InterGalactic Council, and subversively infiltrate the Chimera." Faith paused and pursed her lips, displeasure at the memory obvious. "I suggested we train a construct, or a number of them. You insisted that you should be the one to go. Fa... my sister, blocked the memories of who you had been, so you would not give yourself away. Then she made sure you made it onto a Chimeran ship."

There was another silence as Jasyn felt his heart softening. Then the bitterness rose up like bile in his throat as something else occurred to him. The amount of time that had passed.

"How long?" he finally asked.

Faith raised a brow. "For?"

"How long did it take you to find me? With the amount of resources at your fingertips, I can't believe it took all this time for you to track me down. How long had you known where I was?"

"Oh," Faith answered, tossing her brown and gold hair over a shoulder. "From the first. I knew all along."

Jasyn's hazel eyes widened in surprise and then narrowed in fury. "This whole time?" he demanded. "After you are acting like we have been in love for ages, you knew this whole time where I was and you did not try to get me back?"

Faith's brows drew together and her eyes blazed in anger. "You have no idea what I've been through, who or what I have tried to get back!" she hissed. "I had no idea what Fai.. what had been implanted in you to get you to return," she continued, keeping her voice low although she was quite sure they were alone and the private room had no microphones. "I spent years learning bioengineering and business just to keep up the ruse and keep the company moving forward. I knew where you were and that you were safe. I had to be satisfied with that for a long time." She took a deep breath, trying to control the emotions welling inside her. "Besides," she went on, "*you* were the one that chose to go. *You* insisted that you had a role to play and I had to let you. *You* were supposed to find your way back to *me*! You promised!" Her voice cracked on the last word and a hand came up to cover her mouth. She finally paused and let out a long breath. "I waited and waited," she said, her voice soft and composed once again, "not knowing what to do. Eventually, however, I was able to get spies on the *Resurrection*."

Jasyn's eyes widened again. "Who?" he whispered.

"I had them prod you for some answers, but they were not able to get anything helpful. Not on your mental state anyway. You seemed entirely devoted to the Cause."

"Who?" Jasyn repeated, firmly this time.

"Eleanor, for one."

"Eleanor," Jasyn said, his voice soft again. "My god, if JP finds out..."

"He already has. She's dead. He killed her, of course."

Jasyn felt something twist inside him and he closed his eyes. Eleanor. She had been so kind. And always interested in him. Asking him questions that were unusual, but not enough to arouse suspicion. Now he knew why.

"You're just a puppeteer," he said, his voice low and thick with disgust, "pulling everyone on strings."

His words sank into her like claws and she felt a barrier come up around her, encasing her in a tower more protective than a wall of stone. Oddly enough, it didn't hurt in the slightest. It was familiar, almost comforting. After all, she had built it over a century ago and it had kept her safe ever since.

"I do what I have to do, and I get it done however I need to."

Jasyn shook his head slowly back and forth, forcing a smile that had the look of a leer. "You are just like...well, you know."

Faith's face was so still and her own smile so cold that it could have been carved from ice.

"I've had lots of practice." She stood up. "We'll wait until you have recovered..." she started but Jasyn shook his head, more emphatically this time.

"Don't bother. I'm going to stay at the Castle."

There was a flicker in Faith's gold and brown eyes but otherwise her expression never faltered. "Very well," she acquiesced and headed for the door. "You know where to find me."

"Wait!" Jasyn barked as she reached for the handle. She looked back, surprised.

"What did the 'J' stand for?" he asked.

"Excuse me?"

"JP started out as BG-syn. Bodyguard, synthetic. I know I started as J7, and somewhere it was changed to J-syn. What does the 'J' stand for?"

Faith's face once again became void of expression. "How would I know?" she asked and was gone.

 TWO

- A secret is also a promise, the strength of each are not in the making, but in the keeping.

When Scarlett opened her eyes, all she could see was a figure crouching over her, though her vision was too blurry to make out who it was. She tried to talk but her throat felt like a rusty hinge. She brought her hand up to her mouth and a second later she could feel someone supporting her head and holding a cup to her lips.

The Red Jordan was confused and disoriented. Her ears felt like they were stuffed with cotton. Her head felt like it was stuffed with straw.

From tin-man to straw-man, she thought belligerently. *Am I progressing or regressing?* she wondered. *I'm digressing.*

The only thing that she was sure of was that she was inside of her Fledgling Dragon. The smell and feel of him was all around her. That alone was almost enough to make her weep.

Still, it was bewildering to know that she was inside of him and yet not in her pilot's seat. The last time she had been in her Fledgling he barely had enough room for his one pilot, and it was up front in the cockpit. Yet she had already seen, from the outside, how much larger he had become. The Jordan closed her eyes, trying to remember what had happened.

She had been in town for the celebration of the

Synchronicity.

My god it was packed! she thought, remembering the revelers, dancing and jostling and cavorting, shoulder to sweaty shoulder in the town square. The green-eyed Chimeran Commander had been there, and the blue-eyed elfin Engineer of the Opal Dragon as well. And Mica. She was sure that she had seen the cabbie again but that time he wasn't in a cab but in front of a tent.

Had it been Arwa's tent?

No, it had been a fortuneteller's tent, though it had looked like Arwa's.

She shook her head. It was all so muddled. Had there been an Aridian there? Had she really seen an Aridian? Yes, she was sure of it. It was a female and Scarlett had spotted her right before she had looked up, which must have been when someone smeared the Chlorforgel across her neck.

Had it been the Aridian? Scarlett shuddered. If so, she was very lucky to be alive. She remembered making it to the town walls and staggering out, barely conscious. Fledge had been there, waiting on the crest of the first rising hill. The memory of it brought tears to the backs of her closed eyes.

Scarlett.

"Hmm?" she said, opening her eyes and raising her head just a bit, thinking someone had spoken, then she realized she had heard the voice with her head, not her ears. She eased herself back down.

Fledge?

Her own name came again, warmer this time.

Scarlett.

The Jordan squeezed her eyes shut but this time the tears came, escaping from the corners of her eyelids and running down the sides of her face towards her ears.

Who? she asked mentally, but Fledge's only response was a

feeling of puzzlement. *Who saved me?* she asked.

A sensation of befuddlement was the only response. Scarlett thought that maybe he could not understand her words so in her mind's eye she pictured Bjorn, the tall and lean green-eyed Chimeran Commander. Then she pictured Calyph, his sandy blonde hair over his pointed ears, his almond-shaped eyes blue and full of innocence.

Fledge's befuddlement turned to outright confusion. Scarlett sighed and tried to open her eyes again but they felt as rusty and uncompliant as her voice. She waved her hand and motioned to her neck and the figure was there again, leaning close this time, touching her.

There was a grunt and then she could feel her neck being cleaned with a cloth. She opened her eyes but the figure was still blurred. Scarlett closed her eyes again, concentrating.

She remembered that her knees had buckled and she had collapsed. And she had been caught by strong arms and hefted up. She thought of Bjorn, lean and muscled. She thought of his strong arms and her heartbeat quickened. Fledge's heartbeat responded, though Scarlett had the feeling that it might be in amusement.

Bjorn had carried her once before - lifting her up and carrying her with no effort.

Calyph had caught her up in his arms as well one time and carried her to safety. Had it been to Fledge or to the Opal Dragon? She couldn't remember now, it all seemed so long ago.

Scarlett tried to remember the feel of the arms that had caught her so recently, tried to see if she could discern who it had been.

Green or blue, she thought suddenly as she heard a sound made by the person who was with her now. She thought of Calyph's blue eyes, always so full of concern, and Bjorn's gimlet green eyes, always full of mirth and desire. Desire for her.

His eyes, she thought. *If I could just see his eyes, I will know who it is.*

Blue or green?

Green or blue?

She tried to raise her head but she was gently pressed back down. The figure leaned down again, getting the last of the Chlorforgel from her neck.

Fledge, she thought, *help me.*

A surge of relief washed over her, and a wave of strength as her body was filled with warm, red light. Scarlett reached up to the silhouette above her and wrapped a hand around its neck and pulled the figure down until they were nose to nose.

Blue or green? she thought wildly, forcing her own eyes open. *Green or blue?*

Her own dark eyes, edged with crimson, blinked rapidly - not sure if what she was seeing was real.

Green or blue?

Blue.

The Red Jordan blinked, again and then again one more time – just to make sure – but she was right.

Blue.

It was Blue.

The Blue Jordan was down on one knee and dressed in a black flight suit. Not her usual sparkling sapphire-colored flight suit, but a black one, and she had a matching black patch over one eye, but there was no mistaking the half-elf pilot.

Scarlett fell back down onto the bed making soft sounds like whimpers, till the whimpers grew into soft laughter. Laughter that grew until tears leaked from the corners of her closed eyes once again.

"And just what the hell is so funny?" Jordan Blue demanded, her tone bemused rather than angry. Scarlett tried to answer but only succeeded in coughing, making her laugh harder. "Is that Chlorforgel still kicking your ass or have you lost your damn mind?" Blue asked.

"Both," the Red Jordan managed to croak. Instinctively, she almost asked where they were, but she already knew. She was on a bed and inside her Fledgling.

Fledge has a bed inside him, she marveled.

She tried to clear her throat, trying to get her voice working better, though her mouth was still dry. "Is this real?" she asked.

Blue rose to her feet and then sat down on the edge of the bed and shrugged. "I couldn't say. What might be real to me might not be real to you."

That had Scarlett stumped. With the last of the Chlorforgel off her neck, and the surge of energy from Fledge, the Red Jordan could feel her strength returning. She pushed herself up into a sitting position and took a good look around. The last time she had been inside the Fledgling Dragon he had been no bigger than a fighter craft, with a cockpit large enough just for her. Now, he was the size of a small, very small, ship. She was in the aft end and, looking forward, could see a door to a lavatory, a small galley, and a cockpit large enough for two pilots.

None of it looked real.

But it felt real.

"What happened?" Scarlett asked.

"To you?" Blue responded. "I have no idea. But I do know that you called out to Fledge and I got in before he took off."

"He let you in," Scarlett murmured. It was not a question but Blue nodded, looking slightly discomfited.

"He has been flying with me, and Cyan."

Scarlett nodded, her limp hands resting in her lap as her dark brows pulled slightly together. "And Galen."

Blue's small intake of breath was slight but quick. "Can you see him?" she asked.

Galen, only days before his death, had inserted a microdot communication chip behind the Blue Jordan's left ear, and a similar one on the upper edge of his own jaw line. Even after his murder, the Jordan and the doctor had been able to communicate – physically as well as audibly. Blue did not know whether it was due to the bond they had shared or the manner of his death, but he had stayed with her.

"Not really," the Red Jordan answered, tipping her head to look at Blue. "But I can make out a shadow next to you, where there should be none."

Blue turned her head to look at the doctor's ghost. For her, he was as vivid as he had been when he was alive.

"It's not that, though," Scarlett continued as she looked away, a gentle smile on her full lips. "It's that I can smell him." Her smile widened. "The disinfectant from his lab. Ozone. The lanolin hand cream he used that smelled like lavender."

The ghostly form of the elfin doctor bristled in offense, his black hair falling over his blue eyes before he flicked it angrily out of his face. "I do not use hand cream!" he declared.

"Not anymore," Blue remarked offhandedly, a smirk quirking the corner of her mouth. Galen's ghost sat back sullenly and looked away, his arms crossed over his chest.

The Red Jordan blinked slowly, looking at the curved walls of smooth silver Dragonskin. "He's dead?" she asked, her voice soft.

"Yeah," Blue replied. "He was...killed."

"I'm sorry," Scarlett voiced with sincerity. "Was it the IGC?"

Blue drew in a long breath through her narrow nose and then nodded. "I think so."

The muscles in Scarlett's jaw feathered as she swallowed. "I used to think they were the good guys. I'm really starting to doubt that now."

"Does that mean that we're not the good guys?" Blue asked.

Scarlett moved her head incrementally from side to side. "I

never thought I was a good guy. I was always just serving my own ends."

Blue blinked her eye, wondering if the Chlorforgel was still doing a number on Scarlett. An admission like that was not like her.

The Red Jordan turned her face towards the Blue Jordan, taking in the unusual flight suit with its matching eyepatch, a smirk tucked into the corner of her mouth. "I miss anything else?" she asked.

Blue flopped onto the bed, her head almost on Scarlett's blanketed feet, her lone sapphire eye rolling as she feigned a faint. After three seconds she sat up straight, as if electrocuted.

"Miss anything?" she demanded theatrically. "Miss anything!?!" The Blue Jordan sighed heavily and tilted her head, making her platinum coils shift from one shoulder to the other. "Well, in my personal life - in case you are interested - my eldest sister, who is the head of the GwenSeven Corporation as if you didn't already know, has offered me a job as a military commander in some sort of revolution against the IGC."

She raised her blonde brows and pursed her lips while she waited for what she thought would be astonishment and outrage from the Red Jordan.

Scarlett shrugged. "The Chimera offered me a similar deal."

Blue leaned forward and gawked at her for a number of seconds before she sat back, composed once more.

"Alright," she acquiesced as she held up her right hand, ticking off the digits with her left index finger. "Second, Captain Brogan is in some sort of funk and Blaylock has pretty much assumed control of the Dragon."

That got Scarlett's attention more than anything else since she had regained consciousness. Her head snapped towards the other Jordan, her dark eyes suddenly intent.

"Ah!" Blue exclaimed softly. "Something that interests you! Something *else* that might interest you," she informed, ticking off another finger, "is that Blaylock has some bitch on the Dragon who he is trying to make a Jordan. Most likely a red one, from what I can gather."

Scarlett was now sitting bolt upright, the thin blanket pooling about her thighs. Every muscle in her face, in her entire body actually, had gone taut. Her dark eyes burned with crimson and sparked with murder.

Blue grinned wolfishly. "There you are!" Distracted by what she viewed as Scarlett's return to her formal self, she skipped over her thoughts and happenings regarding Calyph, the elfin Engineer of the Opal Dragon.

For a moment Scarlet was too angry to speak. "How dare they!" she finally hissed. "How *could* they?"

Blue shrugged. "I can't say for sure. But I do know that when Calyph drew fluid from Fledge for your injection, he drew a second vial." Scarlett's dark eyes widened and her hands clenched around the edge of the blanket on her lap. "When I asked Calyph who it was for," the Blue Jordan continued, "he told me it was for Gemma."

Scarlett's brows came down abruptly over narrowed eyes. "Who?"

Blue heaved a sigh that came from her depths, relieved to finally have someone with whom she could share her feelings and concerns. Behind her, reading her emotions more than her actual thoughts, Galen smiled.

"Never thought that person would be Scarlett," he remarked. "Did you?"

The Blue Jordan ignored him and continued talking to Scarlett. "Gemma. GL. A Jordan cadet that Blaylock has a hard-on for in one way or ten others. He's been touting her around the Dragon and she's been sniffing around Fledge. She's a real piece of work."

"I'm sure," Scarlett murmured.

"Anyway," Blue went on, "at first I believed him, it seemed

plausible enough at the time." She took a deep breath and exhaled sharply. She knew she was swimming into dark waters.

"And now?" Scarlett prompted.

Blue drew in another lungful of air. "Now I'm not so sure," she exclaimed on the exhale.

Scarlett's brow furrowed. "What made you unsure? And what happened with the rest of Fledge's fluid?"

Blue froze. She was treading water now. Dark and dangerous water. Not just for Calyph, but for herself. Her tongue already felt paralyzed. She was trying to free it when Scarlett suddenly sat back, her face relaxing with comprehension as she released her death grip on the blanket's edge.

"You injected yourself with the second vial," she said softly.

Blue, her tongue still glued stuck, nodded. The Jordan was a tried and true starfighter. Hand to hand, she had fought Golgoths that dwarfed her in size and strength. She had hunted and killed enemies of the IGC as well as mercenaries paid to kill her. Yet never before had she feared for her life as much as the few seconds she waited while Jordan Scarlett digested the fact that Blue had injected herself with the fluid taken from the Red Fledgling. The half-elf pilot braced herself.

"Thank you," Scarlett said.

Blue remained frozen for a moment. Then she leaned closer to the other Jordan, realizing as she did so that it might be a ruse and the movement might cost her life.

"What?"

Scarlett turned her head so she could fix her crimson flecked eyes on the single blue eye of the other Jordan.

"Thank you," she repeated. "And not just for that, but for looking out for Fledge."

The Blue Jordan sat on the edge of the bed, silent for

many seconds. "Wow," she finally whispered. "You've really changed." Scarlett's immediate glare made her hold up her hands defensively. "Or not!" she was quick to correct.

Scarlett relaxed and cocked her head at the other Jordan. "You're a little different yourself, you know."

A smirk quirked itself into the corner of Jordan Blue's red lips, right where her facial scars began. "More than a little," she admitted. "And…you're welcome."

There was a moment of silence that should have been awkward, but was not. It was broken by a soft alarm coming from the cockpit.

Jordan Blue threw a questioning look at the other Jordan but Scarlett was already on her feet, moving through the strange new landscape innards of her Fledgling. She dropped into the pilot's seat and glanced across the expanded dash as Blue sat in the only other chair.

The color of the light flashed pearlescent white, which meant it could be from one of three Dragons - Pearl, Beryl, or Opal. The odds, however, were that it was coming from Opal, their mother Dragon.

Still, Scarlett hesitated.

Blue did not. She leaned forward and passed her slim fingers over the light on the dash. "This is Jordan Blue," she announced and then waited.

"Jordan Blue?" a voice asked tentatively, making Blue relax noticeably and bringing a smile to Scarlett's lips.

"Yes," Blue affirmed, recognizing the voice of Dareus, the dark-skinned elf who was the Communications Officer aboard the Opal Dragon. She looked askance at the pilot next to her. "I am with Jordan Scarlett," she told him.

"Jordan Scarlett!" Dareus breathed. "Are you headed for the Dragon? As of yet, your coordinates are undetermined."

"We are planning to head for the Dragon," Blue said, guarded. "Just figuring a few things out first. Is everything alright?"

There was a pause long enough for both Jordans to look at each other. Once communications were established it was protocol to be connected to the Captain, or the Executive Officer.

"Well…" the coms man said and paused, "no."

Jordan Scarlett, impatient with his obvious reticence leaned forward. "Who is in command of the Dragon?" she demanded.

Another pause ensued that, though it only lasted two seconds, was enough to make Scarlett's blood pressure skyrocket.

"Technically, the Captain is, of course."

"Technically?"

"I haven't seen him in days," Dareus informed her, his voice soft.

"Where is Commander Blaylock?" Jordan Blue asked, knowing that the Executive Officer had been controlling the bridge for well over a month.

"He is en route to the Beryl Dragon," Dareus answered quickly.

"And Captain Brogan?" Scarlett demanded, not knowing the Captain had been sick and confined to his quarters for weeks.

The Communications Officer lowered his voice even further though the Jordans knew it was likely that he was alone in the bridge with the Navigator, Chiara. Blue had a rising suspicion that they had both been waiting for a chance to be alone. To make this call.

"I think…I mean, Chiara and I both think…he's dying."

Both Jordans froze as if paralyzed and did not even look at one another before they answered in unison. "We're on our way."

Neither spoke their next words but their thoughts were exactly the same.

Take us there.

The Fledglings immediately shot through space with their Jordans, trailing blue and crimson light across the galaxy.

 THREE

- Some secrets are too big to be concealed, so we build entire worlds to hide them.

"Here, drink this."

The woman known to the universe as Faith de Rossi leaned down and handed the dark-skinned young woman a white ceramic mug, steam rising from its depths like vapor rising from a volcanic hot spring. She felt an almost irresistible urge to wrap a blanket around the young woman who her mind insisted was a girl, since she both looked and gave off the air of a rescued refugee, but the villa was plenty warm and she knew that the girl did not like to be touched.

"Thank you," Amberle said, accepting the mug, its rim laser engraved with a concentric circle of repeating G7 logos. "I like hot chocolate."

"I know," Faith whispered.

The girl took an experimental sip and smiled. She was a bit taller and more than a bit thinner since the last time Faith had seen her. Her hair was a bit longer and lighter. Her curls had been bright pink when she had taken the job and left for the Elba moon and Faith had watched it fade via s-cams like a strawberry being bleached by the sun. Now it was dark at the roots, the tight spirals faded to coral pink. Her eyes were the same, though, Faith noted. Not just the color, a bright hazel of brown and green - but the intensity inside them - furtive and relentless, like the eyes of a doe as it drank warily from a steam, watching for predators. Like a doe, her head rose and she looked about uncertainly, her body tense, as if sensing something.

"My friends?" Amberle queried.

"Are being cared for on Callisto," Faith assured her. "They will be taken care of for the rest of their days - which they seem to want to spend on the beaches of Europa," she finished with a smile.

Amberle's smile mirrored Faith's. "They like to surf," she told the de Rossi woman. "Keaton wants to teach me how..." her voice trailed off, as did her smile.

"You are free to join them any time you wish," Faith offered, but her own smile had faded as well, and she had gone as rigid as the girl had been only a moment ago. She did not want her to go. Despite the fact that the young woman was trembling with cyber sickness, and it made her feel guilty as hell, Faith wanted her back in front of a monitor and jacked into the Web. But she was not about to press her.

"No," Amberle said, her hangdog expression awash with her own feelings of guilt. "I would rather keep working."

Faith smiled broadly, a deep breath expanding her lungs and filling her with elation. The girl's hazel eyes brightened over the lip of the mug and she lowered it quickly.

"Maybe," she suggested, "I could go visit them after I finish out our contract."

"I think that is a fine idea," Faith agreed as she accepted a flute of champagne from a young woman in a tailored brown jacket and skirt, her brown hair pulled back into a smooth tail. Amberle watched the young woman and the way her brown eyes moved fractionally behind her black-framed glasses. She knew the left lens had a micro monitor and felt a sharp pang of envy.

"Thank you, Penny," Faith told her PA. "Is Mari preparing a room for our guest?"

"Yes," Penny affirmed. "And I ordered her some new clothes."

"Thank you," Faith said. "And Charity?"

"Is on her way. Her ship was in line to orbit the city. She should be on her shuttle by now and arrive here any minute."

Faith nodded and forced herself into the white wing chair that faced the girl. She did not want to sit. She wanted to pace. She wanted desperately to question the girl about her missing twin and their missing sisters, but knew it was better to wait for Charity. Her brown and gold eyes followed Penny to the bar that stood against the wall which separated the living room from the kitchen and watched her PA remove a glass from a cabinet and set it on the bar. Then she began to fill the ice bucket from the mini freeze in preparation for Charity. Her tawny gaze went back to the girl.

"That might be soon," she said, picking up their conversation where they left off, "if your calculations are correct."

"They are," the girl assured her. "But I was thinking about the other job offer you had for me." Her guarded gaze went to Penny as the PA left the bar and headed for the kitchen. Ms. de Rossi had already cautioned her not to speak of her work to anyone or in front of anyone other than herself or her sister, Charity. Faith's own eyes were bright with surprise.

"You found the Fledgling?" she asked, leaning forward and keeping her voice low though she had already disabled the security microphones on the center floor. The girl nodded and gave her a lopsided smile.

"She found me, actually."

Faith's eyes of gold and brown widened a little more.

"How?"

"The same way you did."

Those tawny eyes widened until they were nearly round.

"The advertisement?" Faith queried.

The girl chortled softly as she nodded, making her faded pink coils of hair bounce. Faith straightened and took a sip of champagne as she thought. She had been looking for her twin, the true Faith de Rossi, for a long time. She had been missing, along with their sisters, Hope and Madeline, for almost a century. Gwendolyn de Rossi, posing as her twin at Faith's own insistence before she left, had been searching for them all ever since.

She had started with high-priced private detectives, some of whom even referred to themselves as WebGods - claiming to be omniscient regarding everything on the Galactic Web. She had told them, of course, that she was looking for her sister, Hope, as well as her own biodentical dyer. It mattered little. They found bupkis.

It was late one lonely night that she was perusing the Callisto Classifieds when she came upon the ad.

I can find anyone it announced with immodest simplicity.

Bemused and intrigued, and also a little tipsy, Ms. de Rossi had sent a secure message to the link attached to the ad.

Find my sister. Name your price.

The response had come - not on the next business day but only a minute later - which was late on a Saturday night, making Faith wonder where the person actually was. What surprised her even more was the response itself.

Most galactic PIs asked the same questions.

Physical description?

Last known whereabouts?

Any idea where she might have gone?

The questions were so stupid that Gwen thought she would have better luck flying around in a space dinghy with an old-fashioned pair of binoculars and looking herself. Instead, the reply had been: *Send me things she wrote. Copies of IMs, DMs, emails, whatever. As many as you can.*

Even more intriguing was that the person did not want to be paid in money or credits but in compute hardware and software.

Ms. de Rossi immediately arranged a vid conference call on a secure net. The surprises just kept coming, along with a good deal of suspicious doubt when she saw that the investigator was a girl in her late teens with a snub of a nose and springy coils of hair that were decidedly pink.

The only thing that kept her from cutting the line was the look in the girl's eyes. They were a hazel brown-green, light compared to her dark skin, but intense and under a pair of feathery brows that seemed always on the verge of a scowl. Despite her young age, those eyes seemed to hold no trace of childhood. Gwen had only seen eyes like that on one other person - her biodentical twin. The look of carefree innocence had left Faith's gaze, she guessed, about the time they turned eight. It sobered her immediately.

"Why the mail and messages?" the supposed Faith de Rossi had asked the girl straightaway. "Other detectives have gone over them, looking for any clue about what they had been planning..." she trailed off as the girl shook her pink hair.

"I'm not looking for where they were going, I'm looking for where they are."

The statement was so simple that it made Gwen feel like a fool.

"And how will you do that?" she asked.

"The way people communicate, especially in the way they write, is always unique. Better than a poker tell but not quite a fingerprint, more like a signature. Either way, they all have specific markings. I'll feed whatever you give me into a program I wrote. After that, it's a lot of searching and cross-referencing."

"Mmmhmm." It sounded simple enough. Too simple. Gwen suspected she was being had. "I'm sending you a small variety of things I've written. I'd like you to tell me what you see."

The girl shrugged as the woman who had identified herself as Faith de Rossi tapped a key on her ghostpad, sending her three different items that Faith had written shortly before she had left in search of Hope. Other messages had popped up on the mainframe periodically after her disappearance, prewritten instructions for Gwen that she had shared only with Charity and decided to still keep private.

Gold and brown eyes had watched the girl's face shift to the right and her body move back as she typed on whatever compute or pad she was using. The girl's hazel eyes moved as they read and then flicked back to the woman on the call.

"One of these is signed Faith de Rossi," the girl said.

"And?" the de Rossi woman challenged. "You said the way people write is like a signature, a tell. What can you tell me by looking at them?"

"I can tell you didn't write any of these," the girl said softly.

Gwen felt the skin all over her body prickle with gooseflesh and her only response was stunned silence. She knew she should laugh and play it off as if she had been trying to trick her from the beginning as some sort of test. Instead, she moistened her lips with her tongue.

"Find my sister. Name your price," she said and for the first time it occurred to her how fortuitous it was to have stumbled upon this girl. The price most people would be naming would not only be astronomical, which Faith - the old and the new - could handle, but it would be the price of a bribe rather than a business deal.

Now the velvet night sky encased the villa, spattered with stars and aglow with the light reflecting off the largest gas giant in the system.

The girl smiled as she lowered the mug and rested it on

the thigh of her pants. The pants had once been maroon in color and certainly had seen better days. "Yeah," she said. "The advertisement."

The woman who was now Faith de Rossi blinked owlishly. "I would not have thought of a Fledgling Dragon to be reading the Callisto Classifieds."

The girl laughed, her small white teeth flashing in her dark face. "Is that a polite way of saying you think I'm full of shit?"

There was another laugh from the foyer making Faith look up and the girl turn in her seat to see they were no longer alone in the room. Far from it.

A woman with white-blonde hair and wearing a cocktail dress that looked like a slice of moonlight stood on the circular platform by the elevator. The fabric of her silver dress shimmered and her slim shoulders were draped with a white fur stole.

"Faith wouldn't say shit if she had a mouth full of it!"

The beautiful socialite shrugged off the stole and it was quickly caught by one of the two assistants that flanked her. Charity de Rossi waved them both away. "Find the kitchen, you two," she instructed and then smiled broadly at Penny, already standing by to hand her a glass of her current favorite cocktail before the PA escorted the other personal assistants from the room.

Charity glanced over her other shoulder to see Geary, Faith's head of security, standing behind her own bodyguard. "You can go upstairs," she informed them before turning back to the living room, her smile returning. Faith had risen from her chair, her lips pressed into a tight line that was turned up at the corners. The girl was looking at her as if she were a space-corgi.

"Sister!" Charity called out, flowing into the room to embrace Faith.

"Charity, you look amazing!" Faith returned as they

exchanged cheek kisses. Once the pleasantries were done, Charity turned to the girl, her green eyes blazing with excitement.

"And you must be Amberle!" she gushed.

The young programmer nodded, wary, but the woman did not reach out to embrace her or even shake her hand. Faith had already warned her sister to avoid close contact.

"And you are Charity de Rossi," Amberle stated, matter of fact.

Charity's head tipped back, exposing a neck that was smooth and white as she laughed. "I was the last time I looked in a mirror!" she exclaimed as she let her head drop back down, her green eyes glittering. She looked at Faith with an edge of tension.

"It's fine," Faith assured her, indicating that the microphones had been temporarily decommissioned for the privacy of her present company.

Still, Charity glanced about. The center of Faith's villa was huge, the living room alone was a stretch of polished darkness that showcased another stretch of darkness - outer space broken by the great glob of Jupiter looming high in the upper right side of the glass wall. She didn't like it. She never had. It made her feel too exposed.

"Maybe we could..." she started as she quickly considered options she knew to be limited. Obviously not a bedroom and she was discomfited even more by the pool area than she was the living room. "Speak in your office?" Charity suggested.

She did not prefer offices, office meetings, or anything of the sort when it came to sitting down for a good talk - but at least they would be behind closed doors. That offered her some comfort. Faith shrugged.

"Certainly. Are you hungry?" Charity frowned and flapped a hand at the suggestion. Faith looked at Amberle and the girl gave her a lopsided smile.

"Not especially, but I could eat."

Faith brought her wrist close to her lips and spoke into the gold cuff that was fastened there. "Penny," she instructed, "please have Cook prepare a..a..hamburger. And some julienned potatoes and bring them to my office. A carbonated cola as well."

There was an affirmative answer from the gold cuff and the de Rossi woman moved her brown and gold eyes back to Amberle. "Let's go into my office," she said, holding out a hand to show the way as the girl nodded and rose to follow the two sisters. They led her, their expensive heels clacking on the black marble, across the living space and up a few steps and slightly to the right through an open door made of dark and heavy wood.

Once they were through, Faith closed the door behind them. Charity sighed in relief as she crossed the room and kicked off her shoes before sinking down into a chair covered in distressed leather. Amberle sighed as well, in hunger.

The room was an immaculate span of polished metal and burnished wood, deep chairs and gleaming compute surfaces. But what caught her attention was the compute monitor and the trace of a ghost pad she could see on the desktop. There was a barely detectable hum coming from the unseen hard drives, making her blood tingle, calling to her. She felt like a derma junkie, spying a derma pin still glistening with promise. She wet her lips with her tongue.

"Please," Faith intoned, holding a hand out towards the huge leather chair next to Charity, inviting her to sit. Amberle approached it and casually lowered herself down, trying not to look at the chair behind the desk. Faith sat on the sofa and turned to face Charity and the girl.

"First, I would like to say how sorry I am about what happened on that moon. I had no idea that those tests were going to be run nor what was happening on the other side. At the time, it seemed like a good place to hide that had a lot of access for equipment that you needed."

The girl gave her a bit of a smile. "Thanks, but don't worry about it. Everything turned out okay and I met some really good people."

She had grown close to the boys she had met on her assignment, Keaton in particular, and it was the first time she could remember making friends. It was a rare occurrence for her.

Amberle felt a pang of remorse for leaving them on Callisto but she knew that Ms. de Rossi had more work for her. Work that Amberle was interested in. What was she supposed to do if she stayed with them? The only surfing she did was on the Web. She already had another job lined up, and had promised Keaton she would go visit just as soon as she was done.

She liked Keaton. And Cooper. She had never met anyone so optimistic. Even Tyler, who had finally been warming up to her.

The thought of them, of the last time she had seen them, gave her a jolt. Mostly it was the image of Cooper, waving at her from a chair. His leg had been propped up in front of him, held tight in an air cast, but his smile had been as wide and bright as ever.

"There's something else," Amberle said abruptly. "Something important I need to tell you."

The sisters glanced at each other worriedly, slowly lowering their drinks as they looked back at the girl.

"I told you about the...workers," she said, swallowing. She looked at Charity, who gave her a nod, silently acknowledging that she was aware of what had happened. Faith had informed her sister about the computer programmers who had been given an experimental drug which turned them into flesh-eating zombies. "And about the children that had also been given something, something that was keeping them children..." This time both women nodded solemnly. Faith had assured the girl that GwenSeven had nothing to do with it. Why would they? They already had anti-aging drugs that worked perfectly. Amberle took a deep breath. "What I haven't told you, yet, is that there were Golgoths on that moon."

Faith looked up abruptly in surprise, almost spilling her champagne, but Charity's green eyes narrowed in disbelief.

"That can't be," she said.

"It is," Amberle affirmed.

"They are not allowed to be even within a light year of the seven systems," Charity argued. "Certainly not here. In the Jovian System!"

"Are you sure it was a Golgoth you saw?" Faith asked softly, though she was beyond doubting the girl at this point.

Amberle nodded. "And not just one. I'm guessing it was an entire company. And that's only what I saw. I don't know if there were more, somewhere else. But, knowing how they move and operate, it is likely."

A silence followed that was gently broken as the door was pushed open by the ample backside of Mari, Faith's housekeeper. The rest of her body followed, carrying a tray with food and drink for the girl. She thumbed a switch on the side of the tray and it obediently hovered where it was placed. She was followed by Bowe, an assistant to the cook, who had brought in a bottle of champagne and a bottle of Varti.

"Why, thank you!" the sisters chimed in unison as he topped off their glasses. He left both bottles on a nearby bar cart, carefully placing the champagne in a magnetic chilling tube.

Mari put down utensils and condiments in front of the girl on the floating tray. "I hope you find everything to your liking; Cook did the best with what she had on short notice."

"I'm sure it will be fine," Amberle said with a smile. "I found I could eat just about anything."

And she had certainly done so on the zombie-ridden moon she had so recently left, including ground roots, leaves, and rodents roasted on sticks in forests. Still, Mari watched her nervously until the girl picked up the burger and took a large bite.

"Delicious," the girl said around her mouth full of food. A smile of satisfaction crossed the housekeeper's face and she departed, followed by Bowe who closed the door behind him.

The silence swam back into the room.

"Who?" Charity finally asked her sister. "Do you think it could..."

But Faith cut her off with a subtle slash of her hand and nearly imperceptible shake of her head, silently shelving the discussion for another time. She looked instead at Amberle.

"Is it really alright?" she asked, indicating the hamburger.

The girl nodded vigorously. "I don't really pay much attention to food," she said, "unless it's something sweet."

Charity, taking Faith's cue, took a deep breath and a sip from her glass as she refocused her attention. Her slim shoulders dipped as she exhaled and relaxed. "Your eyes keep going to the desk," she murmured with a smile. "Do you see something sweet over there?"

The girl's dusky face took on a look that was both knowing and smiling at once. "I can tell you have some really high-tech equipment there. I'd be lying if I said my hands weren't itching to go exploring."

"Feel free," Charity encouraged, her blonde brows high as she gestured towards the compute equipment with the drink in her hand. Amberle looked at Faith, hopeful.

"Be my guest," Faith told her, also extending a hand in the direction of the desktop hardware.

The girl dropped what was left of the meat sandwich, which was most if it, back onto the plate and pushed the hover tray away from her body. She snagged the napkin as she stood up and wiped her hands thoroughly as she made her way to the chair behind the desk. She sat down carefully, almost reverently, and turned on the compute drive. The compute screen flared to life immediately. Her fingers, dark and slim, hovered above the ghostpad. They twitched with anticipation as she looked up and smiled at her employers.

"What do you want to know?" she asked.

"Where is Faith?" they both said synchronously. "And Hope," they added, also in unison.

"I'm quite certain I've found Hope," she assured them as she pulled a small flap of black latex from a pocket in her maroon pants and slipped it over the thumb and index finger of her right hand.

The sisters watched with bated breath as she expertly connected her mini glove to the compute and got to work. The fingers of her left hand danced over the keypad while her other hand moved entire sections of the screen to display in the air to her right. Only moments later, the same hand pulled up and back, the fingers splayed wide.

The tension was palpable as the de Rossis looked on in anxious anticipation.

From the desk sprang a globe of yellow light, swathed with green and gold and coddled in wisps of white.

Amberle sat back, an expression of triumph lighting her young face, dark skin framed by her faded pink coils of hair.

Charity froze, her expression hard and cold.

Faith sighed and sat back in her chair, feeling disappointed and ashamed.

It's my fault, she thought. *The girl is obviously sick. Yet I pushed her.* She let her glass droop and closed her eyes.

Amberle's expression fell, seeing the obvious disappointment on their faces. "It's Venus," she said.

Charity took a drink from her own glass and Faith simply looked at the girl, feeling as if she had sustained a physical blow.

"What?" Amberle asked. "You wanted to know where they are. I can't say for sure regarding...the other Faith - not yet anyway since there are no electronic transmissions there. But this is where Hope is." The girl stood up and walked around the desk, examining the globe. "I can't pinpoint her exact location, yet, but I could with the right equipment."

Faith looked at the floor, feeling guilt-ridden and sick and disheartened. She had no words.

Charity did.

"Venus," she told the girl, her tone as hard as her features, "is the one planet in the Solar System MW1 that is not inhabited. It has never been inhabited."

"It's where she is," Amberle said softly.

"Venus?" Charity demanded, her voice rising. "Are you serious?"

The young woman bit at her full lip, awash with an unexplainable anxiety that bordered on terror but was saved from answering by a low chuckle that turned everyone's head.

"It's not Venus," a voice said from the doorway.

A young man with skin the color of caramel stood there, lean and muscled under a simple yet form-fitting cotton shirt and trousers. His hazel eyes were dark, topped with thick black brows and a head of jet-black hair.

Jasyn stared at the globe of light, a smirk curving up one side of his full lips. "It's a mirror of Venus."

 FOUR

- The deepest secrets are the ones we keep from ourselves.

The Chimeran Commander, who had begun his life over one hundred years ago as the deadliest bodyguard in the galaxies, looked no more dangerous than a teenage choirboy. His smooth but lightly freckled skin, shining auburn hair, and bright blue eyes would have been the perfect camouflage if his angelic face was not already infamous throughout the universe as belonging to a fanatical cold-blooded killer.

JP sat in the dim light of the Officer's Mess Hall aboard the Chimeran Battlecruiser *Resurrection*, watching a news story on the glass flatscreen inset into the wall. The hour was late and the only other person with him was his Executive Officer, Jan Petrov. The light from the screen lit up the boyish face of the Commander and Petrov's blue eyes and white-blonde hair shone, despite the darkness that surrounded him.

The news reel was made to be shown on a holo, so watching it on a flatscreen made the people look a bit balloonish. Despite the cartoon look of the reporters, there was nothing funny about the story. The Bauam was dead. The man who served as head of the One True Church, promoted from the position of Thuaum after JP had relieved the last one from duty by relieving the lecherous man of his ungodly head, had been assassinated that day by a crazed unbeliever.

The killer, the news reported, had snuck a plastic weapon into a baptism and had knelt as if to receive a blessing and then shot the Bauam as he bent over the man. JP watched and listened, a finger curled over his lip in thought and his blue eyes blazing. He turned, those bright blue eyes fixing on Jan as his hand fell away from his boyish face.

"What do you think?" he asked his second in command.

Jan turned his own blue eyes to his commander. "I think if you had been guarding him, that never would have happened." The barest of smiles graced JP's lips. "Did you know him?" Petrov asked as casually as he could.

JP shrugged - not because he did not know the answer, but because it was trivial to him. "I had met him a few times. I had not, however, paid him much mind."

Petrov nodded. He had never formally met the murdered man, but his face had been burned into his memory. He had been a Thuaum then - a lesser priest but still consequential - when Petrov had seen him in person.

"What will happen?" he asked.

JP shrugged again. "The One Church will promote another Thuaum to take his place, of course. I believe the one from Andromeda has the most seniority."

Just as this one was promoted to Bauam, Jan thought, *after you decapitated the last one.*

"I believe I've seen enough," JP said, standing up and turning off the screen with a touch. "I'm sorry," he apologized, glancing at his Executive Officer who had risen to his feet in respect of his commander. "Did you wish to keep watching?"

Petrov shook his head. "No, thank you. I've seen enough as well. But, if it is all right, I'd like to sit here and think a little longer."

JP clapped Jan on one of his massive shoulders. "Of course. I will see you at morning prayers."

Petrov nodded and then sat back down as his commander

left, making his way through the Officer's Mess Hall with less noise than a cat. Jan stared at the blank screen in the dim light of the abandoned room. He had been with JP for many years, over a century, and had spilled an amount of blood that equaled the boy-faced commander in the name of the One and in the name of the Chimera and the Cause.

Truth be told, however, Jan had stopped believing in the One long before Faith handed him over to JP those many decades past, and he could hardly care less about the Chimera. Though he had developed quite the skill and taste for killing.

Still, he had made a promise to Faith, and she to him - but he had not heard from her in so long. Was the death of the new Bauam, the one that had been the head Thuaum the only time Jan had laid eyes on him, some sort of sign? A signal from Faith? She still had one more promise to keep, and so did he.

Jan pondered these things, trying to decipher and trying to decide as he sat, shrouded in darkness.

C3&0

The IGC ship 787, more commonly known as the Opal Dragon, was the same size as a pre-AOC aircraft carrier. More than three hundred and fifty meters long from nose to tail, her pearlescent scales were covered with layers of titanium and she housed a crew of over three thousand in the spaces within her body that the humans and elves had carved out for themselves. They were her humankind, much like children - but more revered were her true children, Fledgling Dragons that were now returning home.

Cyan and Fledge pulled into her starboard side, the vast interior known as Fledgling Bay, and landed gently on the tarmac of silver skin. The feeling of welcome from the Dragon was apparent for both her children and their Jordans. The feeling coming from the crew was entirely different.

They were not to blame.

In the past year alone, the Dragon had been attacked from within and without. A Jordan had been abducted and tortured and rescued only to find she had succumbed to madness. The Dragon had been drawn from her protective armor, unleashed but unable to save another Jordan from the jaws of death nor from one of her Fledglings fleeing the known universe in search of him. And now the Captain had become ill. Deathly ill.

Tensions were high. High indeed.

Worse, however, was the feeling of dread - and resignation.

Jordan Blue and Jordan Scarlett stood side by side inside Fledge, just fore of the galley. Blue glanced at the other Jordan with her single eye as a vertical slit formed in his skin and split open to form a door.

"You okay?" she asked.

Scarlett pushed a burst of air from her lungs in a desperate laugh. "Seriously? I feel like a canary in a coal mine."

You what? Blue almost asked before she understood the reference. Coal miners on Earth used to send a canary down in a cage to test for toxic gases. If the bird lost consciousness or died they knew the air was unsafe.

The Jordan chuckled instead. "You'll be fine." She cocked her head to the side as a set of silver stairs formed on the outside of the Fledgling. "You know, some mines had special cages for the canaries with a small oxygen tank attached so they could revive the bird."

"You're kidding!" Scarlett exclaimed as Blue stepped out onto the stairs.

"Nope," she said as she descended, the other Jordan following. "Though they only did it so they could reuse the canary."

Scarlett rolled her eyes and joined Blue at the bottom of the stairs on the silver tarmac. The stairs lifted and melted back into the side of her Fledgling. The Red Jordan cast her dark eyes around, taking note of the crew on duty in Fledgling Bay.

Security staff (one at the gate of detfleck that separated the Fledglings from the rest of the bay and two at the door that led from the bay), a medic (coincidentally or by fate - depending on your belief - the same medic that had diagnosed her with Space Madness and had sent her packing) were all present as well as the RNC crew to see to the Fledglings.

The tension was palpable. Scarlett felt a shield coming down over her. One, she realized, that was much like the armor that covered the already protected hide of the Dragon. Jordan Blue grinned and nudged her in the ribs with a bony elbow.

"I'll be your oxygen tank," she assured the other Jordan. Scarlett looked at the one-eyed Jordan and smiled as she felt her defenses dissolve.

"In that case," Scarlett chuckled softly, "drop me down the mine."

Blue gave her a lopsided smile with her ravaged face and strode towards the gate in the detfleck that was guarded by a single security sentry and the medic. The detfleck itself was a neck-high fence that cordoned off the larger part of the bay. It was transparent save for the bouncing multi-colored speckles that reflected and refracted the lights. The specks were gold and rainbow-colored and looked like hallucinatory confetti that came and went, like the mist of a waterfall colliding with slanting sunlight. Any living thing that might try to pass through the fence would be reduced to ribbons of bloody meat.

Something tugged at Scarlett's mind as she glanced at the dancing light. Something about dreams. Something she was supposed to tell Blue. But with the stares and the intensity of the bay, it lingered in the corner of her mind.

The walk was short but one that neither Jordan would ever forget. Scarlett took a deep breath, calming her heart and her nerves in a manner that was newly learned. As she let go of her own tension and fear, she could feel the same returned to her. It started with those on duty in Fledgling Bay - bucking at first like a surprised horse - then settling and calming the same way the animal would. She could feel it as it spread like a wave passing through blood and flesh and Dragonkind.

"What are you doing?" Blue whispered, feeling the wave of release as it lapped at her senses.

Scarlett almost asked what she meant, but as she understood the question she could put words to what she was doing. "I'm letting go," she whispered back. "I'm opening up to accept whatever happens."

Blue turned her head to stare in amazement at the other Jordan. "Do I know you?" she asked.

Jordan Scarlett suppressed a smile. "I doubt it. I don't think I know myself."

Scarlett and Blue stopped in front of the men guarding the gate in the detfleck. One was an armed guard, tapping the butt of the gun holstered below his right hip with feigned nonchalance. The doctor was armed as well, though it was much less conspicuous. Scarlett knew that he had a double syringe of sulfur-mercury in the pocket of the medical coat he wore over his crisp civilian shirt. She suspected that he most likely also had a syringe filled with a heavy sedative in case she started acting in a way he did not consider normal.

What the hell is normal? Scarlett thought, trying to stifle a nervous giggle. *I don't know,* the voice in her head answered in a manner that sounded an awful lot like Master Elaeric's. *But you better hope he remembers which syringe is which.*

Scarlett laughed aloud, drawing curious looks from everyone, including Blue who regarded her with a look of incredulity, her blonde brows pulled high over eye and eyepatch.

"This a no-win situation for me," she said with a throaty chuckle as Blue handed over her pistol to the guard.

"Hello Jordan Scarlett," Doc Westerson greeted. "What is a no-win situation?"

Scarlett continued to chuckle softly in a tone of incredulity. "Mine," she said. "I'm trying to act normal, but I don't know what that is. I'm not sure I ever have."

Doc Westerson smiled. "That in itself shows remarkable progress." He produced a microlight and Scarlett opened her mouth as reflexively as a trained seal. "Have you been to see your family yet?" he asked as he exchanged the light for a micro laser waft. She held out her left wrist and the doc ran the laser over it for a carbon DNA scan. Scarlett shook her head and whistled a few bars of a show tune.

"No," she said. "I wouldn't want to take Fledge anywhere without clearance and... I thought it best to visit this family first."

Westerson produced a box from his pocket with her old ID card on top and she placed her hand over it. Matching her DNA and the chip that was embedded in the flesh between her thumb and index finger, the card lit up green and the doc pulled it off the box and handed it to her, the light dimming then disappearing.

The Doc's smile broadened as he stepped back. "In that case, welcome home, Jordan."

Scarlett took a step to the side as he went through the same procedure with Blue.

"And you, Jordan," he asked as he shone the light in her mouth, "have you given any more thought to getting that eye replaced?"

Blue nodded, making his light click on her teeth. He removed it carefully. "Yes. And now that we have another Jordan back on board, I will schedule an appointment as soon as possible."

The doctor nodded his approval as he checked her DNA and credentials. "Welcome back, Jordan," he said, handing over her ID card and stepping back.

The guard returned her pistol and she dropped it into the

holster slung below her hip before walking away. Scarlett kept pace beside her as the crewmen walked by, dipping their heads.

"Welcome back, Jordans," they greeted as they passed, smiling.

"Thank you," the Jordans answered, nodding to them and all others they passed on their way to enter the belly of the Dragon. All heads bowed to them in warm and silent welcome.

"Do you hear them?" Blue whispered as they left the gate.

"Hear what?" Scarlett whispered back.

"The heartbeats," Blue answered softly. Scarlett gave her dark head a quick shake. They were nearing the end of the bay.

"Whose?"

"Everyone's," Blue answered with a glimmer in her lone blue eye. "They are in tune with one another and picking up speed. It sounds... sounds like...." she trailed off with a goofy smile.

Scarlett impatiently yet discreetly poked the other Jordan. "Sounds like what?" she demanded as they reached the opening from the bay into a wide artery.

Jordan Blue grinned. "It sounds like applause."

Scarlett glanced at the crew manning the bay and could see every one of them looking at her. The tension was still there, but it had shifted into something entirely different. Chests were swelled, eyes gleamed. Smiles were pressed into cheeks with controlled discipline and Scarlett felt herself swelling with the same exhilaration. She could feel the Dragon all around her and it felt like an embrace. She was home.

The Jordans left the bay in warm silence and headed to the fore of the Dragon.

Silent as well, until now, was Galen's ghost.

"Were you serious about your eye?" he asked Blue.

"Yes."

Scarlett looked at her questioningly for a second and then,

realizing she was not being spoken to, politely turned her eyes front as they walked.

"Where were you thinking of getting that done?" Galen asked.

Blue smiled. "Where? You don't mean by whom?"

"Well," Galen remarked, "I think that I could..."

"Hard pass," Blue said, cutting him off. "I'd hate for you to fade away mid-surgery. Thanks, but no thanks." She turned her scarred face towards Scarlett. "He wants..." she started but Scarlett interrupted her with a laugh and a shake of her head.

"Thanks, but my imagination can fill in the gaps."

"Chang?" Galen asked.

Blue nodded. "I trust him as a doctor and, possibly even more important, he can get me something black market."

"Most likely won't be a perfect match," Galen warned.

Blue shrugged. "I think I bowed out of beauty contests some time ago. I want high tech and I want it to be one-way only."

Galen had no dispute for that and the three walked on in silence as they neared the Captain's quarters. Scarlett, among all the peculiar things that seemed to be happening around her, suddenly realized something else.

Calyph, the elfin Engineer with whom she had been having a mild affair, had not come out to greet her. Then she remembered he had been in Kayos, the night of the Synchronicity, to get her. The Jordans had beat him back because they had been brought by the Fledglings.

"When is Calyph due back?" she asked abruptly.

"I don't know," Blue replied. "He left to retrieve you while I was gone. I have no idea what craft he scuttled aboard."

Scarlett slowed and looked at the other Jordan. The tension coming from the Blue Jordan, from *Blue*, who never showed any sign of mental stress, let her know that something was way off course.

"What is it?" she asked.

Blue kept her pace, forcing Scarlett to take a few quick steps after her. For a moment the Red Jordan did not think the Blue Jordan was going to answer her, until the half-elf pilot stopped abruptly. Scarlett stopped a step after and gave her a questioning look.

"You need to be careful with him," Blue advised.

"With Calyph?"

Blue nodded. "I don't think he is who he seems to be."

Scarlett shrugged. "Who is?"

"You got me on that one," Blue muttered. She shook her head, making her three coils of white blonde hair shift across her shoulders. "Do you want to change out of those civilians?" she asked, jerking her chin towards Scarlett's clothing. Scarlett glanced down and nodded.

"Yes," she agreed. "A quick change would be good."

Blue smiled. "I'd like to change as well. Meet you back out here in five?"

Scarlett nodded again. "See you in five."

Blue turned and placed her hand on the panel next to the door that opened to her personal quarters on the Dragon. Scarlett did the same at the next door.

Five minutes later, after changing into a crimson-colored flight suit and giving her face a good scrub, Scarlett emerged from her personal cabin, flooded with memory and emotion. She did not look to her left, where the Jordan of the Emerald Fledgling once resided. The door to Blue's quarters opened a second later and the Jordan walked out dressed in a fresh Mylar flight suit of sparkling blue. Her eyepatch, however, was still black. Blue saw Scarlett's grin and shrugged.

"I'll have to get blue ones made," she said, adjusting the patch slightly with the fingertips of her right hand.

"It looks fine," Scarlett assured her. "I'm sure it will do until you get a new eye."

Blue gave her a ghastly smile and together they turned and made their way to the Captain's quarters. They stopped in front of his door and Blue reached out and rapped on it with her knuckles. They waited in silence for a moment.

"Did he know we were coming?" Scarlett whispered.

Blue nodded, though she looked unsure. "He knew I was due back and Dareus said he would alert him when I arrived. She held up her fist and paused, still listening, but the door slid open before she could knock again. There was no one there but Scarlett jerked back. Her dark eyes flicked around the empty doorway.

"You smell that?" she asked softly.

Blue shook her head of white-gold hair as she leaned into the room, her scarred face pinched and anxious. "Captain Brogan?" she called.

"Come in, Jordan," a voice called from around the corner.

Blue walked into the cabin that was well appointed but not sumptuous. She passed through the entryway towards the living room. It had not been cleaned for some time and it showed. There were dirty bowls on the coffee table and a lone candle burned on a side table, black acrid smoke rising from its wick.

She rounded the corner to see the Captain sitting on his sofa in front of a holo fire. A blanket was draped over shoulders that looked atrophied under his pearlescent uniform that was in desperate need of a wash. His silver hair, though relatively short, was longer than normal and flattened in areas where he had lain on it. His cheeks were sunken and unshaved. His right hand gripped his forehead as if trying to contain a splitting headache. It was an unsettling sight for the Blue Jordan.

"Captain Brogan?" she queried, her voice oddly mouse-like.

The hand dropped slowly from his face and his eyes

widened as he saw Blue, dressed in her normal sparkling flight suit rather than the black one she had taken to wearing in mourning.

"Jordan Blue..." he began before he realized that she was not alone. Tilting his head he saw Scarlett appear behind her and he rose to his feet. "Scarlett!" he exclaimed in joyous surprise. "Jordan Scarlett!"

The expression on her face, so reticent that it bordered on shyness and so very un-Scarlett-like, made him unsure of whether he wanted to laugh or cry. As he crossed the room in two quick strides and embraced the Jordans in one great hug, he realized he was doing both.

 FIVE

- The truth isn't always buried. It's disguised as something ordinary.

The young man leaned casually against the doorframe, his crossed arms showing round biceps and shoulders. Faith froze as if a dangerous animal had caught their scent and had paused at the entrance to their den. Amberle shrank back, using the compute monitor as cover.

Only Charity smiled. "Jasyn, please come in." The raven-haired man straightened, uncrossed his arms and took a few steps into the room, still staring at the hologram of Venus that floated in brilliant hues of orange and red and gold above the desk. "Ahem," Charity said, delicately clearing her throat to get his attention. "The door, please," she murmured when he looked at her.

Jasyn, slightly mesmerized by the globe of light, shook off the hypnotic feeling. He put a strong hand on the heavy door, which had swung silently open just enough to let him slip through, and pushed it closed.

His dark hazel eyes went to the young woman behind the desk and she shrank back a little more. "Can you pull up an orrery?" he asked her. "Not the entire system, just from the sun to the Earth?"

Amberle perked back up instantly once she could be of use.

She leaned forward and her fingers danced across the plane of the desk.

Suddenly, the hologram of Venus was thrust to the side so quickly that both Faith and Charity jerked back in surprise. The entire far side of the office, and the office was quite large, was lit up by a swirling globe of golden light so great that they could not see the edges. Between the hologram of the sun and the one of Venus floated another three-dimensional sphere. Mercury, tiny compared to the sun, floated like a gray marble. Venus came next and then Earth, a beautiful globe of blue and green surrounded by a caul of white clouds.

Jasyn stepped between the two planets and grinned triumphantly at the two sisters, much in the same manner Amberle had done only moments ago. The young woman watched, her eyes wide in her dark face, to see if the reception would be different this time.

Faith's countenance was stoic and tight-lipped while Charity's held the suggestion of amusement.

"I'm not sure what I am supposed to be seeing," she drawled. "Why don't you enlighten us, darling?" She took a sip of her drink and smiled encouragingly.

Jasyn looked surprised. "Are you serious?" He looked at Faith but her expression had not changed. "Look at how close these are!" he told them. All eyes went to the holographic spheres floating in the office and the sisters blinked at them. Jasyn's dark brows went up as no one offered any revelation. "Look at the color, and at the sizes of Earth and Venus!" All eyes now moved across the glowing orrery but again neither sister did anything but blink and wait for further clues.

"The dimensions are to scale," Amberle offered.

"Exactly!" Jasyn exclaimed, making her jump slightly. But when she had nothing else to add the young man stuck out his bottom lip and blew a burst of air over his face. Then he snapped his fingers, struck by an idea. "Keep this system here," he told her, "and project on it the same model and scale of Venus as it was a hundred and fifty years ago."

Amberle leaned forward once more and again her fingers thrummed over the top of the desk. There was a pulse of light and she sat back, her eyes darting over the spheres of light and color. Initially, she thought nothing had changed.

Jasyn's smile broadened once again as he waited for them to see. A moment later it hit them all at once.

Both sisters were on their feet, Faith letting out a strangled cry as her free hand went to her mouth. Charity leaned back in an effort to take it all in, her green eyes staring and her mouth open. Amberle's fingers twitched.

"Holy shit," she whispered.

Faith walked precariously to the globe in front of her, as if afraid to disturb it. The gold-colored sphere was turning gently, rotating slowly on an unseen axis. Inside the holographic image of Venus was another planet, this one blue and green and brown and white. It was about half the size of the globe that encased it and its rotation was faster, and in the opposite direction.

"This can't be real," Faith murmured.

"What is real?" Jasyn asked, his voice flat.

Faith gave him a cold glare before turning her eyes back to the image in front of her. "I mean, is it just a mirage?"

"Well," Jasyn said, "a mirage is an optical illusion. This is a physical one."

"To what purpose?" Charity asked, swirling her cocktail as she regained her composure. "And how did you know?"

"I've become wary of mirrors," Jasyn told her, his voice devoid of emotion.

Charity shrugged but Faith looked away from him in dismay and back at the planets. "It's spinning too fast," she mused aloud and glanced at the image of Earth before staring once again at Venus. "It's going about the same speed the Earth is."

Amberle looked at the computer in front of her and then stood up and sidled around the desk. She went around Venus and stood next to Faith, looking inside. Finding what she sought, she pushed her gloved finger through the projection of the outer gases and touched the globe inside.

"I traced the genetic code you gave me and got a hit." Her hand moved under the projection of noxious clouds. "Here." The inner orb was slightly larger than her own head, and the place where she touched was a continent just above the southern hemisphere. "I think Hope is here."

Tears filled Faith's brown and gold eyes and her hand came up to cover her mouth.

"Do you mean,'" she whispered between her fingers, "her... remains?"

Jasyn stepped up behind her and grasped her shoulders gently but firmly.

"Oh no!" Amberle said. "There is someone alive there with the genetic code you gave me."

Faith's body sagged with relief, supported by Jasyn's strong hands.

Charity stood and retrieved the bottle of Varti. "So you are now telling us that there are life forms on Venus? Where nothing has lived, ever?" She shook her white-blonde coiffed hair in disbelief as she refilled her glass and then sat on the arm of one of the large leather chairs, carefully crossing one leg over the other.

Jasyn released Faith and moved towards the desk. Amberle edged away from him and shrugged at Faith.

"There is plenty of life there," she told her.

Faith frowned. "That planet is notorious for being uninhabitable. It is too hot, has too much pressure, and the atmosphere is mostly carbon dioxide." She looked at Charity but was met with blonde brows raised high over green eyes.

"You're not asking me, are you?"

Faith's frown deepened in exasperation and she looked at Jasyn for help. His handsome face was split with a smile showing perfectly made teeth.

"Humans, and elves, have been terraforming less hospitable worlds for centuries," he reminded her, leaning back against the desk.

"And that is what you think happened?" she asked. "That it was terraformed? That someone... that... oh my god...that they..." her voice softened and trailed off as she comprehended the possibilities, and the probability.

The room became silent.

Charity's green eyes flicked back and forth between Faith and Jasyn. "Are you telling me they succeeded?" she asked, incredulous. "Those crazy Zenarchist monks terraformed Venus and the elves simply covered their tracks?"

Jasyn shrugged, the muscles of his shoulders bunching under the snug shirt. "It was what they were trying to do," he told her.

Charity tipped back her white-blonde head and laughed. And laughed. Amberle thought she sounded a little bit crazy. Her brown and green eyes sought out Faith who was staring raptly at the image of Venus.

"I don't understand what's happening," she said softly.

Faith turned to her. "How much history do you know?" she asked.

Amberle blew a burst of air through pursed lips and made her way back to her hamburger. "Mostly just what I've read online. I wasn't very good in school. I dropped out early and took Galactic Web classes to graduate."

In truth, Amberle had hated school. Not the learning, though it was taught at an incredibly boring speed. It was the other kids. Middle school had been the worst. Amberle was teased by everyone about practically everything, and none of it she could understand.

They made fun of her dark skin, though every kid in her neighborhood had skin in varying shades of black or tan. She was teased for being poor, though most had less than her. She was ridiculed for being smart by a sea of people she saw as idiots, a conundrum she could not get her head around.

When Amberle was only twelve, she had begged her parents to drop out and finish her schooling on the Web but they refused. It wasn't until years later, when they saw she could make money from all her time spent jacked into a computer, that they finally relented. Extra income, even a little, helped ease the pressure on their small family.

She took a bite of the burger and waited for Faith to explain.

"You know about our company?"

Amberle looked at her as if she were crazy. "GwenSeven?" she asked after she finished chewing her food. "Of course. Everybody does. You guys make everything, including people." Her eyes flicked to Jasyn and back to Faith.

Charity chuckled and took a sip from her drink, but a slight line formed between Faith's brows. No one had mentioned or even hinted at the fact that Jasyn was a construct. And he was one of the most perfect of those ever made. But it seemed the girl knew. She would ask her later.

For now, the elder de Rossi woman gathered her thoughts and nodded before taking a sip of champagne. "Yes. Well, some years before the Rebellion, we were approached by the Elves of Titan. They wanted to leave known civilization and start over on a terraformed planet or moon, away from technology and war."

"Wait," Amberle said, lowering her burger. "The same elves that blew up in the explosion that wiped out life on Earth?"

"Well," Faith replied, "no one is quite sure what happened.

But, for the lack of better knowledge, it is certainly a possibility."

"It was never proven that the explosion affected Earth," Jasyn added from where he leaned against the desk. "Or if it was a coincidental but unrelated incident."

"Either way," Faith continued, "Venus was where the elves were headed. They disappeared at the time of the explosion, leading everyone to believe they had been evaporated by the blast."

"Our sisters as well," Charity added, again swirling her drink, making the ice clink in the glass.

"But I never thought they were dead," Faith said softly. "I refused to think it."

The girl's eyes drifted back to the image of Venus, a smaller earth-like planet rotating inside it. "That's what he meant," she whispered. "It makes sense, now."

"Who?" Faith asked. "What makes sense?"

"Hellas," Amberle said softly. "A man I met on the Elba moon, where I was starting my work for you. He told me that Hope was within."

A small whimpering sound came from Faith and she cleared her throat to cover it. "And you said you could pinpoint her once you got closer?"

"Yes," the girl agreed. "I'll need a UPG, a Universal Positioning Guide. Then I could program..." she left her sentence unfinished as Faith turned and circled behind the huge desk. She opened a drawer and pulled out a box small enough to fit in the palm of her hand. She walked back around the desk and handed it to the girl.

"Use this when you get closer. It might help."

Amberle switched on the box to see a holographic grid. It was filled with numbers - galactic coordinates. The planets were clearly marked. Two blips of red, one faint and one slightly darker hovered in the image. The faded one hovered close to Earth. The brighter one inside of Venus.

"You had this the whole time?" the girl asked, incredulous. "Why didn't you just use it?"

Faith shrugged as she went to the bar cart and refilled her champagne glass. "For one, I thought it was broken."

"I'm not surprised. This thing has to be a hundred years old!"

Faith shrugged again. "Plus, there should not be more than one dot." She leaned forward and spread her fingers over the image, zooming in. Amberle could now see Mars as well as Jupiter. In the image, now close to Jupiter, were two bright blips - one gold and one green – practically on top of one another.

Amberle eyes went up and flicked between the sisters, noticing the similarity of their rings for the first time. And the differences in the colors of the stones. "You and Charity," she said, glancing back down at the lights in the holo.

Faith nodded. "Hope's beacon had become two beacons, one barely there and both of them where no person was to be found. It was better to think that the tracking device, or the homing mechanism, or the transmission itself had been corrupted somehow - rather than think that something terrible had happened to her."

"And Faith?" Amberle ventured. "The other one...did she not have a similar tracking device?"

Faith held up her hand, showcasing the set of rings there.

"Ah!" The young woman sat down and resumed eating her hamburger, thinking. After a moment, she swallowed. "So, now that we know where at least one of them is, what are you going to do?"

"Go after her," Faith and Charity said in unison.

"How?" Amberle asked. "I know enough to know that nothing, other than a probe, can get through the atmosphere on Venus."

Faith looked at her sister in despair, then at Jasyn. His dark eyes softened. "I think a Dragon could go through it without any trouble whatsoever."

The corners of Faith's lips turned up, but her expression was sad. "I do not consider many things beyond my reach these days," she replied, "but a Dragon could be tricky." Her eyes took on a faraway look, turning back to the fiery orb as she murmured quietly to herself. "Actually, if I took it to the Council I'm sure they would...but do we want to keep this to ourselves, and how long would the IGC take.. could a Dragon...?"

"We definitely want to keep this to ourselves," Charity answered. "And not just because we promised the elves secrecy."

"Could a Fledgling do it?" Amberle asked.

Jasyn shrugged. "If a Dragon could, I think a Fledgling could manage just as well."

Charity's green eyes flicked up to meet Faith's tawny gaze.

"Do you think she would?" Faith asked.

"I cannot say," Charity replied. "I am not sure if she is ready to leave the IGC. But I definitely think she is questioning, wavering."

"Are you talking about Noel?" Jasyn demanded, emotion in his voice for the first time since entering the room. "The one that shot me?"

Both sisters ignored him.

"She's not sure what to think or whom to trust," Charity finished.

Jasyn grunted in agreement and was ignored again.

"We can ask her, though I do not think she is ready," Faith confessed.

"What then?" Charity asked. "Hatch the eggs and fly them ourselves?"

Faith smiled. "An intriguing idea."

"I was joking."

"I know." Faith turned and let her eyes rest on the young woman, less than delicately sticking fried potatoes into her mouth. "I'm wondering if there is another Fledgling that might help us."

Amberle nodded as she licked salt from the tips of her fingers. It was what she had been considering as well. "I think Verdana would do anything for us if we find Jade."

Jasyn dipped his chin and looked from Faith to the girl and then back again. "You're talking about the Fledgling that disappeared and the dead Jordan?"

Faith gave him a nod and took a sip from her glass. "Amberle has found the Green Fledgling."

Jasyn and Charity regarded the young woman with no small amount of surprise.

"She, Verdana I mean, wants Jade back," the girl informed them.

"His body?" Charity asked.

Amberle gave her a nod and swallowed. "Yes. But what she wants even more, and would probably be easier for us to get, is Jade alive."

Charity planted an elbow on her knee and her glass moved back and forth in front of her face like a charmed snake as she smirked at the girl. "And just where are you going to find a living Jordan that has been dead for half a year?"

"Not where," Jasyn corrected. "When."

Amberle grinned at him. "Exactly."

A moment of silence filled the air like a swelling balloon and then was pricked.

"Wait, wait, wait, wait." Charity said, leaning forward as the suggestion sank in. Her green eyes narrowed as she thought. "Are you talking about... going back in time to get the Jordan?"

Jasyn nodded. Charity's face scrunched in puzzlement.

"That's ridiculous," she said. "If you can use the Fledgling to go back in time, why don't you just go back and talk Hope out of leaving? Or stop Faith from leaving?"

"For one thing," Faith said, "no one was ever able to talk Hope out of anything. Faith wasn't very different in that aspect."

Charity harrumphed. "I'll give you that," she agreed.

"Plus," Jasyn added, "time can be tricky. And messing with it can be dangerous. *Really* dangerous. Otherwise, the IGC would already be manipulating it to their own ends."

"Dangerous how?" Amberle asked. She wasn't afraid, just curious.

"If we go back into our past, we run the risk of changing our future, which would alter our current reality."

Amberle laughed at her own feeling of confusion and then, happening to glance at Charity, laughed harder at her expression of absolute perplexity. On her perfect face, the look was comical.

"I think he means," Faith said, "if it was safe to do, the IGC would be doing it. They could use a Dragon to go back and change anything. They could crush the Rebellion before it even starts."

"I see," Charity said, sipping her drink as she thought it over.

Jasyn smiled. "I don't think it would be safe for any of us to go. We have been around too long. We could run into our former selves, or even someone who has known us. I don't know what it would do to our future, or the future in general. I don't know the details of physics, but I think we could end up in a time loop, a temporal paradox, or possibly even rip the fabric of time."

Charity sighed. "You lost me again on that one," she said. "But is it as terrifying as you make it sound?"

"If you could go back a hundred years," Faith proposed, her voice thoughtful as if she might be asking herself, "what would you do?"

"I would try to warn my former self," Charity answered immediately.

"Changing the past," Faith affirmed. "Even the smallest act could ripple out to affect the entire universe. Good or bad, we couldn't know."

"Which," Jasyn added, "makes Amberle perfect for this. If she goes back that far, even her parents would not have been born yet. Her altering anything would likely have little or no repercussions to her future."

"What about the Jordan?" Amberle asked. "What will happen to him? To his own future?"

Faith pressed her lips together and shook her head slowly, almost in apology.

Charity knew the look and knew that Faith did not care much about the life of the Jordan, past or future, not as much as she cared about getting their sisters back. Charity knew because she felt the same way.

"He might be able to prevent his early, untimely death," she offered the girl.

Amberle looked at each of them in turn. What they were asking went a lot farther than programming or hacking. This was involvement on another level, more than just a job. She took a moment to measure herself and see if she was up to such a thing. She blew a lungful of air through puffed cheeks.

"And," Faith added as if sensing her thoughts, "our original contract still stands. Any hardware, software, money, credits… you name it."

The young woman nodded, a small smile gracing her lips at the reminder. She thought of the glasses she had seen Faith's PA wearing and her smile widened.

Or I could skip the glasses and go straight to orbital implants, she thought. The idea made her entire body tingle.

"I'll reach out to Verdana," she said.

Faith gave her a warm smile. "Thank you. Though I think it could wait until morning. How about a shower and some fresh clothes?" She knew the girl had been through hell, and there was no knowing the last time she had slept, yet the disappointment on not getting back behind the compute screen was clear on her face. "And maybe some dessert," she added.

Amberle brightened instantly. "I think that sounds great." She rose to her feet and let Faith usher her from the office.

Jasyn held the door open for them and as they passed by he asked Faith softly, "what did the J stand for?"

"Janitor," she replied under her breath.

The construct found himself unable to repress a smile. His dark eyes swept the room before he left, passing over the images of Earth and Venus. He could hardly believe they had not noticed what he had seen immediately. Then again, it took them a while just to see what Venus had hidden.

Let them keep their secrets, he thought as he closed the door. *I'll keep mine.*

 SIX

- Family secrets are like roots, anchors to an unseen past.

"Happy Birthday!" shouted a chorus of mostly ten-year-old girls, backed by a single set of parents, a sixteen-year-old boy and a grandfather who bordered on ancient – for a human at least.

Jeanette Mattatock leaned forward, holding back the curtains of her dark curls with both hands, and blew out the candles on her cake.

The candles were a bit of a novelty since most cakes were topped with holo candles nowadays. But these were little wax sticks, each topped with a flicker of real flame. The other girls around the table, friends from school and dance classes, watched mesmerized as the little flames went out with a whoosh.

Everyone clapped and Grandpa, the one who both provided and insisted on real candles for every birthday, took a picture with his acrylic. It was the first time he had used the device for a picture and was surprised at the quality. He beamed at his granddaughter as she melted into the small crowd of girls so her mother could cut the cake.

"Why does everyone clap?" Sean mumbled good-naturedly as his grandpa handed him the slim pane of the acrylic. "There's only eleven candles for Pete's sake." He tapped on the acrylic and sent the picture to the printer in his mother's home office, knowing without asking what his grandpa wanted. "But you," Sean continued, directing his eyes to the old man next to him, "if you could blow out all the candles on your cake, I'd clap till my hands bled."

Grandpa gave him a grin. "I don't think they could make a cake big enough to fit all my candles. And, if they did, it would probably burn the place down!"

Sean chuckled and looked away from the grin. He used to avoid looking at his grandpa's smile because of all the yellowed, broken, or missing teeth. Grandpa, however, had relented to Sean's appeals for taking some anti-aging pills, and had grown a whole new set of what he referred to as "chompers." It was a strange sight and Sean wasn't quite used to it. Half the time he couldn't stop staring. It was like looking at a prehistoric teenager.

"I'll go grab that from the printer," he suggested and left Grandpa who was glad to accept a piece of cake from Sean's father, John.

Grandpa took a huge bite of frosting and watched as the girls sat down to confetti cake and pistachio gelato. He was glad that Jeanette was able to have a party. It had been touch and go for the last few months. Jeanette's mother, Rebecca, had found out that her daughter had been ditching her dance classes to hit the arcade in favor of starfighter simulator games. The girl and her mother had been fighting like cats ever since. Sean had asked Grandpa if he thought she was in more trouble for ditching class or for playing starfighter games.

Grandpa had cackled. "Oh, the starfighter games for sure. Your lack of enthusiasm to start flying probably made your mother feel like her children weren't going to run off and join the war like the rest of our crazy family. Jeanette sure surprised her!" Grandpa had cackled again, even louder than before.

"Well," Sean had recollected aloud, "didn't you say the

Mattatocks have always had at least one pilot in the family? And that person is considered the guardian of the family?"

"Yes, but I think your mother was secretly harboring the hope that Johanna would have a child who would follow in her footsteps."

"I think Auntie Jo has reached a rank in the IGC where they don't let you get married or have children."

Grandpa had nodded thoughtfully. "A fact that your mother is either not aware of or is choosing to ignore."

"Probably choosing to ignore," Sean had said.

Sean came back with a printed picture taken of Jeanette blowing out her candles as Grandpa was finishing his cake and the girls were squealing to open presents.

"C'mon, Grandpa. Let's go put this in your book and take a break from all this craziness."

Grandpa was quick to agree. His hearing had been getting better and for being small girls they sure were loud. He put his plate and fork in the kitchen while Sean grabbed a piece of cake to take with him. They left the pod and crossed the hall to Grandpa's door where the old man put his hand on the doorknob, gave it a second to recognize him, and turned the handle. Sean, cake in one hand and Jeanette's picture in the other, followed him inside.

Grandpa's pod had a sense of timelessness to it. He had kept the same furniture and maintained it in the same configuration for as long as Sean could remember. No matter how many times they had moved over the years, which had been quite a few, it was the same old couch, same old rug. There was a clock on the wall – one with a round face and arms – that Grandpa had used to teach the kids how to tell time the way people had before everything was digitized.

The shelves in Grandpa's living room varied but the stuff on them never did. Grandpa had a collection of books that were typed on paper and sandwiched between pieces of canvas covered cardboard. As a Christmas present a few years back, John and Rebecca had them all restored. Grandpa was not pleased at the idea but could hardly argue since the glue holding the pages together in each book had all but disintegrated. The finished product, however, had delighted him since the only thing that was replaced was the adhesive.

Sean left his plate on the small table by the couch, walked past the flatscreen (Grandpa hated watching stuff on a holo) and pulled out the small book from the third shelf that held Jeanette's photographs. He opened it and flipped through the pages of pictures until he came to a blank one and then slipped the newest image into the empty plastic sleeve while Grandpa headed for the kitchen.

As Sean returned the book to the shelf, sliding it in next to his own, his eyes traveled over the volumes that held photos. There were five, all with initials stamped on the spines. His own was the odd man out, sporting a simple SM. All the others were marked JM – though each of the books were different colors. One held Jeanette's, obviously. The others belonged to his father, John, his Aunt Johanna, and their younger brother, Joe Junior. He knew their father had been Joe Senior, of course, but there was no book for him. Or any Mattatock who had come before him.

"Grandpa?" Sean asked.

"Ayuh," the old man answered, returning from the kitchen with a can of Aleket. He dropped down onto his sofa and cracked it open, taking a swig and giving his lips a smack in appreciation.

Sean almost asked where all the other grandchildren were but held back at the last second as he realized he knew. They were dead. But so was Uncle Joey, but he had a book, even though it was barely twice the size of Jeanette's. "What made you start taking and saving the birthday pictures?" he asked instead.

"To be honest, son, sometime when your Grandpa Joe was

just a boy I realized I could not remember how old he was. It was when I started forgetting a lot of things but, for me, that was the worst. When your father was born, I decided I would take a snapshot of him every year on his birthday. That way, if I forgot, I could just go back and count the pages. I did the same with everyone that came after."

Sean chuckled. "But last year I knew you would get frustrated when you couldn't remember how old I was. Why didn't you just go to my book and count the pages?"

Grandpa's mouth twisted at the corner in a humorless smirk. "I forgot I could do that."

Sean laughed and turned to give the shelves a parting glance when something caught his eye. It was on the shelf above the photo albums, on the far-right side of Grandpa's books, just a slim piece of shiny black metal. He didn't know if it was new or if it had always been there, always with the books in every pod, and if maybe he was now just tall enough to see it.

Sean flicked the blonde hair from his eyes and reached up, pinched it between his fingers and pulled it out.

The object turned out to be almost as large as Jeanette's birthday cake, though much thinner. It was a fancy certificate, framed in black chrome behind a pane of glass. Sean looked at it in awe.

He recognized the compass and square insignia of the Masons, framing a capital "G." Above the Masonic emblem was an ostentatious gold seal and below it all was a paragraph of showy words bestowing honors on one Fletcher J. Mattatock for having built the largest structure in the universe.

"Holy shit!" Sean breathed.

Grandpa, who would normally admonish the boy about his language, took a drink from the can of Aleket and grinned, showcasing his new set of pearly whites.

Sean looked at the old man on the couch in amazement. "This has your name on it! Is this you?" he asked, holding out the frame.

Grandpa laughed. He did not caw or cackle - as Sean was accustomed to – he laughed. The sound was as incongruent as the new teeth but, at the moment, Sean noticed neither one.

"Of course it's me!" Grandpa affirmed. "You think I've worked as a babysitter my whole life?" He laughed again and the warm sound filled the podment.

"You were a mason?" Sean asked stupidly, trying to get his head around it. "A *Master* Mason?"

"Ayuh," Grandpa affirmed, taking another drink from the can and smiling his new smile.

"And you…" Sean paused and chuckled in near disbelief, "… you built the largest structure in the universe?"

Grandpa chuckled as well. "Oh, ayuh," he asserted, "but in the record book at the time there were plenty of those little stars."

Sean looked at him, perplexed. "What kind of stars?"

Grandpa twiddled his fingers in Sean's direction. "Those little stars they put in the books for all the excuses and explanations."

"You mean asterisks?"

Grandpa pointed at him with the hand that held the Aleket. "That's them! Asterisks! Yup. Asterisks to let you know it wasn't for being tallest and so on, just the largest footprint. You gotta know moon densities, expandable footings, and steel-crete for something like that." He nodded thoughtfully and tapped a finger on the side of the can.

"What building? Where?"

"The GwenSeven compound on Dione."

"What? You've got to be pulling my leg!"

"Nope."

Sean looked at him, amazed. He realized that he knew a

lot of their family history where pilots were concerned but he never really knew anything about Grandpa. He glanced down at the framed certificate. "Why isn't this hanging on a wall in here?"

Grandpa shrugged. "Got to be a pain to keep taking them down and hanging them up. Easier just to put 'em on a shelf."

"Them?"

Grandpa lifted his chin towards the shelves and Sean followed his gaze. He didn't see any more frames but there was a manila envelope on the top shelf wedged between two of the books. Sean reached up and plucked it out. He put the framed certificate on the table next to his untouched piece of cake, lifted the flap on the envelope and pulled out another certificate.

It was similar to the first, same size and same insignia and seal of the Mason's Lodge, though this one was in recognition for best city planning by an individual. Sean did not know what shocked him more, the nature of the award or the date on it.

"You?" Sean asked. "You planned an entire city?"

Grandpa shrugged. "Not much of a city, really. Not then, anyway. Just a small town but, I will say, it was planned out well and turned out even nicer." A look of surprise flooded his blue eyes. "I owned a restaurant there," he realized aloud. "I suppose I might still own it."

Sean burst out laughing. "A restaurant! Now I know you are joking!"

"Nope."

Sean looked at the award in his hands and then back at the old man on the couch. "A restaurant," he murmured. "What else aren't you telling us, Grandpa?"

"Yes," a voice agreed from the door.

Both Sean and Grandpa's heads turned sharply as their eyes went to the open door of the podment. A woman stood there, dark waves of hair framing a face both beautiful and hard. One arm held open the door while the other held two boxes wrapped in metallic paper and tied with holographic ribbon. She wore a shirt of crimson silk, black leather pants and black boots that came up to her knees.

"Johanna!" Grandpa exclaimed, delighted.

"Auntie Jo!" Sean called out at the same time.

The Red Jordan grinned like a shark.

"What else aren't you telling us, Grandpa?" she finished.

☙❧

Bjorn sat on a park bench in the upper klick of Three Mile City on Io, dressed in dun-colored, nondescript clothes. The outfit made him feel both thrilled, the role of a spy always did, and like a fool.

"You should wear a hat," Lucy had suggested.

The Chimeran Commander had narrowed his green eyes at her, not sure if she was being serious. He suspected that his lovely, dark-haired droid was trying to cultivate a sense of humor.

"Maybe you should wear one," he had replied.

Lucy had smirked at him, causing both his frown and his suspicion to deepen. The park he now sat in, under a great and spreading tree, was full of sunshine and quiet at this time of day. His bodyguard, Julian, watched from some distance away. Bjorn was trying to be as circumspect as possible. Considering where they were, his greatest danger was the person he had been waiting for, but she had yet to make an appearance or enter the building he was surveilling.

The thought of her made him feel warm inside and the awareness of it made him want to laugh. The green-eyed

Commander suppressed the mirth from bubbling out but was unable to keep himself from smiling. He glanced at Lucy and saw that she was smiling as well, her prismatic eyes changing colors.

Bjorn's expression immediately fell, knowing that she was processing his demeanor and calculating what might be the most likely cause. He turned his attention from her to the building he had been watching from over his shoulder. The building that now housed a former teacher of his, one from long ago. He mentally added up the years since he had last seen him and wondered what he looked like. What human aging might have done to him.

He was about to turn back to Lucy when movement caught his eye. He froze, intent on the lone person walking down the sidewalk from the direction of the magnetic tram stop that was less than three hundred meters away.

It was her.

Bjorn knew he should turn his face away, lest she spot him, but he found himself unable to move even a single muscle. After exiting the tram her dark eyes had gleaned the area around her and, seeing nothing to put her on alert, continued on with confident strides down the paved, tree-lined walkway. She passed various sweet shops and coffee kiosks before the path led her into a quaint residential area.

The Jordan was wearing a shirt of crimson silk, black leather pants and black riding boots. The large, dark curls that framed her face blew back in the breeze along with the silk shirt that flattened against her full breasts, making the breath of the Chimeran Commander hitch in his chest.

Now, knowing that he was openly staring and possibly with his mouth open, Bjorn turned his head away, the second before the Jordan turned her own head, her dark eyes sweeping across the park.

Scarlett noted the couple on the bench, a slight line forming between her brows as she saw a tall blonde man next to a dark-haired female, then glancing at the handsome young man purchasing a coffee cone at the park's concession stand. A very handsome young man. Her eyes narrowed for a moment before her suspicions were mollified - reminding herself that she was in the Upper Klick, aka plastic-surgery central.

When Bjorn dared to look again, she was gone.

"That was her!" he exclaimed to his droid. "Did you see her?"

"I did not need to," Lucy remarked.

"Her clothes!" Bjorn exclaimed with quiet excitement as he glanced over his shoulder to make sure she was truly out of sight. "Those are the clothes I bought her in Kayos!" He turned his face to Lucy. "Why do you think she is wearing them?"

"Because she has a lack of any other civilian clothes?"

Bjorn frowned at her and then narrowed his green eyes in suspicion. "Are you trying to be funny again?"

"Yes. Did it work?"

Bjorn's face softened and he chuckled. "Yes," he said, "pretty funny."

"Then why did you laugh now," Lucy asked, "and not before?"

"Because before I thought you were being serious."

"So," Lucy asked as her eyes changed from green and gold to red and gold, "a serious reply generates a serious response, and a humorous reply generates a humorous response?"

"Not necessarily. But it was unexpected, so I wasn't sure if you were joking."

"So, it's only funny when it's expected?"

Bjorn sighed. "Not always, but it is something I cannot explain."

"Cannot or will not?"

"Take your pick," the Commander said, exasperated. "Sometimes explaining shit to you makes life not worth living."

"Are you considering suicide?" the troll asked, sounding genuinely curious.

"I will if we keep having this conversation!" Bjorn hissed. "Can we please return to my first question? Why do you think she's wearing those clothes?"

"There could be any number of reasons," Lucy answered. "She likes the way they look. She likes the way they feel. Or, you can refer to my first response." The dark-haired troll looked sideways at Bjorn, her kaleidoscope eyes changing colors.

"Ha, ha," Bjorn said. "Is it possible she is wearing them because they remind her of me?"

Lucy nodded. "That also is a possibility. But not very funny."

"How would you know?"

"Good point," the troll acquiesced, her ever changing eyes shifting color.

 SEVEN

- Secrets are often just stories that were never told.

Scarlett was greeted warmly by her nephew and grandfather. Across the hall, she was given an even more enthusiastic welcome by the birthday girl who was not only glad to see her auntie and get a few presents she knew would be extra special, but to show her off to her friends.

The girls at the party gave an appropriate amount of oohs and ahhhs as the Jordan's brother embraced her in a bear-like hug. Scarlett did not miss that Rebecca's hug was both stiff and perfunctory. A slight movement of John's head, negligible to anyone but his sister, told her not to ask. The Jordan's own chin lifted in the same manner and she moved away to give Jeanette her presents and watch her open them.

"You gotta admit," John said softly but quite cheerfully, "she's going to impress them a lot more than a birthday clown." Rebecca harrumphed.

Scarlett knelt by Jeanette and handed her two boxes, each tied with a holo ribbon of bright light. The Jordan saw that her niece had lost her round face and plump, childish fingers and sighed. *Damn,* she thought, *she looks a bit like me. Though her hair is curlier.* She shot a glance at her brother, who was also dark-eyed and dark-haired. Rebecca was fair and her looks came though undeniably in Sean.

They both have straight hair, Scarlett mused. *Mine has waves and Jeanette has real curls, actual ringlets.*

The birthday girl tugged on the ribbon encircling the smaller of the presents and it vanished with a showy flicker of light. She eagerly removed the top of the box. There was no way to disguise the crestfallen expression as she forced a smile and withdrew a plush object from the box.

Her dark eyes went up to her auntie. Though she considered herself too old for stuffed toys, she was not about to be rude. Certainly not to her Auntie Jo.

"Thank you," she said politely. "Is it supposed to represent some sort of alien?"

Scarlett laughed heartily, both from the question itself as well as seeing the forced appreciation in her niece's expression.

"I know you might be a little old for fluffy toys," she admitted, "but it has to do with where I have been these past few months, as well as my second present. It's not an alien, but an animal."

Jeanette held the plush figure up and turned it in her hands, now curious.

"The humans call them horses," her father told her. "The elves have another name but I can't remember what it is."

"It also has something to do with my other present," Scarlett said. "Go on," she encouraged, "open it."

Jeanette put the stuffed animal aside and pulled on the ribbon from the second box, making it disappear in an effervescent flash of light. She tore off the lid and this time her face lit up with excitement as she saw what was inside. It was a pair of boots, but none like she had ever seen before. They were heavy and made from some sort of strange material, with pointed toes and a thick heel. They were high on the sides but dipped in at the shin and the back where her calf would be.

"Wow!" she exclaimed pulling one from the box and running a small hand over the stitched leather. "Are these some new sort of flight boots?"

Scarlett laughed again. "No, those boots are worn for riding horses. Damn, they don't teach you kids anything anymore! Do you have a homeholo hooked into a broadband?" she asked Jeanette.

Her niece made a face that suggested her auntie had asked if they had indoor plumbing. "Of course. What do you want..." she started to ask but anticipated the answer before she could finish. "Axel!" she called out, looking across the room. The other girls looked expectantly in the same direction and Scarlett followed their eyes to what looked like a bureau against the wall. "Show me a horse," Jeanette ordered.

The top of the bureau flared with colored light which immediately coalesced into a three-dimensional image of the tall mammal in question.

"I spent the last few months," Scarlett told her niece, "on a planet moon in a town where, instead of mag-trams and aircars, people used these four-legged animals. They would use them to pull carts on wheels or rode on their backs."

The girls all looked at the Jordan with wide eyes that showed they either did not understand or believe the Jordan. Or both. Scarlett shook her head, chuckling.

"Show a horse and rider," the Jordan instructed, directing her gaze to Jeanette, but the holo obeyed immediately and changed to a moving horse, carrying a rider.

"Ohhh!" each girl exclaimed, watching as the new image of the animal repeatedly extended its long legs and pulled them in as it crossed the terrain with obvious speed and a person clinging to its back.

"You rode one of those?" one girl asked, incredulous.

Scarlett nodded. "After I had tamed it, yes."

There was a collective gasp of astonishment, then excitement as they were incited to ask questions of their own.

"You had to tame it?"

"Was it scary?"

"Did it bite?"

"How fast did it go?"

"How did you hold on?"

"Did you ever fall off?"

Scarlett laughed heartily at the barrage of inquiries. "Yes, yes, and very fast – fast as an aircab! You hold on tight, mostly with your legs, and yes, I fell off at first. Some horses do not want to be ridden. But if you are brave and patient, it is wonderful and exciting!"

The girls all oohed again, even louder this time.

"Great," John murmured from the corner of his mouth. "Now she's going to want a pony."

Rebecca forced a smile. "I'd rather buy her an entire farm than put her in a jet."

John laughed softly. "Unfortunately, that's not for us to decide."

Rebecca, who had been moved to a good humor for the first time in weeks, glared at her husband. "It is for now," she told him, "and for the next seven years!"

John took the rebuke with as much joviality he could muster. He had been glad to see his sister, and see her doing so well, and though it seemed she could not have appeared at a worse time, Rebecca seemed to be thawing out a bit. Scarlett showing up in civilian clothes and bearing non-space/starfighter gifts had certainly helped.

"Maybe," John suggested from the corner of his mouth, "we should find out where she's been and take the kids there on vacation."

Rebecca finally failed to repress a genuine smile. "Maybe we should," she agreed.

"Look," Scarlett told Jeanette, extending a long leg to

showcase her own boot, "they're not just for riding horses. I still have mine on, just in case I need to kick someone in the ass."

The girls shrieked laughter from behind their hands. Even Rebecca was unable to contain a chortle, though she shook her head in reproof. Jeanette gave her auntie a long hug and thanked her for the presents before pulling off her shoes to try on her new boots.

Scarlett kissed her niece on the head and stood up. "Enjoy your party. I need to go across the hall and talk with Grandpa." Jeanette nodded vigorously in understanding as she stood up in her new boots while her friends continued their cooing sounds.

The Jordan shot a glance at her brother and his wife as she departed and was glad to see that Rebecca didn't look quite as pissed as when she had first arrived, though the look in her blue eyes was unmistakable. Something was amiss at the homestead and she was holding Scarlett responsible. At least partially.

The Jordan gave them a nod and a smile and headed back across the hall to where Grandpa waited in his chair, a glass of ice water in hand. Her nephew sat in the side chair.

Sean's first instinct, when his aunt had arrived was to follow her across the hall to his podment. He fought it.

Though he was curious to see what she had brought for his sister, and absolutely dying to see his parents' reaction to her appearance, he thought it wiser to stay with Grandpa. He felt it more adult to wait than to follow his aunt back and forth like a child, and possibly be sent back like a child. He had a feeling that the conversation she was going to have with Grandpa was one that he didn't want to miss. When she came back he sat up straighter, feeling that he was certainly more adult than child.

She eyed him carefully, sitting in his chair as if she were weighing the same idea. He felt the gamble paid off immediately.

"What the hell's up your mom's ass?" she demanded.

Grandpa cawed laughter and Sean had a hard time not to do the same. Even stranger, and funnier, he had the urge to reprimand his aunt on her language. Sean found himself snickering and brought up a loose fist to cover his mouth.

"Mom found out that Jeanette has been ditching both her dance and music classes," he explained. Scarlett smiled at the news and then raised her dark brows in curiosity, not understanding what it might have to do with her. Sean took a deep breath and continued. "Instead, she has been going to the 'cade to play in the gaming spheres, mostly those that are in star-fighter simulators."

Scarlett snorted and raised her brows higher. "And?"

Sean laughed. "And she's good. Really good."

Scarlett laughed as well and glanced at her grandfather. "What the hell does that have to do with me?"

Grandpa shrugged. "The kids look up to you."

"That's understandable," Scarlett admitted, "but that's certainly not my fault. Besides, it's in their blood. Rebecca should know that."

"She knows," Sean affirmed. "Doesn't mean she likes it."

The corners of Scarlett's mouth pulled down as she nodded. "Fair enough," she agreed. She glanced at the only other empty chair in the room, gave it a gentle push with her boot so that it better faced Grandpa, and plopped down in it.

"So!" she exclaimed. "How the hell do you know Bjorn van Zandt?"

Sean's blue eyes lit up as they went to his grandpa. He knew from history as well as personal research that Bjorn van Zandt was one of the First Seven and now one of the most prominent leaders of the Chimera.

Grandpa shrugged as if she had asked how much he enjoyed his last breakfast. "I taught him French," he replied.

Scarlett leaned forward in her chair. "You what?" Grandpa's thin shoulders pulled up once again under his crisp green shirt.

"Taught him French," he repeated. "I taught it to a few of the First Seven. He wasn't the best student, but he learned it well enough." Grandpa shifted in his seat and took a sip from the can in his hand.

Sean felt as if there were fireworks going off inside his body. He *knew* he didn't want to miss this conversation.

Scarlett sat back as she found herself, one of the few times in her life, at a loss for words. Not at a loss for questions. Those were flying through her mind faster than a Dragon. *How in the hell did that happen?* she wondered. She knew Grandpa to be of French-Earth descent but not a teacher. He was a mason for Chissake! *Or so I thought. How old is he? A few of the First Seven?*

She considered her training, not as a Jordan but in meditating. She knew questions with any importance would be answered in time. Meanwhile, Grandpa had become stock still, almost frozen. His eyes were focused, but not on anything in the room. His blue eyes were staring dead into the past.

He was thinking of the construct his granddaughter had mentioned. The one with flashing green eyes. Then he was recalling the days of teaching French to the first run of GwenSeven constructs, those they called the Pantheon back then. It brought back memories in such a rush that Grandpa felt like he must be crackling with electricity. He was flooded with feelings of exaltation, crushing sadness, and the fragrance of ...

"Grandpa?" Sean queried softly. He was used to the man drifting off, but now he looked like he might be having a stroke. "Grandpa?" he repeated, louder this time. Scarlett as well was about to call to him when he suddenly came around, not as if waking from a dream, but as if waking to some disturbing news.

He looked at his grandchildren, his white eyebrows drawn together over his blue eyes. "Of all the questions you kids ask, how come you never ask where you came from?" he demanded.

Sean and Scarlett looked at each other, surprised, before looking back at Grandpa. Sean gave an exaggerated shrug. "Because we're from here," he said. "From Io. Even you were born here."

"I know your grandparents were from Earth," Scarlett offered. "From France before it became part of the Euro Bloc. How much farther back were you expecting?"

"Bah!" Grandpa spat, and then waved a hand at them as he gave his head a hard shake. "It's not your fault, it's mine." His wrinkled lips pursed as he tried to assemble his thoughts. Scarlett moved onto the couch. She had the urge to pull Sean onto her lap but she knew he was too old for such things. He did, however, leave his own chair and sank down right next to her.

"I guess I'm not talking about where you came from," Grandpa said, "but who. Whom. Whatever." Scarlett and Sean both kept their lips tight as they fought against smiles. "I always felt that I was supposed to be the historian of our family, the one to pass down all I had seen and been a part of, but I failed." Grandpa sighed and turned his gaze from them, his expression remorseful.

"It's not your fault that you can't remember," Sean consoled. "But your memory is getting better all the time. Maybe it will come to you."

Grandpa chuffed at this, though his expression became even more sad. "It's not that I couldn't remember," he confessed, "though I'm sure that for the last few decades it might have been. But I think it more likely that I didn't want to remember. I suppressed it, you might say." He turned his blue eyes to his fighter-pilot granddaughter who had been uncharacteristically quiet, and patient. "What do you know of your genealogy?" he asked.

Scarlett gave him a dismissive shrug. "I researched it when I was applying to the Jordan TC, checking what I knew they would look into to see if there was anything that might hold up my application or acceptance."

"What did you see?" Sean asked.

"What I had expected, but even more than I had hoped for - that I come from a long line of distinguished fighter pilots."

Grandpa grunted. "Did you see anything that struck you as odd or unusual?" he asked.

"Not at the time, but now that you mention it, yes."

Grandpa waited patiently while Sean thought he might explode with curiosity. He was not, however, going to blow it. He felt as if this was the first real adult conversation in which he been included, and one he would remember forever. He was right.

"Our ancestry is fairly straightforward, since the children have been few and pilots don't tend to live terribly long," Scarlett said. Grandpa nodded, his lips pulled into a thin line. "Also," Scarlett continued, "no divorces, no annulments, no remarriages." The corners of Grandpa's tight lips curled up a bit in pride. "The limbs go up the tree, so to speak, with who married who, up to your branch."

"How high is that branch?" Sean whispered, unable to help himself.

"Pretty high," Scarlett remarked, her dark eyes never leaving Grandpa's blue ones. "Quite a few generations. You'd be surprised."

"I doubt it," Sean murmured.

"Anyway, Grandpa, a long, long time ago, had a child. A girl." Tears welled up in the old man's blue eyes but he held them in. "When it got to Grandpa's name, there was a line next to it - a place for his wife, or at least the mother of his child."

A silence followed that Sean thought might kill him. "And?" he prompted when she didn't continue.

"It was blank," she finished.

"Grandpa!" Sean admonished in a voice barely above a whisper. "You had a baby with...with... someone you weren't married to?"

Scarlett laughed aloud and even Grandpa smiled sheepishly at the boy's shock.

"Don't look so surprised!" he scolded, though his tone was warm. "It was as common then as it is now."

"But, but," Sean stammered looking for the right words, "you're so, so..."

"So what?"

"So Catholic!" Scarlett said, laughing harder. "But," she said, her laughter fading, "that spot should have been filled, even if he wasn't married. That's what was odd about it." She peered at her grandfather, crimson flecks glowing deep within her dark eyes.

"Well," Grandpa said, shifting in his seat, "if there was anything I could have done to have it otherwise, I would have done so in a heartbeat. I loved her with all my heart and wanted nothing more than a life together with her. But there were circumstances that made it literally impossible."

Scarlett cocked her head, as curious as Sean and soon finding herself as impatient. "And?" she prodded. "What might those circumstances have been?"

Grandpa took a deep breath and blew it out through his new white teeth. "Because she was Mira Devereaux, one of the First Seven."

Scarlett and Sean were both struck dumb for long moments. Sean was the first one to speak.

"So," he questioned softly, "we're part construct?"

Grandpa gave him a smile and shrugged. "I never thought of it that way before. But, yes, I suppose you are."

Scarlett shook her head slowly and looked away to the distance, far beyond the walls of Grandpa's pod.

"Motherfucker," she whispered.

 8

- That a dragon hoards gold is a myth. They hoard the truth.

"Wow," Amberle whispered as she entered Faith's personal spacecraft and peered around. Not only was it huge, but it looked exactly like the living room of her villa. There were a few differences, of course, but not many. Jasyn, already on board and standing by the open steel door, smiled at her expression.

"I know," he said. "Why don't you have a seat on a couch? The staff will bring you anything you need."

Amberle edged away from him. She liked him, but he made her nervous. He was always so intense. And intensely handsome. She was not so young or so deep in the Web that it was lost on her. Even his voice was something she could feel in her bones.

She gave him a nervous smile and tossed her pink coiled springs of hair back as she descended the polished granite steps. She crossed over the black glassy floor and priceless Sherpla rugs and sat herself on a white couch.

Faith entered only moments later, talking on a comset and followed by Penny and Geary. She smiled at Amberle as she took a seat and fastened the safety webbing across her lap. Amberle did the same while Jasyn sat himself in a white wing chair facing, but some distance from, Faith. The strain between them was like burgeoning thunderclouds.

Amberle had been given a brand-new acrylic by Penny and was glad for it. Not just the tech, but for something to do. She powered it on as the air filled with chatter, instructions, directions, and tension. Within moments she was deep in the Web.

Jasyn sat with his own acrylic on his lap, its surface as dark as his expression. He remembered the first time he had ridden on Faith's personal craft. He too had been headed to the Last Castle for the first time. The only thing on his mind had been Faith and how much he wanted her.

He looked at her now - the curve of her leg, her smooth throat, glittering eyes - and knew that he still wanted her. Possibly more than before but there was some stubborn anger keeping him away.

What is it? he demanded internally. *Because she knew all along who you are, and you still have no idea? You can't say for sure who she is? She's Faith, she's Gwen, she's Faith.*

Penny and Geary moved away to take their seats while Faith continued her own conversation. The craft disengaged from the villa and put a few gentle kilometers between itself and the elite space community of Iron Rose before taking off like a shooting star.

There is something else, he thought. *Something else that is keeping me from her, something inside of me.* Jasyn's dark brows drew together. *Some memory,* he thought. *If I could just access it, I would know who she is, who I am.*

The craft tilted and the edge of Faith's skirt slipped up her thigh. Jasyn clenched his jaw and looked away.

If Amberle felt impressed by Faith's spacecraft, she was absolutely awed by the Last Castle on the Distant Shore. Charity's residence was a fairy-tale castle, with squat towers and tall spires, though the obsidian edifice seemed more appropriate for a villain or a wicked queen. Amberle's dark skin looked pale in comparison as they approached the black towers that gleamed in the magnified sunlight.

She was speechless as they walked through the halls carpeted with long rugs, walls made of stone and sometimes paneled in polished wood. Many rooms had fireplaces, both real and holographic versions. In some places art hung from the walls, while others were adorned with a type of rug different from those on the floors - ones that were silky smooth and had art woven into them.

They reached a room where Faith's attendants and security left them and they were greeted by Charity and her normal household entourage— three personal assistants, three bodyguards, three butlers, and the tallest human Amberle had ever seen.

The man was slim with blonde hair, a reddish blonde beard, and blue eyes that stared straight into her. He made the young programmer immediately nervous.

Charity greeted them with her usual aplomb, kissing Faith on both cheeks before she moved to Jasyn who bore the same gesture with infinite patience. Possibly not infinite, as it evaporated when the tall human moved towards them.

"Hello, Amberle," Charity greeted, clasping her hands together at her waist, knowing the young woman did not like to be touched. "This is Nathan," she said, introducing the man looming over her shoulder.

"It is a pleasure to meet you," he said, stepping forward. He was so close and so tall that she had to tilt her head back to keep her eyes on his face. Her faded pink coils of hair trembled between her shoulder blades as he extended his hand.

Amberle swallowed. Though she did not like people touching her, it was shake his hand or be extremely rude. She grasped his large hand with her slim, dark fingers. "You as well," she returned, relaxing her grip on him immediately and trying to back away.

The Engineer, however, held on a moment longer and when he did let go, he drew his fingers sensually across her palm. Amberle had to clench her teeth to keep from shuddering.

Jasyn began to move forward but Charity stepped lightly between them.

"A table has been set for high tea in the Conservatory," she informed everyone with a charming smile. "If you will follow me?"

She turned and walked away down the corridor without waiting for a response from anyone, silk skirt whispering confidently with her brisk strides.

The others followed her from one hall to another and then to a wide staircase. One set of stairs led down while two more - one on the right and one on the left - curved up and around. Charity ascended the right-hand set of stairs, one pale hand on the polished mahogany banister to keep steady on her stiletto spiked heels with the rest of the party in tow. They crossed a broad hallway and into an enormous circular room with a domed ceiling made of glass.

Inside was a garden of gargantuan proportions. Topiaries made of multicolored rose bushes dominated the beds where smaller droves of flowers bloomed in the filtered light. Gurgling fountains created streams that made their way between the shrubs, bubbling over smooth stones to create gentle falls and swirling pools before disappearing into the ersatz earth.

The young programmer realized that a few of the rose topiaries, the really big ones, were in the shapes of eggs. They were taller, and much wider, than she was. The blooms were tightly packed and bursting with color, save for two of the enormous eggs; one black and one gray. She had never seen roses in black or gray before, but they were as eye-catching as the eggs of yellow, orange, violet, and indigo.

A tiled path snaked between the manicured beds, leading them to a large gazebo in the center of the vast atrium. Charity's guards and aides melted away down smaller paths as the golden-haired de Rossi ascended the few steps into the vaulted gazebo.

Amberle blinked her hazel eyes at what she saw.

First, she had never before seen a table shaped like a triangle. Second, the entire area bespoke of a delicate opulence she had never witnessed.

Fine China plates had been set out, along with hand-painted teapots, jetting steam from their spouts, and matching teacups on saucers. Porcelain dishes held sliced fruits and julienned vegetables, along with bowls of dips and sauces. There were breads, scones, and pastries along with honeys, jams, and jellies. Tiered silvered trays offered tiny sandwiches with the crusts cut off and bite sized morsels of cookies, cakes, and chocolates.

Faith was the first to sit and Nathan was quick to slide into the seat next to her. Amberle glanced at Jasyn and saw the muscle in his face ripple as he clenched his teeth together. Keeping his expression frozen, he pulled out a chair for Charity and sat himself between her and Faith.

Men dressed in black jackets over pressed white shirts appeared with decanters of alcohol and bottles of champagne which they began to open.

Amberle slipped into one of the chairs on the empty side of the triangle.

Immediately, a butler appeared at her side and poured steaming tea from a pot into her teacup. He then placed a silver set of tongs on the plate in front of her. She looked around, trying to hide her confusion amidst the pop of champagne bottles as he continued around the table, pouring tea for the others. The only eye she caught was Jasyn's.

He gave her a slight smile and looked from the tongs to the tiers of delights on the table, silently encouraging her to help herself. Amberle gave him a broad smile in return. She might indulge in a big meal now and then but when it came to snacking, she was a champ. The young programmer began to heap her plate while the others were served champagne and cocktails.

Amberle sampled a flaky pastry layered with honey and nuts and found herself with sticky fingers. A man was by her side in a moment, offering her a moist towel on a silver tray. She thanked him, cleaned her hands, and selected a less messy morsel. The others (she couldn't help but think of them as "the grown-ups" even though she herself was an adult) were talking what sounded like politics. A subject in which she had zero interest.

She tried the tea which, while not bitter, was not much to her liking.

"Would you like milk or sugar for your tea?" a butler asked, leaning down towards her shoulder. "Or some lemon, perhaps?"

"Mmm, sugar?" she suggested. She was not a tea drinker, so she had no idea. Sugar, however, was hardly ever a bad idea.

The black-suited gentleman leaned closer and, with a tiny set of gold tongs, carefully dropped a cube of sugar into her cup, and then added one more.

Amberle stirred it and took another sip. Her face lit up and she smiled at him. "Much better! Thank you!"

The man smiled and backed away.

The young programmer had just bitten into a crustless sandwich filled with ham and cream cheese (a combination she would have never concocted in her wildest imagination but found to be amazing) when a man from Charity's security detail entered the gazebo and leaned down to speak softly in her ear. Her green eyes flicked up to meet Amberle and she gave a nod to the man, dismissing him.

"The Fledgling has entered our air space," she said, indicating the artificial atmosphere that surrounded the watery moon of the Distant Shore.

Amberle could feel her heart begin to beat faster. She wiped her mouth with a napkin and stood, her laden and unfinished plate forgotten in her excitement. The others rose as well and followed as Faith led them this time, back down to the main level and through two hallways until they were at a large elevator. It stood, waiting with its double doors open.

Faith whispered something to Geary, who had appeared out of nowhere as he was prone to do, and he gave her a nod and moved away - clearly not liking what she had said. She entered the lift with Charity, who had also dismissed her guards. Amberle joined them, followed by Jasyn and Nathan.

The Engineer smiled at her and ran a finger down the length of her arm. Amberle stiffened as the doors shut and the elevator began to descend. He did not touch her again, but she could feel the weight of his stare and the ride down seemed to last forever. She was glad to feel the slight jolt when they reached the bottom and breathed a sigh of relief as the doors slid open.

Jasyn was quick to step out and look around, Amberle right on his heels to do the same. The construct was looking for any signs of danger. The young woman was simply curious.

They were in an immense cavern underneath the fortress. The area was well lit and it had the feel of a military hangar. The stone floor had been ground down and polished into a smooth tarmac that Amberle guessed could hold a platoon of fighter jets.

Or a dozen Fledglings, she thought. *Even as they grew. This place is enormous.*

Currently, the vast hangar only held one small space-capable jet and a sleek luxury craft that seemed to be mostly glass, but they were dwarfed by the titanic amount of space around them. The tarmac dropped off on one side a good hundred yards away, a slope of obsidian rock that disappeared into the rough dark waters, while the other side stretched away under the Castle.

More than just the Castle, she thought, *this hangar must cut through the entire island.* Squinting to see further back, she could discern huge support pillars, mostly black stone but some were reinforced with dark titanium. Each column was as large as a family-sized podment.

Her gaze swept to the right and she saw an area with desks and chairs and very low-key computer components. Behind them, attached to the obsidian wall of the cave were metal boxes she supposed housed electrical breakers. Next to the elevator they had just exited was a shadowy alcove that she thought most likely a stairwell.

Amberle's hazel eyes were drawn to the entrance of the cave. It was a wide slit of light that opened onto the oceanic surface of the moon.

The young programmer could hear water everywhere. The crash of the sea against the rocks outside the cavern, the splash of smaller waves on the platform where she stood, and a constant dripping from some of the farthest walls.

All of it was background noise.

Inside her there was a strange thrumming. It was something she had never before felt. She could feel it building, becoming more intense, and she knew it was from the approach of the Fledgling - coming closer, heading for the only entrance to the cave from the outside.

It built inside her like an oncoming storm and she clenched her small hands into fists as it grew and grew. Her heart began to beat a little harder and her breath began to come a little faster.

Then it faded.

Verdana had changed course and was moving away.

Verdana? Amberle queried mentally. She had not intended communication; she was simply at a loss as to what the Fledgling was doing.

Had she changed her mind?

The young woman was about to ask Faith for a compute she could link to when the thrumming inside her body resumed. She turned her dusky face back towards the entrance in the rock above the choppy waters.

Within a heartbeat the opening became obscured, filled with the body of the Fledgling as she dove from the light and into the murky shadows of the cave. Amberle clasped her slim hands in front of her chest as she watched Verdana approach. The faded pink coils of her hair trembled with excitement.

The Fledgling was the size of a small one-man fighter jet, but instead of a pointed nose there was a snout. Eyes of curved diamond glass panes were where the windshield would be. Her skin was silver that gave off a shimmer of brilliant green, as if dusted with crushed emeralds.

She passed the other craft and turned gracefully so that she was facing the people on the tarmac. And pointed towards the only exit.

Her belly was smooth but, as they watched, four legs pushed out and the Fledgling landed before them on claws tipped with silver talons.

Amberle blinked in surprise as she heard a soft voice inside her head.

Girl.

The young woman laughed, delighted.

Amberle, she thought deliberately. *My name is Amberle.*

Amberle, Verdana corrected, surprised and curious. The girl had not spoken aloud, but with her mind. It was something the Jordans on the Opal Dragon, after three years together, were just learning.

Amberle, Verdana repeated, her silver body emitting an emerald glow.

Amberle clapped her hands like a child and looked around at the others in the small group.

"My God," Charity murmured. "We have ourselves a Fledgling. Can you believe it?"

Faith laughed for the first time in weeks. "I can," she replied. "I just can't believe it took me this long."

"Well," Charity conceded, "it's not like they have them at the local market."

Faith laughed again. "And I certainly thought it would be through our dear little sister. After all, she is a Jordan." She turned her tawny gaze to the girl. "We have Amberle to thank for this."

Amberle gave her a nervous, lopsided smile.

"Let's not get too excited," she told the others. "We need to get her to agree to the work that needs to be done first, then get Jade. One thing at a time."

Jasyn smiled despite the unsurety of his own feelings. The smile evaporated a second later when Nathan put his hands on Faith's shoulders and leaned down to speak softly in her ear.

"Would you like to stay and watch me work?" he asked Faith, giving her shoulders a gentle squeeze.

"Yes," she agreed, "I would. You don't mind?"

The Engineer gave her a lecherous smile. "Not at all," he said, keeping his face next to hers. Faith blushed while he kept the contact for a few more moments.

Charity's gaze slid to Jasyn. His dark hazel eyes blazed with murder but, other than that, he seemed under control.

"I might watch for a while as well," Charity announced,

bringing her wrist to her mouth and speaking quietly into the silver bracelet there. When she was done, she looked at the dark-haired construct by her side. "Jasyn, darling, would you mind scooting a few of those chairs over here?" she asked, pointing at a few high-backed leather air-chairs behind the desks that lined the curved wall.

Jasyn dipped his dark head in acquiescence and moved away as Amberle listened to the Fledgling. Then she turned to look at the rest of them, her face lit up.

"Is that okay?" she asked.

"Is what okay, dear?" Charity replied.

Amberle's look of excitement fell slowly. The enormous cave was silent save for the distant sound of waves, crashing on the rocks. "What Verdana asked," she said. "Is that okay?"

Charity glanced at Faith, who had kept her brown and gold eyes fixed on the girl.

"Did you guys hear her?" Amberle asked. The eyebrows of both sisters went up in surprise.

"She is speaking to you?" Faith asked. "You can hear her?"

Amberle nodded. "You can't?" she asked, feeling stupid. It was obvious by looking at them that she was the odd one out.

"It's not out of the ordinary," Nathan interjected, his hands still on Faith's shoulders though he had straightened to his abnormally tall height. "Fledglings often communicate through one person, usually their Jordan." He gave Faith's shoulders another squeeze, "I'm going to make sure all my metals are in order," he told her before moving off to the neatly stacked rods of lithium and titanium.

Amberle gave a sigh of relief at his words, though she was discomfited by the words from Verdana. Faith's scrutiny did not miss it.

"What is it?" she asked the girl softly after the Engineer had moved away.

"Verdana doesn't like him," Amberle said, keeping her own voice low.

"Then she is a good judge of character," Jasyn said as he guided the chairs over, nudging two towards the de Rossi sisters.

"No thanks," Amberle said as he held the third one out for her, "I'm too fidgety to sit."

Jasyn nodded and there came a chime from the lift that led up to the castle. The doors opened and two butler droids floated out. One held a bottle of champagne glistening with condensation by one metal limb, a magnetic chill bucket with another, and four champagne glasses with a third. The other droid held an ice bucket, a silver tray topped with short glasses of heavy crystal, and a decanter of cut glass full of dark liquid.

They floated over to where the four waited and began preparing and pouring the drinks.

"What did she ask?" Faith asked Amberle, ignoring Jasyn's snide remark as she lowered herself down into a chair that bobbed slightly under her weight. "When you asked if it was okay."

"She wants to know if she can stay here," Amberle said, giving them an expression that was a bit sheepish. "She hasn't come right out and said it, but I get the feeling she wants to stay hidden."

Charity gave a snort of laughter and then a small yelp of surprise as she dropped into her own chair, a bit less gracefully than Faith, making it bounce so hard it nearly tossed her out. The chair righted itself and the younger de Rossi quickly recovered and accepted a proffered glass of liquor from one of the droids.

"Well," she said, settling into her seat, "how fortuitous!"

"We would be happy to oblige her," Faith said as she took a glass of champagne from the outstretched metal limb of a droid. Amberle smiled and turned back towards Verdana as

Jasyn and the de Rossi sisters watched, entranced that she was communicating silently with the Fledgling.

"Fortuitous indeed," Charity murmured as she sipped her drink.

Nathan, having checked his materials, rejoined the group. Jasyn took a step closer to Faith's chair.

Amberle watched their silent exchange even as she had her own. She took a tentative step forward.

"I let her know that she is going to need some changes made. She seems willing, but nervous. She wants to know if I can go inside," the young programmer told the Engineer, "while you work. Can I?"

"Certainly," he agreed. "At least, until I need to pressurize the cabin. Until then, I'm sure you'll be a great comfort to her."

Amberle smiled and trotted away towards the Fledgling, her coils of hair bouncing. As she neared Verdana, a small hole appeared in the silver skin and a silver ladder formed against its side. Amberle felt like she might burst with excitement.

The young woman grabbed the first rung and hauled herself aloft, shimmying up the rest of the ladder and pulling herself up and into the temporary door that closed once she was inside.

Amberle, grinning from ear to ear, looked around the small space as she felt the thrum of excitement around her.

Though she was not tall, she had to bend over to keep from hitting her head on the low ceiling. She was behind a single chair, obviously a pilot's chair, nooked into a cockpit that faced the clear eyes of the Fledgling Dragon.

"Whoooaah," Amberle whispered.

Sit down, Verdana encouraged.

"Really?" Amberle asked aloud.

Verdana glowed, inside and out. *Yes, really.* Something about the girl touched her starfire. The girl stepped forward and slipped her slight frame into the lone seat.

Amberle's brown and green eyes slid over the console. Though the Fledgling looked like a military fighting jet on the outside, her dash was smooth and unmarred with the normal dials and digital screens. Amberle stretched out her hands over the dash console of dragonskin, sensing what was beneath - communications, connections, webs... knowledge. She sighed.

What, Verdana breached softly, *do they want to do to me?*

Amberle pressed her lips together. Her fingers twitched out of habit, as if ready to type, then she began to speak as she realized it was not necessary to type anymore. Then it struck her that she hadn't been speaking aloud save for once since the Fledgling had arrived.

They want to make you bigger, she thought, and immediately felt that Verdana had heard, and understood.

For Jade? Verdana asked.

Yesss, Amberle sent back hesitantly, *but also for their own ends.* She sensed now that Verdana was even less mature than she was. It gave her both a feeling of camaraderie and a need to protect the young Dragon. She could feel the tension around her.

What does that mean?

Amberle stuck out her bottom lip and sent a blast of air up and into her coral pink colored spirals of hair. *I don't know,* she replied. *But I will do whatever I can to help.*

Around her, the Fledgling glowed.

From inside, the girl watched as bars and rods of different types of metal floated by. The Engineer, using only his mind to move the materials he needed, placed and melted the metals all over the Fledgling Dragon.

"Does it hurt?" Amberle asked aloud.

No, Verdana answered, and then sent the girl an image of a child putting on a coat. Amberle smiled in understanding.

They sat in companionable silence for the entire morning, breaking it occasionally with questions and answers mostly sent by images and thoughts.

They took a break for lunch, for which Amberle was eager and grateful. She was starving and glad to see that the plate she had made for herself upstairs had been brought down. She attacked her heaped array of snacks and sipped on a carbonated water.

Then Amberle watched, from the outside, as the Engineer finished the growing. She kept up her mental conversation with Verdana. Reassuring her as metals were melted around her body and the Engineer guided a droid inside to pressurize and grow the cabin.

At the end of the day, when it was obvious that things were wrapping up in the hangar, the others began preparing to go back upstairs, into the Castle.

"We'll finish tomorrow," Nathan said, his hand raised as he guided the remains of unused metals into piles against a rough, black wall.

"She's not done?" Amberle asked, her hazel eyes sliding over the smooth and shiny (and much larger) Fledgling.

Nathan smiled as the metals seemingly organized themselves into neat rows. "She is done with her physical growing," he told the girl. "What comes next is for us, or you - rather. She will be internally fitted with a galley, a bed, and a lavatory." There was also an upgraded weapons system to be put in, but he did not feel the need to mention that to the girl.

"Until then," Charity said, rising a little unsteadily to her feet, "it's time for dinner. And another cocktail or two."

The others smiled in agreement, except for Amberle.

"I'd like to stay here," she ventured softly, "if that is alright."

Verdana had not asked her to stay, but the girl could sense feelings of uneasiness and loneliness coming from the Fledgling. They were feelings she recognized. Ones she was well acquainted with.

"All night?" Charity asked, surprised. Amberle nodded.

"Why, of course," Faith told her. She turned her eyes to the dark-haired construct. "Jasyn can bring down some dinner for you. Blankets, an airbed, whatever you need."

"Yes," the Engineer said, stepping up behind Faith and putting his hands on her shoulders. He was so tall that he looked over the top of her head at the construct. "Maybe he can stay, keep you company."

Jasyn's expression darkened with fury and the air became so heavy with pressure that Amberle thought her ears might pop.

Danger, the Fledgling warned.

Yes, the young woman sent back. *But not for us.*

"Charity can send a droid," Jasyn said through perfect, clenched teeth. "Besides," he said, putting his glass down on a floating tray, "I promised Faith's security detail that I would make sure that she made it safely to her room tonight."

Faith would not be surprised in the least to find out that Geary, her head of security, did indeed make Jasyn promise to see her safely to her room. She knew, however, that it was just as likely that the construct did not want her alone with Nathan. And she did not miss how he had freed up both his hands.

"Of course," she agreed quickly, stepping away from the Engineer and looking at the girl with her eyebrows raised over her eyes of brown and gold. "Is there anything in particular you would like?"

"Ice cream?" Amberle asked, hopeful.

Faith's lips pressed down to hide her smile. "I was thinking of dinner."

"Ice cream?" Amberle asked again.

The corners of Faith's lips quirked up. She suddenly remembered another young girl, the only one she had ever really known. But she had been very different from Amberle. "I'll send down some spaghetti," she told her. The girl gave her a resigned smile. "And some ice cream," she added, making the girl's face brighten. "What would you like?"

"Chocolate," Amberle answered immediately. "Or anything with chocolate. Or chocolate with anything in it."

Everyone was now smiling, everyone except Jasyn. His black stare was still fixed on the Engineer.

Faith gave the girl a nod and then turned and headed for the elevator that led back up to the Castle. Jasyn fell into step right behind her, Charity and Nathan following. The two droids trailed behind, carrying empty bottles and dirty glasses.

Once in the elevator, Charity asked Nathan about what he would be needing the following day and Jasyn leaned down, putting his lips close to Faith's ear while the socialite and Engineer talked.

"What did the J stand for?" he whispered.

Faith could feel the heat rush through her body at his nearness, at the feel of his breath on her neck. Then she felt a rush of anger at the way he had been behaving of late, and at keeping a distance between them.

"Jailer," she said from over her shoulder.

Then the lift came to a halt and she was through the doors even as they were still opening. Jasyn smiled at her back as he followed.

♋

Amberle sat down in one of the forgotten air chairs and carefully pulled her feet up onto the seat. She hugged her knees and looked thoughtfully at the newly grown Dragon Fledgling. She knew Verdana had cybernetic wiring and was somehow hooked into the Galactic Web, which was how she had seen the advertisement and made contact. Amberle now wondered how deep her connection was, and what her clearance might be.

Before even a few minutes had passed, there was a chime at the elevator and its doors opened. Two droids, Amberle could not tell if it was the same two from before or different ones, floated into the vast space of the cave.

One carried a tray with steam escaping from beneath the silver domes that rested there. Another limb held a tray topped with a carafe of lemonade along with a glass and a bucket of ice. Behind it drifted a metal box, its sides coated with frost. The other droid carried seemingly a much lighter load, holding only a metal disc in one limb and a small plastic package in another.

As they neared, the second droid dropped the disc. The circular piece of metal, about the size of a dinner plate though much thicker, began to unfold over and over. Metal snapped and clicked until there was a bed not much bigger than a cot. Amberle watched as a pad on the cot began to fill with air. While the mattress was inflating, the droid opened the plastic square - a pillow and blanket practically exploding into being as they were released from the compression cube.

Meanwhile, the other droid had expanded a table in front of the young woman and was carefully placing plates and utensils down for her. It set down the glass, poured a measure of lemonade, and then retreated to the waiting elevator, leaving the frosted silver box behind. The second droid followed.

The young programmer pulled the table closer to her chair and lifted the silver domes off the plates and set them aside. There was enough spaghetti, meatballs, and garlic bread to feed three people. Amberle ate it all.

Completely stuffed, she leaned back in her chair. Listening to the sounds of the surf outside, she looked at Verdana and knew that - in one way - she was still hungry. As if hearing her thoughts, a circle opened in the side of the Fledgling and, what looked like melting silver, formed itself into a set of stairs along the side.

Grinning, Amberle wiped her hands and hurried to the slender staircase. She climbed up and in and looked around, her eyes wide.

The first thing she noticed was that she could stand all the way up without bumping her head. She had seen how much bigger Verdana had become on the outside, but it seemed entirely different inside. So much empty space. Yet she could sense a feeling of pride coming from the Fledgling.

Amberle crept into the cockpit and slid into the pilot's chair. She marveled at the smooth expanse of Dragonskin and chuckled.

"I don't know what to do without a keyboard," she said softly. "Or at least a glove."

Three different types of keyboards rose up out of the smooth console before her, offering her choices. And her right thumb and index finger glowed silver, the same place where her silicone glove would normally go.

But, Verdana sent, *you can just tell me what you want.*

Amberle grinned again. And went to work.

Sometimes she spoke, sometimes she typed, sometimes she just let the Fledgling glean her thoughts.

She paused after two hours of being immersed in the Web only to go back into the cavern and open the silver box coated with ice crystals. As she had suspected, it was filled with different kinds of ice cream. She selected one, a lone bar dipped in chocolate, along with a pint-sized container of another. She grabbed a spoon off the table and, though she knew Verdana could keep her warm, she took the blanket off the makeshift bed.

Back inside, she finished both desserts while she read and watched and researched. Finally, when she felt she had learned enough of Jade, and had a good idea of what Verdana was capable of, she decided where to go after the lost Jordan. And when.

Amberle was thinking of exploring more of what Verdana could do when she felt her seat moving underneath her.

What's happening? she asked.

The chair was flattening, stretching out, and the girl realized it was becoming a bed.

You need to rest, Verdana replied.

But, Amberle started, only to feel the Fledgling shush her.

For being so childlike, the young Dragon was being quite motherly.

Reluctantly, the young woman lay down and pulled the blanket over her. She wished she had the green jacket she had gotten on the Elba moon. But Faith had taken it and given it to someone to find out where it had come from.

Thinking of her jacket made her think of Keaton. She wondered where he might be and what he might be doing. She realized she missed him. She even missed Cooper and Ty, but she wished Keaton was there.

A small tendril of silver melted away from the bed, like the tail of a snake. It slipped up and, like a small and sparkling finger, touched the edge of the girl's blanket.

Amberle smiled and closed her eyes.

 NINE

- A secret is only dangerous when someone dares to believe it.

Calyph returned to the Opal Dragon via an interstellar shuttle. The trip back from Kayos seemed to take forever, making the already anxious Engineer downright jumpy. He missed Scarlett by mere minutes, for which he thanked his lucky stars. He needed to see Jordan Blue first. The sooner the better.

He found her in Fledgling Bay, talking to a weapons tech. He waited until she was alone and then sidled up to her as casually as he could muster. Her expression turned sour at the sight of him

"I'd like to talk to you," Calyph said, keeping his voice low. "Someplace private. Preferably not on the Dragon."

"I bet you would," Jordan Blue answered, making no attempt to hide the contempt in her voice. "I certainly wouldn't mind having a word with you either. Where do you suggest?"

Calyph swallowed. "We're going to be rounding Neptune tomorrow and stopping just outside the orbit of Triton."

"And?" the Jordan prompted. She knew about the stop. The Dragon would be taking on supplies, a few new crew members, and filling the water tanks with fresh water. The stop was expected to take three days.

"It only has a few cities," Calyph continued, "but the largest is Salacia, and there will be a number of people taking shore leave there. I can take a transport. There is a bar named Atlantis II, on the far side of the downtown sprawl. I'll be there at 1500."

The Jordan fixed her eye on him for a second before giving a brief nod and walking away.

"What are you after?" Galen asked after she had left the bay.

"He has secrets," Blue said.

"Who doesn't?" the doctor's ghost muttered.

Blue's face scrunched to the side in an expression of distaste. "Not like his. He is a liar and a betrayer. But he is also an Engineer, and metallurgists are hard to come by, especially ones that are cleared to work on Dragons, and their Dragon children. I can't kill him, or even turn him in, just because he smells to me of lies and deceit."

Galen grunted.

The Jordan dressed the next day in one of her sparkling blue flight suits, debating only momentarily if she should wear her sidearm. The inner part of the system, closer to Jupiter and Saturn, was mostly populated with humans and elves. Out here on the edge, however, there were numerous alien colonies, and not all as overly friendly as Golblis.

Blue attached the holster to her belt and dropped her pistol in it.

She left Cyan at the IGC Base and took an aircab across the sprawl.

The Jordan arrived at Atlantis II ten minutes before 1500 to find Calyph already there and waiting. He had actually gotten there an hour earlier, just to be safe. He stood up from the bench he had been warming, greeted the Jordan with a nod and then moved towards the hostess stand.

Blue's eye traveled over the bar and the patrons, taking it all in with her sharp gaze.

"Mmmm," she muttered. "Ritzy."

The place was huge and filled with the atmosphere of a discotheque on a New Year's Eve though it was a regular weekday afternoon. The main building was a pavilion with numerous bars and lounges. There were many pools, some for swimming and some for the aquatic lifeforms in attendance.

The Jordan could see large eyes perched atop glistening stalks peering from the water and tentacled limbs holding cocktails. Some cocktails were nestled into depressions along the edges of the pools with tubes that led back under the water.

Along with the amphibious aliens were scantily clad humans and elves, dancing and splashing while enjoying libations under the magnified sunlight.

The pulse of music came from unseen speakers, though it was slightly muted in the cavernous entrance.

The wait staff was comprised entirely of shungapods, water world lifeforms that did equally well on land. They were soft-bodied invertebrates, but having eight limbs made them excellent waiters. Four of the limbs were shorter and primarily used for ambulation while the other four were mostly used as arms. They scuttled everywhere with surprising speed - taking orders, delivering drinks, dropping off platters of food, and clearing tables.

The Jordan saw there were underwater barstools in the pools, semiprivate booths in and out of the water, and lounger sun beds of various shapes for the variety of species. Set back away from the pools were completely private cabanas cordoned off with heavy blue drapes.

Blue drew stares from eyes on stalks as well as those in heads.

"Maybe I should have worn a swimsuit," she said, smiling broadly.

"Everyone still would know who you are," Galen said in her

ear.

The maître d' at the host stand was a short human with slicked back black hair and a tiny black mustache. He gave them a grin as they approached, showing an obscene amount of teeth.

"Calyph Bette," the Engineer informed the small human. "I reserved a private cabana."

The Jordan leered at him, the scar in her right cheek rippling. "I don't mind people staring at me," she told the Engineer.

"Well, I do," he responded, which was true. And no truer than the present. Blue shrugged and followed the maître d' through the day club.

A number of humans with eyeshades floated around the main pool on plastic inflatable rafts – some flat, some shaped like starfish or mertails. Half a dozen Golblis floated alongside them with no need for inflatables.

The music was louder here, thumping out beats that she could feel pulsating under her skin.

"We are a little busy," he apologized, almost shouting to be heard, as he led the Engineer and the Jordan past two small freshwater lagoons and halfway around what looked like the second main pool. He finally stopped in front of a private cabana and pulled open the heavy drape. "Nonetheless, your waiter should be here in just a few minutes. Ten, at the most." He stepped aside while the Jordan entered and glanced about then he bowed and let drape fall.

There were two chairs and a small sofa of white plastique with blue cushions. Small side tables held fruits and nuts. The table against the back curtain was lined with bottles of water. There was a remote to control the music being piped in as well as the four holos that flickered in the upper corners of the tent. A slim stand by the entrance was stacked with plush towels that had been folded into the shapes of stars.

The heavy drapes helped mute the maniacal beats and squealing screams coming from the pools.

"Ten minutes," Calyph muttered as the man left. "More like twenty. And that is if we are lucky. I'll get the first round at the bar." He glanced at the Jordan and raised a blonde eyebrow over a slanted blue eye. "Champagne?" he asked.

"You know it," the Jordan assured him as she sat herself down on the small couch.

The Engineer gave her a curt nod and ducked out of the cabana.

Blue examined the tray on the table next to her. It was silver and divided into sections, each section holding dried fruits, salted almonds, and potato crisps. She selected a dried apricot and munched on it while she waited for Calyph. It was sweet but had a slight numbing effect on her tongue and lips that was not unpleasant.

Galen's ghost held the heavy canvas drape slightly open with one finger, peering outside for a moment before letting it drop and joining the Jordan on the couch.

"You watch out for him," he warned as Blue selected a candied pecan and popped it into her mouth. It had the same numbing sensation as the apricot.

"Who?" she asked. "Calyph?"

Galen nodded. "People with secrets are not to be trusted."

"Unless you know what their secret is," she countered, helping herself to some peppered pistachios.

"Even then," Galen warned, reaching out to stroke her face with his thumb.

"That's strange," he murmured, frowning.

"What is?"

"Your skin. It feels...overly smooth. Like glass."

"You're touching me right now?"

Even though he had been dead many months, she had

always been able to feel his touch. Though, lately, he had seemed less – and she cocked her head as she looked at him – less *substantial*.

Before he could answer she turned her head and coughed. A bit of pepper from the pistachios was trapped in her throat, making it itch and tingle. She coughed again, harder this time, and the doctor's ghost tried to rub her back but again encountered what felt like glass between them. Glass that was thickening and becoming stronger by the second. He felt a bolt of apprehension rip through him as Blue coughed again.

Calyph entered, shouldering the canvas curtain aside, carrying a glass of champagne in one hand and a dark bottle for himself in the other.

"Not a moment too soon!" the Jordan growled, choking the words out. She accepted the proffered flute of sparkling wine from him and took a long drink as the Engineer sat down heavily in the chair. Galen stared at him. He was watching the Jordan closely while he took a long pull from his bottle. Watching her intensely.

"No!" Galen shouted. "Don't drink it!" He lunged at her and swung at her arm, trying to knock the glass away, but his hand passed right through her.

The doctor's ghost sank to his knees, his blue eyes lit with fear.

The Jordan guzzled half the glass, ostentatiously cleared her throat, then cleared it again. "Ugh! Ahem!" She took another drink and let out a huge belch. "Oh!" she sighed. "That's much better."

Calyph smiled. "The Grevin pepper doesn't agree with you?" he asked.

"Obviously not," Blue admitted, taking another dried apricot from the tray in hopes the numbing spices used on it would soothe her irritated trachea.

"No, no, no!" Galen shouted to no avail. He took another

swipe at her hand, wanting to knock the drugged fruit away and again his hand passed right through her arm. He slumped back down, his mind racing as he tried to determine how he could help her.

"Cyan!" he shouted. "Cyan!"

But, from the Fledgling, there was no response. Having been cut off from the Jordan apparently cut him off from her Fledgling. His ghostly blue eyes lifted hopefully as the fabric of the cabana rippled.

A pair of tentacled limbs snaked into the split in the drapes and pulled them apart to admit a shungapod, holding a tray atop another of its arms, four short legs propelling it into the cabana.

"Another round?" it warbled, its watery voice coming from the area where all the appendages met underneath its soft bulbous head. Two inky black eyes blinked from the mottled gray and black skin that covered the slick body.

"Absolutely," Blue acquiesced, her drink already almost gone. Calyph gave the creature a nod and it disappeared back through the drapes.

Calyph sat back in the cushions, the neck of the dark bottle held loosely between his fingers as he rested his elbow on the arm of the chair. "I'd like to tell you a little bit about myself," he said. "About my past."

Blue's expression brightened. "This should be good," she said as she settled back into the sofa. She took a sip from her near empty glass. *Damn,* she thought, *that pepper really did a number on me. I can hardly taste the champagne.* She almost turned a quizzical eye to Galen but Calyph starting speaking.

"I grew up on Chandlier. Do you know where that is?"

The Jordan nodded. "It's in the Flower. IGC hub. Big meeting place for dignitaries. Lots of embassies."

"That's right," Calyph agreed. "We lived in the small suburb of Proyect. My father worked at the embassy there."

"As an ambassador?" Blue asked, impressed.

Calyph laughed softly. "As a clerk."

"What did your mother do?"

The Engineer took a drink from his bottle, surprised that she would ask, but answered truthfully. "She worked for an Apothecary. I would go in and help her in the back sometimes when she worked extra hours, which was every chance she could get. We were very poor." The Jordan nodded and took a sip from the bottom of her drink while he continued. "I did not fit in at school, and not just because we were poor. As a child I learned that the only thing more cruel than other children were alien children. I was ostracized because of my race and because of our poverty, but there was another child there more despised than myself. An Aridian."

The Jordan nodded again in understanding as she finished the bitter champagne. Aridians were feared by many and avoided by almost all the rest. "You two became friends," she surmised aloud.

"Close friends," the Engineer agreed. "Very close. We spent every moment we could together. We swore that we would always take care of each other, and that together we would get out of the poverty-stricken life we seemed doomed to live in forever."

Galen's head lolled back in boredom. "You're breaking my heart," he murmured sarcastically as Calyph went on about growing up and falling in love.

What is the point of this story? the ghost wondered. *Trying to befriend the Jordan? Earn her trust? Garner some sympathy?* It didn't seem likely. What did seem likely was that the Jordan's champagne had been drugged as well as the food. Her relaxed pose was becoming more of a slouch. Galen's face came down quickly as it turned to Noel.

"He's stalling!" he shouted at her. "Stalling for time!" the doctor's ghost bellowed to no avail. "You need to get out of here!"

But the Jordan was putting the pieces together herself, despite a relaxed sleepiness that was creeping into her.

"Scarlett said she saw an Aridian at the festa as she was trying to make her departure from Kayos. Right before she was smeared with enough Chlorforgel to knock out a Golgoth." Blue gave Calyph a wan smile and shook her blonde head slowly from side to side. "You two planned on taking Scarlett, and Fledge as well?"

Calyph nodded as he took another drink from his bottle and Blue clucked her tongue at him.

"Stupid," she chided. "And dangerous. But I'll admit, you've got more nerve than I gave you credit for. Still, sharing such a secret with me is even more foolish..."

The Engineer kept a sharp eye on her as her thoughts continued in silence. *It's because they don't plan on using Scarlett anymore,* she realized. *And they plan on me not telling anyone. Only one way that could happen.* She turned to look at Galen but he was nowhere to be seen. She also realized, belatedly, how numb her other senses were.

"Shit," she mumbled, rising to her feet to find herself unsteady. "Fuck," she tried to exclaim but it came out as a slurred mutter while she almost stumbled backwards into the couch.

Calyph rose as well, gauging how much the drugs he had given her were working and wondering if he would have to restrain her. Galen, meanwhile, could feel the field that separated him from Noel continue to thicken, pushing him back until it felt as if he were watching her from the outside of a glass cell.

Just then, their waiter returned, the tray with their drinks held high with one limb while another was used to push open the heavy drapes.

"Thank go.." the Jordan began, no longer wanting her drink

but in dire need of sending a distress signal - a call for help - through anyone.

But the shungapod, instead of handing the Jordan her glass of champagne, hurled the tray at her head and lunged for her body.

Blue's reflexes, even in her drugged state, moved faster than her ability to understand the situation. With one arm she blocked the tray flying at her head and with the other hand she pulled her pistol from its holster.

The shungapod, however, was already swinging another limb and it struck the Jordan's wrist. The pistol went flying over the back table before it hit the curtain and clattered to the floor. Blue turned, groggy and slow, as if she had just awakened from a long nap, and felt the shungapod jump onto her back, limbs wrapping around her body and pulling it to the ground.

The half-elf pilot fought back but it was like a drunkard trying to kick off bedsheets. Concentrating the best she could, she lashed out, trying to hurt the creature, but the damn thing was so soft everywhere that the Jordan's blows had little or no effect. Frustrated, she opened her mouth to yell out but another limb slipped around her neck, choking off any sound.

Galen went wild, shouting at the Jordan, the Engineer, and the shungapod, all while crying out to Cyan to do something but he was cut off from everyone. He banged his hands against the field that separated them but it was as hard and as impenetrable as a wall of Perspex.

Blue brought up both hands, grasped the arm around her throat and pulled down, restoring her flow of air enough to breathe and then drove an elbow back towards the creature's brain but the bulbous head slipped away.

Her gaze darted up as one arm-like appendage rose up, exposing three needle-like tips glistening with fluid.

The sharp prongs were once used by shungapods a millennia ago, to paralyze prey. Now the shungas mostly had them removed since they, like most civilized species, bought their food already killed, cleaned, and wrapped neatly in plastic.

Calyph's Aridian lover, Tara, had a hell of a time finding one that still had both the prongs and the venom sac. The Doppelgänger had taken the shunga's form, and life, and then spent over a week in the body getting used to the feel and learning to move it with strength and speed.

Blue gasped and finally yelled for Cyan herself. Immediately she was enveloped with turquoise light and a renewed strength poured into her. Her hands dug into the limb around her neck and tore it away as she rolled to her left, her eyes searching the ground for her fallen gun.

The shungapod gave a quavering curse in Anglicus as it went with her, wrapping its leg appendages around the Jordan's thighs and dragging her back. It cursed again as Calyph danced away and quickly stepped close again, just on the edge of the fray.

"What's taking so long?" he cried out, jumping away again as they rolled back, Blue trying to disentangle herself and disable the shunga.

"She's really strong!" Tara warbled through the shunga's throat. The limb with the poison prongs flailed about as she tried to keep it away, wanting to be able to land it somewhere she could really drive it in. She tried for the Jordan's neck but the pilot saw it coming and flung it away, keeping her hand clear of the spikes. She tried for her stomach next but the Jordan was able to free a leg and kick away the pronged arm with a booted foot. She swung again and almost landed it in her thigh but the crazed Jordan threw another elbow into the Shunga's face.

Though the Aridian was protected by all the squish around the shungapod's brain, it sent her head flying back and all her arm limbs flailing. Blue struggled into a sitting position and tried to pry off the lower limbs. Tara snaked three arms back around the pilot's torso and aimed this time once more for the neck. The Jordan, her arms momentarily pinned, ducked and shoved back with her shoulder.

Knowing her moves were being seen and thwarted, Tara gave up on a precision hit and began slapping wildly with the needle-tipped arm. On her third frenetic swing, the pointed end of the arm came down hard onto the Jordan's shoulder, driving the spines through the fabric of her Mylar flight suit and into her flesh.

Blue cried out, more in dismay than pain, and her body began to go limp, the strength draining away in a flood as the turquoise light about her faded.

Under her body, the already soft form of the shunga softened even more, four of its limbs drawing in and melting into the torso while the other four shifted - muscle and sinew replacing soft tissue as toes and fingers formed on the budding hands and feet. The bulbous head shrank and hardened.

The Aridian shrieked in victory and delight as she retook her natural form – a diminutive, almost stick-like body topped with a rather large and almost perfectly round head. Long curtains of straight hair fell on either side of round eyes so prodigious they took up two-thirds of her face. It was a form that was hardly threatening, unless one knew what she was.

Slender fingers wrapped around the Jordan's throat and a soft voice whispered in her ear. "I don't know how long the paralytic lasts or what kind of creatures may process it better, so let's not waste time."

The Aridian closed her enormous eyes and concentrated. Blue fought to make her breathing erratic and therefore harder for the predator to match, but the paralytic was making her breath slow and even. The Rogue Aridian matched her breath perfectly, the tips of her long fingers lightly caressing the Jordan's skin, gently extracting her DNA.

"Ssshh," the Aridian soothed, "it will be over soon."

Calyph moved closer, watching intently as he sank to his

knees.

Blue tried to close her eye so she could think better but was unable to perform even that one small function. Instead, she stared helplessly at the canvas wall of the cabana, the bottom half anyway, seeing people pass in the form of shadows and feet of all shapes and sizes, oblivious to what was happening behind the curtain. Thoughts of Galen and Cyan flickered through her mind, along with those of her sisters, the Dragon, Scarlett, and the IGC, but she knew she did not have time to speculate about them now.

She's going to turn into me, she thought. *I have to be ready for that, and ready to kill her the second she does. Jesus, how? I can't even move my eye. But my brain is still working, and my lungs, thank Christ. So think!*

The urge to close her eye to focus her thinking was strong, but all she could do was stare at the canvas curtain, its strip of light cutting down the middle, and the shadows of day trippers as they partied in and around the pools.

The shungapods' venom is tetrodotoxin, and the fact that I can breathe means it was a small amount, no doubt due to the fact that the ancient ones ate small fish and other little aquatic animals. It's a neurotoxin, but not enough to kill me. My body will eventually burn it off... burn it off...

Blue stared at the gap in the curtain and tried something that should be as natural to an elf as breathing. It was something they had brought from the old worlds. From the cold worlds. Long ago it had been a survival mechanism. Now, it was simply something taught to young elves like a party trick, something akin to wiggling their ears. Noel had never taken it for granted and had honed it during her time at the Jordan Training Center and she tried it now – to raise her body temperature.

It was hard to tell if it was happening. She was already plenty warm from her struggle and now lying on and being held by the Aridian she was even warmer.

She willed her heart to beat faster, harder.

The Jordan focused upon her organs, her bones and tissues, and mentally pressed from her core - driving pressure out to the skin that covered her body.

The Doppelgänger was too engrossed in her own body's processes to notice. It was aware that the change was not happening, was being thwarted somehow. She dug her fingernails into the Jordan's neck, drawing blood, then morphed a finger into a slim tentacle with thin, membranous skin. The tentacle stroked the small, bloodied cuts like an animal licking a wound. She kept her round eyes closed, scowling deeply as she concentrated.

Calyph watched the now silent struggle with growing dismay. He had seen Tara take other forms before, and it was always quite fast. Sometimes disturbingly so.

"What's taking so long?" he whispered.

Blue, startled, glanced at him.

And realized she had moved her eye.

She blinked.

Feeling was returning, but not fast enough. Her body felt as if it were burning up with fever. Internally, she pushed harder and raised her temperature more. Now she could feel it, a hot flashing and throbbing as if she had come down with the glom flu. She could feel a sheen of sweat begin to form on her brow.

Then suddenly, just as she felt her muscles begin to twitch, the Aridian cried out in anger and loosened her hold in frustration.

"I can't!" she shouted, furious. "Her DNA is protected!

"What?" Calyph demanded.

"Her DNA has a copyright!"

"What does that mean?"

The Aridian let go of her prey in disgust. "She's not real!"

The elfin Engineer, his blue eyes wide with shock, slowly

moved his gaze to the Jordan. The half-elf pilot, just as surprised and filled with a terror-like dread, felt that enough of her strength had returned and, before that strength could flee in shock, rammed her elbow back and into the Aridian's head.

This time, without the shunga's mantle to protect it, it cracked against her face and drove her head back into the concrete floor, knocking her unconscious.

Blue pushed herself away from the limp body and sat up shakily on her haunches, her breath coming in ragged gasps. She turned her eye to Calyph, who was watching her with fearful eyes full of trepidation. She could not venture to guess which of them was more shocked, or which of them now had a more dangerous secret.

 ONE ZERO

- Is it more important in this life to know what is real, or who is real?

Scarlett made sure to say good-bye to the birthday girl and give hugs to the others before she left. She met Sean and Grandpa back in the hallway that separated their pods.

"I want to speak with you more about our family tree," she told Grandpa. "When I have more time."

Grandpa nodded sagely and gave her a glimpse of his new pearly whites. Scarlett did her best not to grimace or cringe. Instead, she flicked her dark eyes to Sean.

"You're looking after him?"

"Yeah," he agreed. "I mean, yes ma'am."

Scarlett laughed. "I'm still Auntie Jo to you," she assured her nephew. "But keep watching after him." She turned her dark-eyed gaze back to Grandpa. "I'll request a few days of leave so we have more time to catch up. Maybe we can have a family picnic or some shit."

"Language!" Grandpa admonished.

Scarlett laughed and gave him a kiss on his cheek, surprising him. He could not remember her doing such a thing in over a hundred years. She reached out to tousle Sean's blonde locks but instead pulled him close and kissed the top of his head. He was equally shocked and pleased.

"You two behave yourselves," she ordered before she turned and left.

Smiling, the Red Jordan exchanged the hallway of the podment for the sunbathed aggregate concrete pathway that would lead her back to the tram station. She had not taken a dozen steps down the sidewalk before all her senses started to buzz.

Nothing that screamed of an immediate threat, but something was off and the focus was on her. It had the same feeling of walking into a room full of people when all conversations seem to pause and every eye turned in your direction.

Without slowing her pace, she glanced about the park. Same gentle knolls of grass and the appearance of blue sky. The same couple still sat on the bench with their backs to her. Two parents with a toddler were in the silica pit, encouraging the youngster to take a few cautious steps. The handsome man who had been getting coffee was nowhere to be seen.

But he's here, though, Scarlett thought. *Whoever the hell he is, he's here somewhere.*

Her dark eyes searched the park, not seeing the missing man nor anything out of the ordinary. Her gaze passed over the couple on the bench once more and, as it did, she was hit by a smell that wanted to make her knees buckle. It was not an unpleasant smell. Far from it. The skin under her right arm and down the side of her ribcage began to tingle.

Shit.

With her eyes back on the path in front of her as she walked along, Scarlett reached up and gave the stud in her ear a gentle squeeze. A voice spoke into the same ear almost immediately.

"Upper Klick Security. Is this an emergency?"

"No, not at all," Scarlett answered. "Would you please connect me with Transit?"

"Certainly, ma'am."

The line went silent for second before another voice came through her com transmitter. "Upper Klick Transit, how may I help you?"

"This is the Red Jordan of the IGC Opal Dragon," she informed the voice from Transit, though she was sure he was quite aware of who she was. "Is it possible to secure a private car at the Daybreak Metro Station?"

"Unquestionably, Jordan." There was a moment where she could faintly hear quick clicking noises, presumably typing. "I can have a tram there for you in a minute and a half. It has three cars, but you will have the train exclusively to yourself. Will that suffice?"

"Absolutely."

"Excellent. It will be the red train, platform three. Arriving now in less than a minute, but it will wait for you for as long as you need. It is AI controlled, you only need to tell it where to go and it will get you to the station closest to your destination. Is there any other assistance I can offer?"

"No, you have been more than helpful. Thank you."

"My pleasure, Jordan. Thank you for visiting Upper Klick."

The line went silent and Scarlett shook her dark locks out behind her. She could sense that the couple had left the bench and were casually following her from a distance. She had no doubt now that it was Bjorn and his lovely troll, Lucy. Nor did she doubt that the handsome man getting his coffee in the park earlier was his bodyguard.

One of them, she thought as she could now sense others joining the haphazard parade with forced nonchalance. She mentally tsked herself for her lack of attention before when a voice spoke up inside her head.

Do not judge yourself too harshly, the voice whispered. It was the voice of Elaeric, the former monk who had taught her mediation, among other things. Scarlett's full lips turned up at the corners. *You did not take notice then because there was no threat. Their only intention was to watch.*

Now that their intentions have changed, she silently surmised, *so has my attention. Interesting.*

She left the park behind. Modest podments still continued on her left but on her right was a row of small stores. Some sold convenience items but most were redolent of sugar. A candy shop, a donut stand, and a cupcake store. A gelateria and an ice cream parlor.

And what might those intentions be? she wondered lightly, her smile growing.

The sidewalk widened and trees lined the path. There was a separate sidewalk in front of the shops, speckled with wrought-iron tables and chairs. Families and couples made use of them, eating sundaes and sipping malted shakes.

Scarlett had the distinct feeling that her followers were shortening the distance between them. They were pulling together. Closing in on her.

Far from afraid, the smile on the Jordan widened more.

This was going to be much more fun than a birthday party.

The housing on her left dropped off and the tram station began. Platforms and access bridges surrounded cement cradles split by gleaming rails. Sleek, bullet-shaped trains hummed, waiting.

Scarlett took in the entire scene with a sweep of her dark eyes. Past the sweet shops and sundry kiosks was a line of aircabs, the latest news broadcasts flowing around their sides in holographic streams.

The sight of them resurfaced a memory that gave Scarlett a shiver, and a quirk to her smile. She turned towards the platforms and trains, feeling her pursuers close in and slow down.

The first platform was teeming with adults and children in

various athletic uniforms, off for a day of competitive sports. The six blue passenger cars were filling up quickly. Scarlett took an escalator up and had another look around from atop the platform bridge.

The next cradle held a golden train mostly populated by teenagers since the first stop would be at the local mall. There were a few adults on board, most of them making their way to the bar car. It was not scheduled to leave for another four minutes. Past the ten-car gold train bound for the bustling shopping center was a much smaller one. It was red, only three cars long, and completely empty.

Scarlett grinned and took the first escalator down. She tossed her dark hair over her shoulders and boarded the gold-car tram bound for the mall.

⊰⊱

Bjorn felt that he could hardly contain his excitement as he and Lucy rose up from the park bench and began to follow Scarlett from a distance. From the corner of his vision he could see Julian slip from the shadows of the coffee stand, followed by Diego. He knew that Micheal would not be far behind.

They trailed at what he hoped was a safe enough distance to go unnoticed, yet he felt horribly exposed. If Scarlett happened to look back, she would recognize him immediately. He slowed his pace and draped an arm around Lucy's shoulders. He tried to dip his head as if in conversation with her and did not miss the smug look in her eyes as they changed color.

"If you make one mention of my need for a hat," he warned, "I will squeeze the life out of you."

"But I am not a living being," Lucy pointed out, as if he needed such a reminder. "Are you implying you will short circuit me somehow?"

"Yes," Bjorn affirmed, looking sidelong at Scarlett's backside as she passed the sundry shops. He saw her reach up to her ear and, though he was too far back to hear her, he knew what she was doing. "Can you monitor that call?"

Lucy's eyes shimmered, changing colors. "No," she answered after a moment. "It's a secure line."

"Damn. Who do you think she is calling?"

The eyes on the droid flickered. Lucy thought the question opened up a near endless amount of possibilities for a joke, but could sense Bjorn's already abnormally high tension and answered plainly.

"She just left her only family, so it is likely not one of them. It could be any number of military personnel, but also unlikely that she would call from here rather than back on her vessel."

Bjorn's handsome face wrinkled in a scowl. "Enough of the unlikely possibilities. What is most likely?" He felt Lucy's shoulders move slightly under his arm.

"She is approaching a transit station. She needs to get back to the spaceport. It is quite likely it was an inquiry about transportation."

Bjorn grunted. "Seems almost overly simple."

"Aren't most things?"

Bjorn grunted again.

The Jordan slowed as she made her way into the open-air tram station.

Bjorn and Lucy slowed as well, though there were people here that offered excellent camouflage. The Chimeran Commander did his best to blend in with the others out on a weekend outing.

He watched Scarlett take the escalator to the pedestrian bridge and glance around. Quickly, he turned Lucy so they were both facing the other direction. He watched as Julian approached and passed them by before pausing a few meters away, his eyes going everywhere. Diego came next and paused before reaching Lucy and the Commander.

Bjorn risked a peek over his shoulder in time to see Scarlett descending on the other side of the bridge and then watched through the windows of the blue tram to see her board a car on the next train, a golden one. He followed with haste, jerking his head in a silent order for the others to follow.

He took both escalators as if they were stairs, ascending one and then descending the other quickly. Looking into the gold-painted train he could see Scarlett making her way to the bar car up front and realized they were only a few feet away from each other. The only things separating them were a pair of chairs and a pane of glass.

Bjorn averted his face, wishing that he really did have a hat.

Damn that Lucy!

Thinking of her, he looked back to see the droid approaching casually, flanked by Julian and Diego. Micheal was not far behind them. Bjorn jerked his chin at the golden train as he boarded a car, motioning for them to get on the same train but the next car back.

Scarlett made her way to the bar car, glancing at the holo showing the time to departure. It turned from two minutes to one minute while she watched. The line to order a drink was not long, but put her close to the door, opposite to the side she had entered. Gentle warnings began to sound to stay clear of the doors, as the tram would soon be departing. Scarlett kept a safe distance.

Bjorn was close. His party was not far behind him but he was the closest to the Jordan. His smell filled her nostrils and she was aware that her entire body was now tingling. Especially between her legs.

She did her best to ignore it.

The Jordan looked up at the brightly light cocktail menu, absently perusing the variety of drinks while she counted the seconds in her head.

CR80

Bjorn passed casually through the train until he was in the passenger tram next to the bar car. He forced himself to back off but found he could not keep from staring through the double set of sliding doors at Scarlett's profile.

Her face was turned up as she scanned the selection of libations. Her dark hair formed loose natural waves that fell away from a strong straight nose and high cheekbones. Her breasts were round, pushing against the crimson silk fabric of her blouse, threatening the buttons that held it closed.

An unseen speaker advised to stay clear of the doors as the tram would soon be departing. The first stop, it assured, would be the Luxor Shopping Center.

Bjorn hardly heard. A random parent in the bar car tried to get in line for a drink, blocking his view. Bjorn frowned and absently pushed at the crotch of his pants with the heel of his hand, adjusting his growing erection as he moved to the side to keep his eyes on the Jordan.

She smiled at the man trying to join the queue and stepped back, letting him go in front of her.

Just then the tram gave its final gentle warning regarding its forthcoming departure.

Scarlett's face turned and this time Bjorn was not quick enough to turn away. The Jordan and the Chimeran Commander locked eyes and he could hardly believe that she showed no signs of surprise or consternation. Instead, she smiled at him. And slipped out the closing doors of the tram.

Bjorn, not to be outmaneuvered, had the long-honed reflexes of a pilot. Though the closing doors next to him were on the side of the train opposite the side Scarlett had used, he leapt through them - his body turned sideways - and landed on the concrete platform as the tram began to move down its track. As the cars slid past, he saw the surprised faces of Lucy and his bodyguards still on the train. Julian gave him a fierce scowl and began hurrying through the train, looking for a way out.

On the other side of the departing tram, Scarlett glanced about to see if she had been followed.

Gold car after gold car passed by, picking up speed as the train left the station.

The platform on which she stood was empty.

Smiling, she turned and headed for the red train in the next cradle. On each car, where the destination was usually marked, the word *Private* was illuminated in holographic letters.

The last few cars on the gold train finally passed by, leaving Bjorn exposed on the other platform. He had no need to worry. Scarlett had already turned her back to him and was approaching the next cradle which held a train of only three red cars.

The tram took a retina scan from the Jordan and opened its doors for her. All the doors. Scarlett boarded the first car as Bjorn ignored the warnings on his platform and jumped down into the empty cradle. He jumped easily over the metal rail, pulled himself up on the other side, raced across the concrete, and boarded the last car of Scarlett's train just as the doors were closing.

The tall Chimeran ran a hand through his blonde hair, pushing it away from his green eyes as they darted around the empty compartment. His heart was pounding and his erection had not subsided in the least.

The red train gave a hushed sigh and left the station, gliding smoothly on its track, picking up speed as it went. The Jordan jerked back and wrapped her hand around an upright silver rail to keep herself steady. She was not thrown off balance from the movement, but from the instant realization she was not alone.

Once again she was filled with Bjorn's scent and her skin sizzled. The heat was like hands on her body - gliding over her breasts, her hips, between her legs. Her face snapped back over her left shoulder, back to the cars attached to her own.

Scarlett, her eyes narrowed and her nostrils flared, turned on the heel of her boot and strode past the empty seats. The doors between the first and second car opened at her approach with a barely audible hiss. As she walked through them, the far doors of the tram opened and Bjorn stepped into the middle car.

For a second that seemed to draw out like a spool of electric thread, the two just stared at each other, like gunfighters of an age long since passed.

Bjorn could not help but admire the Jordan from across the short distance. The black leather of her pants wrapped her strong legs like a second skin and the silk of her crimson shirt clung to her chest.

The Chimeran, however, was dressed in the drab clothing of a civilian. To Scarlett, it only accentuated his features. The sand-colored shirt stretched across his broad shoulders and the brown pants he wore hung low on narrow hips. His golden hair and green eyes shone as if illuminated.

Simultaneously, the pair took a step closer to each other. And another. And another.

Bjorn felt as if he was being pulled by a magnetic force.

To Scarlett it was as if tendrils of electricity had wrapped themselves about her extremities and were reeling them in.

Each took another step. Then another.

When she and Bjorn were a meter apart she once again grabbed one of the silver poles that went from the floor to the ceiling of the tram and held herself steady in one place.

He was the first one to break the silence

"Hello, Scarlett."

The Jordan laughed. Not a giggle or a chuckle, but an all-out laugh.

The Chimeran commander smiled at the sound and cocked his head, curious. "What's so funny?"

Scarlett shook her head, still laughing though it was now fading into chuckled huffs. "You."

"Me?"

"Yes, you. The way you greet me every time as if we work some mundane job together. As if I just saw you yesterday."

Bjorn's smile widened. "Would you prefer I shout profanities at you?"

Scarlett laughed again. "I think it would surprise me less. Or at least put me in a mindset better able to defend myself."

"You don't need to defend yourself against me," he said softly, taking a step closer.

Scarlett tightened her hand around the rail she still held, but did not move.

"Why are you here?" she asked instead.

"I want to know if you have considered my offer."

"Don't be ridiculous," Scarlett scoffed.

"About asking?"

"About thinking I might consider it."

Bjorn took another step closer and Scarlett felt herself inundated with heat. She lifted her chin, ignoring it the best she could, which was hardly at all.

"But you *are* considering it, aren't you?"

"No," she said, knowing all too well that she was lying. She had indeed considered it, many times. The scenario of it had played through her head the way confrontations like this with Bjorn had played through her dreams as she slept.

A piercing feeling swept through her and she was acutely afraid that she might be dreaming, right here and now.

"Is this real?" she asked aloud.

The golden brows of the Chimeran Commander clenched minutely, slightly narrowing his gimlet eyes. "Define real."

And just like that, Scarlett knew that there was no real. Only perception.

And, just like that, her perception changed.

Suddenly she felt as if her chest were expanding, as if filling with air - her shoulders becoming more broad. Her head swelling with vision and knowledge.

The shock of revelation hardly had time to sink in - for at the same time she realized that she had crossed over the first steppingstone of which Master Elaeric had told her about enlightenment. A short conversation that now felt like eons past but had really been not that long ago.

Forgive the past completely.

She knew that she had done just that.

How?

That was a matter to meditate upon at another time.

Now, Bjorn narrowed his green eyes at the Jordan. Something inside her had shifted. The sexual tension was still there, taut and electric. But there was a ripple of energy that went through her and passed through him.

"What was that?" he asked.

Scarlett's smile was a bare glimmer on her face. "I'm not sure. But can we please cut back to the chase? We're not on some backwards moon. This is one of the most advanced places in the seven systems. Our every move is being recorded. Every word."

"Lucy?" Bjorn intoned.

Scarlett cocked her head, nonplussed, her eyes widening slightly as she heard the voice of Bjorn's troll come through the unseen speakers on the train.

"All outgoing communications have been blocked," the droid assured smoothly.

Bjorn took yet another step towards her. They were now less than a foot away from one another. "You may speak freely," he encouraged. She could feel the heat from his body, the electricity of their proximity and, of course, his smell. Her legs weakened, especially at her knees.

"Oh?" Scarlett spoke innocently. "Thank goodness. In that case, you can go fuck yourself."

Bjorn laughed as he rolled his eyes, not put out in the least. Scarlett, however, was disturbed at how his laughter made her feel.

Warm.

Warm and safe and thrilled all at once. She scowled.

"Again, would you please get to it? To what do I owe this visit?"

"Did you look into what I told you the last time we talked?" Bjorn asked, his expression solemn for what she thought must be the first time. "About the Amliss attack? About your father?"

Scarlett sighed. "To what end? It would be ridiculous to lie about something that would be easily disproved."

"So you believe me?"

The Jordan let out another deep breath. "Yes."

"And your thoughts about the IGC?"

The muscle along Scarlett's jaw tightened, as if trying to hold in her words.

Bjorn's blonde brows raised. "Your thoughts?"

"Are not what they used to be," she admitted.

The Commander's expression softened and his green eyes glimmered with hope. "Have you considered my offer?"

"Of course," Scarlett answered. "But you don't see me in

Chimeran coveralls, do you? Flying a Chimeran jet?"

Bjorn smiled. "I think the Commander's chain I gave you would suffice. And I'm not sure I'm ready to let you into another one of our fighters just yet."

Scarlett's lips turned up at the corners. She glanced out the window to see they were passing through another station. The train slowed, for safety's sake, then picked up speed again. It was a private hire that would not stop until she reached her destination. Or until she asked it to. She looked back at the Chimeran, looking up to meet his eyes with her own.

"Why are you here, Bjorn?"

The Commander moved incrementally closer and wrapped his hand around the silver rail that Scarlett still held, just above hers, so their fingers were against each other. Their bodies were merely inches apart. The scent of him invaded more than her nostrils. It seeped into her skin and ran through her veins, making her dizzy. Her entire body was engulfed in passion and she tightened her grip on the rail to keep from pressing against him.

"I love you, Scarlett."

The Jordan's face went slack and her dark eyes widened, the flecks of crimson in their depths flaring like fanned coals.

"What?" she blurted, too stunned to speak for a matter of seconds. "You, you're crazy. That...this...you're just trying to..." the Jordan stammered, trying to find the words.

Bjorn smiled again. He had never seen her frazzled. It did not last long.

Scarlett drew a deep breath in through her nose and let it out quickly through pursed lips. She lifted her chin and shook her dark hair out behind her.

"Don't be ridiculous," she admonished.

"I would do anything for you," he said.

"Would you quit this war?"

Bjorn sighed. "How did I know that would be the one thing you asked?"

Scarlett smiled. "And?"

"I would stop fighting, if that was what you asked of me, but I would not stop helping my people."

Scarlett's smile widened. It was a bold offer, almost too bold to believe.

"How did you infiltrate the Dragon?" the Jordan asked bluntly.

Bjorn shrugged as if she had asked him how he put on his pants in the morning. "Chris helped me abduct the Engineer."

"Chris?" Scarlett asked, galvanized. "Chris who?"

Again, Bjorn shrugged. "I don't know his last name. I've always just known him as Chris. We took the Engineer and after some -ahem- questioning, he told me how to release the starfire."

The Jordan gave him a dark look and he continued quickly.

"Chris gave me a uniform and got me aboard the Dragon. You know the rest."

Scarlett racked her brain but did not come up with much. Though she knew most people only by their last names, as they were referred to on a military vessel, she also knew quite a few people named Chris, both male and female. None, however, whom she thought could get a Chimeran aboard the Opal Dragon. She doubted it would be hard to find out if she really dug, she would just need to show Bjorn some pictures. What interested her more was how completely open he was being with her.

"We could both leave this war," he said.

Scarlett shook her head. "I won't leave my Fledgling. Never."

One corner of Bjorn's mouth quirked up. "Of course not. Who or what would try to stop you?"

The Jordan returned his smirk. "The InterGalactic Council for one - a fleet of Dragons."

"I don't think they would. The IGC might try or want to try. But the Dragons?" Bjorn shrugged. "You tell me."

Scarlett's dark brows drew together.

He was right. Opal would never attack Fledge. Neither would Cyan, she was sure of it. No matter what orders they were under. She wondered briefly if any of the other Dragons would and discarded the idea immediately. They would not kill their own kind. An idea began to form in her mind but she felt Bjorn's hand close over her own and all thoughts flew like wisps of paper in the wind.

"Do you realize how vast this universe is?" he asked, his hand protectively encasing her own that still held the silver rail. "How full of possibilities? We could go anywhere, do anything."

Scarlett gave him a look full of suspicion and amusement. And warmth. Bjorn did not miss it. His hand tightened over hers.

"We're coming to my stop," she informed him.

The Chimeran's eyes looked deep into her own. "That can mean so many things."

"I know. But, for now, I'm being literal."

"Lucy, stop the train."

From wherever the droid was, she overrode the directives of the tram and closed the brakes.

The train screeched on its rail at the sudden command, its occupants leaning dangerously forward and then lurching back as the inertia shifted. Scarlett - despite her hold on the safety rail, found herself pressed against the Chimeran Commander. Instinctively, Bjorn's arm wrapped around her waist and held tight to keep her on her feet. It was probably a good thing, the Jordan realized. She had never been more unsteady in her life.

Everything was brought into sharp relief. The feel of his leg against hers, the bone of his hip. The strength of the arm holding her. His eyes so green they seemed to glow. And his smell. His goddamned smell.

She pressed against him, unable to stop herself. Her breasts flattened against his chest and she pressed her sex against his. She could feel her own breath, hot against the place where his shoulder met his neck.

Scarlett heard him gasp, yet the Chimeran kept perfectly still as the train completed its unscheduled stop. When it did, with one last jerk, Scarlett stepped away.

"It would be better for one of us to leave here," she breathed. "I'm not sure how many cameras your droid can override, but half of the ones at the next station are going to be IGC. Alarms will go off somewhere if that happens."

Bjorn took a step back as well and nodded. "Of course. I'll get off here and have one of my guards pick me up so I'm not seen on any footage that might bring you into question."

"Thank you."

Scarlett wet her lips with her tongue. Though she knew he had to go, for her sake more than his own, she found she didn't want him to leave. In fact, the opposite. She realized she wanted him to kiss her first. She wanted to feel his hands on her body. She wanted...

Bjorn smiled as if reading her thoughts and took another step back as the doors slid open.

"The next time I see you, Scarlett, I hope you are wearing the necklace I gave you." He leapt lightly to the ground, a flatland of close-cropped blades of green and gold, then turned and grinned rakishly at her. "Or nothing at all!" he called as the doors closed.

Scarlett shook her head and laughed softly as the tram began to move once more. She watched Bjorn until he disappeared and then she collapsed into an empty seat. Her legs were shaking.

"Balls and shit," she whispered.

 ONE ONE

- After learning a secret, you may never wake up the same.

Blue took a deep, shuddering breath. She could still feel the effects of the tetrodotoxin. They were fading, but slowly. She turned her face to Galen, still trapped behind the pane that separated them but visible now, her eyes full of accusation as the questions poured from her in a flood.

"Is it true? Am I not real? Did you know? Did you play a part in this?"

Calyph's terrified gaze followed the direction of her stare, but he saw nothing nor no one else in the cabana.

Galen's head shook vehemently, his black hair whipping his face before he looked down with a scowl. "No," he told her, though his tone did not carry its normal note of surety. It was quite the opposite. The Jordan looked at him suspiciously, the fingers of one hand coming up to settle the eyepatch that had come askew in the struggle. She saw his countenance light up and his face lifted. "Did you ever find Faith?" he asked. "Did you get your rings?"

Blue's scarred face became a mask of confusion. "I went to see her, after I had circled Saturn for days, trying to decipher what you tried to tell me in that hangar on Leoness. She didn't say anything about any rings and I didn't think to ask. I thought you were referring to the planet."

Galen shook his head, gentler this time. "No. The rings of Saturn were actual rings, the kind you wear as jewelry. They were made by your grandfather and biometrically matched to his DNA so he might easily distinguish his granddaughters from their biodentical dolls. The stones on them glow when worn by the real daughters of Christa de Rossi. He made a set for each, and left behind three more for those he thought might come later."

"Constance, Grace, and me," Blue said softly. Next to her, the Aridian stirred, moaning softly, bringing her attention back to the present, and the danger it presented. The Jordan turned her face to the Engineer and smiled crookedly. "Your childhood friend?" she asked, indicating the waking Aridian.

Calyph had remained crouched on the cement floor of the cabana, swarmed by a hundred ideas of what to do and too mortified to do any of them. The only thing he was sure of was that he could not leave Tara. Otherwise, he would have already fled.

"Yes," he said softly.

The Jordan sneered as she leaned over and grabbed the round head. She could feel the Aridian beginning to blink her round eyes under her fingers. Palming the round head as if it were a Mayer ball, she lifted it slightly before slamming it back onto the ground. The face rolled to the side, the body limp once again.

"No!" Calyph shouted as he lurched forward. "Don't hurt her!"

"Hurt her?" Blue asked. "I should kill her."

"No!" he cried out again.

"You too for that matter," the Jordan continued as she settled a knee onto the female's thin chest. "I won't be safe again until I do. And I refuse to live the rest of my days looking over my shoulder, or always wondering if the person behind me is really this bitch."

"Please," Calyph pleaded. "She won't, I promise." His shoulders sagged in desperation. "I'll do anything you ask."

"You're right," Galen said, his voice flat. "You should kill them both."

Blue kept her knee on the unconscious creature's chest, pinning her to the ground. She agreed with Galen, but she knew that Calyph had his uses. The Aridian too, if she could be controlled. The Jordan winced, knowing that Faith would undoubtedly think the same, then felt herself shrug mentally.

Fuck it, she thought. *Better to be the player than the pawn.*

"That second shot of Fledge's fluid," she said narrowing her eye at him, "that wasn't for Gemma, was it?"

Calyph swallowed and shook his blonde head. "No. It was for Tara. Blaylock had asked about it but hadn't asked for it. Not yet, anyway."

"It wouldn't have worked," Blue told him. Calyph's brows went up. "It works on the Captains," she continued, "because the Dragons are already familiar with them, and the bond. The Jordans need to be there at the birth, when the Fledglings hatch, to form that first bond. The Fledglings need to be comfortable with the person, drawn to the person. You would have been better off giving the triptych to yourself."

Calyph's crestfallen expression made him look more bewildered and lost than ever. He needed Tara. She was his anchor whenever he was adrift. She made all their plans and big decisions. He couldn't let the Jordan hurt her, much less kill her.

"Get my gun, Calyph," Blue ordered, her voice flat.

"You're not going to kill her, are you?" he pled softly. "Please, Jordan. She's all I have."

"Then get the gun and don't get any ideas about using it, or I'll break her neck."

The Engineer moved slowly, carefully retrieving the Jordan's weapon. It had slid across the cement and would have kept going but the sight piece had snagged on the heavy drape. Calyph used his fingertips to pull it free, turned it so he could hold it by the butt, and stood up.

The thought of using it on her did flick through his mind. It would be practically soundless and he could slip away with Tara. She could figure out where they would go and what to do once she came around. It could be hours before the Jordan's body was discovered.

He turned, gun in hand, to see Blue watching him intently. She had slipped a hand behind Tara's round head and had the other one clasped over her forehead. The Jordan's eye narrowed at him as if reading his thoughts. Her nostrils flared slightly and he could see her grip on Tara's head tighten.

Terror chased all thoughts of mutiny from his mind. The Engineer carefully turned the pistol again so he was holding it by the muzzle and crept back to the Jordan, abject.

"Put it in my holster," she instructed.

Calyph did as he was told and backed away carefully. Almost distantly, he heard a squeal and a splash, followed by loud cheers and laughter from outside the cabana. Music pulsed and throbbed. The noise of the crowd rose and fell like waves upon a beach. He could hardly believe only minutes had passed since they had arrived, and no one was aware of what was happening only a few meters away from the raving revelry of the water club.

Still, Jordan Blue eyed him with suspicion. He could feel her measuring him, calculating. Suddenly, he felt that she had decided to kill them both after all. He braced himself, thankful for - if nothing else - he and Tara would be embarking upon their last journey together. He readied himself mentally, as best as he could.

"I want you available to me at all times," Blue said sharply. Calyph's sigh of relief was so great and so loud that he almost collapsed. "You, and your troll," Blue demanded, "are to do whatever I ask, without question."

Calyph nodded eagerly. Demands were good. It meant she needed him, or at least was willing to keep him around. She could make him her slave if she wanted. He had been Tara's slave since he had known her, it would be nothing new. Thinking of her, his blue eyes darted to the Aridian's limp form. She looked so tiny in her own body, so vulnerable with her huge eyes closed and mouth slightly open.

"I'll do anything you ask," he assured her. His gaze drifted to his love, who he knew would have the final say in anything he did, but that would only be if she was with him. He had to keep her with him, keep her safe. He looked pleadingly at the Jordan.

"We'll bring her along," Blue told him. "But," she warned, "if you try anything, at any time, I'll kill you both." The Jordan turned her eye next to Galen. The pane of glass that separated them had attenuated to a thickness no more than a film of ice on a frosted pond. "Suggestions?" she asked.

Galen only looked back at her, making her frown. Though his expression was calm, his eyes bore an unusual intensity, rather than his usual softness or open curiosity. "What do you think?" he asked pointedly.

Blue expelled a gust of air from her lungs as she quickly considered her options. "Well," she said looking at the unconscious form on the cement floor of the cabana, "I can't just leave her. And I don't want her to wake up until I know how to contain her. God only knows what she might turn into or do to me."

The Jordan shivered slightly and Galen's narrow blue eyes narrowed further as he watched her reason aloud.

"I can keep her sedated if I get her to Cyan. She's small enough that I could throw her over my shoulder and tote her out of here, but any number of razi-droids could and would snap pictures like crazy of a Jordan carrying an Aridian from a club." Her eye flicked back to Calyph. "What were you giving me?" she asked.

"To sedate you?"

"Yes."

"Rohypnol."

She didn't bother to ask if he had any left, she simply held out her right hand. "Give me the rest of it," she demanded. Calyph reached into his tunic and produced a vial that was half full of amber colored liquid.

Blue took it from him and, flipping the top open with her thumb, turned back to the Aridian and used her other hand to hold up the female's chin while she dumped the remainder of the vial into her mouth. She waited a few moments for the liquid to travel down the Doppelgänger's throat.

The Jordan had no idea how long it might take to go to work on the Aridian, or if it would even have the same effect it had on a human.

"Only one way to find out," Galen murmured as if reading her thoughts.

A gruesome smile spread across the Jordan's expression as she drew back a hand and slapped the Aridian hard across the face.

Calyph stifled a cry as Tara's huge eyes fluttered open before slipping closed once again as she muttered something intelligible. Blue smiled, satisfied, as she twisted her body to see the Engineer.

"Hand me that towel," she instructed. Calyph looked around and spied the one she meant. It was the one the "waiter" had worn draped over a tentacle.

He handed it to the Jordan and Blue threw it over her shoulder before sticking her hands into the Aridian's armpits and pulling her into a sitting position. The Aridian complied reluctantly, slumping over with another slurred opinion. The half-elf pilot leveled her gaze at the Engineer.

"You are going to prop her up," she instructed, "and walk her out of here like she is any other raver that overdid it today."

Calyph nodded as she continued. "I'm going to be following you with my hand on my pistol." Calyph swallowed and nodded again. "You are going to get in an aircab and I'm going to get in right after you."

"From there?"

"I'll take it from there," Blue assured him. She put an arm under the Aridian and hefted her up but couldn't hold her. The small form was a slack dead weight that wanted to slip back down to the floor like a giant fish. "Help me with her," she told Calyph, unable to keep the grin from her face as the Aridian lolled about. "She's like a puppet with cut strings. A surprisingly heavy one."

Calyph slipped an arm around Tara's tiny waist and Blue slung one of the small arms over the back of Calyph's shoulders. The Jordan pulled the towel off her own shoulder and draped it over the female's round head that was already bent so low that Blue expected it to drag her down. It was what made her so hard to hold erect.

The Jordan's grin widened and she looked at the Engineer, her hand on the butt of the pistol she wore on her hip as a silent reminder. To Calyph she looked like a shark. One that had been mauled by another shark. Galen watched as the last of the barrier between Blue and himself dissolved into nothing.

Blue jerked her head towards the tent flap in the cabana. Calyph, supporting the dead weight of his lover, walked through it. The Jordan followed closely behind with Galen trailing her, his eyes watchful and wary. Now more than ever.

The sunlight hit her full in the face as she left the cabana and she blinked rapidly, smiling broadly at those who gave her nods of recognition and the others that also recognized her but were too open-mouthed to move. She moved with a nonchalant grace, the man in front of her supporting a thin girl so drunk that he was practically carrying her.

The Jordan's lone eye darted upwards to where a few razi news-drones were headed their way and, though she didn't like it, kept the smile on her face. As luck would have it, as they were about to exit the club to hail a cab and the drones were closing in, a socialite wearing no more than a holographic bikini showed up with an outrageously large and loud entourage.

There were screams of delight at the appearance of the S-System's most popular vocalist. All heads turned and the drones zipped away in the other direction, blissfully allowing the Engineer and his ladies to slip away and into an aircab unnoticed.

"That was advantageous," Blue remarked as she gave the cab their destination. It banked on its cushion of pressured air and sped for the private spaceport.

Calyph, who was trying futilely to keep Tara upright, saw the Jordan tip her head and smile. Though he was still terribly afraid of her and of what she might do, his curiosity got the better of him.

"So you really do talk to ghosts?" he asked. It had been a rumor that had been circulating on the Dragon recently and was something that he normally would have ignored, but he had seen too much of the Blue Jordan to discount it.

"Only one," Blue confided with a smile that was crooked and bittersweet. "Umbra in machina. The ghost in the machine."

"When did you learn Latin?" Galen asked.

Noel laughed. "I didn't. I'm sure, just like most people - doctors excluded - I pick up phrases here and there. Like *Carpe Diem* and shit like that." Galen gave a snort of laughter at that one.

"I suppose so," he agreed.

"Where are we going?" Calyph asked.

"To see my sister, Faith. And get some answers, mostly the one to prove that I'm no construct. That she meddled with my DNA I have no doubt, she obviously had the balls to dick around with my prosthetic eye. I wouldn't be surprised to find she had altered the DNA of every living de Rossi, for one reason or another under the impression that she was doing it to protect us." She threw a look of disgust at the form slumped against Calyph. "Which," the Jordan admitted, "I guess she did."

Galen laughed softly. "You don't like that she saved your life today, do you?"

"No," she answered, "I don't."

"She's damned smart," Galen said. "And that's coming from me. Hope once said that Faith was always eight steps ahead of everyone else. Thank god she was this time."

Blue nodded in agreement but her mind was no longer on Faith. It was on the way that Galen, though his tone was light, stared at her intently.

Since when has he done that? she asked herself. The answer that came to mind was immediate and gut-wrenching. It made bile rise in her throat, burning it, but she kept her expression placid. *Since always.*

The Engineer, who had suddenly gone as white as a sheet, paid no heed to the conversation of which he was only getting one side. It was no wonder. He was in a whole heap of trouble. It was not, however, what had drained his face of blood.

Calyph, who had only just recovered from the debacle at the water club, had gone pale at the thought of meeting Faith de Rossi. She was undoubtedly the most influential, most wealthy and most powerful woman in the universe.

If Tara could replicate her, even for a short amount of time, they wouldn't need Fledglings or Jordans or anything. They could escape with more money than they could ever spend in their lifetimes. The question was, how?

Calyph swallowed hard and tightened his arm around the unconscious body next to him. Tara would know.

ONE TWO

"Man is not what he thinks he is, he is what he hides."
  –André Malraux

Petrov splashed water on his face from his bathroom sink and then wiped it roughly with a towel before throwing it on the floor. It had been a tough day aboard the *Resurrection*.

JP had killed two crewmembers. One on purpose - a mechanic with bad news about their jets - and another mechanic, by accident, who had unfortunately been standing too close to the other.

JP had a mighty reach.

His blades increased that reach by another half meter of razor sharp steel.

He carried two, one up each sleeve, and Petrov carried his third - a back up if they had dealings with Golgoths. Petrov, however, did not keep it concealed in his sleeve but wore it in a sheath that hung from his belt.

The Commander killing the mechanic was undeserved, it wasn't his fault they had four jets that would not fly unless fitted with parts they did not have, but it was no surprise. JP killing the second mechanic was both undeserved and a surprise. Mostly because it was unintentional.

How many deaths aboard the ship in the past six months have been unintentional? the XO wondered. *Is he getting sloppy? Careless? Or is it simply inconsequential to him who dies or why?*

Petrov grasped the sides of the sink and lifted his face to the mirror. He did not like what he saw there. His eyes, ocean blue with the irises ringed in gold, looked back him, condemning him.

He thought back to the day he had met Faith de Rossi. What it had taken for him to find her, to get to her. It had been a long road. It had been many roads. An entire century had gone by since then but his memories were clear as crystal.

There had been lying.

Begging.

Stealing.

All while living with the horror that was in his head.

He had been living with the horror for months when he saw the broadcast of her, speaking at some event or accepting some award. He could not hear the broadcast, but he saw her. There was no doubt she was quickly becoming one of the most wealthy and influential figures in the universe. He had known who she was and it was like the voice of the One spoke inside his head.

He knew she was the only person who could help him.

So he went to find her. He spent all his money just to get to the moon that was closest to his. Then he worked as a field laborer to get passage to the next. And worked again to get aboard another ship. The next moon had no fields to work, only mines. So he worked the mines till he had enough. Each moon, each job, wore him down a little more. Not his body – he was big and he was strong. But his spirit began to flag. Each one was getting him closer to Faith, but not fast enough.

At the next spaceport, though it took him two days to summon the courage, he stole a credentials card from a man at a bar and bought a ticket. Two days was much quicker than a season in the fields. He did the same at the next port, this time taking a chance on a well-dressed man that was getting tipsy, and bought a ticket all the way to Titan.

Titan, however, was no backward moon in the outskirts of the system. It had higher security protocols and cameras everywhere. The fear of being jailed, or worse, when he was finally so close to his goal, kept him honest one last time. Petrov found work in a hydrocarbon plant long enough to get a ticket to Dione.

He walked from the spaceport on Dione to the GwenSeven Headquarters and collapsed at their front door.

The One was with him that day.

When the doors opened he was met by a PA so mortified by Petrov's appearance that he was calmly calling for security before Jan could explain why he was there.

Then Faith herself walked in from another door and stopped short as the words she was about to speak died on her lips.

"Dr. de Rossi!" Jan exclaimed. "Please, I need to speak with you."

"...yes," the PA was saying over his comset. "Reception. Please hurry."

Then Faith held up a hand. "No, Thomas. Call them back, everything is fine."

The PA, his dark eyes round behind his spectacles, contacted their security department once again as Dr. de Rossi beckoned to the bedraggled man who had shown up on their doorstep.

"Come with me," she said.

Jan Petrov had followed.

She led him to her office and motioned to one of the chairs by her desk. He sank down as she retrieved a bottle of water from a miniature fridge. Jan took it gratefully and drank it all down at once. He licked his lips and felt how chapped they were. He had not realized how thirsty he was, how dehydrated.

She got him another bottle and sat down across from him. He ignored the second bottle and told her his story. What had happened. The horror.

"I want them all dead!" he had declared vehemently when he was done. "I want to kill them! Every one of them!"

"I'll take care of it," Faith replied.

"I don't want it taken care of! I want them dead!"

"I heard you the first time."

Jan had looked her is disbelief. "Do you mean…"

"Yes," she said. "I do."

Jan collapsed for the second time that morning, this time falling forward in relief over the desk between them. He closed his eyes and tears burned behind his lids.

"You realize, of course, this will not happen overnight."

"As long as I am alive to see it," he whispered.

"There will be something I will need you to do.

"Anything."

She measured him for a long moment with her eyes of brown and gold. Then she had switched off the security camera to her office.

Commander Petrov gazed at his reflection over the sink. Over the decades, Faith had fulfilled her promise to him. Almost. She had one more to go.

When that happened, he had a promise of his own to fulfill. He hoped it would be soon. Looking in the mirror, he knew he was running out of time.

Petrov straightened and left his quarters in search of JP.

Light years away, Grandpa gazed at his own visage in the

mirror over his own bathroom sink. His blue eyes were clear and his skin, which had been getting as thin and crinkly as old paper, was smoothing out. He still sported a fine map of wrinkles, but they were not as deep as they had been. His wispy hair was filling in as well, becoming thicker and there was now as much blonde as there was gray.

It's like traveling back in time, he thought with wonder.

He bared his new teeth. Now *that* was something. He cared little for his smile, which was mostly why he had never done anything about his teeth as time and age wore them down. It did not occur to him, however, what an effect it had on his eating.

He believed his diet of soft foods was because he liked what he ate, and he knew he would always love pastries, but until recently he failed to realize what he had stopped eating.

Crisp foods. Crunchy foods. Foods with substance.

Like steak.

"Speaking of which," he told his reflection, "I am quite sure there is some in the fridge." He turned and left his bathroom, the light dimming and then going out completely after he was gone. He went into the sunny kitchen in his podment and made himself a hearty steak and egg breakfast.

His body was changing too. He wasn't so damn skinny anymore. He did not know if that was due to him eating more, and more healthy foods, or from the pills Sean had gotten for him.

He sat down at the table in his nook and dug into his breakfast. One thing the pills were doing for sure, was improving his memory. What he remembered more and more were the people, the family that had filled his life over the decades. Hell, over the centuries. It brought both joy and sorrow.

Grandpa forked a bite of steak into his mouth and chewed, his mind thoughtful and far away. He supposed his loss of memory had been a mercy for a while. He had lost so many whom he had loved. Still, that was no excuse to forget them.

Grandpa looked up, startled. There had been a knock on his door. Nobody ever knocked on his door, at least not that he had heard in the past seventy years or so. He almost yelled "come in!" but realized that the door had an automatic lock. It was programmed for his hand.

He had no idea how the damn thing worked - if it took his print, DNA, heat signature or what. He just knew that it opened the door for him, as well as the rest of the family. So he was more than a little surprised when, after wiping his mouth with a napkin and crossing his living room, he opened the door to see Sean standing in the hallway.

"What are you doing out here?" he asked, his now blonde and gray eyebrows going up over his blue eyes. "Is the door broken?"

Sean smiled and pushed his own blonde hair away from his own blue eyes. "No, I just don't feel right walking in on you unannounced anymore."

Grandpa smiled. "Afraid you are going to catch me doing something I shouldn't be doing?"

Sean chuckled nervously. "Yes," he admitted.

Grandpa chortled, a sound that was steadily changing with the rest of him. It was a sound laugh, not a caw or a cackle.

"Son, the day you catch me doing something I shouldn't, especially here in my living room," Grandpa laughed again, harder this time, "is the day I toss those pills in the chute."

Sean chuckled and followed Grandpa back into his podment.

"Besides," Grandpa continued, "my home is your home. Always has been, always will be. You walk in here whenever you want."

"Okay."

"No gaming today?" Grandpa asked as he went into the kitchen to clean up his breakfast. He did not have to ask Sean why he wasn't in school. He knew it was Saturday.

Lord above, he thought, *why didn't I start taking those pills years ago?* He smiled as he zipped the dishes through the washer and put them away. *Because you were so far gone, old man,* he answered himself, *the possibility never even occurred to you.* Then he frowned as he closed the cupboard. *Or because you didn't want to remember.*

"No," Sean answered. "Not now, anyways. Jeanette has ballet class."

"But you think she's at the arcade?"

"I'm sure she's at the arcade."

Grandpa laughed and poured himself a glass of tomato juice and added a splash of French vodka. "Need my vitamin C," he told Sean with a wink. "Blackberry?" he asked while the refrigerator door was still open.

"Yes, please." Grandpa pulled a can of sparkling blackberry water from the shelf and handed it to his grandson. "Thanks," Sean said, following Grandpa into the living room.

"So," Grandpa said as he plopped down into his chair, "are you here for some stories, or to avoid an uncomfortable situation with your sister?"

Sean laughed as he sat in the other chair and popped open his can of bubbly water. "Both?"

Grandpa laughed. "What do you want to know?"

"Well, you said before I never asked about where we came from. Who we came from. Feel like telling me?"

Grandpa gave him a smile both wistful and nostalgic. "Son, I think that is the reason I have held on for so long. I would love to tell you." He took a sip of his drink and his smile widened. "Do you want me to start from now, and go backwards, or start from the beginning?"

"From the beginning," Sean said immediately. "That's how all good stories start." He wiggled his butt on the chair, settling in for a good story. He couldn't remember the last time he had done so.

Grandpa laughed. "Not all the good ones," he said. "In fact, I'm not going to start when I was born, or even growing up right here in Three Mile on Io. Though, back then, it was only One Mile."

"Damn," Sean remarked, impressed as always by how much Grandpa must have seen over the years.

"I'll start by telling you when I left Io," he said and the look that came on his face was dreamy with wonder. "Good God, son, I wasn't much older then than you are now."

Sean could appreciate the comparison. *So many years!* he thought. If his math was right, and it usually was, Grandpa was talking about close to three hundred years ago. *So many years!*

"And I bet I looked quite a bit like you do now," Grandpa said. "I'll be damned. I always thought you looked like your mother, and you do, because Jeanette favors your father with her dark hair and dark eyes. But, these days, when I look in the mirror and see my eyes and hair now, much more like they had been back then, I suppose you do have some of my looks."

Sean, who had filled out in the last year and was now taller than Grandpa, smiled. "So the dark hair and dark eyes, that must come from Grandma."

Grandpa smiled all the way to his eyes. "Indeed it does."

"So?" Sean prodded. "What happened?"

Grandpa laughed and took a sip off the top of his drink. "I left Io when I was seventeen."

Sean set his own drink aside and rubbed his hands on his thighs. He had heard many stories from the old man over the years but had never been as excited to hear one as he was now. And he knew this one was going to be a whopper. And he wasn't wrong about their ages - Sean would be seventeen within the year.

"I traveled on a cryo ship to Esodire, a dreamless nap of over five years. My body hadn't changed, hadn't aged a bit, but my identification card - what now has evolved into the credentials cards everyone carries - said twenty-two. So twenty-two I was. I was already a Journeyman, and on a crash course to make Mason and Master Mason. I was hired by an elf named Cronus, a bioengineer who wanted to build a research facility. But...are you okay son?"

Sean laughed. He knew his fists were clenched and his blue eyes were probably bulging from their sockets, but he couldn't help it. "I'm fine, I just can't believe what I'm hearing. I mean, I believe it, but I want to curse, or laugh, or howl every time you finish a sentence."

Grandpa chuckled softly. "Well, keep it together if you can. I'm just getting started!"

"I know!" Sean agreed and then cawed laugher. He slapped a hand over his mouth and nodded for Grandpa to continue.

"I had completed the plans and he had bought the land, but before we were to begin construction he met with his granddaughter, Faith de Rossi." A whimpering noise came from Sean but he otherwise held his tongue. Grandpa continued. "Faith pitched Cronus on an idea of making artificial humans. Constructs."

"Were you there?" Sean asked, leaning forward in his seat. "At that meeting?"

"I was not part of the meeting," Grandpa said with a smile, remembering how he had been sent into another room like a child who was not to hear the grown-ups talk. "But I was there."

"Holy shit!"

Grandpa laughed. Looking back, he realized he had been at quite a few meetings as GwenSeven grew and evolved. He might not have been a part of those meetings either, but he had certainly been there.

"Anyway, instead of building the complex for Cronus and his research, I ended up building a compound for Faith and her sisters, and their dyers. It was where they created the first constructs." Sean made a small squealing sound but otherwise kept quiet. "The first phase was creation; the second phase was instruction. Skills, including languages, were determined for each construct. The ones that were to learn French were tutored by yours truly to give them a true French accent. One of them was intended to be a high-level executive assistant."

"Mira Devereaux," Sean said softly. "I looked her up. She was beautiful."

"She will always be beautiful."

Sean swallowed. "What happened to her?"

Grandpa took a deep breath to steady himself. "Son, I can't say for sure what happened to her and, because I can't, I want to believe that she is alive. And happy. Somewhere."

 ONE THREE

- Secrets can turn blood into strangers, and strangers into blood.

Jasyn had resigned himself to the space next to Geary in the security room on the upper level of Faith's villa. They stood apart, and silent, in front of the monitors that showed almost every room in the enormous residence, including the security room where they were now. The only places excluded were Faith's personal quarters.

Geary did not trust the construct, but that was neither new nor unusual. Geary didn't trust anyone. It was one of the reasons that made him good at his job.

In the room with them were Tom, Geary's second in command, seated next to DJ. DJ had been with the team for a year and was proving to be a good addition to the de Rossi security contingent.

It had been a busy day at the villa. Jasyn, along with the Engineer named Nathan, had arrived in a special craft from the Last Castle to retrieve the Dragon egg that had thus far remained safely hidden and dormant at the bottom of Faith de Rossi's swimming pool.

Nathan, whom Jasyn liked not at all and trusted even less, had loaded the craft and sent it back to the Castle - deciding to personally stay and follow in the morning. Jasyn had decided the same. Faith had guest rooms and the dark-eyed construct meant to see that Nathan stayed in one of them.

Tonight, DJ had taken the seat next to Tom in front of the bank of monitor feeds. Geary, next to Jasyn, stood behind them. His eyes flicked from screen to screen, but constantly went back to pause on the only one that Jasyn was fixated upon. The one that showed Faith.

She was in her living room, staring out through the curved floor to ceiling glass wall into the vastness of space beyond. It was not entirely dark outside, it never was. From the far-right corner of the wall came a pinkish-orange glow where Jupiter loomed in the distance.

Stars pricked the black of space and the walls of the room itself gave off a soft, ambient glow. From the peripheral vision of both men, they could see the tall and lanky Engineer move from the camera in the hallway to the view of the cameras in the living room. He crossed the room, approached Faith without hesitation and stood behind her, putting his hands on her shoulders.

Tom, exhausted from the day but amused at the moment, watched Geary and Jasyn from the corner of his eye as they watched Faith. He could see the tension that flooded both of them and his eyes flicked to the monitor where the Engineer was massaging Ms. de Rossi's shoulders.

The second in command of de Rossi security was tired. It was the end of his shift and DJ was there to relieve him. It was time for him to check out for the day, but he found he was unable to do so. He stifled a yawn and rubbed his face with his palms and then rested them on the long slim stretch of the desk beneath the screens. Enough years on the job had honed his senses to know when shit was about to hit the fan. He simply had to see what was going to happen.

Jasyn, however, had apparently seen enough.

A scowl distorting his handsome face, he turned to leave the room and was stopped by the grip of Geary's strong right hand around the thick swell of the construct's right bicep. Jasyn looked at the head of de Rossi security, his black eyes full of surprise yet glaring with unbridled ferocity.

Geary slowly shook his head. "We are not to disturb her during her personal time, not without reason - reason that typically involves her safety."

"I," Jasyn hissed, "am not *we*."

"Possibly not," Geary acquiesced, not moving nor lessening his vise-like grip on Jasyn's arm, "but you, and by your own choice I believe, have elected not to be part of her personal life."

Jasyn expelled a great breath of air through his nostrils and, with his teeth clamped tightly together, turned back towards the monitors. Geary released his hold and turned his own gaze back to the screens that showed the expanse of the living room. His breath hitched as he saw the Engineer lead Faith to the couch, coax her down, and slip off her shoes.

Shit. Geary thought, scowling. *This is not going to go well. No matter what happens. This is going to be bad.* He felt his own jaw tighten reflexively, the muscles along his lower face rippling.

The head of security watched Nathan carefully set down the heeled shoes, sit on the opposite end of the couch, and scoop up a delicate foot before he began to massage it slowly.

Geary's sharp eyes went first to Faith's face, looking for any distress. When he saw none, his gaze flicked to Jasyn, whose distress was enough to fuel a rocket. A small vein pulsed in his temple under his tan skin.

At least he is keeping it controlled, Geary thought with a flicker of approval, his steely eyes going back to the monitors.

Ms. de Rossi took a sip of her champagne and laughed at something the Engineer said.

Tom shifted in his seat, his exhaustion fading as it was replaced by a tingle of excitement. He knew it was only a matter of time, and precious little of it, before the construct defied Geary. Jasyn's dark eyes were intent on the monitor, his jaw clenched as tight as his fists. Tom had a feeling that Jasyn would be heading downstairs any second, no matter what Geary said or did.

The com-line from the Private Community of Iron Rose Security rang, startling him. He wasn't wearing his earpiece so he simply leaned forward and touched the button under the monitors that would open the link.

"de Rossi security, this is Tom."

"Hi Tom, it's Al. You have a Dragon Fledgling headed your way."

"The blue one?" Tom asked, the weariness that had been bone-deep suddenly nonexistent.

"I believe so, but the Jordan was not very cooperative. Do you want me to put her through or do you want me...".

"No," Tom interrupted, a smile making its way onto his face. "Put her through right away." There was a click and then Tom could hear a murmuring from the com. "de Rossi security," he said once again.

"Tom!" a female voice exclaimed. "Is that you?"

Tom's smile grew till it was nearly ear to ear. "It is."

"Lovely. This is Noel de Rossi," she said and then laughed as if her name were the funniest thing in the world. "Faith's sister, remember?"

"How could I forget?"

Tickled laughter came again from the speaker. "I'd like a word with her."

"I'll let her know!" Jasyn quipped and was gone from the room before Geary could make a grab for him.

"Ms. de Rossi is indisposed at the moment," Geary announced as he leaned towards the com, frustration clouding his face.

"Docking now," the Jordan announced back.

"You will need to remain there until you are cleared," Geary ordered, his eyes flashing to the monitor where he could see Jasyn entering the living room of the villa. The security man seethed with indecision. He knew that neither Jasyn nor the Engineer were an immediate threat to Ms. de Rossi, but a confrontation was certainly brewing and he did not think it appropriate or safe for it to be in front of her. Nor could he let an armed Jordan come barging in with her own storm. "Do *not* let her in," Geary commanded before striding out the door.

Tom rubbed his hands on his thighs, watching the monitor and listening for the com. DJ hoisted an eyebrow at him and then turned his own eyes back to the monitors as well.

Blue rose from the pilot's seat inside her Fledgling and headed aft past the small galley towards her sleeping quarters. Calyph lifted his blue eyes towards her with a questioning look from where he sat on the bed next to the female Aridian. Her limp body was surrounded by a glow of greenish-blue light. The Jordan gave a nod of satisfaction at the sight of the still unconscious Doppelgänger.

"Keep her that way," the Jordan said. Calyph dipped his head in acquiescence though her words were not for him but for her Fledgling. Cyan knew and she felt a slight hum in her head as he acknowledged her request.

She turned from her sleeping quarters and faced the wall that was composed of silver Dragonskin. As soon as she did, an area three meters high began to melt away, exposing a sealed doorway that led into the titanium shell of Faith's villa while forming a seal around it.

Waves of cold came from the metallic shell and steam formed where the Fledgling kissed its skin.

"Cyan?" she asked. Cyan, knowing what she was after without having to ask, pinged the villa. She waited patiently as the ring echoed through the metal, adjusting the holster on her hip. Four seconds ticked by and Cyan pinged the villa again. Still, there was no response.

※※※

"I said, get your hands off her," Jasyn was saying as Geary descended the stairs and stood on the foyer to the living the room.

The voice of the raven-haired construct was low but the menacing tone was as obvious as the control he was forcing. He stood looming over the lanky Engineer who reclined, seemingly unworried, on the couch. Faith was reclined against the other end though her body had gone as taut as a wire. Nathan kept massaging her foot.

"Jasyn," she admonished softly, but the construct's dark eyes stayed focused on Nathan's blue ones. Geary slipped silently across the black marble of the foyer and into the living room. If the confrontation got physical, he needed to get her away from it.

"Stop looking at me like you're going to kill me," Nathan drawled. "I'm an Engineer, boy, and we are especially hard to come by. Companions, however..." Nathan shrugged and left his sentence unfinished.

Christ, Geary thought, *how stupid is this man?*

But Jasyn's expression had oddly melted from one of hatred into something akin to hunger. Hunger that was about to be fed.

※※※

Blue watched the door for a few moments longer, waiting to hear the bolts slide from the hatch and the hiss of the seal as it broke, but nothing came. She took a few steps back towards her cockpit so she could see that her com line with the villa was still open.

"Tom?" she called. "You didn't forget about me out here, did you?"

Tom, sitting with his knuckles against mouth as his eyes went back and forth between the monitor showing the living room and the one that showed the airlock, sighed. His eyes went to DJ as he spoke into the com.

"No, Jordan, I have not forgotten you. I just can't let you in right now. Your sister is busy, but we will let her know as soon as possible that you are here and requesting an audience."

In the Fledgling attached to the airlock of the villa, Blue turned her face to Galen's ghost and gaped at him.

"An audience?" she whispered. "Like she's fucking Oz?"

Galen laughed and Noel shook her head, smiling. She looked at the still-closed hatch with growing impatience. If Cyan could have opened it, he would have done so already. She tapped the toe of her right boot, thinking. Then something else occurred to her. She looked at Calyph, so quickly and with such intensity that he jerked back involuntarily from where he sat on the edge of her bed.

"Anything you can do?" she asked, motioning with her head towards the door.

Calyph smiled. "Of course."

After all, moving metals was what he did.

There was a short pause and then Blue finally heard what she had been waiting for - the sound of greased metal bolts sliding back into their cradles, and the sound of the wheel turning on the other side of the hatch.

In the security room of the villa, DJ's eyes widened and Tom was sure his own heart skipped a few beats as he watched the wheel on the inside of the airlock door began to spin.

"Are you doing that?" DJ asked.

"No!" Tom replied, holding his hands up and away from the controls before jumping from his seat and nearly running from the room. "Shut down the elevator!" he commanded over his shoulder as he bolted.

"As if," DJ laughed under his breath as he did as he was ordered, "shutting down the lift is going to stop someone able to open those doors."

"Stay put," Jordan Blue similarly commanded Calyph as she put the bottom of her boot against the hatchway and pushed it open.

Calyph nodded as he watched her disappear into the airlock. Cyan closed the hole he had formed but remained docked against the villa. The elfin Engineer waited a few seconds and then began to gently shake Tara, trying to bring her around.

Blue stepped into the airlock and glanced around as the door swung shut behind her. She could hear the automatic fail-safe kick in to seal the port as she regarded the lift momentarily and then took the stairs that spiraled down around it. The first set of stairs took her down to the next level where Tom was not only waiting for her but blocking the next staircase down.

The Jordan gave him a beaming smile but hardly slowed as she circled the lift.

"Tom!" she hailed, pulling her pistol from her holster. "Good to see you again!"

Faith's security man hardly had time to register the greeting, much less reply to it. His heart was beating so fast at the smile from the Blue Jordan as he took a step closer to block the stairway that he was slow to register she was drawing a weapon.

When his reflexes finally kicked in, they took him off balance.

"Here you go!" she called as she tossed her laser pistol over his left shoulder. "I'm sure you're wanting that."

Tom moved instinctively and caught the weapon easily, but his jerk to the left allowed her to sidle past his right side and slip away down the stairs. Tom cursed under his breath and, tucking the Jordan's weapon into the back of his pants, raced after her.

☙❧

"Well, well, well!" Noel de Rossi announced with an overabundance of good cheer. She crossed the black marble floor to the edge of the foyer and looked down on the proceedings in the sunken living room as she spread her arms wide. "What do we have here? It must be a family get-together since everyone looks so pissed."

Tom came to a stop beside her, feeling Geary's glare like heat on his skin.

"I did *not* let her in," he assured his boss.

The head of de Rossi security took a stealthy step closer to Jasyn, flashing his steely gaze at the Jordan.

"Then how the hell did she open the port?" he asked. He took another step, bringing himself within less than an arm's length of the construct.

Blue grinned and answered for him. "I have an Engineer with me."

There was a whisking sound, soft and quick and accompanied by a flash of movement so instantaneous that it was only discernible once it had stopped. Geary's eyes bulged as he stared at his own gun, snatched from the inside of his jacket by Jasyn, now held against the head of the Engineer.

"I guess your type is easier to come by than you suspected," the construct said with a great deal of satisfaction.

Geary's eyes flicked to Tom only to see that he had been disarmed in the same manner and with the same lightning speed by the Jordan, who held Tom's gun aimed at Jasyn.

"Don't make me shoot you again," she warned, though her

voice was light and teasing.

"Why would you?" Jasyn asked, the corners of his lips turned up and his eyes fixed on the face of the Engineer. "What is this man to you?"

The Jordan's blonde eyebrows went up as she considered. "You're right." She drew the gun back into the hollow of her shoulder, the barrel pointing up towards the ceiling.

Geary was considering reaching for his second weapon when Faith pulled her foot from Nathan's grasp and sat forward, straightening up on the couch.

"Enough," she admonished. "Jasyn, give Geary back his gun and return with him upstairs." She turned her gaze from the dark-eyed construct to the man still lounging on her couch. "Nathan, I think it best for you to retire to your room for the night, feel free to summon Mari for anything you might need. I have family business I must attend to."

With that said - she stood, picked up her shoes, and strode from the living room, heading for her office.

Jasyn turned the gun in his hand and handed it to Geary, never taking his eyes from the Engineer. Geary returned his pistol to the holster under his jacket and waited for the construct, ready to grab him if necessary.

Jasyn leaned down towards the lanky man still sprawled on the sofa. "Sleep tight," he whispered. Then he straightened and walked away, heading for the staircase. He did not look at Faith as he passed her.

Blue flipped around the sidearm she was holding and offered it to Tom, butt first, smiling. "Sorry," she said, slightly abashed as she gave him an apologetic shrug. "Reflexes."

Tom did not look amused but he found it impossible to be angry with her. "Thanks," he said, taking the weapon and returning it to the holster against his ribs.

Blue gave him a lopsided grin. She had an almost irresistible urge to kiss him. Not romantically, but a big comical smack on the lips. Instead, she reached out and drew her fingertip lightly from his cheek to his chin.

"Thanks, Tom," she said softly. He stared, wide-eyed as she turned and followed Ms. de Rossi.

No one, however, was more shocked than Galen. He chased after Noel as she headed for where Faith waited at the door of her office.

"What the hell was that about?" he demanded. Blue simply smiled, tossing her coils of hair over her shoulder.

Tom looked around quickly, blinking owlishly in surprise, but Geary was whispering some nugget of advice to the Engineer who was glaring at Jasyn's feet as they went up the stairs. Blue walked past her sister and into her office. Faith stepped into the room and closed the door behind them. Galen was with them, and still upset, seething with angst but Blue pointedly ignored him and turned her iron hard gaze to her sister.

"Where are my fucking rings?" she demanded.

Faith returned her stare for a long moment, taking one deep breath and then another as she took measure of her sister and then walked calmly to her desk, circled behind it, and opened a drawer. She retrieved a small package and tossed it down onto the mahogany panel of the workspace.

It made the rattling sound of a die being cast.

Blue's eye flicked down to see a small acrylic box. Something about it filled her with excitement and trepidation. Like it was calling to her. Unable to stop herself, she reached forward and snatched it up.

Faith watched silently, her face inscrutable and her mouth pressed into a tight line. Even the ghost of the elfin doctor had paused his jealous ire and stared openly, mesmerized.

Noel lifted the lid of the box and saw a large ring with three stones nestled into a square of velvet. On closer inspection she saw it was three rings, each one topped with a sparkling sapphire. Her eye flicked to Faith's hand and saw a similar band of three rings, though they were crowned with a trio of topaz stones that gave off a golden glow.

Blue felt the breath hitch in her chest as she pulled the rings from their velvet nest and in her peripheral vision she saw Galen flinch, as if he meant to stop her but then stopped himself. She held them up before her eye, examining the different markings on each band with a soft wonder.

Smiling gently, she held her left hand aloft and used her right hand to slip the rings onto her index finger. Astoundingly, they fit perfect. Blue held up the hand and turned it, appreciating the craft and the fit and the beauty of the rings.

But no glow came from the stones.

None at all.

ڃڀ

Jordan Blue sank down into one of the chairs that faced Faith's enormous desk, her beautiful yet ravaged face devoid of any expression. A thousand things went through her mind.

Maybe they're not on the right finger. Maybe I'm just not a de Rossi. Maybe maybe maybe ....

But she knew. In her heart, she knew. She looked up and, seeing the expression on the Faith's countenance, she knew for sure. Her lone blue eye flicked to Galen, the ghost of the only man she had ever loved and saw the same knowledge in his eyes. The feeling was that of being punched in the gut. Hard.

Faith circled back around the desk and seated herself on its surface, pushing herself back far enough to cross her legs.

"Mother brought you to me when you were four months old," she said.

"Me?" the Jordan asked, looking up at her.

Faith shrugged, indifferent, as she continued in a voice that

was almost dreamy with recollection. "You were beautiful."
Her eyes focused suddenly and fixed on Noel. "And dying." The
Jordan closed her eye as she listened to Faith. "Mother had
already been to dozens of doctors, specialists and, of course,
all kinds of Zealot priests including her Sauam. You had a
degenerative disease, which by itself might have been treatable,
but it was coupled with an alien virus that was making your
heart shrink. One doctor had suggested a heart transplant,
another an artificial heart. They all told mother, however, that
the likelihood of survival would be next to nothing because of
the virus."

Noel opened her eye. "So she brought me," the Jordan
stopped and let out a great breath of air, "the baby," she
corrected, "to you."

Faith nodded. "There was nothing I could do."

"You're not that kind of doctor," Blue said, her voice edged
with bitter irony.

Faith refrained from answering her with anything but a
nod, her own lips pressed tightly together.

"So what did you do?" Noel asked.

"I gave mother a slow-release tranquilizer and took her and
the baby to the main GwenSeven Medical Center."

"At the GwenSeven compound?" Noel asked. "Where you
make constructs?"

Faith nodded. "Mother went to Charity's castle. The baby
went to Medical and I went to the compound, where I made
a four month old female from my own and Charity's base
genetics, to make sure the degenerative disease would not
carry over, and then overwrote the base with the DNA of the
child."

"What happened to the baby?"

Faith swallowed. "We kept doing everything we could to
save her, including a heart transplant and, for a few weeks, I
thought we were going to succeed. But, in the end, we failed."

"What happened to the baby?" Noel repeated.

"She was cremated there, on the Distant Shore. We had the ashes compressed into a diamond. Charity has it embedded in her chest, just below her left collarbone."

The Jordan planted her elbows on her knees and leaned forward, putting the tips of her fingers to her temples as if she were getting a headache. "I can't believe it," she whispered. "I'm not real."

Faith slipped off the desk and wrapped her fingers around the Jordan's left wrist and gently pulled her hand from her head. "You are as real as I am," she said quietly. Blue gave her the smallest of smiles and her lone eye filled with a tear.

"Thank you for that. But I can only imagine what it is going to cost me."

Faith let go of Noel's wrist and, putting a hand on either side of her own hips, grasped the desk and leaned back on it. "What do you mean?"

"Is how you planned to turn me to your side? If I did not come on my own accord?"

Faith shook her head. "No."

The Jordan regarded her with no small amount of surprise. "But you could. This is your spade in the hole. One call and I would be exposed. Turned out of the IGC just for starters and God only knows what else. Experimented on? Executed? Both, probably."

"You're my sister," Faith said softly. "Why would I want any of that?"

The Jordan shook her blonde head in frustration. "Leverage? To get what you want?"

"You're my sister," Faith repeated.

The Jordan exhaled sharply and sat back in her chair, blinking away the tear that kept trying to gather in her eye. "You still want me to," she paused to chuckle softly, "join your side?"

"I do."

"And you are not going to hold the threat of exposing me over my head if I don't?" Blue asked, smiling.

Faith shook her head, also smiling.

"Do you expect me to respond emotionally because if this?"

Faith's laugh was light and short. "I expect you to make your own decision in this."

The Jordan pursed her lips. "And you are not trying to sway me in any way?"

"I will always try to win you to our side. Family belongs together. But I must put this to you - now that you know, how easy will you rest? Will you live in fear of being exposed? Of the IGC doing any of those things you just suggested? Of losing your Fledgling?"

Blue's face fell bit by bit and then collapsed entirely. She could think of nothing worse. Not Galen's death. Not even her own. Her eye lifted to meet the brown and gold eyes of her sister.

"What do you want me to do?" she whispered.

Faith's smile was gentle. "Whatever is in your heart. Think about it. But don't take too long. The universe is sitting on a powder keg, and the fuse has already been lit."

The Jordan's head dipped, understanding. It was all too easy to imagine that fuse, hissing and sparking as it ran its snake-like course through the galaxies towards an explosion that might mean the end of all life. At least life as she knew it.

Slowly, she lifted her lone eye to meet Faith's tawny gaze once more.

"Did Galen, know?" she asked.

Faith's expression was as stoic as ever.

"I never told him. But..."

"But what?"

"Noel," she said softly as her shoulders pulled up in a shrug that looked apologetic, "he had more doctorates than I had earned at that point and was closer to you than I ever was. How could he not know?"

Blue let out a sigh so deep that it felt it came from the toes of her boots. "You're right," she agreed. "About a lot of things, it seems." Her thoughts were not only on Galen but also the IGC. The government she had committed her life to was not panning out to be what she had always believed them to be. It looked as if they might be worse than the people she was fighting. People, she realized now, who were just like her. "And, once again, you've given me a lot to think about."

"And yet, there is still much more to discuss. I'd like to schedule a meeting, for lack of a better term, at Charity's home. And I would like the other Jordan to be with you, if you can arrange it."

Noel's eyebrows went up at this last request, but she nodded. "I think I can. Meanwhile, however, I have quite a few other fish to fry," she said, her thoughts now going to the two she had hostage in her Fledgling. Thoughts of Galen. Of Scarlett. Of the situation back on the Opal Dragon.

Faith nodded. "Tom will meet you at the airlock."

The Blue Jordan stood and then froze before she burst out laughing. Faith drew back in surprise for moment, startled and curious. Noel looked at her, her blue eye wide and a little crazed. "I honestly don't know what to do right now."

Faith gave her a gentle smile. "Follow your heart. You're not made of tin, you know."

A small chuckle edged with hysteria slipped from the Jordan's red lips but she gave her sister a nod and headed for the door, letting herself out. The living room was oddly deserted but she could feel the presence of people from seemingly everywhere. She took the stairs up and around the lift, past the security level and to the airlock.

Tom already awaited her there. He held out her pistol.

"Thank you," Blue said, accepting it and dropping it into the holster on her hip.

Tom frowned at her, tilting his head. "Are you okay?" he asked.

Blue returned the frown. "Yeah, why?"

"You don't seem yourself."

The right corner of her lip quirked up and she almost asked him how he would know what her normal self was, but she nodded instead. "Just preoccupied."

He gave her a nod and a look that suggested he doubted her answer as he went to the door and released the airlocks. "See you soon?" he asked.

Blue finally smiled as the doorway opened with a hiss, revealing the inside of her Fledgling. "Probably."

Tom returned her smile and stood aside as she entered Cyan.

The ghost of Galen followed her, silent as a grave.

 ONE FOUR

- A secret lives only as long as silence keeps it company.

The Blue Jordan boarded her Fledgling and glanced aft, back to her sleeping quarters. Calyph waited there on the edge of the bed next to the Aridian, still comatose in her aura of aqua-colored light. The doorway behind Noel disappeared, melting closed as Cyan sealed back up before disengaging from the villa. She looked at Galen's ghost, still silent but paler than ever.

Never before had she wanted so badly to be alone. To be able to think quietly, to mentally go over everything she had discovered in the last ten hours and decide what she was going to do.

Yet here she was, in her Fledgling that was seemingly full of people and problems.

Well, she thought, *one thing at a time.*

Leaning back against the counter that separated the galley from the cockpit, she crossed her arms over her thin chest. She blew out a deep breath and regarded the doctor's ghost with her lone eye.

"You knew," she sighed.

"I did not," Galen denied in a hoarse whisper. His throat worked as he swallowed. "Not for sure."

Noel closed her eye. "Galen." His name came out like a soft reprimand.

"Of course, I suspected…"

Blue opened her eye and cocked her head at him. "Suspected what exactly?"

"I knew you were different. Special. I was always trying to figure out what it was, but never could."

"And that's why you stayed with me. You knew, but you still wanted something. The one thing that every scientist is after. Proof."

"I stayed with you because I loved you."

"You knew."

"I don't care what she says about you, you are real."

"I don't think anyone really knows what that means anymore. But I can't go on living a lie. And you knew. You knew that I was a lie."

"You are not a lie. You are real. Our love is real."

A smile glimmered on Noel's red lips. "I have no doubt about that - about our love, I mean. And for that, I am truly grateful."

"But?"

"You've been quiet lately," she observed aloud instead of answering, "but I can feel you watching me. And it seems like you have been…fading. I think it has been because you have become more and more sure of what I really am. Now that you know, I think you might fade away completely. And I think I am ready for that."

"Because I knew?"

"Because you knew. And never told me."

"What would you have done? What difference would it have made?"

Blue shook her head. "I would have known. I wouldn't have to find out from a stranger, one trying to kill me. And confirmation from a sister I hardly know."

Galen felt a stab of pain and knew he deserved it. He could see a tear glistening in her eye.

The shoulders of the Jordan trembled in what could have been a laugh or a sob. "The ghost in the machine," she acknowledged softly. "I can hardly believe I said that jokingly, only a few hours ago, having no idea how true it was." Her brows drew down over her eye and eyepatch. "Or did I?" she wondered aloud. "Did I know, somewhere down deep inside of myself?"

Galen returned her frown. "You are not a machine, you are as real as they get. But I hope a part of me does stay with you forever."

The Blue Jordan gave him the slightest of smiles and a look of approval through her shimmering eye. She dipped her head slightly and the tear finally spilled out and down her cheek.

"You will. Goodbye, Galen."

The ghost of the elfin doctor could only nod. His throat was twisted with pain, as was his heart.

The Jordan closed her eye. *What is real?* she asked herself.

Whatever you make it be.

The Jordan opened her eye. Galen was gone.

"Still," she murmured, "better safe than sorry."

She did not bother herself with a spoon this time, or even a small knife. Her slim fingers went to the side of her neck and slid up until they found the small bump behind her ear where Galen had implanted the communication link.

With the nail on her index finger, she pierced the skin and dug the tiny metal disc out of her flesh.

The Jordan, feeling a thin trail of blood begin to slip down her neck, tipped her head to the side. It was caressed with bluish light that at once took away the sting and stopped the bleeding. She looked down at the pellet of metal covered with minuscule droplets of blood, and then flicked it away.

"Keep that for me, would you?" she asked as the pellet was swallowed by the silvery wall of Dragonskin. She stared for a moment at the place where it had disappeared and then wiped her cheek with the back of her hand and let out a long, shuddering breath.

She thought she would feel crushed, heartbroken, lost.

But what she really felt, inside, was Faith. Not that she was beginning to understand her, but that she was becoming her. The surprise she felt was barely a flicker. *After all,* she thought, *she is my mother. Her and Charity both. As much as Christa or as much as Opal - my Mother Dragon.*

She took a moment to compose herself, pressing the heels of her hands into her eye sockets. Then she circled the counter that separated the galley from the sleeping quarters and looked at the elf sitting on her bed.

The Aridian was still unconscious, despite Calyph's efforts to revive her, cloaked in a shroud of sea-colored light.

"Are you alright?" he asked earnestly. Blue was touched by his consideration, despite the fact she had taken him hostage.

"Yes, thank you. Just putting my ghost to rest."

Calyph licked his lips. "Have you decided what are you going to do with us?" he asked fearfully.

"Well," she said, straightening her small form as she considered the near future, "I need to get you back on the Dragon before you are missed. How long was leave allowed for Neptune?"

"Forty-eight hours for non-security personnel."

Blue nodded thoughtfully. "No problem there. As for her..." she said, looking at the comatose Aridian.

"Please don't hurt her," Calyph pled. "Or..."

"Turn her in?" Blue asked. "Because she will certainly be put to death?"

Calyph hung his head. "Please," he whispered.

Blue gave an exaggerated sigh. "Well, I certainly can't let her run amok! Especially knowing what she is after!"

Calyph looked up at the Jordan. "I will make sure she doesn't come after you, or Scarlett. I'll do whatever you want," he promised. He sounded to the Jordan like he meant it. She might think him a liar but there was nothing fake about how afraid he was now.

"Shit," Blue muttered. "I need time to think."

Especially now that I'm keeping my own counsel, she thought, disconsolate. *Alone.* She felt a pulse of warm blue light and smiled.

But I'm not alone, am I?

The pulse came back, even warmer. Blue cocked her head as she eyed the rogue Doppelgänger.

Can you keep her like that? she sent. *For a long time if need be?*

The pulse that came this time made her laugh. It was the Fledgling equivalent of flubbing lips and rolling eyes. He could keep her that way indefinitely, if need be, with no more effort than breathing.

She racked her mind over what she should do and came up with nothing plausible every time. Then it struck her. She shouldn't decide on her own. She was not alone, and she had more than her Fledgling. She had more than her sisters by blood. She had Scarlett. She needed to talk to Scarlett.

It occurred to her with cold clarity that Scarlett, once given the truth, could very likely turn her in, or shoot her. She had certainly tried in the past.

But Scarlett was different now, wasn't she?

"Would she?" the Blue Jordan asked aloud. "Would she try to kill me?"

Calyph glanced around, wondering if her friendly ghost had returned, then realized she was probably talking to her

Fledgling.

Blue cocked her head again and, though Cyan didn't answer with words, the feeling she got from him was doubt. He did not feel that the other Jordan would hurt her.

Decided, at least on *that* course of action, Noel turned on her heel and strode through the inner body of her Fledgling. When she reached the cockpit she dropped into the pilot's seat and touched a red light on the dash.

A hologram of Fledge flared to life above the console. Blue touched another light, also red, and opened a communication link between the Fledglings.

"Jordan Scarlett?"

The reply was both quick and firm.

"Yes."

"This is Jordan Blue."

"That would seem obvious for a number of reasons."

Blue's head tipped back on her neck, her three platinum coils of hair slipping down her back. She was amazed at how Scarlett's voice and demeanor made her feel instantly better. Her shoulders sagged as she considered how much and what she could say over the com-link. It was very little.

"I need to speak with you before we return to the Dragon. In person."

"Before we return?" Scarlett echoed. "Where are..." she began to ask, trailing off. In her mind's eye Blue could see the other Jordan pulling up a similar hologram of Cyan over the dash of her own Fledgling, including coordinates. "What are you doing out here?" Scarlett asked. "We're practically in the same quadrant. I thought you were supposed to be in the Neptune..."

"Something came up," Blue interrupted. She was again racked by what to say and what not to say, which felt like pretty much everything. Even what she had already said, about speaking in person could be interpreted in different ways. Though she was sure that there was no way the IGC could hear what was going on inside her Fledgling, they were on an IGC line. God only knew who could be listening.

Blue chewed her lip, suddenly wondering if there was some sort of code she could use. The Jordan almost laughed aloud at the thought.

But the Red Jordan did not need a code. Blue had said enough. She needed to talk. In person. She knew it must be hella important for the half-elf pilot want to speak to her in private. And not aboard the Dragon.

"I still have thirty hours of personal leave," Scarlett said. "Of course I would enjoy meeting you for a drink somewhere. I'm certainly going to need it if I must listen to your current amorous conquests."

The Blue Jordan collapsed in her seat as if her bones had been suddenly removed. She could barely believe that Scarlett had not only caught on to her need for privacy, but had lent her aid in the subterfuge. She straightened back up.

"Well, you're never going to believe the guy I met today." She glanced to the aft end of her vessel to see the terror in Calyph's eyes.

A laugh came from over the com. "I think I could say the same," Scarlett chuckled. "Drinks are definitely in order."

But where? the Red Jordan pondered. The only place she knew in the Jovian system was Io, and it was obvious that even the Upper Klick could be infiltrated. She almost laughed aloud. *Infiltrated. Io is not an IGC ship. Anyone with a bankload of credits is welcome.*

"Race you back to Neptune?" Blue challenged.

"You have any place in mind?"

"Anywhere but a water bar."

Scarlett's laugh was soft over the com. "There's an Erish bar on Triton in the old city of Tiberius. It's as decrepit as the city, and twice as nasty, but they have a great meat pie. It's called…"

"Finnegan's Wake?"

Scarlett laughed again. "You know it? How?"

"I like good food. And the stew is better than the pie. But you're right, the place is filthy. I have to make a stop, but I'll beat you there by half an hour." Her slim fingers began to move over the console, entering coordinates.

"The hell you will," the Red Jordan countered, entering coordinates into the dash of her own Fledgling. "But, even if you do, you're still buying."

"Deal," Blue agreed.

The two Fledgling Dragons shot across the galaxy, trailing blue and crimson light.

ﾎﾎ

Scarlett arrived first.

Though they had started from roughly the same area, Blue made a necessary stop to rendezvous with the Opal Dragon. Fledgling Bay was mostly deserted and, for that, the Jordan was grateful. Many officers and enlisted as well were taking leave and the skeleton crew still aboard was busy manning and tending to the massive living craft.

An area a meter wide and two meters high opened in Cyan's side, just fore of the galley, and a set of silver steps led from the opening down to the matte silver tarmac of the bay.

The Blue Jordan jerked her head in the direction of the exit. "Behave yourself," she told the elfin Engineer by way of *goodbye and get out.*

"I'll do anything you want," Calyph reassured Blue for what she thought must be the hundredth time. "Just…"

"Please don't hurt her," the Jordan finished. "Yeah, yeah,

yeah. You don't have to come find me when I get back, but don't make it hard for me to find you."

The Engineer nodded obediently as he rose and headed for the exit. He cast one last worried look over his shoulder as he descended the stairs. Blue reclaimed her pilot's seat and let Dareus, the Communications Officer on the Opal Dragon, know where she was headed.

"Must be some party down there," the Coms Man commented warmly but a chill went down the Jordan's spine.

"Well," she remarked, trying to keep her tone light, "there are a number of them, but I think I'll try another bar this time." She looked at her watch and could hardly believe how much had gone on in the last twelve hours.

Cyan, his egress point once again a seamless part of his skin, rose up and glided through the membrane of the bay door and out into the freezing vacuum of space.

Blue checked Scarlett's coordinates and saw that the other Jordan was just entering the artificial atmosphere around Triton. She opened a com line between the two Fledglings.

"Hey," she said.

"Hey, yourself," the Red Jordan answered.

Blue licked her lips and glanced aft at the comatose form on her bed before looking back out through the eyes of her Fledgling.

She was about to suggest they skip Finnegan's, and not just because of the shit show she had already encountered on Triton that day. She knew the conversation they were soon to have needed to be completely secure. Yet to say such a thing over an open IGC communication line would arouse immediate suspicion if they were being monitored. She could only assume they were. It was safest to assume that they were. It always was.

"Wait for me at the airfield, would you?" Blue asked. "I'd like you to come aboard Cyan and check out something in the galley. I'm not sure if it is something I should have looked at."

"You got it," the Red Jordan agreed, the mystification she felt masked by the strong tone of her affirmation. She took Fledge down to the surface, found the IGC secure airfield, and landed amongst other craft from the Opal Dragon.

As Fledge settled down on his legs, Scarlett sat back in her seat, her dark eyes far away. She was damned curious as to what Blue had going on, but her mind was consumed with thoughts of Bjorn.

She could still smell him, could feel the places on her body he had touched.

She thought about what he had said. Had he really told her he loved her? The bigger question was, did he mean it? And Chris. Who the hell was Chris? Besides a traitor. Abducting the Dragon's Engineer was serious shit. It went way beyond hiring an illegal Chimeran nanny.

And all this on the heels of finding out about her family tree.

The dark-haired Jordan rose and went aft towards her small bedchamber to change from her civilian clothes into a crimson flight suit. She tucked her riding boots under the bed and pulled on her flight boots. It felt surprisingly good to be wearing Mylar again and she smiled at the thought of it. Catching her reflection, she saw the IGC patch sewn over her heart and her smile faded.

Scarlett headed back to the cockpit and sat down to wait. She drummed her fingers on the arm of her pilot's chair and hoped that Blue did not have any surprises for her. The Red Jordan thought she had enough revelations for one day. Christ but she wanted a drink. She mulled over the events of the past eight hours, took slow breaths, and waited for the Blue Jordan.

Watching the holo above her dash console, Scarlett saw Cyan approach and land outside, not far from Fledge. She stood and smoothed down her crimson flight suit as Fledge opened and sent down a flight of stairs for her.

The Red Jordan descended, the heels of her flight boots making hollow clanging sounds on stairs that retracted, seeming to melt backwards into the Fledgling, once she reached the ground. As she crossed the tarmac to the other Fledgling that waited there, an oval melted from his side and he formed his own set of stairs. The Blue Jordan stood in the opening, waiting, her right hand resting on the butt of her laser pistol.

What the hell? Scarlett thought as she approached the stairs and climbed quickly to the top. If something had the Blue Jordan that cautious, it was serious. The half-elf pilot stepped aside to let Scarlett in, threw her gaze like darts around the airfield, then led the way through Cyan as he closed the hole in his side. Blue stood aside again when they reached her sleeping area, giving Scarlett a full view of the figure on the bed, deep asleep.

"Holy shit," Scarlett whispered.

"Recognize her?"

Scarlett snorted. "They all look the same to me. You think she's the one who smeared the Chlorforgel on me at the festa?"

"I know she is."

Scarlett wrinkled her nose. "She smells like Calyph," she said, her dark brows drawn together in a frown.

Blue's light eyebrows shot up in surprise. "Well," she said, "that's not really surprising. Considering."

"Considering what?" Scarlett asked but realized the implication almost immediately. "Ugh. Are you serious?"

Noel nodded. "They've been together since childhood, so I was told."

"Is Cyan keeping her that way?"

Noel nodded again. "She attacked me and tried to replicate me, though you were her original target."

The Red Jordan pulled a face, grimacing. "I was reeling

from that Chlorforgel. If she had gotten me out of sight, I would have been easy prey. I managed to wipe some of it off, but then Fledge was there. And…"

Bjorn, she almost said. *Bjorn was coming for me.*

"And," she continued, "you think her and Calyph are (and here she chuckled softly, knowing her next words were Grandpa's) in cahoots?"

"I know they are," Blue affirmed, not diverted in the slightest by Scarlett's oddly ancient phrase. "What should we do with her?"

Scarlett looked at her in surprise. "How the hell should I know?"

"I don't know," Blue admitted, "but I think we should figure it out together. That and some other things."

The Red Jordan let out a great breath of air and nodded. She had some items to discuss as well. She used the heels of her hands to scrub her eyebrows. "I could really use I drink. I've had a hellava day."

The Blue Jordan barked laughter. "Don't even start with me. I could use a nip myself, but I don't entirely trust any conversation outside our Fledglings. Even at Finnegan's. How about some champagne?" she suggested.

Scarlett shrugged. "It's better than nothing."

Noel went up on the toes of her flight boots, excited. "I feel like I'm entertaining," she admitted, scuttling past Scarlett and into the galley. Scarlett shook her head and followed the other Jordan who was already pulling a bottle from the cold compartment before opening a cupboard to retrieve two cups.

"Classy," she remarked, leaning on the galley countertop, resting her weight on her forearms.

Noel smirked as she, to Scarlett's surprise, quickly and expertly removed the wire cage and the cork with a soft popping sound. "Cleaner than Finnegan's."

The Red Jordan chuckled as she straightened and accepted a cup from Blue. "True," she agreed. "Though I'd like to make it there to eat. The food really is outstanding."

"Who knew the Erish could cook?" Blue asked as she filled their cups. "The only things they brought with them from Earth were potatoes and cabbages."

"And whisky," Scarlett told her.

"And whisky," Blue agreed.

They touched their cups together in salute and each took a drink. Scarlett's nostrils flared slightly and her dark eyes narrowed as she lowered her cup. "No Galen?"

The Blue Jordan's jaw clenched for a second, making her scar ripple. Otherwise, her expression remained stolid. "No Galen."

Scarlett shrugged with indifference and glanced around for a chair but the only place to sit were the two seats in the cockpit. She looked at Blue who nodded in silent agreement.

The seats swiveled slightly towards them as the Jordans approached. Then, after they had sat themselves, the chairs turned towards one another.

"You first," Scarlett said, crossing one long leg over the other and taking another drink from her cup.

Blue took a deep breath. "You were right."

Scarlett sniffed. "Of course I was." She uncrossed her legs and recrossed them. "Though I'm not sure what you are referring to."

The Blue Jordan took another deep breath, expanding her lungs until she thought they might burst and then let it out in a rush. "I'm not real."

She said the words as forthright and plain as she could, her muscles wound tighter than springs. She was not sure how she expected Scarlett to react, it certainly wasn't with a nonchalant shrug.

"What's real?" the Red Jordan asked.

Blue scowled at her. "I'm being serious, Scarlett. Really not real. I just found out that I am a construct."

The Red Jordan gave her one of her shark-like smiles. "There seems to be a bit of that going around."

"What the hell is that supposed to mean?"

"I found out I'm a little construct myself."

"Bullshit."

"It's true though. Or, at least, that's what I was told. That I am descended from one of the First Seven. I'm inclined to believe it."

"Are you just trying to one up me, like always?" Blue demanded.

Scarlett laughed. "Do you think I would try to one up you on something like this? And do you think it's something I would admit to anyone else?"

Blue held her cup of champagne between her knees as she balled her hands into fists and held them against her temples. "Why isn't anything ever simple?" she demanded.

Scarlett graced her with another smile and another salute from her cup before she took a dainty sip. "Because then it wouldn't be fun."

Blue scrunched her eye shut. "Uuggh!" she growled. "And when did we change places?"

Scarlett laughed softly. "I think we are both just starting to find out who we really are. Probably not an easy thing for anyone. Even more so for us. What makes you so suddenly sure you're not who you thought you were?"

"Remember when I told you I caught Calyph pulling an extra syringe of Fledge's fluid?"

Scarlett nodded and Blue continued. "It wasn't for the cadet, like I originally thought. Though Blaylock had run the request up the flagpole. It was for her." Blue motioned to the back end of the ship with her platinum blonde head.

From there, she told the Red Jordan everything that had happened, ending with her conversation with Faith. By the time she finished, both their cups were dry. Blue got up to retrieve the bottle.

"Do you have anything to eat?" Scarlett called after her.

"Peanut butter and crackers," Blue called back.

"I'll take some crackers, if you don't mind."

Blue returned with the bottle and a plain brown box. "I don't mind at all." She handed the cardboard container to Scarlett and refilled their cups. "Sorry, it's not much of a selection."

"It's more than I have in my galley," Scarlett told her, pulling out a round cracker and popping it into her mouth. She expected it to be stale but it was surprisingly crunchy. Salty.

"You haven't had the time," Blue reminded her. "Now you," she instructed. "I doubt it's a long story, you've only been back a matter of days."

Scarlett told her of the conversation she had just had earlier that day with her grandfather. When she finished, Blue sat back and sipped from her cup.

"Do you think it's important?" she asked.

Scarlett laughed. "I think it's important no one finds out."

Blue chuckled. "No shit. I mean," Blue sighed, her demeanor beginning to soften, "do you think it makes a difference? That we are different? Not just from each other of course, but from everyone else?"

Scarlett lifted her chin. "No. Our Fledglings chose us. There were others there, pilots just as trained and qualified. Yet they chose us."

Jordan Blue gazed at her, her lone eye unfocused and far away. "You're right," she admitted softly. "We are special," she said, and then laughed at what she had said, shaking her blonde coils.

Scarlett cocked an eyebrow at her. "Why is that funny?"

"My mother used to tell us that, to myself, and all of my sisters - that we were special, just like everybody else." The Blue Jordan lapsed into the soft jets of laughter that came with remembrance.

"But you and your sisters are a little more unique," Scarlett mused aloud. "Anomalies, born of human and elf. If that is not special, I don't know what is."

Blue, who had been reclining in her seat, leaned forward. "And you," she said, pointing to Scarlett with her cup of champagne, "you are as much so, or even more if what you say is true. The constructs were not built to produce progeny. So if you are just that, and come from one of the First Seven, well - that is quite extraordinary indeed."

"I'll have to look into that before I believe it," Scarlett told her, though - in truth - she already believed it to her core. She cleared her throat and straightened. "There's something else," she said.

Blue's blonde brows went up again and stayed that way as she listened to Scarlett relate her encounter with Bjorn.

"Sooo," she said when the Red Jordan had finished, "we both have job offers?"

Scarlett laughed but after a moment the mirth drained from her face. "Did it ever occur to you to ask what our numbers meant?" she asked.

Blue shook her head. "Not at all. We are soldiers. We are told what to do, and we do it."

"Something about it always bothered me."

"Of course it would," Blue told her with a smirk, "you hate being told what to do."

Scarlett laughed softly. "I know, I know, but this is more than that. The fact that I wore a number on my arm for three years, and never questioned anything about it." She looked at Blue, searching her ravaged face. "Do you know what I mean?"

"If you're talking about swallowing everything you are fed without asking what it is, then I know exactly what you mean. I feel like I have been played a fool, a child, a savant. And between you and me, I'm done with it. Instead of questioning nothing, I'm starting to question everything."

"Including this?" Scarlett asked, her right hand rising up as four fingers gently caressed the patch sewn over her left breast. The patch of the IGC.

"Especially that."

"I have been having the strangest feelings," Scarlett said softly. "Feelings that contradict each other."

"The feeling that everything is falling apart, and the feeling that everything is coming together?"

Scarlett stared at the other Jordan, the crimson flecks in her dark eyes flaring like embers. "Yes," she said. "That is exactly it."

Blue gave her a crooked smile. "I feel the same. What do we do?"

Scarlett shook her head. "I don't know. At least I don't know now. Which means I think we just wait. Wait and see."

A high-pitched sound came from the coms dash, making both Jordan's jerk so hard they nearly dropped their cups. The box of crackers fell from Scarlett's lap to the floor. She took no notice. It was an emergency signal. They both sat bolt upright as Blue reached out and touched the flashing light on her console.

"Jordan Blue," a voice addressed formally over the com line. Both Jordans recognized the voice of their own Communications Officer, Dareus, aboard the Opal Dragon. "Leave is cancelled. All ships are to return to the Dragon at once. Captain…"

The voice of the coms man cracked on the last word and Scarlett clutched the other Jordan's arm, a painful lump expanding in her throat, strangling her.

Blue shook her head. "It's not Brogan," she whispered. "We would have felt it." She hoped.

Dareus cleared his own throat. "Captain Condliffe is dead."

ONE FIVE

- A well-kept secret isn't silent, it whispers to those who are ready to listen.

The Jordans were stunned. Not just at the news, but to be given such news from Dareus rather than their Captain went against standard operating procedure. If not the Captain, then certainly such information should have come from the ship's Executive Officer.

Blue and Scarlett listened, wide-eyed, as the Dragon's Communications Officer related that Captain Condliffe had hung himself in the closet of his room on the last dimlight. There was no note.

The young Captain had been deeply depressed about the loss of Beryl's eggs and the massacre of the would-be-Jordans on his ship, but it still came as a shock to all those aboard and all who knew him. He had been a strong man and a good Captain, certainly not one to desert his crew and plunge them further into darkness.

Dareus informed the Jordans that, immediately upon hearing the news, Captain Brogan had retreated to his own quarters and regressed back into the same funk that had gripped him after the death of Jade – the same time that Scarlett was on forced medical leave and Blue was emotionally absent.

Dareus and Chiara, the Navigator, had held whispered debates on whether or not they should inform the Jordans. However, once they received a communication that Commander Blaylock was on his way back to the Dragon, the discussion ended. They notified the Jordans and hoped they would return quickly.

They did.

The Jordans, having the fastest ships outside of the Dragon, were the first ones to return from Triton. It would be almost an hour before the next ships arrived. It would be a good two hours before everyone on leave was accounted for and loaded onto the larger transports.

The security check in Fledgling Bay was mercifully short and the Jordans hurried from the bay to the fore of the ship that housed the Commander of the Opal Dragon.

Scarlett paused long enough to look at Jordan Blue, and then rapped hard on the silver door with her knuckles. There was another pause as the Captain…

looked? listened? sensed?

…the pilots waiting outside. Then the door slid open and the Jordans peered around the entryway and into the Captain's private quarters.

"Come in!" They heard him call. "I'll be right out."

The Jordans entered the hallway and the door slid shut behind them. Scarlett wrinkled her nose.

"Can you smell that?" she asked, keeping her voice low.

"Is it me?" Blue asked, her voice soft but her eye wide with concern.

Scarlett laughed quietly. "No!" she whispered hoarsely. "It's coming from somewhere in here. The last time we were here I thought it was the Captain, since he looked like he hadn't bathed in a while, but he smelled fine when we saw him a few days ago." Her dark eyes darted about, curious and concerned. "I could probably find it, if I had the time."

Blue's eye opened even wider. "Well, you literally can't go sniffing around the Captain's private quarters!" she hissed.

"I know that!" Scarlett hissed back. She looked around, a frown creasing her dark brows. "It's not that it is simply a bad smell, though it is, but it gives me a really bad feeling."

Blue considered this for a moment. "It's your heightened sense. Close your eyes end tell me what it smells like, and not just that it's bad. What the smell *feels* like."

Scarlett closed her eyes and breathed deep, her frown deepening.

"Hello, Jordans," the Captain said, entering the hallway and startling them both. His appearance was even more of a shock.

His face, in dire need of a shave, had again taken on a haggard look and his skin was ashy. He had pulled on a pair of coveralls that were wrinkled and dirty and hung on a form that, once lean and muscular, looked withered. His iron gray hair was long enough to form a few small greasy curls that clung to the nape of his neck. His looks were almost sufficient to make Scarlett reconsider the source of the bad smell in the cabin, but she was certain it was not coming from him.

As if hearing her thoughts, he took a deep breath through his nose, but it caught along the way and he coughed into his fist, turning his face away. He must have felt the stubble against his hands for he gave the two pilots a sheepish smile.

"Forgive my lack of military discipline, but the last time I shaved I shook so hard I cut myself. I called Clarence, he runs the barbershop in the Atrium, and he is going to come personally to give me a shave. And thank you for meeting here," he said. "Commander Blaylock thought it would be more private than the bridge, considering the nature of our discussion."

Blue could hardly believe that he had regressed to such a condition in only twenty-four hours. But, all things considered, he really had not had time to fully recover in the few days since

Scarlett had returned. She opened her mouth to ask him what had happened, but a resounding knock came from the door.

"Come in!" the Captain called.

As if speaking the devil's name was enough to summon him, the door slid open, and the Executive Officer came into the narrow entryway. He appeared surprised, and none too pleased, to see that the Jordans had arrived before him. His dark eyes, however, went to the Captain.

"Jim," he said, his voice oddly sympathetic. "How are you doing?"

The Captain's expression, at first a pathetic attempt at stolidity, dropped. "Not well," he admitted. "Please," he invited, "come in."

He turned and trudged, almost tripping on his own feet, into his small living area where two couches and two chairs were positioned around a low table. One wall held a holo-fireplace, dark now but topped with a thin ledge that served as a mantel of sorts. On the ledge was a fat candle on a small plate that burned with a lurid light. A considerable amount of wax had run down and gathered, forming lumpy canyons on the sides of the candle and pooling around its bottom. Most had been caught by the plate.

Scarlett looked away from it and took a seat in one of chairs once the Captain had seated himself on a couch. Blue sat down next to him at a respectable distance and Blaylock assumed command of the other chair.

"There is going to be a service for Captain Condliffe," the XO announced. Brogan's whole body seemed to clench in pain and Blue restrained the urge to put a hand on his knee to comfort him.

"Where?" Blue asked. "And how soon?"

"On the Lucca moon. In eight days. Three of the Dragon Captains will be there, including Captain Brogan and the Captains of the Silver and Copper Dragons."

Brogan frowned at this. "That goes against protocol," he said. "Having us together like that." Blaylock nodded in understanding. "It has been waived, in consideration of the situation. Condliffe was a great man, and well-loved. It is only fitting that you and your Jordans be there."

Brogan shook his head. "You will go in my stead."

Blaylock's hazel eyes expanded at this, as if he just sustained a blow. "But, sir! You were close to Captain Condliffe, you mentored him, you..."

"I am quite aware," the Captain said softly, his face turned away and his pale eyes staring at the candle burning on the mantel. "I will be on the Beryl Dragon for his interment. I will see him laid to rest." His last sentence was barely a whisper.

"Captain, I know the Council showed great leniency for Captain Todd and Captain Hunter to attend the funeral service as they knew Condliffe personally. But I cannot imagine that, on *top* of that, to have the Beryl and Opal Dragons so close together..."

"They will," Brogan stated calmly, staring into the flame of the candle as it danced. "They will do it for me."

Blaylock was stunned but not dissuaded. "Sir," he argued, "I suggest our places be reversed. After all, it will be at the interment that the IGC will announce Condliffe's successor. I don't want to seem overly confident, but I think it likely that I will be the..." his words trailed off as Brogan turned his pale eyes back to his second in command, pinning him to his seat.

"I will spare you the suspense. Commander Slater is to succeed Captain Condliffe. He has already assumed command in principle. The IGC will make it official at the interment."

The Jordans watched the exchange silently. It was obvious that the Executive Officer was struggling with the situation and trying not to let it show. Both Jordans tried not to make it apparent how smug they were about it.

"I have *ten* years of seniority over Slater," Blaylock said softly. "And I was to be rotating to the Beryl Dragon next year."

The Captain nodded to show he understood, but held out his hands, palms up, as if to say he was powerless in the decision.

"Slater has been on the Beryl Dragon for five years and has the beginnings of a bond with the Dragon, and solid bonds with the crew."

"Still," Blaylock said stolidly, regaining his composure. "You should be at the service."

"Look at me, Commander," Brogan said with half a smile. "I should not be seen by anyone in this condition."

With that, Blue could not agree more. She did not think it would be good for him to be seen by even his own crew, maybe *especially* by his own crew. It was probably a good idea that he had confined himself to his quarters. Blaylock drew a deep breath in a continual effort to control himself.

"Who will be in command of the Dragon if we are both gone?" he asked, unable to restrain a sneer. "The Navigator?"

The Captain did not miss the heavy sarcasm but did not rebuke him. "I will, since I will be taking the Opal Dragon to the second system for the interment. Jordan Scarlett will remain aboard, and in command, while I am aboard the Beryl Dragon. Jordan Blue will accompany you to the service."

All eyes in the room widened at this news, but none more than those of the Executive Officer. He looked like he had been sucker-punched. Blue could hear Blaylock's heart hammering like a madman striking a drum and wondered if the others could hear it as well. She hoped it would explode.

To his credit, he pulled himself together in a mere few seconds before the Captain spoke again.

"It does, however, open the Executive Officership of the Beryl Dragon. I can put in a word for you to rotate early, if you would like."

Blaylock was able to restrain his fury, but not mask it. "And serve under Slater?" he fumed, his hands balled into fists.

"I understand if that rankles you, and - clearly - it does. I can also recommend that you remain here and rotate instead to the Copper Dragon when the time comes."

Blaylock, blinking his eyes rapidly as if in an effort to keep them in his skull, struggled for control. And found it. "If you will excuse me then?" he asked as he stood, giving his opal-colored flightsuit a sharp tug. "There are arrangements I need to make."

The Jordans rose to their feet.

"You are dismissed," the Captain acquiesced.

Blaylock turned and left the Captain's quarters without another glance, much less a departing remark, to the Jordans. Once he had gone, a great whoosh of air evacuated the Captain's lungs as he sagged back into his couch. It was obvious that he had been exerting a great amount of will to confront his second in command.

Both Jordans knew it was something that would have been unheard of in normal situations, but this situation was going from abnormal to dangerous.

"We should be going as well," Blue said softly, watching her commander take a series of slow deep breaths before giving her a nod as he rose shakily to his feet. The Red Jordan was turning to leave when the flicker above the fireplace caught her eye.

"Sir?"

Brogan turned his pale eyes to Scarlett. "Might I inquire about the candle?" she asked him.

The Captain gave her a small smile. "Are you going to reprimand me for having an open flame on a ship?"

The Red Jordan blushed. "I would do no such thing. It just seems odd. The only times I've seen real ones they have been much smaller, and on cakes - birthday cakes actually. A tradition my grandfather always insists upon."

"Ah!" Brogan exclaimed softly. "They are also used for another tradition, one called keeping a vigil. Are you familiar with the term?"

Scarlett nodded solemnly. "It is a time for quiet mediation, when a loved one dies."

"Like Jade," Blue whispered.

The Captain nodded. "And that was the reason I first lit it. But it is also lit when someone dear is gone, to help them find their way home."

"Like me," Scarlett whispered.

Brogan nodded again. "I put it out when you returned," he paused and his throat worked as he tried to swallow, "but I lit it again when I received the news of Captain Condliffe."

Scarlett put a hand on his arm, Blue put a hand on his other and he gave them a brave smile.

"Thank you, Jordans. Please see to your assignments. I am going to clean up and get as presentable as possible."

The two pilots smiled back and each gave him a nod of assent before they took their leave. They left his quarters and headed down the Artery towards midship.

"He's sick," Blue said, almost under her breath. "Really sick. What do we do?"

"Well," Scarlett answered, keeping her voice equally low, "what do you do when you're sick?"

"See a doctor?" Blue ventured.

"Exactly."

⚜

Blaylock left for his own quarters, never having been so angry in his life. And he had been angry many times before, murderously so. He was so furious now that he thought he might literally explode. It was all he could do to not scream in fury as he passed through the Artery and down the vent shaft.

Crew members could see that fury in his eyes and gave him a wide berth.

The Executive Officer of the Opal Dragon could not believe that the IGC was going to give the command of the Beryl Dragon to Commander Slater. The man was nothing but a gorilla in Blaylock's opinion.

It should have been a double suicide, he thought vehemently as he let himself into his room. A room that was hardly bigger than those of the Jordans.

And Brogan! What the hell is he clinging to? The centuries long rule of Captains is at an end. I'm not the only one who sees that.

The XO went to a cabinet against the wall that was topped by three glass decanters and a pair of short glasses. Blaylock filled one glass nearly to the top with a synthetic scotch from one of the decanters and drank it down in a single quaff.

I can hardly believe he suggested that I rotate to the Copper Dragon, he thought, raging.

The scotch - synthetic or not - hit his stomach like a ball of fire and went to work calming his nerves. *There could be worse places,* he mused, his boiling insides settling down to a simmer. *Gemma is on the Copper Dragon, and Captain Todd is going to have to go someday. Most likely sooner than he expected.*

The Executive Officer poured himself another three fingers of the scotch and took a sip, frowning because it was the Opal Dragon he wanted to command. Mostly because he wanted to cow the stupid Jordans who had plagued his life for the past three years, especially Scarlett.

But, his calming mind reasoned, *when the Fledglings grow into Draconae, they won't be here anymore.*

He brightened suddenly as he wondered if maybe the

Jordans could be used as Dragon fodder, their dead bodies providing genetic material for reproduction. Then - just as quickly - dismissed the idea. They were females. They would not provide seed for the female Dragons.

"Damn them!" he shouted and hurled his glass against the wall where it shattered, showering the side of the room with glass and golden liquid. Chest heaving and his whole body near to jumping up and down with his wrath, Blaylock forced himself to calm down enough to pour another draught of liquor into the remaining glass.

Again, he brightened with a quickness that was frightening. He realized that being at the funeral service he might be able to conquer something that was previously an unsolved problem. He drained his glass and left it on the cabinet before he headed to a small alcove in his room that held a desk, and his private compute with a private and secure com-line. He might be able to be with Gemma sooner than they had hoped. And be in command of a Dragon faster than he could have believed.

But, first, he had to make sure he was not fired upon like the rest of the fishes that were to be in the barrel.

☙❧

Doc Westerson left the exam room in the medical center, typing on his acrylic as he walked into what served as a both a waiting and reception area.

"Do I have anything else scheduled today?" he asked David, his head nurse, finally looking up to see that there was someone, or *someones* actually, waiting for him. Not one, but two Jordans to be exact.

He tucked his acrylic under his arm.

"Um, yes," David said, standing up behind a small desk. The Jordans stood up as well as the Chief Medic entered the small room.

"We would like to have a word in private with you, Doctor Westerson," Scarlett said. "If you do not mind, of course."

"Of course not," he said, turning and holding out an arm towards the hallway to his office as a young human left the examination room, rolling down his sleeve and looking at the Jordans with open curiosity before giving them a nod.

"Jordans," he greeted.

They both gave him a nod in return and started down the hallway, pausing before the closed door.

Westerson, the Chief Medic on the Opal Dragon, opened the door and ushered them inside. "Please sit down," he invited, gesturing to the two low-backed seats that faced his desk, while he circumnavigated the desk and sat in the high-backed chair behind it.

His eyes were a muddy green and filled with intrigue as he folded his hands on top of the surface next to a small compute monitor.

"To what do I owe this visit?" he asked. "Neither of you is unwell, I hope." His eyes moved to Scarlett and rested there, though it was Blue who spoke.

"Someone is certainly unwell," she agreed, "but neither of us."

Westerson studied them for a moment and then sat back in his chair. "I see."

"Do you?" she asked.

"All too well," the medic answered, a sour look on his face. "So I will tell you before you ask - I cannot and *will not* divulge any medical information regarding the Captain. I have an oath to uphold."

Scarlett had to bite her tongue not to remind him that he had previously shared a bit of her own personal information with the Blue Jordan. Then again, she was not the Captain.

Blue, also aware of this, spoke quickly. "Certainly not. I have a...friend, a dear friend, that is ill. I want to help her."

The doc cleared his throat, eyeing the Jordan with suspicion, though not unkindly.

"How thoughtful of you. What are her symptoms?"

Blue looked at Scarlett, unsure. The Captain had certainly not shared any of his symptoms with them, they could just see that he was sick. Terribly sick.

Scarlett, however, did not need to be told, she knew what she had seen. She straightened in her chair.

"Loss of appetite. Possible nausea and or vomiting. Anxiety. Depression."

"Problems concentrating and thinking," Blue added, jumping in as she realized that, like Scarlett, she knew enough just by what she had seen. "Poor motor control. Deteriorated hand-eye coordination. Problems with memory."

Westerson frowned deeply. "Difficulty walking, maybe breathing?" he asked, unable not to.

The eyes of the Jordans widened slightly.

"Yes," they whispered in unison.

Doc Westerson looked down and rubbed his forehead between his thumb and fingers.

Also in unison, they leaned forward.

"What is it?" Scarlett asked. "Do you know what it is?"

"I know what it sounds like," Westerson admitted, "but in case it might be a friend we have in common, here on this ship, it would not be possible. It couldn't be."

"Would you have tested for it?" Blue asked.

"No!" the doc affirmed, not aware of the way she had phrased the question. "That only happens with small amounts, over a prolonged exposure of ingestion. And there is no way that is possible."

"Wait, wait, wait." Scarlett ordered. "I have the feeling there is something I am missing here. Can someone please clue me in?"

Westerson took a deep breath and looked at her before turning his muddy green eyes at the other Jordan.

"You're thinking mercury poison, aren't you?"

Blue nodded.

"It does sound like it," he agreed. "But, like I said, it would have to be small amounts, ingested over a long period of time. And no food on the Dragon, which is mostly simstrate anyways, has any heavy metal in it, even in trace amounts. For just that reason."

Blue had the urge to tilt her head, to listen for Galen and his advice. She swallowed hard and looked back at the medic.

"What if he was breathing in in?" she asked, forgetting that her hypothetical friend was supposed to be female. "Every day? All the time?"

"That would certainly do it," Westerson agreed. "But, again, how? If there was some sort of breakdown or leak, there would be a huge number..." but his argument was falling on deaf ears. The Jordans were looking at each other.

"The candle," they chimed together.

"That's what I smelled," Scarlett said.

"Mercury vapor is odorless," the doc informed her.

Blue turned her face back to him and gave him a savage smile. "To normal humans," she told him.

"If that is the case," Scarlett said, addressing the medic, "what do we do?"

"Get rid of the source, or get him away from it immediately," Westerson said quickly. "I'll need to get him on chelation therapy, also immediately."

Blue fixed her glittering eye on the medic. "Better yet, and faster, get the Engineer and take him to the Captain's quarters."

Scarlett fixed her own eyes on him. "And don't tell anyone."

The medic was both a good doctor and a good man. He gave them a nod and left the room without asking any questions. The Blue Jordan looked at Scarlett after he had gone.

"You never told me what it smelled like," she said.

The crimson in Scarlett's dark eyes burned like hot coals as she looked at Blue.

"Betrayal," she said. "It smelled like betrayal."

❧❦

An hour later, Jordan Scarlett - along with the Dragon's Chief Medic - stood outside the door of the Captain's quarters. She had suggested that only her and the doctor go while Blue waited for Calyph. Having everyone show up at once would look alarming.

"Besides," Scarlett had told the other two when they were back at Medical, "if he is angry at us for interfering in his personal life, or we are wrong, there's is no need for anyone else to get into trouble."

Blue wanted to say that it was not his personal life if it affected his ship and his crew, but kept her mouth shut.

Doc Westerson, who had agreed to Scarlett's suggestion, now looked at her as they stopped in front of the silver door to the Captain's quarters.

"Do you know what you are going to say to him?"

Scarlett, for the second time that day - and as far as she could remember was also the only time she had knocked on her Captain's door twice in the same day - rapped her knuckles on the silver Dragonskin and cocked an eyebrow at the medic.

"How about I say we want him to marry us?"

Westerson gave a loud snort of laughter in surprise. He quickly put a finger on his upper lip and shook his head. "You really caught me off guard on that one, Jordan."

Scarlett smiled and faced front.

This time, when the silver door slid open, the Captain stood there. Gray brows drew together under his disheveled crop of iron-colored hair as he saw the two waiting before his quarters.

"Please come in," he invited, standing aside, his pale eyes worried in his sunken face. The Jordan led the way into the foyer and beyond into the living area of cabin. It had been tidied, a little, but the smell was as cloyingly poisonous as before.

"Do you smell it?" she asked the medic as they stopped before the dark holo fireplace.

The medic shook his head in the negative as the Captain joined them, his face a mask of concern.

"Is everything alright, Jordan?" His eyes went to Doc Westerson. "Has there been a relapse?"

Scarlett's heart melted in her chest from the fact he was worried about her health over his own. She licked her fingers and pinched the wick of the candle burning on the mantel. It went out with an angry hiss.

"No, sir," she said, "but thank you for your concern. This is about you."

The Captain opened his mouth as if to argue, and then closed it.

"Sir," Doc Westerson said, "may I take a blood sample?"

The Captain paused, on the brink of questioning them, but he was no fool. He knew he was not well. He nodded and pushed up the sleeve of his pearlescent coveralls. It rose easily over his wasted arm.

Westerson pulled a mini kit from his pocket and popped it open. He swabbed the commander's inner elbow then produced a micro-syringe; a tiny gun equipped with a small hypodermic. He placed it against the alcohol swabbed skin and pulled the trigger. A thin needle shot into the Captain's arm and a clear capsule filled rapidly with blood. The needle went back into the gun with a snap. The medic pulled out the capsule and pressed it into a fitting in the kit he had brought with him.

Numbers that were meaningless to both the Jordan and the Commander lit up on the readout but they could see the throat of the medic work as he tried to swallow. He looked at the Jordan and gave her a solemn, almost terrified, nod.

Scarlett reached up and touched the com stud on her ear.

"Get Calyph here. Now."

"What's going on?" the Captain finally demanded. He waved away the liquid bandage the doctor was preparing and just let his sleeve slip back down his arm.

"Sir," Westerson said, "you have mercury poisoning."

"I what?"

"Have mercury poisoning. I could start you on chelation therapy but I think the Engineer could get the majority of it out of your system, and much quicker."

"How?" the Captain asked. "How did I get mercury poisoning?"

"I think that is a subject best discussed with your Jordans," the Doctor advised. "Now, would you like to come to Medical or should we do this here?"

"Here."

"I'll need you to lie down. You could lie on the couch or..."

The Captain shook his head. "My bed will be better."

A knock came at the door.

"Come in!" he called.

There was a swishing noise as the door opened and another as it closed. Jordan Blue and Calyph entered the living area a moment later. The Captain turned and headed towards his bedroom.

"Jordans," the medic asked, "if you would please wait here?"

The Commander shook his head. "No. I want my Jordans with me."

Westerson nodded and followed him, along with the others, into the bedroom. All tried, out of respect, not to glance around. They failed.

To the Jordans, the room did not look much different from their own. A little bigger, a little dirtier, but not much. There was a dirty coffee mug on the dresser. An over-used pair of coveralls on the floor in the corner. The bed looked slept on, but not slept in.

"I will need to you to undress down to your shorts," the doctor advised him.

The Captain pulled off his boots and tossed them aside, then unzipped his coverall and stepped out of it before tossing it into the corner. Scarlett felt her jaw clench looking at his wasted form. His skin was gray and looked like a second set of coveralls. Loose ones. She could see his ribs. He laid down on the bed without having to be asked.

Brogan stared at the ceiling and waited.

The Engineer stepped forward, took a deep breath, and stood over the Captain. He held out his hands, palms down, as if he were a magician preparing for a trick. To everyone else in the room, it was no less astounding than magic. Certainly more terrifying.

Within a few seconds the Commander's body began to tremble as if plagued with ague. He gagged and retched, turning his head to the side as he dry heaved. Blue put a reassuring hand on his shoulder. Then every eye in the small room widened as what appeared to be silver pins, or needles, began to rise from the skin of the Captain.

Eyes widened even further.

The pins appeared as if they were trying to melt and coalesce to form a blanket of quicksilver but the Engineer kept pulling them out, and up.

"Doc?" he intoned, his voice quavering.

The medic had gone as still and pale as a corpse. Keeping his eyes on the figure on the bed, he held up a vial that was obviously and obscenely too small for the amount of mercury the Engineer had pulled from the Captain.

"Shit!" Calyph hissed quietly after glancing at the vial.

"What do you need?" Scarlett asked.

"Something to hold it, anything." He voiced a hoarse chuckle. "Anything bigger than what the doc has."

Jordan Blue darted to the side and grabbed the small waste can next to the Captain's desk. "Here," she said thrusting it forward. "Will this work?"

The Engineer nodded. "Hold it steady."

Blue did so and he began to guide the liquid metal from where it hovered over the body on the bed and funnel it into the small steel can. As the mercury departed, the Commander gasped for breath.

"Get him some water!" the doctor commanded.

Scarlett rushed from the room and found a small kitchenette off the living area. She drew a cold glass of water from the tap and hurried back in time to see the last droplets gather at the bottom of the waste can.

"Here," she said, kneeling by the bed.

The Captain, his skin cold and clammy, sat up. He accepted the glass and drank it down in huge gulps until he choked. He turned away, coughing into his shoulder. He laid back down as Blue cautiously handed the vessel over to the Engineer.

"I'm going to take this back to my quarters," he told the others. "I'll put it in an airtight container and keep it there until you let me know what you want me to do with it."

The others nodded as he left and then turned their eyes back to the Captain.

"How are you feeling?" Westerson asked, fitting another

capsule into the micro gun.

"Weak," the Captain admitted. "But better. Much better."

The doc took another blood sample and tested it. The surprise he felt was plain on his face. "Amazing," he whispered. He cleared his throat and looked at the others with his muddy green eyes before they settled on the Commander. "It's practically all gone. And amazing that you are alive with that much mercury in your system. I would still like you to have a few sessions of the chelation therapy."

The Captain nodded and closed his eyes.

Scarlett picked up a light blanket that had been folded at the end of the bed and shook it out over the Captain. She glanced at Blue who gave her a nod.

"Thank you," Scarlett told the medic. "If you don't mind, we would like a moment."

"Certainly," Doc Westerson agreed. He gave a slight dip of his head to the Captain who dismissed him with a nod of his own.

"Doc?" Blue asked. Westerson paused, his eyes on the Jordan as she jerked her chin in the direction of the living area. "Take the candle to Calyph, will you?"

"Is that where it was coming from?" Brogan asked.

"We think so," the medic affirmed as he dipped his head again in acquiescence to Blue's request and left the Jordans with their Captain.

When the three could hear the door slide shut, the Captain's pale eyes lifted to find Jordan Scarlett's dark ones.

"I know what you are going to ask me," he said with a sigh. Scarlett's brows rose with the unspoken question. "You want to know where I got the candle." Scarlett nodded and the Captain fought against another sigh. "From Commander Blaylock," he told them, his pale gaze shifting to the Blue Jordan. "He knew it would mean a lot to me, keeping a vigil for the one I lost, and the one who had to find her way."

Scarlett swallowed against the lump in her throat, but it was Blue who asked the next question.

"Scarlett was gone for months," she said. "That seems like a long time for one candle. Has it lasted that whole time?"

Captain Brogan shook his head and the sigh he had been holding back escaped his lips. "That candle was the seventh one I have lit. Commander Blaylock gave me a box of them."

The Jordans looked at each other, locking eyes. Scarlett's fists had clenched involuntarily and she slowly forced them open. Blue's one-eyed gaze was hard and steady.

"Jordans," Brogan advised, "do not jump to conclusions. And do not do anything rash."

Blue and Scarlett turned their faces back to him.

"Have we ever?" they asked in unison.

Brogan sighed once more. "Balls and shit," he whispered.

 ONE SIX

- The deeper you dig, the more fragile the world becomes.

Verdana took Amberle where she wanted to go. More than that, she took her to *when* she wanted to go. Into the past.

It was where (and when) Verdana wanted to go as well. To get Jade. To see him. To save him.

The girl supplied the when, Verdana supplied the where. She zeroed in on his DNA as soon as they entered the atmosphere of the tiny moon where he had been born and raised.

After a sweeping flight over green hills and valleys and hamlets, they found him trekking through a forest at a run with someone in pursuit. Verdana was overjoyed.

It was so like Jade to already be on an adventure! She overshot the forest and landed in the small valley towards where he was headed and waited.

A few moments passed in silence and then there he was.

He crested the hill at an all-out run and came to a skittering halt, almost falling over, before he regained his balance and stood looking down at her in amazement. He was dressed in country garb, chocolate-colored hair tumbling over his jade-green eyes.

The girl, the Fledgling human called Amberle, had done

as she had promised. There he was, younger and just as enthralling as he would be when she would choose him to be her Jordan, almost a hundred years from when they were now.

Jade Jade Jade! she thought with exaltation.

Amberle disembarked to speak to the young elf as he trotted towards them. The Fledgling got the distinct feeling he was in some sort of scrape. It made her beam inwardly at him.

Verdana listened to them, intrigued.

Within a minute he had boarded the Fledgling on Amberle's request for help and his unquenchable desire for adventure. And, she suspected with a mental grin, due to his intent on getting out of the situation he was currently in - which meant getting away.

Verdana, feeling she might burst her new seams with joy and gratitude, listened to the sound of his voice as he talked and it filled her with warmth. At the girl's request, she lifted easily from the field and the Fledgling coasted through the air at an easy pace while the two inside chatted. Then the girl placed her dark fingers on the silver dashboard and let Verdana know where she wanted go. And when.

Verdana, theoretically stretching her new wings, took them to where (and when) the girl had asked.

That was when a strange thing happened. It was like nothing she had ever experienced, though she was very young. There was something she could only grasp as a *ripple.*

A ripple in her thinking. A ripple in her memory.

The Fledgling knew without a doubt that there was nothing she would not do for her Jordan. But suddenly, she could not remember which one of the dear beings in her body *was* her Jordan. She felt a strange deep love for the male elf, but was quite certain that it was the dark-skinned young woman that commanded her.

They soared over lakes and rivers, on what felt like (those feelings coming from Amberle) a wayward mission. Indeed, it did take an unruly turn when she was left to hide in a cave while her young companions went off into the forest. Upon their return, however, she was allowed to blast a nasty group of alien Golgoths to smithereens.

Feeling smug, they finally left the moon in the Outer Banks behind.

Verdana took them, trailing emerald light through the dark of space, to the far side of the ringed giant, Saturn.

જ્જ

Amberle announced their arrival to de Rossi security and Verdana eased them down into the artificial atmosphere. She flew them over the watery moon of the Distant Shore where the sun, almost nine hundred million miles away, had just set. They dipped into the hidden hangar under the Last Castle.

"Wow!" Jade exclaimed, looking through Verdana's eyes at the cavern that stretched out farther than he could see. If not lit by a number of lights, most hanging down, he would hardly be able to see at all.

They were received by the same party that had seen Amberle off - the de Rossi sisters, Jasyn, and Nathan.

Most of them were even dressed the same, or very similar to, the last time she had seen them. Faith was in a suit of white with gold chains hanging from her neck and ears. The construct wore dark pants and a shirt that was tight across his chest and around his arms, though this time it was made of a shimmering silver material. The lanky Engineer was once again, or still, in pale mechanic-style coveralls. Charity was the only one markedly different, wearing a cocktail dress of silver and green that covered only her breasts, barely, and the area between her upper thigh and hips, barely.

Even the droids were there, though Amberle could not tell if they were the same ones, setting up a table with flatware and plates of food. The young adventures disembarked the Fledgling and Amberle made the introductions.

Jade, the young elf who had returned with her, had a slight build, brown hair and shining green eyes. He was uncharacteristically quiet, stealing bold glances at Charity and her drastic amount of bare skin.

Amberle had an almost irresistible urge to cry out *got him!* as if she had just landed a big fish or brought down a fleeing stag, but she was too agitated to be funny. Her departure from Jade's world had not been as smooth as her arrival. She and the elf had just left an encounter with a number of Golgoths on Jade's moon of Erebos and it still had her rattled.

Faith greeted them with warm welcomes but the young woman cut her off, trying her best not to be rude but impossible not to be blunt.

"I need a gun."

Faith froze, unblinking, her hands clasped tight. "Excuse me?'

"I need a gun," Amberle repeated. "I'm not backing away from this mission, but it has become more dangerous with each step I take. I don't want more money, or more software, but I want a gun."

Faith began to shake her head but the dark-haired construct gave her a nod. "I'll take care of it," he assured.

"What happened?" Charity asked before taking a drink from a glass that was as long as her arm, filled with sparkling purple liquid.

"There are Golgoths on Erebos," Amberle told her.

"Golgoths," Faith asserted, making sure she had heard her correctly. "Like last time, on the other moon. You are sure?"

Amberle sighed through her nose and lifted her chin, realizing she did not have to turn towards Verdana or even ask. The Fledgling responded to her thoughts without the need for words.

In the midst of those gathered, the Fledgling projected a life-size holographic image of the aliens that had gathered before her. The tall Engineer, though he was closest in height to the creatures, jumped back.

"Jesus!" he shouted.

The handsome construct, who had stepped instinctively in front of Faith, stared at the hologram before he shifted his dark hazel eyes back to Amberle and gave her another nod.

"But that's all the way out in the Outer Banks," Charity said. "They shouldn't be there any more than they should have been on Elba."

"And at the same time," Amberle noted aloud.

"The timing could just be by accident."

"There are no accidents," Jade told her, his voice soft.

Charity returned his somber expression and sipped her drink.

"Please," Faith implored, "have something to eat while I make some calls."

She moved away quickly and Amberle looked meaningfully at Jade as if to assure him she had made the right decision. He looked back at her. More than just satisfied, he placed his hand over his heart as he stared into her eyes, showing he was in her debt. A blush crept up over Amberle's dark cheeks and she looked away.

Seeing the places being set for them by the droids, she jerked her chin towards them and headed away, the elf on her heels.

"Thanks," Jade said as they sat down at the small table for two, facing each other. "For not wasting any time on that."

"What can I say?" Amberle asked. "I'm wise beyond my years."

Jade laughed as he sat down and gave her kick under the table. Amberle kicked him back and loaded her plate with gravied meat and mashed potatoes.

Faith returned after only three calls, the only ones she really needed to make, and watched the pair with a feeling of horror and shame.

Jade was covering his mouth, which was full of food as he laughed, and kicked Amberle under the table. Amberle laughed and threw a slice of cooked squash at the elf.

They're children, she thought. *Practically babies.* Faith herself was over three hundred years old and, for her race, not even middle-aged.

She knew Jade was thirty years old, at least he was from when they snatched him, which was barely an adult by elfin standards. She was not sure of Amberle's age. When she had done a search for her on the GW she could not find her birth record, but knew it could not be more than twenty human years.

What am I doing? she asked herself, wavering for only a moment before she answered herself - and quite firmly - *I'm doing exactly what Faith de Rossi would do.*

Faith watched them joke and laugh as they ate - like a couple of kids on their first date. She felt another stab of guilt and quashed it immediately.

"Are you going to let them get a night's worth of sleep?" a voice asked from behind her. She did not need to turn to know to whom the voice belonged. Nonetheless, Jasyn stepped forward and into her peripheral vision and took a drink of dark liquid from a short glass, his eyes also on the young pair enjoying their dinner.

"It's the least I can do," Faith answered, taking a sip from her own glass - though hers was champagne. Jasyn snorted softly and she ignored him.

"What did the 'J' stand for?" he asked.

"Judge," Faith replied, turning her head so that their eyes met.

There was so much sorrow in that gaze that Jasyn nearly broke. He wanted to tell her that he did not judge her, that he never had. But Faith turned away and walked to where the two were enjoying a simple supper.

She offered them rooms upstairs but when dinner was done and it was time for bed, both Amberle and Jade passed over the offer to sleep in the castle and instead opted to stay inside the Fledgling.

Faith gave them a smile and a nod as they headed back for the living ship that had brought them.

"You can have the bed," the young woman told the elf, trying not to sound overly uncomfortable. "I'm fine sleeping up front."

Jade shrugged and climbed into the bed in the aft end of the Fledgling, deciding beyond a doubt that it had been the most exciting day of his life. He had lost his virginity, was chased by a jealous husband, rode inside a Fledgling, saw live Golgolths, and traveled through time. It was preposterous.

Something inside told him that it was just the beginning. He laced his hands beneath his head and closed his eyes, trying not to think of the beautiful young woman sharing the close space with him.

Amberle reclined in the pilot's seat and placed her hand firmly onto the armrest. Silver tendrils snaked out of armrest and slipped over, under, and between the young woman's fingers, forming a mesh glove. Amberle smiled and jacked into the Galactic Web.

Sleep, Verdana urged.

I will, Amberle agreed. She thought back over the day, also almost unable to believe how many things had happened. *Was I really sleeping here, in this same spot, only twenty-four hours ago?* she wondered. *Was it only just this morning that I left to find Jade?* It seemed incomprehensible that so much could happen in so short of time.

Thinking about it made her realize just how tired she was.

Still, she started a search for trending videos as something else occurred to her, but she was getting sleepier by the second.

Are you doing that? she asked as her eyes drooped.

There was no answer, just a feeling of satisfaction as the young woman's eyes closed altogether.

The Fledgling reshaped the seat into a bed and wove a silver blanket over her sleeping form. Protecting her two passengers in a soft emerald glow, even she rested fitfully.

☙❦☙

In the morning, Amberle and Jade awoke to find a breakfast laid out on the table in the hangar. The two said little to each other but ate quickly, hurried by their excitement more than the press for time.

"You seem nervous," Jade remarked.

Amberle almost replied with a scathing remark, thinking for a moment he might be making fun of her. His voice was soft but there was a sparkle in his pale green eyes that held nothing but kindness. She gave him a lopsided smile.

"I'm always like this," she told him, "though I'm getting better. You should have seen me a month ago."

A month ago, she knew, she had been much worse. She had been all but shaking with Cyber Sickness, practically blinded by natural light, irate and repulsed by human interaction – especially touch.

She wiped her mouth with a napkin and rose from her seat. Jade did the same and together they made the short walk back to the Fledgling Dragon where the de Rossi sisters waited along with the dark-eyed construct. There was still no sign of the lanky Engineer.

Faith stood before them in an impeccable cream-colored suit edged with gold, her hands clasped in front of her body.

The skirt of her suit was short, exposing long, pale legs. She wore golden shoes with high heels, and a heavy gold chain necklace. There were hectic patches of color on her face and her eyes were red from lack of sleep.

"Bring back my sister," she commanded, "or any trace of her."

The young woman and the young elf both dipped their heads in solemn acquiescence. Charity de Rossi was possibly in the same attire as the night before but it was hard to tell as she was covered with a silver robe. One that covered very little of her. She had a drink in her jeweled hand, though it was still not even eight on the clock, and she raised it in salutation.

"Good luck finding her," she said with a smile that showcased perfect teeth. "And even more luck if you do."

The young adventurers gave her nervous smiles in return.

But it was the devastatingly handsome black-haired construct that surprised Amberle the most when he approached and put his arms around her.

The young woman froze, not just from his touch - which she had learned to bear without panic but still did not like - but from the fact that he was fastening a belt around her waist. He cinched it so it rested on her hips and slipped a laser pistol into the holster that hung from the leather strap.

"Don't trust anyone," he advised softly before he pulled away from her and took a step back.

Amberle's shoulders sagged. "But I was just starting to trust people!" she hissed at him with a frown.

Jasyn shrugged apologetically as he smiled at her. "Life is all about knowing who deserves that trust, and who does not."

His dark eyes gleamed while, at his side, Faith stood as still as a statue, her lips pressed together into a tight line.

"Good luck and Godspeed," Charity bade them, raising her drink in salute once again.

Amberle and Jade glanced at each other and then boarded the Fledgling without another word until they were seated.

Verdana snaked safety webbing over both of them.

"Wow," Jade finally whispered. "That felt pretty tense. Or intense. I'm not sure."

"Both," Amberle agreed as Verdana lifted off the tarmac, tucked in her legs, and raced out of the hidden cave and into the bright light over the crashing waters of the Distant Shore.

# ONE SEVEN

- Not all locked doors need a key. Some just require the right question.

Blaylock tipped his head to the side and dug his index finger into the minuscule space between his throat and the neckline of his shirt. He pulled his finger around in a half-circle, trying to loosen the collar that felt like it was strangling him. He could not remember the last time he had worn a suit and tie. Decades, probably. All he knew was they were not any more comfortable now than the last time.

He had grown used to the feel of his flight suit, though it angered him to no end that said suit was going to remain one of an Executive Officer.

Damn Brogan for sending me on this mission when he should be the one keening over Condliffe's stupid life!

Blaylock kept his eyes forward and his face impassive as he fumed internally.

Probably afraid that is exactly what would happen. Start wailing like some delrah.

Jordan Blue stood at his side, dressed once again in her sparkling black flight suit that she had so recently given up. With her form so thin and the glints of light thrown from her shimmering garment she looked to Blaylock like the blade of an obsidian knife.

Her presence annoyed him greatly, though he was heels over head thankful that it was not Scarlett. The Red Jordan had gone from annoying to insubordinate to damn near mutinous.

Blaylock mused, for the hundredth time, on the best way to get rid of her. For someone who had proven to be half-crazy and twice as dangerous, it seemed to distress no one but himself.

The doors to the *chiesa* – a building that had once been a Catholic church – opened. Captain Hunter and Captain Todd both entered and walked solemnly towards the front. Jordan Blue watched them with her one eye as they strode down the aisle.

The Captains were both fairly young, like the demised Condliffe, but that was the only thing the men had in common, other than their rank. The Captain of the Copper Dragon was ginger-haired and lean. Blue saw that the other was more stolidly built with short dark hair that was shot with gray.

No, she saw, looking more intently. Not gray. Silver.

She looked back at Captain Todd and realized that he might not have started out with ginger hair.

Will my hair turn blue someday? she wondered suddenly. Though it sounded both intriguing and plausible, something made her doubt it, despite the fact that her eye had begun to change color.

Scarlett's hair had not changed color but her eyes were slowly being kindled with flecks of crimson.

The two Captains took their place, also up front, but on the other side of the aisle. They each gave a solemn nod to the representatives from the Opal Dragon. Blaylock and Blue returned the gesture like time-lapsed mirrors.

Blaylock somewhat suppressed a sigh of impatience. They now only waited on the official that was to represent the IGC. Blaylock wondered who it would be. He cursed Barin Trey for going and getting killed.

What an idiot! the commander thought bitterly. Barin had been a great ally. Now the IGC Director of Artificial Intelligence was some old doctor, undoubtedly already swayed by the money or, worse, the ideology of Faith de Rossi.

Still, Blaylock supposed the AI Director would be an unlikely choice to represent the IGC at the funeral. He wondered again who it would be and knew that it could present an opportunity to make a new alliance within the governmental structure.

At that moment, the doors opened again, this time with a loud *BANG!* as if blown open by a strong gust of wind, to admit the unknown IGC attendee. Blaylock, along with every other person present, turned to stare. The XO of the Opal Dragon felt his heart sink and his balls shrivel as they pulled up tight against his body. His face snapped back to the front and he fixed his dark hazel eyes forward, even as Blue looked with curiosity over her left shoulder.

Though not as terrified as Blaylock, a frisson rippled over her skin as she turned her own eye back to the front.

Khasper, the Captain of the Iron Dragon stood for moment, surveying the scene inside the chiesa and then strode down the center aisle, the barely audible sounds of hushed gasps and murmurs following in his wake.

He was tall and lean and almost as thin as Jordan Blue. His skin was as white as the belly of a dead fish and his hair was blacker than a starless night.

The elfin Captain reached the front and was momentarily undecided on where to stand. He glanced to the left to see Captain Hunter and Captain Todd standing next to each other.

They gave him a solemn nod which he did not return.

His dark eyes swept to the right and barely registered Commander Blaylock before those black eyes fell on the Blue Jordan.

Noel, as ever overcome by sheer curiosity but still

mandated to military composure, spared him a single glance before she too dipped her head in deference and fixed her face forward.

Khasper, however, did not. He moved to stand next to her, his black eyes intent.

Blue could feel the weight of those eyes like a touch as they roved over her body before staring fixedly at her face. His lips parted to give a glimpse of teeth that, though they were small and square, looked sharp.

The Jordan stole glances at him from her peripheral vision. His dark hair appeared to be white at the temples and over his ears but she realized it was just the reflection of the lights of the chiesa, shining in the depths of his coal black hair.

Then the reverend approached the pulpit, clearing his throat, and the weight of those eyes shifted away.

The reverend was a non-denominational religious man, though he was undoubtedly once Catholic, as was Condliffe's family and seventy percent of his home moon. Knowing that everyone who had been called was now present, he began his sermon.

He had barely begun talking about life and how precious it was when Blue tuned him out. Though she could see from the side of her eye that Khasper was facing the pulpit, she had the distinct feeling that he was looking at her.

The reverend droned on for another two minutes when things began happening all at once with the force of a load of bricks being dumped on the chiesa.

The first thing that hit Blue, making her rock back on her heels, was Cyan's voice as it filled her head.

Danger! he warned.

Then her mind's eye was filled with what he saw - fighter jets unloading a barrage of laser fire - her real eye saw Khasper flinch.

She turned her head in time to see the two Captains on the

far side of the aisle straighten as if galvanized by an electric current. A Klaxon went off only a second later, blaring and echoing between the walls of the church.

"Christ!" Blaylock cursed as a murmur rose like a wave throughout the congregation.

Khasper turned to Blue, seemingly unfazed. "Find me when it is done," he told her. Before she could ask what *it* was, he vanished.

"Nice," she whispered.

A human male, aging with wisps of white hair fluffing over his ears, stepped in front of the preacher and leaned down to speak into the microphone. "Please stay calm," he advised. "Unless you are military personnel, please remain in your seats." He looked down at the first row of officers. The Captains each had a hand over one ear to drown the noise of the Klaxon while they listened to their com lines. "First row, please go first, then the second and so on."

The Captains left quickly, almost at a run. In Blue's mind she could see the image Cyan was sending her, that of fighter jet streaming towards him. She returned the image of Khasper as he disappeared.

Blaylock looked at the Jordan to tell her that he would remain with the civilians but as he did so, she vanished. Blaylock stared at the space she had been, his heart thumping with trepidation and his blood boiling with anger.

ᘓᘔ

Captain Brogan stood in a small formation with five other officers aboard the Beryl Dragon. Standing next to him was Commander Slater, Beryl's newly made Captain. In front of them, on an air gurney, was her former commander, Captain Condliffe.

The skin on his body was ashy gray except for the ligature

marks - a pale red ring around his neck where he had tied the thin cable that had killed him. Brogan felt his hands clench involuntarily.

Someone should have covered that up, he thought, angry. He kept his eyes trained on Condliffe's body, knowing that if they strayed they would fix on the Chief Medic.

Doc Kuri, the head medical officer aboard the Beryl Dragon, stood solemnly at the end of the row of four other men and one woman. He had purposely left the marks bare in the hopes that someone else would notice.

Hoping someone would see how low and uniform the angry red line was. He thought anyone would be able to tell the ugly ring, at the center of the young Captain's neck rather than under the chin, looked more like a strangling than a hanging. To suggest it, however, would mean treason if he had no proof.

Besides, who would do such a thing? Condliffe was loved by all on the Beryl Dragon. Something Kuri did not account for when anticipating someone would notice. Brogan had been his mentor, Slater had been his best friend. The Communications Officer had, silently, been half in love with him. She held her composure but did nothing to hold back the tears that streamed freely down her face. The Navigator simply watched in stunned silence.

The last officer, if he could be called that, was the Engineer whom Brogan had brought from the Opal Dragon.

He might be good at what he does, Kuri thought, *but he sees little else.* The Doc kept his own eyes fixed forward, lamenting inwardly.

Everyone present could feel the sorrow that seeped from the Beryl Dragon.

Calyph stepped with the floating gurney as it moved, guiding it into the cyclopean column of swirling fluid in the belly of the Dragon. Captain Condliffe went in feet first, his body naked save for a swath of silvery fabric that wrapped the bottom of his hips to the tops of his thighs.

The young Commander was swallowed by the column - legs, torso, necklace of a dying red bruise, to the thick brown curls on his head. Brogan bit down on his tongue as this last disappeared into the column, remembering tousling those curls when the dead man was just a goofy-assed aviator that could fly like he had the devil in his sights.

Calyph ran a hand over the column, making sure it was sealed and a small noise came from the Communication Officer's throat. Brogan, who was supposed to say something to the small group turned his red-rimmed eyes now to Kuri, who was already staring at him with an intensity that momentarily surprised the words from him.

Yet in that moment, when their eyes met, there was a jolt that shook the Dragon and glances darted everywhere as alarms went wildly echoing through the ship. Slater turned on his heel and took off at a dead run with everyone but the Engineer following in his wake.

"Wait here!" Brogan ordered Calyph over his shoulder as he followed the others out of the belly and headed for Fighter Bay.

ᘓᙣᙔᘔ

Jordan Scarlett stood in the bridge of the Opal Dragon. She was dressed in her normal crimson flight suit, though there was a black band around her arm in remembrance of the fallen Captain Condliffe. There was another band above it that was pearlescent, marking her as the Interim Commander of the Opal Dragon.

She did not sit in the Captain's chair at the helm but instead stood next to it - arms crossed over her chest, feet apart and braced as if she expected the Dragon to move suddenly.

Despite the reassuring sounds of soft blips and beeps from the navigation board and the murmur of the coms, her blood was racing.

Something was coming.

She could feel it.

The port side door to the bridge opened and Scarlett was surprised to see Calyph's troll wheel in before stopping a few meters away from her. She cocked an eyebrow at it and turned her gaze back to look through the eyes of the Dragon.

"No word from Beryl?" she asked Dareus. It was a stupid question. Of course he would have told her if the other Dragon had been trying to reach them, but she was antsy.

"None, ma'am."

Breathe, she told herself. Seven seconds later, she found herself looking at the Gunnery Officer.

"All quiet on all quadrants?" she asked him.

Gunnery Officer Anatoli glanced at the panels in front of him and nodded. "Not a ship in sight other than our own. Beryl is just over 1AU away, roughly 93,000,000 miles, or 150,000,000 kilometers." He touched a light on the panel and a holographic image appeared of Opal's sister Dragon over the console.

Scarlett resisted the urge to sigh or pace. She kept perfectly still, despite the fact that her nerves were tingling. At least they weren't tingling up and down her right side.

She glanced at the troll who also seemed to be staring out expectantly into space.

Was there something that it knew? It certainly was not equipped with any auxiliary senses. Still, she had the feeling it was there for a reason. Her gaze slid over the control panels of navigation and coms, then the screens the Gunnery Officer was minding.

Again, her dark eyes went to the troll. It could answer all sorts of questions. But not the ones she was after. She knew the tricky thing with the droids was asking the right questions.

Her eyes flicked over the officers in the bridge. Maybe it wasn't that she was asking the wrong questions, but she was asking the wrong people. It occurred to her at the same moment that the anxiety she was feeling might not be her own.

Opal? she queried mentally, tentatively. *Do you sense any danger?*

Otherlings! she replied instantly.

Scarlett's shoulders dropped and she felt her heartbeat quicken even more.

Where? she asked.

Pictures and numbers ran through her mind, but without an astral map, she had no idea what Opal was trying to tell her. It didn't matter. Alarms were now sounding. The Beryl Dragon was under attack.

More alarms went off on the other side of the dash. Copper and Silver were also under attack.

It's highly coordinated, was her first thought. *To attack three Dragons within seconds of each other.*

But not us.

She mentally counted down from three and still nothing.

Not us.

"Enlarge the holo of Beryl," she instructed the Gunny. The quadrant for the Beryl Dragon swelled, filling the area above the console. A Chimeran battle cruiser had entered the sector and had dispatched two dozen fighters that were engaged in a fire fight with the jets now pouring from the side of the Beryl Dragon.

"Should I dispatch ours?" the Gunnery Officer asked. It was a question he never would have raised to Brogan, but Jordan Scarlett was not Captain Brogan. She was an IC serving for what should have only been a few hours. A few eventless hours.

Scarlett shook her head. "They would nearly be out of

fuel when they got there and wouldn't last more than another two minutes when they did. And, yes, Gunny, I know that we could get the Dragon to cover half that distance in a blink and get them there to help, but that might be their ploy - to get the Dragons closer together. Besides, it's a distress signal, not a distress call. They will let us know if they want us to intervene."

The Gunny nodded in approval. She was right, and she was keeping surprisingly calm. Scarlett let her hands drop to her sides.

"Meanwhile," she instructed, "show me a holo of the Lucca moon, including the Silver and Copper Dragons. The huge chunk of space projected above the console disappeared in a blink to be replaced by the Lucca moon and the hell that surrounded it. The Dragons, far apart and on opposite sides of the moon, were taking heavy fire along with the surface of the moon itself.

But not us, crossed Scarlett's mind again. *Not us. Why? The obvious is that they are after the eggs, and we don't have any. But neither does Beryl. They can't take down a Dragon without a nuclear fallout that would incinerate them as well. And they are strafing the shit out of that moon. What are they after? What do they have that we don't?*

Her gaze went to the great glass eyes of the Dragon and saw her reflection, standing with her hands balled at her sides and her legs braced. And she knew.

"Dareus!" she ordered, "open a direct line with Captain Brogan's personal communication band."

The slim dark fingers of the Communications Officer moved so fast they were a blur.

Aboard the Beryl Dragon, Captain Brogan had entered Fighter Bay and was headed for his personal jet when the comlink surgically embedded in the upper scapha of his right ear gave a single, low but long, bleep.

The Opal Dragon.

He paused at the bottom of the ladder to his jet and ran his finger over the implanted com, opening the link.

"Commander Mattatock," he greeted, his tone both formal and firm. Ninety million miles away, though it was only to be expected, Scarlett felt a ripple of surprise and pleasure for him to address her that way.

"We are aware of the attack you are under, Captain. It is from a Chimeran Battle Cruiser with only short-range fighter craft."

"I expected as much, but I did not accompany Commander Slater to the bridge. I am heading back to you."

"No," Scarlett said. She could hardly believe she uttered such a thing and, though she could not see the faces of the other officers, she was sure their eyes were as round as eggs while they listened. "I want you to stay where you are," Scarlett ordered.

Brogan stood with one hand resting lightly on the ladder to his personal craft. He knew that Opal was not under attack. Not only would Scarlett have informed him of that immediately, but he would have felt it.

The Interim Commander turned her head towards the troll. "What is the absolute farthest reach for ship detection in our panel?" she asked.

The circular head of the droid swiveled so that its optic band was facing her. "General visage is one hundred million miles, unless given exact coordinates to search."

What do you see beyond that? Scarlett sent to Opal.

Otherlings. Just Beyond.

Scarlett's hands tightened involuntarily into fists, but otherwise she was outwardly calm. "Captain Brogan," she addressed, looking once again through the eyes of the Dragon, "despite the circumstances, I believe you are safer where you are for now."

The Captain weighed her words, fighting his compelling instinct to immediately return to his ship. "My personal craft can outrun any of those fighters," he assured the current commander of his Dragon.

"Then send it by remote, as fast as it will go."

Brogan's response was near immediate. "Yes, ma'am."

He ascended the ladder to his craft and climbed in just enough to pull the remote chip from it before he backed down the ladder. Jumping from the second to the last rung, he landed on his feet and quickly powered up the jet before sending it out and on its way.

On the Opal Dragon, Scarlett's gaze snapped to the Gunnery Officer. "Bring back the holo of Beryl!" He immediately had it up and the Beryl Dragon was once again shown as a hologram over the console that was two feet high and four feet long.

"Spin it," Scarlett ordered. "I want to see the port side, but keep the same proportional aspect."

The image of the assault on the Beryl Dragon turned in time for those in the bridge to see a lone craft, leaner and sleeker than any fighter, jettison from the port side bay and shoot into space - away from the battle.

Of the twenty Chimeran jets engaged in the fight, ten broke away to follow the lean craft into the black. Another ten spewed from the underbelly of the Battle Cruiser, also in pursuit.

"Holy shit," Dareus whispered.

"Battle stations!" Scarlett shouted. "Sound the alarm!"

Wide-eyed as they were, the officers in the bridge were military trained and obeyed without question, though there was no threat they could see.

"Battle stations!" the Gunnery Officer echoed, the words a loud affirmation in the bridge as they went into his comset and were broadcast throughout the ship. "Sound the alarm!"

The hands of the Communications Officer blurred again over the dash. Alerts were sent to the IGC Military Command and a general announcement aired throughout the Dragon as a Klaxon began to sound. The gunny was about to glance questioningly at the Interim Commander when a Chimeran Battle Cruiser came crashing into radar on the furthest edge of their quadrant, barreling towards them at twenty kilometers a second. The math ran through Scarlett's head as she calculated the speed and distance.

"Make ready to defend, ready to attack!" Scarlett called out.

"Make ready to defend, ready to attack!" Anatoli echoed.

"Time to dispatch those fighters, Gunny," Scarlett said. "She'll be close enough to release hers in eighteen minutes. I want every J-8 ready when she does."

"Yes, ma'am," the gunny answered. He pressed the button on the side of his comset and began issuing orders to the pilots in Fighter Bay.

ONE 8

- The best kept secrets are the ones hidden in plain sight.

"Oh hell yeah!" Jordan Blue shouted as she found herself standing in the cockpit of her Fledgling. She dropped into her seat as Cyan shot forward then canted sideways to avoid the laser fire coming at him.

Blue stretched her hands forward and Cyan filled them with a wheel as he let her take over manual control. Her mind raced as she took it all in, starting with the immediate threat. They were being fired upon by three fighters trailing close behind. She braked hard and banked left, letting the fighters go by before she unloaded on them with a single blast of Dragonfire. All three ships were incinerated.

Her eye darted over her com board, seeing the many requests for communications before she looked back up through Cyan's eyes. "Enlarge that view," she instructed, and her vision was immediately filled with the fight ensuing on the far side of the moon. She had a single glimpse of the Iron Dragon as it blinked from view.

"As swift as your Captain, I see," Blue murmured as she turned her attention to the Silver Dragon who was under fire. "And not leaving without your Captain," she said. Her eye went next to the fighter craft leaving the fight to swarm down upon the moon.

"Race you there!" she whispered, grinning, as she took Cyan down in a plunge. Her grin dissipated as she saw they were all bound for the chiesa.

"Oh shit," she said, her voice low. "They know. They knew."

She recalled Captain Brogan's words when Blaylock had told them of the service, and who would be there. It went against protocol, having two Captains together - even more so for three. For the express reason that should an attack come, an enemy could take them all out in one fell swoop.

Blue pushed the wheel, taking them into a deeper dive, urging Cyan to go faster. She intercepted the attack just as it came, but was too close to the moon to for Dragonfire. She used laser fire instead. It was just as deadly, if her aim was true (and it always was), but it was more time consuming.

As the third enemy fighter went spinning off without a wing and the fourth was crippled, the fifth and then sixth and seventh went shooting by her. Blue turned and followed.

Instead of racing to catch them, she slowed so she could get behind the last one. She picked him off first, then sped up to catch the other two. She rolled Cyan to the right, firing at one Chimeran fighter jet and then rolled left towards the other, blasting it to oblivion.

As the Jordan circled around she saw the jet she had crippled heading straight for the building full of mourners, and IGC military. Its weaponry was shot out but it continued down, picking up all the speed it could.

"Shit, shit, shit," she muttered, each word growing louder as she realized exactly what the Chimeran intended. The Japonesa had a word for it. *Kamikaze.* The pilot was intent on a suicide dive, smashing his fighter into the chiesa. Blue followed but knew that if she fired on him she would strafe the church as well.

"We need to get under him," she said, her voice low. Cyan, with more speed than she had ever felt from him, was there in a heartbeat, burning in between the chiesa and the incoming jet. Blue flipped him over so he was belly up and then lasered the fighter into ash. The Fledgling then rolled upright and the Jordan took in the scene below.

Captain Hunter had left on his transport for the Silver Dragon. Captain Todd, however, stood with others in the shadow of the chiesa with his hands over his ears, shouting into his com-link. His transport had all but been destroyed in the attack.

"Take us down," Blue commanded. "We need to get him to his Dragon."

Cyan swooped low, pushing out his legs for a fast landing. He hit the ground hard - his heels and talons digging trenches into the earth. Blue held tight to the arms of her seat until the force of their arrival settled enough for her to jump to her feet without being thrown around. She rushed towards the galley as he opened a door for her and formed a set of silver stairs against his side.

"Captain Todd!" Blue shouted as she leaned out but the Captain of the Copper Dragon was already running towards her at an ungainly trot.

Blue could see that he was injured, but not where. She took the stairs against the Fledgling by holding the slim rails and sliding down. She burned the hell out of her palms but ignored it. Captain Todd waved wildly at her, mutely ordering her back into her Fledgling. She ignored that too.

Blue ran like mad trying to get to him, her back to the fighter bearing down on them both. She could hear it coming, a building roar that tore and pushed the air with a heat that screamed.

She heard the muted yet deafening thuds of hot rounds a second before she was thrown from her feet by a barrage of artillery that left her on her back with her ears ringing. She curled up instinctively, throwing her arms over her face as chunks of earth began falling like dirty hail. When enough of the clumps had settled so she could see, she leapt to her feet and again ran for Captain Todd.

The air was filled with smoke, dust, and screams.

Her eye watering and the sound in her ears muffled from the salvo of fire, she made her way to where the Captain lay on his side, one arm flung over his head to protect it as best he could.

Alongside with whatever injury he had sustained before, now most of his right thigh and part of his calf was missing. Luckily, Blue supposed, it had missed the bone and been hot enough to cauterize the wound. Still, he was in bad shape. Parts of him were smoking from laser fire that had come with the first onslaught of fighter jets.

Blue dropped to her knees and wrapped her arms around him, willing Cyan to get them back on board. Nothing happened. Apparently that ability was limited to her and her alone. Exhaling sharply, Blue left one arm hooked under his and hauled him into a sitting position. Captain Todd bit back a scream.

"Get out of here, Jordan!" he commanded with as much force as he could muster. It wasn't much.

"Not without you, sir. Cyan!"

This time the Fledgling responded with what he could, surrounding the Jordan with a turquoise-blue light and infusing her with a surge of strength.

"Push up with your left leg!" the Jordan shouted, her pointed ears still ringing and half deaf as she pulled the injured Captain up. This time he did scream, but he complied. She got under his right side and held his right arm over her shoulder.

"We have less than twenty seconds before that fighter can turn for another run at us," the Captain told her, his breath coming in ragged gasps. His face was streaked with sweat and grime and blood. "You need to go."

"When I say left," Blue told him, "you are going to plant your left foot down and lunge, when I say right, you are going lean on me." He looked at her doubtfully and she gave him the most reassuring smile she could. "It'll be just a like three-legged race at a JTC picnic."

Captain Todd's eyes closed, leaking tears.

"Left!" Blue shouted. The Captain planted his left foot and heaved his weight forward.

"Right!" Todd leaned on the Jordan and she yanked at his form and together they staggered ahead.

"Left!"

The processed was repeated. And repeated again. And again.

Together they lurched towards Cyan but they had only made it a half dozen yards before the Jordan could see the fighter circling back. "Left!" she shouted, urgency fueling her determination. "Right! Left!"

They were almost to Cyan's stairs when the jet opened fire. Clods of dirt exploded in a line, racing towards them as Blue tried to heave the Captain up the steps. At this point, however, he was close enough for Cyan to pull on his own, sucking in both the Captain and the Jordan as the hot rounds ricocheted of his wings and cut into the earth next to his silvered talons.

His door closed as the Captain collapsed on the floor and Blue ran for the cockpit. Cyan was already rising from the ground as she dropped into her seat.

She opened a communication link with the Copper Dragon as her Fledgling shot through the air and up into the atmosphere.

"This is Jordan Blue," she announced. "I have Captain Todd. He is in critical condition. I will be entering Fighter Bay…".

"The Womb!" Todd ordered with the strength he had left. "I want you protecting the eggs!"

"I will be entering the Womb, under Captain Todd's orders.

I want an entire medical team already cleared and waiting."

"Copy that, Jordan," a voice responded.

Blue's lone eye scoured the moonscape but it looked like the worst had come and gone. Even the Dragons were being abandoned by the Chimeran fighters. Cyan cleared the blue of the moon's atmosphere and entered the cold black beyond. He streaked through space, covering millions of miles in seconds.

"They don't..." Captain Todd gasped.

Blue turned her head to see him and her eye widened. She had forgotten about the comatose Aridian laid out upon her bed. She had no idea what would happen should the secret she was harboring be found out, but she needn't worry at the moment. The injured Captain was flat on his back, situated with the top of his head pointed aft and he was too immobile to turn and take a look.

"They don't what, sir?" Blue asked.

The Captain raised his head so he could see her. "They don't have picnics at the Jordan Training Center." His head dropped back down and Blue could hear him laugh softly, despite the pain he was suffering.

"You are right about that, sir," she agreed before turning to face front. "But this would be their idea of one," she said under her breath, "if they did."

The Copper Dragon became visible in the distance and then grew before her. Short minutes later she was guiding Cyan through the nitrogen field that protected the vast open space in the port side of the Dragon and set him down on the copper-colored Dragonskin floor.

Blue bolted from her seat before he was even settled. She thrust her hands under the Captain's arms and began to move him as carefully as she could toward the door as it opened. Still, his face was a mask of pain.

"Cyan?" she asked but there was no need. The Copper Dragon was already encasing her Human Dragon Child in waves of golden light, easing his pain even as the Jordan slid him to the door where an air gurney was waiting.

With the help of the Dragon's Chief Medic she pulled him onto the floating cot and followed him as it descended. She began to back away as he was surrounded by medical staff but he caught her by the arm. She looked into his brown eyes, seeing clearly the bursts of copper stars within them.

"Thank you, Jordan Blue," he said. "Not for saving me, I was already beyond that when you landed - but for coming for me, and getting me back here."

Jordan Blue gave him a solemn nod as his eyes bored into her for an eternal second, and then slipped closed and his hand slid from her arm.

Then he was being whisked away by medics and floating nurse droids. She followed slowly, stopping at the gate in the detfleck.

The wake of activity around the injured Captain was filled with a deafening silence.

Blue handed her pistol to a guard and opened her mouth so the doctor on watch could look around with a penlight. She went through the rest of the security requirements automatically while her eye traveled over the section of the bay that was the Womb.

Her gaze was drawn, of course, to the eggs. Each was the size of a two-man space pod - one a brilliant orange and the other bright yellow. Safe in their cradles, they were surrounded in a half-circle by ten crew members of the Dragon dressed in coveralls the color of copper wire, armed with laser rifles and wearing double holsters of photon pistols.

Next to them were a group of people that Blue knew could only be cadets. Eight would-be Jordans, dressed in ashy gray coveralls, stood singly and in pairs talking quietly.

Blue recognized one immediately and her lips pulled down at the corners as the security man returned her sidearm. The

Jordan gave him a nod as she accepted the pistol and dropped it into the holster on her hip, her eye still fixed on the dark-haired elf.

Gemma was watching the departure of the Captain with a look of distaste. Blue frowned.

She is not happy to see him return, she thought with a touch of unease. The cadet finally turned her narrow face and, her dark eyes spying the Jordan, gave her a thin-lipped smile.

Blue remained by the gate in the detfleck and listened. As usual, the first thing her ears picked up were the sounds of heartbeats: the security man and the medic. The seven men and three women guarding the eggs. Strong beats, ready for battle and full of relief that the Captain had returned. The beat of the cadets, strong with an undercurrent of nervousness.

Except Gemma.

Blue could hear the pulse of her heart, angry that the Captain had returned. It was almost enough to distract the Jordan.

Almost.

Blue turned her face to the eggs and began to move towards them. The heart of the Copper Dragon, made of starfire and also glad at the return of Captain Todd, beat steady and slow like a bass drum.

But there was a note in that beat, a note of sorrow.

Is it for Captain Todd? she wondered. *Or for ...*

The Jordan neared the line of armed guards and, other than their own heartbeats, the silence was maliciously alive. The tallest guards were in the center and one, with dark blonde hair and gray eyes that were slightly close-set, nodded as Blue stopped in front of him.

"Jordan," he greeted formally.

"Where is your Engineer?" she asked.

"He is aboard the Silver Dragon," he answered. "The IGC

has been short-handed so he has been rotating back and forth every four months, monitoring both the Dragons and their eggs."

The black-clad Jordan swallowed down her fear and gave him a small smile. "May I?" she asked, inclining her blonde head towards the eggs. The guard hesitated for a moment only because of the situation occurring outside the Dragon. But, knowing that she was a Jordan - an IGC officer just shy of being a commander, he dipped his head and stood aside.

Blue passed through their line and, after a few strides, stopped in front of the progeny of the Copper Dragon.

She reached up and gently laid a slim-fingered hand on the rough surface of one egg and then reached across to the other.

She took a deep breath, waiting. Then she took another.

Nothing.

No heartbeats.

She kept her face impassive as she regarded the eggs before her.

Dead?

No.

She thought back to the Womb at the time when Cyan had hatched. It had been hot. Stifling. Most of the cadets had stripped down to their smallclothes. It was warm here in the bay, but not hot.

Blue's keen eye swept the area once again. The cadets had not changed from the coveralls they arrived in from the Jordan Training Center. She knew the Dragon kept the area warm for the eggs, but the eggs produced their own heat as well.

Because these are not eggs, she thought. *They're decoys. The real ones are gone and have been for some time.*

"Balls and shit," she whispered.

Captain Brogan, bereft of his transport back to Opal, left the bay of the Beryl Dragon that was still dispatching her combat jets. He made his way to the bridge, crew members stepping aside respectfully as he passed.

The bridge of the Beryl Dragon was a mirror of the one on his own Dragon, save for the officers at the controls.

Captain Slater stood amid the swarm of activity in the control room, calmly issuing orders. His Executive Officer, Commander Wu, stood by the Coms and Navigation Officers.

The holos over the control dash, however, were not of Opal and Beryl. They were images of the Lucca moon, and the Copper and Silver Dragons.

"Holy hell," Brogan whispered. Looking up, and out the eyes of the Dragon, Brogan could see that the nearby conflict was already falling apart. The Chimeran fighters were breaking away and heading back to the Battle Cruiser.

"Most of them are pursuing your craft," Slater informed the other Captain.

"Why?" Brogan asked. "They have to know they can't catch it."

"They know," Slater assured him. "But they are following as fast as they can. Opal has not been attacked, but another Battle Cruiser has entered her quadrant."

He jerked his head at the Navigations Officer and a holo of the Opal Dragon appeared above the right side of the console, the massive cruiser approaching her at top speed.

Brogan felt his hands clench involuntarily.

The cruiser cut her engines but the laws of motion kept her burning through space at an outrageous clip. All in the bridge watched as fighter jets spewed from the side of the gigantic battleship identified on the holo as the *Carthage.*

The same moment, the Captain's Bloodjet entered their visual field followed by the fighters from the *Resurrection.*

"The hounds to the hunter," Brogan said, his tone like acid.

Slater nodded.

They watched as the fighters from the *Carthage* descended on the Bloodjet, each swooping down to fire a single shot into the cockpit.

"That's strange," Slater murmured. "You would think they would be trying to blow it to bits."

"Maybe they are trying to draw us out," Wu said softly, his hand resting on the back of the Communication Officer's chair.

By then, the fighters from the Opal Dragon had arrived and were firing upon the Chimera. The enemy, having treated the commander's private craft like a game in a carnival, was now chased off quite easily. The tattered steel and blasted glass of the Bloodjet was proof of their accomplishment. Her Captain stared at the remains of the craft. Unsettled as much by the sight of his ruined jet as he was of the idea rising in his mind.

"Shit," Brogan muttered.

"Sir?" the coms man queried, his voice loud but not quite firm as he turned his eyes to Captain Slater. "I have Admiral Kasey."

"Put him through the open line," Slater said. The Communications Officer nodded and turned back to his board.

"Admiral?" Slater affirmed aloud.

The IGC Admiral's voice came over the open com to the bridge. "Captain Slater. You are to take the Beryl Dragon to the following coordinates. A string of numbers in a rainbow of colors appeared above the navigation dash. "I am sending the Opal Dragon in the opposite direction."

"Yes, sir," Slater agreed, glancing at Brogan. The message on the other Captain's face was clear. He wanted to get back to his Dragon, not farther away from it. Slater did not blame him. "The fight is over. We will depart as soon as I have all my pilots back on board, sir. I am recalling them now."

There was a barely audible grunt from the Admiral before the communication was cut.

"Thank you," Brogan said earnestly. He touched the com embedded in his ear, opening a link with his own bridge. "Commander Mattatock," he called out.

"Yes, sir," Scarlett answered immediately. "Not to worry, sir. The Dragon is not under attack and the..."

"I am aware of that, thank you. Now I need you to get me back aboard my Dragon."

On the Opal Dragon, Scarlett clenched her jaw. She could not physically expose the Captain to what was happening. She wanted nothing more at that moment than to be in Fledge, tearing the brazen Chimeran fighters to bits. Fledge would have no problem with those little shits.

Fledge.

"Captain Brogan," she said.

"Yes?"

"I am sending my Fledgling for you. Please get yourself to the starboard side bay."

"Yes, ma'am," he agreed immediately. He dipped his head quickly to Slater and Wu. "Commanders," he acknowledged and turned briskly and strode from the bridge, making haste for the bay - stopping along the way to collect his Engineer.

Doc Kuri, a deep furrow between his dark brows, watched them go.

Scarlett, focusing in a way she had never done before, communicated her wishes to Fledge. She thought he might be reluctant, but he surprised her.

By the time the Fledgling had retrieved Calyph and Brogan, the Beryl Dragon's fighters had returned and the mighty IGC Warship disappeared from sight. The Captain and the Engineer were back aboard their own Dragon within minutes while the Chimeran Battle Cruiser *Carthage* was undergoing the massive effort to leave the scene as quickly as possible.

Calyph followed Brogan as he hurried to the bridge, feeling the Dragon move - an amazingly gentle shift as she prepared to shoot through space.

Back aboard his own ship everyone stepped deftly aside, most stopping in their tracks to stand at attention. Brogan hardly noticed as he rushed to the helm in a forced effort not to break into an all-out run.

Opal cloaked him in a blanket of feelings, mostly tearful gratitude at his return. He sent back what he could as he hurried along. Reaching the bridge, Scarlett turned and heaved a sigh of what he thought must be relief to relinquish the burden of command.

Indeed, Scarlett was relieved. She pulled the iridescent band from her arm immediately. "The Captain has the conn," she announced.

"The Captain has the conn," Anatoli echoed.

"Thank you, Jordan," Brogan returned. His solemnity dissolved seeing her, seeing everyone, his crew. To see the ones he held so dear went far beyond mere relief.

"Do you know how much that jet was worth?" he softly reprimanded Scarlett, a smile edging his lips.

"Not as much as your life, sir," she responded. She attempted to return his smile, but it faltered. Brogan felt his own expression fall.

"What is it?" he asked.

Scarlett lifted her chin. "Captain Todd is dead. Jordan Blue rescued him during the battle but he passed away shortly after she had him back aboard the Copper Dragon. Captain Hunter has been grievously wounded."

Brogan closed his eyes and let his head drop, but only for a second. He lifted his head and fixed his eyes on Chiara. "You have the coordinates the Admiral sent?"

"Yes, sir."

"Show me."

A hologram formed over the console that displayed a string of numbers and the quadrant of space the numbers represented. Also visible was the moon that had so recently been attacked.

"It makes sense," Scarlett commented. "It is probably the last place the Chimera would be looking for us. Yet, should they return, we are the best equipped to engage them."

"And Commander Blaylock is still there?" Brogan asked, looking to Dareus.

"Yes, sir, though he has secured a jet and is making ready to leave."

"Well, this will shorten his trip considerably. Let him know where to meet us. We can make it there in less than a few seconds." He turned his eyes to Chiara. "Take us there," he commanded.

# ONE NINE

- Reality is just a story we tell ourselves.

Faith, having taken up a temporary residence at the Last Castle, had brought most of her staff with her. Mari was there to see to her wardrobe and the rest of her personal belongings as well as to assist Penny whenever needed. Geary was there, of course, and had brought Tom and DJ as well. A skeleton crew had been left behind at the villa which included a number of security men as well as the cleaning staff along with Cook and Bowe. Charity already had enough cooks in her kitchen.

Faith set up a makeshift office in a parlor suite close to the conservatory. It was brightly lit, mostly from the artificial sunshine that streamed through the floor to ceiling windows that also gave a magnificent view of the gardens.

A desk had been set up with a compute and three monitors, close to the windows but situated so that she did not have her back to them. She would have preferred the privacy of her bedroom suite but she wanted to be close to Charity.

Charity as well preferred to work in the privacy of her bedroom suite, though hers was not just multi-roomed but enormous. An entire tower of the Last Castle belonged to each of the sisters, but Charity was the only one who used hers to the fullest.

The bottom floors of her tower were thousands of square

meters and staffed with enough people to run a corporation or crew a ship. The middle floors were full of artfully racked clothes, night clothes, dresses, suits, shoes, and jewelry. The second level from the top had a bath, shower, steamer, sauna, and styling room where her hair and make-up was done on a daily, sometimes even hourly, basis depending on her schedule.

The top room of the tower ensconced her bedroom suite which included a living retreat with two chairs and a couch that faced a fireplace, a sumptuous, canopied bed with tied back drapes and covered with seven pillows - all in different shapes and sizes. On the far side of the bed was an alcove that housed a woman's vanity. Her own ingress to the GwenSeven mainframe.

There was a smaller, but still quite large, bathroom. And, of course, a small (small in comparison to the others) closet.

However, with things being as they were, she had cried off her many social engagements and sat working in the same room as her sister. A feather-weight acrylic was held in one hand while the other tapped and skimmed, her white lacquered nails clicking on its surface.

Here, instead of bodyguards, the women were flanked by personal assistants. Most waited in the wings while others, like Penny and Aide, hovered close to their employers.

Nathan, who was always a distraction, had been dismissed to work in the underground hangar or indulge in any leisurely pursuits that did not involve the de Rossi sisters for the afternoon.

Still, Jasyn lingered in the parlor with a diabolo menthe in his hand, watching Faith as she worked. Occasionally his gaze would drift to Charity and he would smile. He had remarked the previous day after she had been on her acrylic for hours without a cocktail in sight, that he had never seen her so industrious, or sober.

"Don't tell anyone," she had replied with an impish smile, motioning for two of her personal assistants, "it would ruin my reputation."

Jasyn had returned her smile and shook his head even as it occurred to him that she ran the finances for the largest corporation in the known universe *and* was a Director in the financial branch of the InterGalactic Council.

She must work all the time, he thought, *behind closed doors. When does she sleep?*

His dark hazel eyes went to Faith, knowing that she worked round the clock. How many times had he awoken in the middle of the night to find her side of the bed cold and looking around only to see her a few feet away, sitting in front of the mainframe?

He would watch her sometimes, her finger gliding across the ghostpad as it went from letter to letter instead of typing, afraid even the slightest noise might disturb his sleep. She was always considerate in those kinds of ways.

Faith glanced up, as if sensing him watching her, and he averted his gaze. He felt slightly ill. The dark-haired construct put his glass down on a side table, deciding the normally refreshing drink had too much syrup in it.

Don't be an idiot, he told himself. *You feel sick about what is happening. You put up a wall in anger and she put one up in defense.*

The trouble was, he had no idea how to break through either one. His eyes went back to Faith, who had promptly returned to whatever business was occupying her morning.

She had just taken a call on her comset when one of Charity's many assistants entered the room and spoke quickly to Aide. Aide was at Charity's side moments later, speaking quietly and quickly. Charity stood and handed her the acrylic she had been using.

"Have Chaz give her clearance," she instructed before her eyes went to the PA who had brought the news. "Have Chihiro clear the hangar," she told her. The PA gave her a nod and disappeared. "And you," she said, addressing Emily, Aide's own PA. "Get me something to drink."

"What would you like?"

Charity exhaled a sigh of impatience. "I don't care, use your imagination." Realizing what she had just said, her green eyes went to Emily whose brown eyes were large with consternation. Charity sighed again, softer this time. Emily was a construct. She had little to no imagination. "A Nero Ruskie," she told her before turning her attention to Faith.

The older de Rossi had finished her own call quickly and risen to her feet.

"We have a Fledgling on approach," Charity informed her.

"I surmised as much." She took the comset from where it was hooked over her ear and gave it to Penny. "Amberle?"

Charity nodded as Emily handed her a short crystal glass with dark liquid over a single but large cube of ice. She took a sip and gave a nod to show both she approved of the drink and was ready to go.

Faith led the way from the room with her sister on one side and Penny on the other, Jasyn following close behind. Guards, who would normally fall in around them, watched from shadowed alcoves.

They exchanged one hallway, their heels clicking on the stone floor, for another. They took another off to the left, away from the access to the towers where the stone floor led towards the lifts.

Geary stood alone in front of the open doors of the elevator that waited to take the de Rossi sisters down beneath the castle. Penny broke away from the group, taking up a post on the side of the elevator opposite Geary.

She knew all too well that whatever meetings were happening in the hangar these days were strictly private. No attendants, no security detail.

Not officially, anyway.

Geary's steely eyes, however, met with Jasyn's dark ones in mute acknowledgement. The construct gave him a barely perceptible nod in return. The two had developed a strange and entirely silent kinship along with a mutual respect due to the fact that they both strove to keep Faith protected at all costs.

Charity drained her cocktail and handed the glass to Penny. The de Rossi sisters entered the lift first, followed by Jasyn. Each of them turned around to face the doors as they closed. Faith drew in a long gulp of air and blew it out.

Hope! she thought with a fervor that burned all the way down her body. *After all this time! And possibly Faith, the* **real** *Faith, if she had gotten Hope, there was a chance they could be together.*

The elevator began its descent, and Faith felt her breath begin to come faster and she blinked back tears. Keeping her eyes focused on Jasyn's broad shoulders, her hand reached out seeking Charity only to find Charity already reaching for her.

Their hands clasped, they waited with bated bath as the lift came to a smooth stop and they both gave the hand they held a gentle squeeze before letting go. The doors opened and Jasyn led the way out, his dark eyes going everywhere before narrowing as they spied Nathan.

The tall Engineer approached the small group just as the green Fledgling dipped into the opening to the cavern and rushed towards them. It braked hard as it went by, turning with tight precision and landing gracefully on the tarmac of the hangar.

The gust created by its passage blew Faith's hair in a chaotic whirl that she hardly noticed. Nathan reached down and smoothed her locks, brushing them away from her face.

Jasyn froze, fists clenched, but Faith either failed to notice or chose not to notice that as well.

As the young Fledgling Dragon settled on its haunches,

silver skin glimmering green, she was only vaguely aware that she was again holding hands with Charity. A set of steps melted down from the door that was opening in its side and, after a moment, Amberle's fluff of pink coils over her dusky face popped out to look around.

Spying those waiting, she gave her jacket a tug and exited the Fledgling. Faith realized she was squeezing Charity's hand with a near bone-crushing force and loosened her grip. Charity seemed not to notice either way, her green eyes intent upon the young Dragon and the young Jordan.

When Amberle reached the tarmac the steps retracted and the door irised closed, becoming smooth Dragonskin one more.

Amberle stood before them alone.

The young Jordan took a second to gather her courage, lifted her chin and began walking towards them, her expression fixed.

"I think I'm going to need another drink," Charity said softly.

"I think we all will," Faith replied under her breath as Amberle reached them, then she lifted her chin as well. Despite the way her gut was wrenching inside her, Faith stepped forward and forced a smile. "You must be tired," she said. "And hungry."

Amberle's shoulders dropped. She gave Faith a sheepish smile and nodded. Jasyn looked at Faith and swallowed down the sore heat that burned in his throat. He knew how disappointed she had to be yet was making the effort to care for someone else instead.

She is not cold-hearted, he told himself in a silent but harsh reprimand. *She never was. And I need to find a way back to her. But I need to find a way to remember her first. Remember us.*

He followed the small group back to the lift and up into the castle.

They returned to the Castle proper, Nathan accompanying

them this time along with Amberle. Faith had used the gold cuff on her wrist to call Penny as they were departing the hangar and the parlor was already prepared by the time the small group arrived. Charity had also made a call to her head of security via a similar device, a slim silver bracelet, to have any microphones and cameras in the parlor disabled.

A number of servants from the bar staff appeared as the small party entered the room, along with a butler guiding a pair of floating trays. Everyone found seats in a circle of couches and chairs, Jasyn moving with a deft quickness to put himself between Nathan and Faith.

As they were served libations, the butler held out a small plate towards Amberle and lifted off a golden dome. The young Jordan, expecting food, was surprised to see a small towel, carefully folded into the shape of a flower with steam rising from it.

"So you may freshen up," the man told her.

Amberle took the hot damp towel and used it to clean her hands and, after a moment of deliberation, gave her face and neck a quick once over as well. The butler gave her a smile as she put the used towel back on the plate. He set up a table close to her and took items off the floating trays and placed them down.

Though he seemed kind, Amberle oddly missed the droids that normally waited on her. She eyed the plates of spring rolls and small meats with picks in them for easy eating along with dipping sauces. She was hungry, but she knew she would need to do some explaining before she jumped on the mini buffet.

Thirsty, she drank down a large glass of water and then met the eyes of the others as the serving staff drifted away. She glanced around nervously and, though it felt like they were alone, her eyes fell on Charity.

"Is it okay talk?" she asked. The de Rossi socialite gave her a smile and nodded. The young Jordan relaxed somewhat in her chair. "You were right about Venus," she told them, "and the elves. They are there. Hope is not. But her daughter is."

Charity's green eyes went to her sister, but Faith was staring at Amberle, tears shimmering in her own eyes.

"Can you describe her?" Faith asked softly.

Amberle nodded quickly. "She was dirty, covered in blood..."

Faith's brown and gold eyes widened even as her brows drew together over them. "That's not quite what I meant."

"Oh," Amberle said. "Sorry. She is slim, with red hair. *Really* red hair."

Jasyn saw Charity's fist clench involuntarily and the breath hitch in Faith's chest as the young Jordan continued.

"Her eyes are narrow, like an elf, and they are brown and green and gold."

"Did she have my sister's rings?"

Amberle swallowed, her dark throat moving almost imperceptibly. "Two of them. She said that one had belonged to her father."

"Hope must have given one to the monk," Charity surmised aloud, slightly surprised.

"Hahn," Jasyn said softly in realization or remembrance, the name coming to his mind unbidden. "His name was Hahn."

Feeling she had given them enough for the moment, Amberle selected an item from the tray. Pinching the silver pick between her thumb and finger, she dipped the skewered morsel into a sauce at random and ate it. She placed the pick on an empty plate and had tried three more meats and sauces before she realized the soft conversation in the room had paused and everyone was looking at her.

"Tell us more," Faith said. "Do you know why she was dirty and bloody? Was she hurt? Is she alright?"

Amberle finished chewing the piece of poultry and nodded.

"She was armed with swords and knives. She, and the elves,

had been fighting a battle. And losing."

"What happened?" Nathan asked.

"Jade and I got there just in time. We broke up the battle and chased off the nasty creatures they had been fighting. Verdana really scared the hell out of them. And torched quite a few."

Charity's eyes widened over the rim of her glass and Nathan chuckled softly.

"And you spoke with her?" Faith prodded.

"Yes. She showed me the rings, two of them, that she carried with her. She said the stones would grow brighter if she put them on. She also said she had not seen her mother since she was a child. I got the feeling that she did not remember her, not very well at least."

Tears filled Faith's eyes once more and she blinked them away. "I want you to go back for her."

Now it was Amberle's turn to blink rapidly, in surprise. "She doesn't want to come."

"She will."

Amberle's feathery brows went up over her green and brown eyes. "I'm not so sure. She really had her hands full."

Faith's chin lifted. "Were there any other people there? Fighting alongside her and the elves?"

"Yes."

"Describe them."

"There were some men, very tall." Her eyes went to Nathan. "Like him."

"The natives to Eris," Charity mused aloud, "were Nordic, from Earth. Must be them. Some of them. There was also a race of elves, Sylvan I believe."

Amberle nodded. "There were a few elves, different from most of the others. They looked like children."

Charity nodded. "That's them."

"I want you to go back," Faith repeated, insistent.

Amberle shook her head, her pink coils of hair brushing her dark cheeks. "You don't understand, she did not want to come with me. And I could hardly force her. Speaking of which, I can hardly do anything! I have a weapon I don't know how to use, a Fledgling I am only barely acquainted with, and a job that has no fixed description. Who am I? What am I? What am I supposed to do?" she demanded.

There was a moment of silence before Charity rose to her feet and plucked a cocktail from a tray and handed it to Amberle. "The eternal questions," she answered, "we all ask ourselves."

Faith rose with a frown and removed the glass from Amberle's hand and replaced it with a small bottle of soda as Charity retook her seat.

"Were there any others there fighting with her?" she asked pointedly as she leaned back against the arm of a chair. "Ones who looked like humans? Extraordinarily beautiful humans?"

Amberle swallowed and nodded. "Yes."

Charity turned her green eyes to Faith, blonde brows raised in astonishment. "Marco's people?"

"I'm certain of it," Faith answered without looking at her sister. She kept her own eyes fixed on the Jordan. "I want you to go back for her - for my, for *our*, niece. I am quite sure she will come willingly."

Amberle puffed out her dark cheeks and blew out a burst of air. "I'm guessing you know what I need to do to make that happen?"

The corners of Faith's lips pressed into her cheeks in what might have been a smile or a grimace. "You are going to make her an offer she can't refuse."

Amberle rolled her eyes and let them fall back down to Faith. "I want to meet the other Jordans."

Faith gave her a nod. "I can arrange that."

"And I need to learn how to shoot."

"I can arrange that," Jasyn said.

"Is there anything I can do for you?" Nathan drawled, his voice almost a purr. "Adjustments to your living quarters in your Fledgling? Anything to make you more comfortable?"

Amberle swallowed. There was no one who made her more uncomfortable than the tall Engineer. "I think I'm okay. But thank you."

"Let me know if you change your mind," Nathan told her, his smile wide and lecherous.

Now it was Jasyn who rolled his eyes.

"Of course," Amberle answered, her own gaze darting nervously to Charity for help.

The white-haired socialite, always able to break any tension, heaved a sigh and rose up from her small sofa. Nathan reached out a hand to help her to her feet.

"But, speaking of personal quarters, we have a suite of rooms prepared for you, Amberle. Sleep in your Fledgling if you like, though there is a real bed if you choose to use it. Along with a tub and a shower, and closets full of clean clothes."

"That actually sounds wonderful," Amberle admitted.

"Again," Nathan said, "if you need any help…"

"Oh, Nathan!" Charity admonished. "Help *me* to the bar."

"With pleasure. Which one?"

Charity's laugh was light but genuine. "Any of them!"

 # TWO ZERO

- Truth is like a Dragon's shadow, sometimes you are the only one who can see it.

For the Dragons living in the new Age of Dragons, the recognition of spatial coordinates was as good as being there. The Opal Dragon made the crossing, halfway across the star system, in a matter of seconds.

For those working in the bridge the movement was slight, a rocking as if being in a vehicle that had just gently accelerated and carefully braked. Those on their feet braced themselves or placed on hand on a console or bolted chair to keep steady. Those seated barely noticed. Everyone continued as if nothing had happened.

The ship settled outside the orbit of Lucca; the Copper and Silver Dragons had both departed, both leaving the system. Captain Brogan turned from the sweeping view of the moon and motioned to Scarlett. She followed him to the pit, took the few steps down, and took a seat facing him.

"Tell me everything that happened while I was on board the Beryl Dragon."

Scarlett recounted everything to him.

When she was done, Brogan planted his elbow on the arm of his chair and his hand came up, his thumb resting under his chin and his forefinger over his upper lip.

"They were after the Captains this time. That's what you think?"

"Yes, sir."

"Anything else occur to you? Anything odd?"

The eyes of the Red Jordan glanced up from where she was sitting in the pit. Dareus and Chiara were at their consoles, as usual. Major Hearth, one of the Dragon's Security Officers was in the bridge, engaged in a hushed discussion with Anatoli. Even the Captain's personal steward was there, wiping down the chairs at the helm.

The Jordan was hesitant to voice her thoughts in what felt like such a public manner and then she realized that it was exactly what Brogan wanted her to do. If he had wanted their discussion to be self-contained, he would have raised the privacy wall around the pit.

"I think it is beyond the shadow of a doubt that the Captains were targeted," Scarlett said. "More than that, I think it was their aim to make sure each Captain was killed but not annihilated. That there was enough of each body to be returned to their Dragon. If that is the case and I am correct in my assumption of what it means, then the Chimera are privy to some serious shit. IGC intel that is classified to officers O-5 or above."

Captain Brogan regarded her for a few moments with his pearly blue eyes. Then his hand dropped from his chin and his gaze fixed on the opalescent band that Scarlett had returned to him. He folded it and folded it until it was no more than a small square. He looked up and met Scarlett's dark eyes with his own.

"You saved my life today, Jordan. That's twice now, in less than a fortnight."

"You've saved mine plenty."

Brogan gave her a grunt and a begrudging smile.

"Commander Blaylock is on approach," Dareus announced.

The Captain made a face that the Jordan did not miss.

"Is there something else you would like to discuss?" she asked, her voice soft.

Brogan nodded. "There is. A few things to be honest. But this is not the time or place. I need to speak with my XO." He rose to his feet and the Jordan quickly did the same. "Thank you again, Jordan Scarlett. You are dismissed."

Scarlett left the bridge quickly, not wanting to see or speak with the returning Executive Officer.

She was not that lucky.

The Jordan was within steps of her personal quarters when she rounded a curve in the Artery and found herself face to face with Blaylock. And the shock of him could not be more if he had shot her in the gut.

Her dark eyes went wide, glints of crimson burning in their depths, as his smell filled her nostrils. It was the same as it had been before, acrid and sterile, and she had always assumed it had simply been the smell of his soul, if he had one.

Now she knew different.

It was like the smell of a med cen. Or a hospital.

What brought it home this time with the speed and force of a punch from a pugilist was that he was wearing a suit, rather than a uniform.

Scarlett recalled the last time she had seen such a man, an IGC Official, who had been wearing a suit rather than a uniform. A man who had been in the hospital room where her father had been lying, covered in bandages, refusing medication or anything for the pain of his wounds because he had wanted to remain lucid.

Wounds that, though severe, were supposedly not fatal. That was what the doctors had assured her brother. Scarlett had believed otherwise until only months ago, when she considered the possibility that the IGC Official who had been debriefing her father had also pressed a derm pin full of poison into the neck of Joe Mattatock as he thanked him for his service.

Even more recently, she felt positive that the man had undoubtedly done just that. Now, she was certain that the man who had done so was the one standing before her.

Her breath came out through her parted lips in a soft rush of wet heat.

You bastard! was what she was about to say, a murderous rush of blood beginning to race through her veins when a voice spoke inside her head. It was motherly and smooth, like a swath of silk being pulled across her brain. It was the voice of the Dragon.

Careful, Opal warned with quiet urgency, *he's dangerous.*

Scarlett's parted lips pulled back to reveal her teeth.

So am I, she responded silently. She felt the mother sigh, not in exasperation as most did with Scarlett, but with amusement and pride. The smile on the Jordan widened and she saw it register on the face of the Executive Officer.

He began to acknowledge her recognition with a smile of his own and she realized that she knew something else as well. His betrayal and ambition had no bounds. None.

"Hello, Chris," she said softly.

All amusement drained from his face.

"That's still Commander Blaylock to you," he reprimanded, his tone like a slap. "Or *sir*. You having command of the Dragon for a few moments does not exchange our places!"

"Yes, sir," Scarlett agreed.

He knows that I am on to him, she thought, *but he doesn't know to what extent. And he doesn't care.*

The smile returned to the junior commander's face as it twisted into a leering grin.

"Mind your words, Jordan, to myself as well as others. You would not want to rant or share far-fetched suppositions to anyone. It might sound like paranoia and a sure relapse into

SM. You could find yourself once again on medical leave.
Permanently this time. I could have you gone by dimlight and
you would never see your Fledgling again."

Scarlett's blood, already hot, began to boil. If not for her
training in stillness she might have done something so rash
that Blaylock would unquestionably have his way and she
would be back on forced leave. Possibly for good.

Instead, she opened her mind to the Dragon.

Hold him.

Scarlett was unsure of whether she was understood, or the
command obeyed. After all, she was not the Captain, not even
interim.

But she was a Jordan. Human-dragon-child. Daughter of
the Dragon.

She took a careful step closer to the Executive Officer. He
narrowed his eyes in suspicion but did not move.

Moving like a curious cobra, Scarlett swayed - moving away,
and then moving back quickly towards him so she was even
closer, her face right in front of his own.

The Executive Officer, smug with his threat, but
uncomfortable with the Jordan so close, tried to jerk away in
response but found himself unable to move back. Unable to
move at all. The color drained from his face as Scarlett took
another step, putting her body up against his.

She tasted her victory, though she did not smile.

She pressed in close, then leaned in even closer, till her
cheek was almost touching his cheek and her lips were
alongside his ear.

"And I could kill you with a thought," she returned softly.

Commander Blaylock found both his mind and body
paralyzed and fought against the fear that welled inside.

The Jordan stepped back, measured him with her dark
gaze, and left him there. When she rounded the corner out of

eyesight, the Executive Officer felt the strength return to his limbs. He staggered forward but kept on his feet.

Forcing himself to keep his breathing steady and even, he looked around the empty corridor. If he had been startled by the way Blue had disappeared right in front of him, he was deeply disturbed about what Scarlett had just done. He knew it had to do with the Jordans receiving the triptych.

Damn that Brogan! I knew we should not have given it to them. Moreover, I should have had Calyph draw a vial for Gemma when it was an opportune moment.

Fists clenched in anger; he turned to head for his personal quarters. Captain Brogan could wait. The Executive Officer was now sure it was time for him to leave the Opal Dragon. And for another Captain to meet with an unfortunate accident. But first, he now had a debt owed to Jordan Scarlett, and he knew just how to pay it.

હ⁊૭

"Congratulations on a job well done," JP said.

Jan Petrov bowed his head in response.

The Chimeran Commander addressed his officers, not in the bridge of the Chimeran Battle Cruiser like most Commanders would but in its chapel, which most Battle Cruisers did not have.

The chapel, one of the few areas of the ship to be carpeted, was dimly lit by faux candlelight. On the walls to either side were sconces of wrought silver that held plastique candles. Eight rows of wooden pews were split down the middle by a narrow aisle. The aisle led to an altar that displayed the symbol of the Zealot Cassar Church on the far wall – two circles laid side by side, touching but not crossing.

The two circles signified the two faces of the One – the creator and the destroyer – but the way they touched made the

symbol look like a more rotund version of the Chimeran logo –
the symbol of infinity.

JP stood in front of the altar, like a priest ready to deliver a
sermon. Also like a priest, he wore a heavy linen cassock that
belled out around his feet and a high, round collar that was
notched at the throat.

Petrov stood before him at the end of the aisle, seven pilots
lined up behind him. JP motioned for them to sit and they took
seats in the front pews, joining the officers already there.

The officers who were not on duty in the bridge had
already been called to the chapel. They were not the only ones
listening, the entire crew could hear the Captain's voice as it
was broadcasted throughout the entire ship.

"This was the most coordinated and successful attack," the
angelic-faced Chimeran said, "in the history of the Revolution."
There was an abundance of smiles and nods from the officers.
JP sighed. "Yet," he continued, "to be honest, I feel we are still
falling short of any real achievement."

Expressions softened on the face of the officers in the
bridge and a solemnity, more solemn than usual, filled the ship.

"The responsibility of this falls on my shoulders, not yours,"
he told them. "And I can assure you I am taking steps to change
that. I mean to see that this step is one that leads us forward.
That this battle starts a momentum that will bear us like a ship
coming to shore upon a wave."

A statement such as this would surely have been applauded
or cheered aboard any other ship, but the *Resurrection* was
not like most ships. Instead, eyes closed and heads bowed in
prayer. Some in fear. JP was not like most commanders like the
Resurrection was not like most ships. If he was displeased it
meant danger. Often the life-threatening kind.

"See to your stations and stay the course. I will see those
not on duty tonight at evening prayers." He held up two fingers
and inscribed a pair of circles in front of his chest.

Those seated rose gratefully to their feet to leave but JP motioned at Petrov to retake his seat. The others carefully cast their gazes aside, hoping that they would not be asked to stay as well.

They were lucky.

As they silently filed down the aisle and left the chapel, JP took a seat in the pew next to his Executive Officer.

"I meant what I said on a job well done," he told him. "Not just in this attack that you led, but your whole plan for it. Still..."

"It's not enough," Petrov said softly.

Both men sat facing the same way, their eyes fixed forward.

"It's not that," the young-looking commander consoled, his normally perfect forehead creased in consternation. "It's just that it is..." he trailed off as he searched for a way to explain.

"Not fast enough?" Petrov demanded in a hoarse whisper.

JP nodded. "Though I always believed, and still do, that patience and perseverance will win out in the end, I am feeling something different these days."

"A sense of urgency?" Petrov ventured, keeping his eyes still fixed on the wall before him, the altar just within his vision.

"Yes!" JP agreed with enthusiasm. "A sense of urgency! Like we have been chipping away at some great wall in order to bring it down, when we should just jam an imploder brick into a crack and blow it down!"

Petrov finally swung his face to the left to meet JP's blazing blue eyes with his own. "I have an idea."

JP nodded encouragingly and Petrov let out a deep breath and then cast his gaze down as he thought. JP's heart went out to him for it looked like it was no easy task for the bull-shouldered Executive Officer.

A furrow formed between Jan's golden brows.

"Maybe we are being too direct," he suggested.

JP's own auburn brows raised at this. "Too direct? What do you mean?"

Petrov's scowl deepened. "Maybe we need to be more... more sneaky."

JP leaned forward, attentive. "Tell me more. I am quite curious as to what you are thinking."

The face of his Executive Officer hardened. To the Chimeran commander, he looked like a young, but quite large, child struggling with an arithmetic problem. It made the expression on the Captain soften.

"I'm thinking," Jan said slowly, "that maybe instead of trying to break down the front door, we should try sneaking in the back."

〇〇〇

Blue passed through the membranous field of electrified nitrogen as she entered the starboard side Fighter Bay of the Iron Dragon. She had left the Copper Dragon without a word upon hearing the silent scream inside her head. She knew then that Captain Hunter had passed.

The Jordan checked first with her own Dragon, who had already fought off a small number of Chimeran jets. She let them know that she had been requested for an audience by the Captain of the Iron Dragon. Scarlett, of all people, had acquiesced and had let her know that Brogan would recall her as he saw fit or necessary.

Cyan landed amidst an array of combat jets. Blue peered about from her seat. The bay was immense but there were few people there other than some mechanics working on a variety of craft.

No fence of murderous detfleck, not even a security detail. The Jordan knew that it had been a long time since the Iron Dragon had eggs or Fledglings to protect.

Over eight hundred years.

Still, it was an IGC ship. A Dragon.

I guess if you can see anyone coming, she mused, *you can shoot them down long before they can become a threat.*

Even so, the lack of obvious security unnerved her a bit. She stood and tugged down on her black Mylar flight suit. Cyan opened and formed stairs for her on his side. Blue glanced aft before she left, regarding the unconscious Aridian for a moment.

I have to do something about her. And soon.

She ducked out of the opening and descended the stairs and as she did so was hit with the smell of the Dragon. Cyan closed up as soon as her boots were on the tarmac and she didn't blame him. Her mother Dragon, Opal, had a metallic smell but it was slight. Just an undertone, like the scent of ozone that came from the laundry bay.

The Iron Dragon smelled, well, like Iron.

Old Iron.

It felt like she was holding a handful of metal coins in her mouth. Saliva poured from her glands and she had to fight the urge to spit. The Jordan inhaled deeply through her nose, letting the smell fill her. She did it again as she walked away, letting herself habituate, letting it become a part of her. By the time she had crossed the living space of the hangar she hardly noticed the smell at all.

As she left the bay and entered a monstrous-sized Vein she came to a complete stop. She had announced herself upon approach to the Iron Dragon and had been informed by a monotone voice where she could land.

That was half an hour past and she had now been aboard for many minutes. But there was no one to greet her, no one to direct her. Yet what *really* set her nerves tingling, was that no one was looking at her. She got a glance now and then as she passed a pilot or a mechanic but a disinterested glance was all it was. It was more unnerving than if everyone had stared at her.

Well, it's a Dragon, she thought. *Its layout can't be much different than any other.*

She turned towards the fore of the ship and started walking, her chin high and her eye curious.

Indeed, it was like any other Dragon - in that barracks and services were in the aft (tail) of the ship. Before long, her strides brought her closer to the middle of the ship and she found she herself in the Atrium.

The Atrium on the Opal Dragon was a semi-open, ovoid space, three stories high midship. The Lower Atrium was lined with social bars, clubs, and a few light drugbars. The Mid Atrium was full of shops that provided all kinds of goods or services interspersed with a few apothecaries, coffee shops, and com-link cafés. The Upper Atrium consisted of all kinds of eateries, from snack counters to intimate vitro dining.

This place was nothing like it.

For Blue, it gave the impression of being in the lower Klick of Three Mile on Io. She had been to another place once that was also similar. It was a city on Indasia called New Shanghai, a metropolis shrouded in perpetual night.

The main street of the city, she recalled, had been lit with neon and halogen lights and lined with seedy shops that sold damn near everything. If one left the main drag, they were confronted with countless alleys filled with food carts, steam, and a racket of noise.

This is what the belly of the Iron Dragon was like. And not just three levels like Opal had. Blue counted three below and three above. And like New Shanghai, it was a crowd of hookah bars, clubs, drug dens, smoke shops, food carts and darkened apothecaries. And, from what Blue could surmise, most of the crew.

She began once again to make her way to the fore of the

ship, again curious that no one spared her more than a glance. Even those were few. Walking through the Atrium, the Jordan noticed something else. The crew was entirely elfin.

Hair colors and hairstyles were different, but there was no mistaking the thin faces and slight body frames. The slightly slanted eyes and pointed ears.

It makes sense, Blue thought, *for Khasper to have a crew of elves. If they prove themselves loyal, they will be around a long time. A real long time.*

The light was murky and full of shadows, though it was not dimlight on the ship. And the Atrium was so wide across that she could hardly see the other side. Though she knew the Iron Dragon dwarfed all others, being inside gave her a perspective she could not have imagined.

Walking along, Blue noticed narrow passageways between the shops and bars that looked like alleys in a city.

People lurked there - some crew, some who must be workers on the ship employed in the many businesses in the Atrium - distinguishable by their clothes. The crew wore iron-gray flight suits. The others wore whatever they wanted.

The great, dimly lit space in the belly of the Dragon seemed to go on and on, punctuated only by the alleyways dividing the boba carts and ramen stands like city blocks. Dark, narrow streets tapered into walkways that led deeper into the Atrium like capillaries in tar-blackened lungs.

When the Jordan finally reached the end she continued past the quarters where the officers lived and still the bridge was nowhere to be seen. She took an air shaft up to the next level and found more housing, mostly that of the Executive Officer.

Damn, I know this Dragon is enormous but this is crazy!

She went up one more level and then one more before she found the bridge. Once she was on the right level, it was impossible to miss. No guard, no doors, it looked more like a medical center than a control room for one of the deadliest ships in the universe. At least not like the one she was used to on her mother Dragon.

There was not just one communication dash with a single officer, but a communication center with many boards, screens, and holos and a number of officers. The same with navigation. Huge rectangles of acrylic panes displaying everything from weapons to coordinates were suspended from one end of the bridge to the other.

There was no sunken pit with chairs and cushions so the Captain may relax while discussing matters with his staff.

Instead, there was one great chair of white plastique with padded black leather surrounded by those great panes of holo-projecting acrylics.

Khasper sat in it, flanked by a steward and the steward's aide on one side and the Executive Officer on the other. There were three, smaller acrylics in front of him and he was studying one until the Jordan entered the bridge.

The Captain looked up and over to her and smiled, beckoning to her. His teeth were very white and, like before, looked very sharp.

"Jordan Blue!" he greeted as she joined him.

"Captain," she responded, dipping her white-blonde head.

"Here so soon? I thought you might stop in the Atrium first to…. refresh yourself."

Blue gave him a lopsided smile, the scars in her cheek rippling. "I prefer to handle business first."

The corners of Khasper's thin lips pressed into his narrow face. "The human in you, I suppose." One corner of his mouth quirked up higher than the other. "In that case," he exclaimed, "let's get to it!"

He planted his palms on the arms of his chair and pushed his lithe body up and out. "Let me start by giving you a tour of my ship."

Blue's eyebrows raised at this. Considering the size of the Iron Dragon, such a thing could take days.

"This is the bridge!" he announced, spreading his arms wide. Blue suppressed a smile. "I guess that just leaves my personal quarters."

This time the Jordan was unable to hold back a smile that showed her perfect teeth.

Khasper turned to his steward as Blue's gaze roved over the others close by to gauge their amusement at the Captain's roguish remark.

There was none.

Suddenly, she noticed that in the same way that no one looked at her due to indifference, no one looked at Khasper at all.

On purpose.

Not a soul looked the Captain in the eye, not even his steward as he took orders to have dinner and drinks sent to his room. Not his Executive Officer as Khasper gave him directions on what he expected for the next twelve hours aboard the ship.

They kept their gaze carefully averted, as if to make eye contact - even accidentally - might invoke some mythical curse.

Finished with his instructions, the elfin commander shifted his focus to the Jordan. "Come!" he ordered as he strode past her. Blue followed, curious as ever, noticing that the others now refused to make eye contact with her as well.

Down two levels and heading more to the middle of the Dragon, they arrived at the Captain's private quarters as three elves, dinner having been delivered, were departing. They gave the pair respectful murmurs as they left, their almond-shaped eyes downcast.

Jordan Blue gave a low whistle as she looked around. "Pretty posh," she remarked. Khasper gave her a shark-like smile and let her look around while he pulled a freshly opened bottle of champagne from an icy chill bucket and filled a chilled flute to the brim with golden bubbles.

The Jordan absently touched the patch over her right eye as she looked around in astonishment.

Captain Brogan, of course, had the largest personal space aboard the Opal Dragon. It was spartan compared to what she was seeing.

The most remarkable feature, other than the size, was that the eyes of the Iron Dragon continued down below the bridge to the Captain's quarters, offering a magnificent view of space. Blue immediately thought of Faith's villa with its great, glass windows. Especially since the floor here was also black polished marble. Yet Faith's floor was softened by thick white rugs and her furniture was white. Here, there were no rugs and everything was black. The only accents were inlays of iron.

"Do you like it?" Khasper asked, handing her the flute of champagne. Blue accepted and took a sip as she nodded.

"I do."

"I fashioned it after a penthouse apartment I saw in New Tokyo, centuries ago. Is that what it makes you think of?"

Blue smiled. "No. It actually makes me think of something quite different, but not a place."

Khasper's black brows went up over his black eyes as he took a sip from a steaming cup with no handle. "Please," he intoned, "share what it makes you think."

"Seeing this," Blue tried to explain with a shake of her head, "makes me think of my own Dragon, and of my Fledgling. And it makes me think that anything is possible."

The Captain gave her an appraising smile and tilted his head to a low table of polished ebony that faced the diamond glass eyes of the Dragon. The table, flanked on three sides by low slung black leather couches, had been set for dinner.

Blue took the seat on the right-hand side of the table and Khasper sat on the long couch, but close to her, on her left. He removed the iron lids from the small cast-iron pans and poured oils and sauces from cruets into tiny ebony dishes for dipping.

The Jordan was unfamiliar with much of the fare but did not hesitate trying any of it, including the slices of raw fish. Especially when fed to her by Khasper via the tips of his ebony chopsticks.

Both the Captain and the Jordan, both being so slight in form, were sated after only a short while – by the food at least.

Khasper refilled the Jordan's glass. He thought she would recline back with it, but she took a sip and set it back down on the table. She sat leaning forward with her forearms placed over her black-clad knees.

The Captain reached out a long-fingered hand, waxy smooth and fish-belly white, towards her cheek. Blue, unlike any other being that would most certainly be repulsed by the corpse-like hand and draw away, instead leaned towards him, her body tingling with curiosity and a shrill of excitement.

His fingers, strong and colder than those from a grave, traced the scar that ran across her face. She felt a shiver that thrummed within her bones but it was not one of repulsion, like she might have suspected, but a cold undulation of sexual desire.

Khasper felt it as well and a slow smile spread across his face. There were many that would suffer his touch, but the list of those who had ever enjoyed it was a short one indeed.

"What is it that you like, Jordan Blue? Besides champagne, of course."

The Jordan picked up her glass then sat back and crossed one leg over the other, giving the dark Captain a broad smile. "I like stories," she confessed. "Do you know any good stories?" Her smile widened slightly and the toe of her boot ran itself up the outside of the Captain's leg.

Khasper returned her lecherous smile with one of his own as he grasped the Jordan's boot and gently slid it from her foot. He did the same with the other and relaxed back into his chair.

"I know lots of stories," he confided, letting her continue to massage his calf muscle with her toe. "What kind of story are you in the mood for?"

"Oh," Blue exclaimed softly, as if the whole topic was as blasé as the weather, "you know, the usual. Love, danger, determination, espionage, etc." She laughed lightly and took a sip of champagne.

Khasper, still smiling his wanton smile, leaned forward and ran a slim fingered hand up her thin leg encased in black Mylar.

"And what type of story do you prefer - fiction or nonfiction?"

"Nonfiction, of course, since it is more titillating - as long as it is racy and exciting. I do not waste time being bored by mundane politics and matters of the state."

Khasper's smile widened into a grin as he slipped his finger under the hem of Blue's black flight suit at her ankle and began to caress the smooth white skin underneath.

"Yes," he said.

Blue waited for him to continue and, when it was apparent that it was all he had to say, she laughed. "That's one hell of story!"

Khasper's smile widened, showcasing his teeth once again that, though square and perfect, had an edge to them that scnt an imperceptible shiver up her spine. His dark eyes looked deep into her own. "But you aren't really after a story, are you? You are after answers."

Blue's face softened into a smile that was both knowing and appreciative. "But you don't know what story, what...answer, I am after," she said.

The dark Captain gave her another glimpse of his teeth. "Yes to all of them."

Blue laughed again. "But you don't..."

Khasper fell back into his chair, his head lolling on his

shoulders in mock exhaustion. "What? What?" he cried before leveling his face to hers again. "You want to know about the other Jordans? About my Executive Officer? About the Eris conspiracy?" Blue's eye widened in surprise as he went on. "Yes, yes, and yes!" he exclaimed with ersatz impatience but real joviality.

The Jordan took a sip of champagne to give herself a moment to pull it together. "First of all," she said, "let's put a pin in that last one. As for the first two, if you are so ready to admit the truth to the rumors, why are they rumors at all?"

Khasper smiled again. "Because you are the only one I have ever admitted them to."

Blue's surprise doubled. "Why me?"

The smile on the dark Captain widened. "You are different," he said. "And I have the feeling you would hear the lie in my voice."

Blue felt a chill run through her blood. "You know what the triptych did to me? How?"

His smile faded into nothing. "I make it my business to know."

The Jordan put her half-empty glass down on the table next her. "Then I think the time for bedtime stories is over, and it is time for bed."

Khasper's smile returned in a flash and, as he pulled her to her feet, the light in his cabin disappeared. Blue was right. His teeth were sharp. And he liked to bite.

❧❧❧

The next morning, nearly half of an hour before the Iron Dragon began to move out of dimlight, Jordan Blue slipped into her black flight suit that she guessed would cover most of the bite marks but cared little for the ones left exposed. As she zipped up the front, the dark Captain came from the bathroom fresh from a shower, a towel wrapped around his thin waist and another in his hand. He gave her a grin as he used the second towel to scrub his wet, black hair.

"Thanks for last night," he said, "you were unreal." Blue returned his grin, not letting his choice of words reflect in her countenance though they in fact struck a chord within her that started her heart racing. "As you always were, and still are," he finished.

Now Blue's expression faltered. "Not always," she remarked, keeping her tone as light as she could.

Khasper's grin widened. "Don't worry, your secret is safe with me."

The Jordan felt as if she had been punched in the gut. He knew, somehow, that she was not real. A multitude of possible denials and dismissive replies ran through her mind. None stuck.

"How did you know?"

"I make it my business to know. Though, personally, I would not have known on my own. Ferrous knew, and that was enough." He dropped the towel in his hand and slipped his arms around Blue's waist.

"You won't tell the IGC?" she asked.

"The what?" he asked in return. Blue frowned. His question was not playful or teasing, but genuine. Then it seemed to dawn on him. "Ah!" he exclaimed. "Them! No. That would serve nothing, as do they." The Jordan hoisted an eyebrow at this last comment but he tightened his grip on her waist before he continued. "I meant what I said, your secret is safe with me. I like you, Jordan Blue. I hope I see you again."

Blue finally relaxed in his embrace and returned his smile. "I like you too, Captain, and hope for the same. I'd like to hear about that Eris conspiracy you mentioned."

A soft chuckle came from deep within his throat. "Maybe

next time."

Blue gave him a lopsided small and turned to leave. She was a step away when he grabbed her by the wrist.

"And Jordan!" he exclaimed, holding her tightly with one hand. She turned back with a smile, but Khasper was not smiling. His narrow face was solemn. "Don't ever bring an Aridian aboard my vessel again."

Blue's scarred face went slack. "You knew of her, too?" The communication between the Captain and his Dragon was beyond supernatural.

"I only allowed it because you have kept her adequately sedated." The barest of smiles finally ghosted his thin lips. "And because I wanted to spend the night with you."

Blue gave her blonde curls a small shake in exasperation. "I haven't figured out…".

"There is a device called a Schakel…"

"I know, but the keys to them are universal, like handcuffs. And I can't get one without being seen somewhere. What am I supposed to do? Order one on the GW with my completely traceable credentials card and have it delivered to the Dragon?"

Khasper laughed softly and Blue thought the sound must be like the sound of fingernails scratching at the inner lid of a coffin.

"They can also be custom ordered by those who have the money and the connections. I am sure you know who I am thinking of, as it is also someone who can deliver such an item in the clandestine manner you require."

The Jordan's lips pressed down in a frown. "I think I know who you mean."

"I know you know," the Captain said with a smile. He pulled her close once more and kissed her goodbye.

 TWO ONE

- What is more real, what we see or what we believe?

Jan Petrov strolled leisurely along the sidewalk next to the mall. With his white-blonde hair and striking blue eyes, he fit in perfectly in the Upper Klick of Three Mile City on Io.

He walked by a martial arts studio where a bearded man in a black gi was instructing a group of small children as they punched and kicked at holo boards. He passed a dance studio and his blue eyes darted over every child there.

Nope, he thought.

The tall pilot continued and entered the mall, a great edifice built in the shape of a pyramid. He found a lift, there were four, one at each corner of the mall. He touched the light that would take him to the second level, then changed his mind and touched the blue light. The canted elevator, creeping up at an angle, stopped just before the highest floor. Petrov stepped out onto the level that held mostly specialty shops and mini day-spas.

He went into the Apothecary and made a quick purchase. He expected it to be wrapped in something effeminate, possibly embarrassing, but the sales lady put it in a silver box and then into a black, unmarked bag-box with small handles.

He thanked her and left, this time taking the elevator down to the second level. He exited the lift and entered chaos. Lights and noise and smells attacked his senses. This level was entirely comprised of shops made to entice young adults, teens and tweens. Stores sold animated toys, cheap trendy jewelry, handheld consoles and the playing chips that accompanied them.

It also enclosed the arcade, rows and rows of electronic games. Dancing games, flying games, fighting games. They beeped and screeched and thumped out music. It was accompanied by the high-pitched screams of adolescent fury and joy. The air was odorous with the aroma of fried foods and sugar. Lights and lasers flashed.

Petrov swallowed and entered the gaming area, hoping the bag made him look like a shopper rather than a predator.

He need not have worried.

Another handsome man, his hair darker than Petrov's but his blue eyes no less bright, was searching the area for his son. The Chimeran pilot saw that he even held a similar black box-bag.

The man looked at him with a nervous smile. "Any idea where Chimeran Pilot is?"

Petrov chuckled, and then laughed. He just couldn't help himself. "No," he answered. "Any idea where I can find Chimeran Revolution?"

This time the man chortled soft laughter. "I think that one is actually called Chimeran Rebellion."

Petrov shook his head with a beguiling smile. "I can never keep it straight."

The man sighed and looked into the madness of sirens and strobes. "Once more into the breach, eh?"

Petrov grinned. "You first."

The man straightened his shoulders and walked boldly into the fray. The Chimeran Commander was about to take a similar, parallel route, when his quarry skipped right by him, her dark curls bouncing.

〇〇〇

Penny approached her employer and stood next to her, a patient yet expectant expression on her face. Faith was quite familiar with Penny's expressions and knew that her PA had a call for her. An important one.

"It's your sister," she said. She did not look at where Charity was reclined on a sofa as the socialite raised her white-blonde brows. "The Jordan," Penny specified, extending a velvet lined box with Faith's jeweled comset nestled inside.

Faith plucked it out, hooked it over her ear and pressed one of the jewels.

"This is Faith de Rossi," she said.

"Heya, sis!"

Faith was unable to restrain a smile and Charity sat up straighter on the couch. "Hello, Noel," Faith said. "It's good to hear from you." She listened to the chuckle that filled her ear from the com. "Did I say something funny?"

Noel laughed again. "It's not what you say, it's how you say it. Like we are some normal family."

Faith's smile widened. "I could berate you for not visiting enough, not doing your share of family responsibilities. Perhaps shout some profanities or accuse you of not returning my hair drier. I am guessing that is more of what normal sisters do."

"How dreadful!" Charity muttered, making a face. She waved a jeweled hand at a butler and then made a beckoning motion, silently requesting a cocktail. The Jordan, wherever she was, laughed outright.

"You might be right," she agreed. "And maybe we are becoming more normal, whatever the hell that is, because I called to ask you for something."

"And what might that be?"

"Do you know what a Schakel is?"

The ever-growing smile on Faith's face dissipated. "I do. Are you alright?"

Noel laughed. "Of course I'm alright, or I wouldn't be talking to you. Or the person talking to you would not be asking about a Shackle. Can you get me one? One of the custom jobs?"

"Of course I can. How am I supposed to get it to you?"

"Are you at your home?"

"No, I am at Charity's castle."

"Even better."

"Where are you?"

Noel rattled off a list of numbers. Faith's lips pressed together into a line.

"I'm not that knowledgeable about galactic..." she started but was cut off by Noel's laughter.

"I know. I was just fucking with you."

"Why?"

"My nature, I suppose." She laughed again as if she had made a joke.

"Are you drunk?"

The Jordan looked at the glass of champagne in her hand. It was her second. "Certainly not. I am roughly two and half million kilometers from Saturn."

"Can you come here?"

"I can."

"Can I expect to see you soon?"

There was a pause while the Jordan called up the coordinates for the castle from Cyan and did the math in her head. "I can be there in a couple hours."

Then there was a pause on Faith's end, as she calculated as well. "Can you bring your fellow Jordan?"

"Scarlett?" Blue asked, surprised. As if there was another fellow Jordan she could bring.

"Yes."

"Am I in danger of losing my job offer?"

"No. You are still my first choice."

A sigh came from the com in her ear and Faith cocked her head, waiting. "Believe it or not, you might be starting to be my choice as well."

Faith could not keep her jaw from dropping open, even if it was slight.

"I'll be there in a couple hours. Pretty sure Scarlett will be with me."

The Jordan was about to cut the link when Faith spoke up. "Noel!"

"Yes?"

"There is a hangar behind the castle. No need to tear up Charity's lawn."

The Jordan smiled. "Alright," she acquiesced. "See you soon."

"Love," Faith whispered as the link was cut. Her tawny eyes went to Charity who had her hands and shoulders up in a comically exaggerated shrug.

"Well?" she demanded from the couch. "What the hell is going on?"

"She's on her way," Faith said as she calmly removed the comset from her ear and handed it to Penny who had suddenly materialized by her side. "She is finally on her way to us."

Jordan Blue found Jordan Scarlett in her personal quarters. The door had opened as soon as Blue had knocked on it, but the other Jordan had not called out any sort of welcome.

"Scarlett?" Blue queried quietly into the cabin. She took a step inside and looked around. "Scarlett?" she whispered, lowering her voice even further as her eye darted about the room.

She knew the other Jordan was there. She could hear her heart beating. It was slow and steady. Still, there was no sign of her. Blue was about to call out again when she spotted the Red Jordan, sitting cross legged on the floor, her eyes closed.

Blue straightened from the crouch she realized she had crept in with. "What the fuck are you doing?" she asked.

"Meditating," Scarlett responded without opening her eyes.

"What?" Blue asked.

Scarlett's dark eyes cracked open. "Meditating," she repeated. "It's a practice…"

"I know what it is," Blue said with a chuff of air. "I just can't believe you are doing it."

Scarlett gave her a look of tolerant exasperation. "I do it every day."

"Really?"

"Yes. It helps quiet the mind. Maybe you should try it."

"Fuck that."

Scarlett laughed and twisted, stretching her back. "So… you are here for…?"

"Yeah," Blue said.

"Yeah?" the other Jordan responded, her lips quirking up at the corners.

"What are you smiling at?" Blue asked.

"For some reason," Scarlett responded, "I am brutally reminded of Jordan training, when you would come looking for someone to join a pick-up game of IG War or Battlefront."

Blue laughed. "I can't believe that was only a few years ago. It seems like forever."

"I know," Scarlett agreed, "but still..."

"Like yesterday," Blue finished. "Sooo," she continued, "how would you like to join me for a game of... Fledgling Inspection?"

The corners of Scarlett's lips pressed down, not in a frown but in an attempt to suppress a grin. Her dark eyes flicked about and knew instantly that Blue wanted to speak with her privately. A place where they would not be seen nor heard.

"Yours or mine?" she asked.

"Let's start with yours," Blue suggested. "I'd like to see how your galley is equipped."

"Eh," Scarlett responded as she rose to her feet, "not well. Let's stop by the mess hall galley and pick some stuff up."

And they did. Dry goods, canned goods, and a few bottles of red wine that Scarlett had taken a liking to.

Blue glanced around as a steward filled two boxes. They had passed through the steaming and bustling kitchen area and stood in the part of the galley that served as a pantry aboard the Dragon. Shelves were stocked to their edges and there were pallets of boxes and crates, some quite large, still waiting to be unpacked.

"Would you like help taking these to your Fledgling, Jordan?" the steward asked Scarlett, but the Red Jordan shook her head.

"Thank you, but we can handle it."

He gave her a nod and returned to his duties while each Jordan picked up a box and left through the busy kitchen area and the Mess Hall.

The deception is complete, Scarlett thought as she and Blue made their way to Fledgling Bay, *and my galley is now stocked. How convenient.*

They went through security together, the process taking

only slightly longer because the supplies they carried had to be inspected as well. Blue even helped put away the groceries in the galley before she sat down, cracking the top off a split of champagne she had brought along for herself and drinking it straight from the miniature bottle.

"So," she said. "Have you ever thought about leaving the IGC?"

"Jesus!" Scarlett hissed, her dark eyes darting about as if to see who might be listening.

Blue made a face. "They can't hear us," she assured the other Jordan. "Trust me, if they could monitor the Fledglings, I would have been arrested weeks ago."

Scarlett relaxed, somewhat. "Still," she said, keeping her voice low, "I don't think that is something we should discuss, at least not here."

"So that is a yes," Blue said, her voice flat.

Scarlett filled her lungs with air and gave the other Jordan a quick nod. "Just a thought, though. Not anything for certain."

The right side of Blue's lips edged up into her scar. "Nothing in this life is certain. How would you like to go for a ride?"

♣☦♢

Jeanette took a seat on the Red Line tram and took note of the man that boarded when she did. He was tall and blonde and, even at eleven years old, she knew he was quite handsome.

He sat a few seats away and pulled a pocket acrylic from his jacket. The dark brows in her heart-shaped face drew together slightly as she observed his features. He looked familiar.

The man glanced up from his acrylic and saw her staring at him. Jeanette quickly averted her gaze, but from the corner of her eye she could see that he was still watching her with a slight intensity.

She glanced back and he cocked his head, narrowing his eyes. "You look familiar to me," he said, his voice carrying a tone of curiosity. Jeanette, of course, had been lectured most of her life about not talking to strangers - but that had stopped when they moved to the Upper Klick. She guessed because it was the safest place on the entire moon.

She laughed. "I was thinking the same thing," she said. "Maybe I go to school with your kid. But it would have to be in the middle school," she advised, "I graduated from elementary school last semester."

She was very proud to not only to be at a new school, but one that was divided into semesters. It felt very adult. But the man shook his head.

"No, I don't have any children. But I am sure I have seen you before." He turned his face to the window, thinking, while Jeanette's curiosity grew and grew. He looked back suddenly, his face bright. "Is your last name Mattatock?" he asked.

Now Jeanette's face lit up. "Why, yes!"

The man snapped his fingers. "That's it!" he exclaimed. "I know your aunt!"

"You do? Auntie Jo?"

The man laughed. It was a warm sound. "Well, we call her Jordan Scarlett, but yes. And that would make you Jeanette. You have a brother named Sean."

"That's right!" she agreed, enthusiastic. He must know her Auntie Jo really well.

"You look quite a bit like her."

Jeanette giggled. "I get that a lot."

"She's a great pilot."

"She's the best!"

"I've heard your brother has started training with your

father."

All the good cheer drained from the girl's heart-shaped face. "Yeah, well he's not that good. I'm way better."

"Is that so?"

"Yes, it is. I've beaten every pilot game in the sphere and made it up to level seven in a real simulator."

She was glad to see the look of surprise on his face.

"A real simulator? Level seven? But you are only what, twelve years old?"

It made her feel even better that he thought she was older, even though he looked doubtful of her claim.

"Only eleven," she confided, "but I'll be as good as my Auntie someday. I could probably be better if they would let me start training, but I can't until I'm sixteen."

"Why so late?" he asked. "We start training our pilots at thirteen."

"What?" Jeanette asked, leaning forward. Sixteen seemed like a lifetime away. Thirteen was practically around the corner. There was a beep and they both looked up at the holo showing upcoming stops.

"My stop is next," the man said, tucking the acrylic into an inner pocket of his coat. "It's been very nice talking with you. My name is Jan, by the way." He gave her a smile and slid forward slightly to the edge of his seat, ready to stand when the tram came to the stop.

Jeanette felt ready to burst. *Thirteen!*

"Do you live here?" she asked. "Close by?"

"Heavens no!" Jan told her. "I live on a ship. But if you're really interested in early flight training…, do you have a credentials card by chance? I could give you my information."

"No," Jeanette said, crestfallen. "I'm too young."

Jan gave her a sympathetic nod as the tram began to slow. "I'm sorry. I forget how restricted your rights are down here."

He stood up and held the silver bar next to his seat to keep steady as the car stopped. Jeanette stood and did the same.

"Thirteen?" she asked. "Really?"

"Of course," he said. "If we want the best pilots, then we want them training as soon as they can. We could probably even make an exception in your case, considering who your family is, and if you are as good as you say you are." His last words were delivered with a smile that held a trace of suspicion.

"I am!" Jeanette declared. Now she was sure she was going to explode.

She could start training, real training, now?

Jan cocked his head as the doors slid open. "I'm on my way to have coffee with my boss. Do you want to come with me? We could ask him."

"Yes!" Jeanette agreed immediately. She scooped up her dance bag but he stood, blocking the open doors. His face was suddenly serious.

"Are your parents going to be alright with this?"

Jeanette's shoulders sagged. "If I'm back by dark they'll never notice."

"I don't want to get you in trouble."

The tram beeped and announced the doors would be closing soon. His concern washed out any fears or hesitation Jeanette might have been harboring about strangers.

"It's fine, it's fine!" she assured emphatically, motioning for him to get going. Jan laughed and stepped from the tram carriage and Jeanette followed close behind as the doors slid closed.

Smiling broadly, she went with him to a car park and a sleek air car. Jeanette whistled appreciatively and Jan laughed.

"Don't be too impressed," he said as he opened a door for her. "It's a rental."

Jeanette giggled as she slid into the seat and pulled the safety web across her lap. She had trouble with the buckle, however, and Jan had to help her after he got in his side of the car.

As he leaned over to assist her with the clasp, a chain slipped forward from the top of his shirt and hung in front of his neck. Jeanette's dark eyes went wide as she saw that the platinum links were an endless chain of figure eights, the symbol for infinity.

But by then, of course, it was too late.

☘☙

The Jordans were granted clearance for patrol by their Captain and took off from the Dragon, trailing streams of light. They headed towards the sun, but their trip was far shorter than a journey to the only star in the system.

The Fledglings had just passed Saturn when Cyan began to slow and Fledge followed him to a stormy, watery moon. Scarlett checked their coordinates and saw they were in what was referred to as a dead zone. An unnamed, unrecorded satellite. But there was life there, she saw on the scan. Life where there should be none.

They passed through a massive electrical storm as they descended into the atmosphere, and their arrival was no less shocking. Thunder boomed and lighting flashed over a moon almost completely covered in water.

Scarlett followed Blue as she dove and then leveled out, zooming over the angry ocean towards an immense island. The landmass was rocky, but mostly covered with grassy lawns and trimmed hedges. In the center was a building, as dark and large and frightening as Ferrous, the Iron Dragon.

Obsidian spires reached for the sky as if trying to catch the light that flickered there before every boom that shook the atmosphere.

Jordan Blue had taken over manual control once Cyan had returned them to the atmosphere of her sister's residence and she circled the colossal edifice, looking for the hangar that Faith had told her to use.

She did not see anything on the first pass, but she could hear what beckoned to her. Holy hell, she could *feel* them.

"Seven circles," she murmured aloud. "Can you hear them?"

The only open line she had was to the Red Fledgling, and the Red Jordan responded.

"No. But I feel something. It's calling to us. What do you hear?"

"Heartbeats. Always, that is the first thing I hear. You don't...wait, what do you smell?"

"Fire," Scarlett told her as they swooped down past the crevice that led to the hangar. "Dragonfire, though it is dormant. There are Dragon eggs down there."

"Yes," Blue agreed. "Did you see the opening?"

"Yes," Scarlett said. "We can get it on the next pass. It's hard to see, but I feel like something is pulling us there, drawing us in. How many of the eggs do they have?"

Blue banked hard, pulling Cyan around to go back the way they had come. "All of them, Scarlett. They have them all."

 TWO TWO

- Some friends, like secrets, take a lifetime to reveal.

Jordan Scarlett flew low over the choppy waters of the Distant Shore, following Blue towards the flat gap they had spotted at the base of the massive island.

"Are we going to have enough room to maneuver in there?" she asked Fledge.

An image appeared over the console, looking like it had been drawn or copied from a blueprint. The schematic showed the castle and the massive rock on which it, along with all of its grounds, sat amidst the waves. The island was short, only a few meters above sea level, but tremendous in girth. What was above the water was deceptively small in comparison, like an iceberg.

"Wow," Scarlett said as they dove for the cave-like opening.

"We could fit an entire platoon of Fledglings in here," Blue said over their private link. "Which is probably their plan."

Scarlett realized she was no longer flying Fledge. She had let go of control as they entered the darkness and he had taken over. Yet he sent her no questioning images, no queries on where she wanted to go.

It was as if he knew.

The Fledglings had begun to brake as soon as they had

entered the cavern but already it was opening up to the vast space beneath the castle, lit by a variety of diodes, halogens, and fluorescents.

The Jordans felt their breath sucked away at what they saw.

A small group of people stood talking on the tarmac but the Jordans took no notice of them. They were too busy staring at the Fledgling that awaited them.

Verdana.

She sat in a glow of green light, her glass eyes shining.

Cyan turned, stretched out his legs, and landed by her side. Fledge did the same and landed on her other side, flanking her.

Both Jordans were out of their seats and out of their Fledglings as fast as they could move. Within moments they were standing together in front of Verdana, quietly voicing questions to one another, when the others joined them.

The small group was quite familiar now to Jordan Blue, except for a young woman with dark skin and spiraled hair that was a light, dusty pink in color. Since she knew everyone else, Blue made the introductions.

"Scarlett, this is my sister, Faith de Rossi. My sister, Charity. And their pet Chimeran. I'm sorry, I don't think I ever got your name."

"Jasyn," the dark-haired construct with the perfect face replied, his tone flat.

"And Jasyn!" Blue announced. "This is Jordan Scarlett," she said holding out a hand towards the Red Jordan.

"It's a pleasure," Scarlett said as the others offered similar sentiments. "And this is?" she asked, looking at the young woman wearing a hip holster that held a laser pistol.

"I'm Amberle," the young woman said, stepping forward. "The Jordan of the Green Fledgling."

Blue and Scarlett gaped at her.

"The what?"

"Excuse me?"

Amberle smiled. "The Jordan of the Green Fledgling," she repeated.

The other Jordans blinked at her in amazement. Amberle's smile widened and she looked at Verdana. The other Jordans followed her gaze and from the nose of the Green Fledgling was projected a scene that looked like it could have been a holo movie, but more real.

Three-dimensional light formed two people sitting in the cockpit of the Fledgling. One was clearly Amberle. The other was...

Blue cried out in surprise, loss and terror.

The other was Jade.

Younger and wearing civilian clothes, but unmistakably Jade.

For Blue it was like seeing the image of Galen's ghost for the first time and she knew that if Jade had come back in some way she could quite possibly lose her mind.

Scarlett also made a choked noise and clutched at the other Jordan.

"He's... he's not... it can't be..." Blue stammered.

"Shh!" Scarlett shushed. "It's not now, it's a replay." It was a horrible explanation, but it was all she could manage.

"...Verdana needs someone," the image of Amberle was saying. Jade's face had an unusually serious expression, but it softened.

"I think that's you," he said quietly. His green eyes looked into the ones of the young woman facing him.

The young woman laughed softly. "I can't be a Jordan," she chuffed. "Jordans are trained fighters, and the most experienced pilots in the universe."

"I think all you really need," Jade countered, "is to be chosen by a Fledgling. Everything else, you can learn."

"She didn't choose me, she found me."

Jade smiled. "Kind of the same," he told her. And, when she frowned at him, "There are no accidents," he added.

The image faded and was replaced by a new one. The young woman with dark skin stood facing Jade outside of Verdana. The background was a blurred green and the sky was bright. Scarlett guessed they must be on a moon, some place with grass and sun.

Jade reached out and cupped Amberle's dark cheek in his slender hand. "You do that, Jordan."

Amberle laughed. "I still don't know how that's going to work. I don't know the first thing about being a Jordan."

"Are there Jordans in your time?"

Amberle nodded.

"Find them. Learn from them."

His words hung in the air as the new image dissolved and a choked sob escaped from Blue's throat.

"He was younger there," Scarlett said softly.

Amberle nodded. "By more than a hundred years."

Scarlett looked at her. "But you were the same. How?"

Blue's hand came down from her mouth and her eye was cold and wild. "You went back?" she asked. "You used Verdana to go through time, backwards?"

Now even Jordan Scarlett's face was pale and slack. "Never," she said, her voice barely above a whisper. "We are never supposed to do that. You could…"

"Yeah, yeah, yeah," Amberle agreed impatiently. "I could throw things out of whack. But I'm here now and he's back where he should be and things are…well, as good as can be expected."

There was no way she was going to mention that there was some sort of, and undisclosed, threat of Golgoths in their solar system as well as in the Outer Banks. *And, oh yeah, Verdana is also carrying my egg. Fertilized by Jade.*

Instead, she puffed out her dark cheeks and expelled a great breath of air, rocking back on her heels. "It's about time for lunch, isn't it?" she queried, looking at Faith with raised brows.

Faith gave her a nod and began to turn towards Charity when Blue spoke.

"The Dragon eggs," she said. "They are down here, aren't they?"

Faith dipped her head in acknowledgment.

"I would like..." Blue started when Scarlett gave her a poke in the ribs. "We would like," Blue corrected, "to see them."

"Very well," Faith acquiesced. "Let me call Nathan. I can reach him on the..."

Jasyn's face contorted in disgust. "I can do it," he informed her and the others. "You don't need him for everything," he said as he walked away. "Or anything," he added, though by then he was far enough away for his words to be lost in sounds of the waves. Almost.

"Nathan," Blue said, remembering the man she had seen on Faith's couch. "He's your Engineer? The one who was in your villa?"

"Yes," Faith admitted.

Blue gave her a lopsided smile. "I believe Jasyn dislikes him more than he does me."

"Jasyn does not dislike you," Faith corrected, "he just doesn't like that you shot him."

"What?" Scarlett asked, frowning at Blue.

The Blue Jordan waved a dismissive hand. "Remind me to tell you about that later."

The Red Jordan stared at her but the other Jordan had turned her eye to the construct, returning with a small device in his hand. He glanced around at the group which had gone suddenly still.

"Go ahead," Charity encouraged.

The dark-haired construct held up a remote that was about the same size and shape of a metal coin. With his thumb, he depressed a tiny node in the side, and then dragged his thumb a quarter way along the edge of the disc.

Two seconds later, there was a vibration that ran through the platform on which they all stood. Both Jordans straightened and looked at the water, lapping roughly at the edge of the tarmac.

The blunted tips of the ovoid-shaped eggs emerged first.

Six of them, each no less than two meters wide and four meters high, rose from the waters of the Distant Shore. Mist and droplets sprayed in all directions, the water catching and reflecting lights in a rainbow of color much like a fence of detfleck.

Scarlett felt her knees buckle as she was overcome with memory. She grasped at a dream she once had. Her and Blue, in a tropical rain forest. Mist from a waterfall, catching the rays of the sun, reflecting it in all the hues of the rainbow. Blue asking her what she didn't see.

Then the memory of leaving Elaeric's cottage for the last time. Looking into the meditation room. And realizing what it was that she did *not* see. And the voice of Opal, of her mother Dragon, telling her to remember. To tell Blue.

"Holy shit," Scarlett whispered.

"I know, right?" Jordan Blue whispered back, awed by the sight of the six Dragon eggs rising from the water.

"Yes," Scarlett agreed softly, "but it's something more. Remind me later to tell you." Blue nodded, her mind disengaged as she watched the water stream from the sides of the eggs.

They rose upon fields of circular propulsion and then came to a stop. They were all huge, all breath taking. Even Coal and Stone, though they had no color, were no less gem-like as they dripped and sparkled in the light of the cave.

As the small group admired the miracle before them, they all watched as the shells seemed to shift. Seemed to ripple. Scarlett's sense of smell flared within her nostrils, filled with the scent of Dragonfire encased within each shell. It was growing, burning.

Glancing at Blue and seeing her single eye opened wide she knew that Blue could hear their heartbeats pounding.

The Red Jordan looked suddenly at the young woman, supposedly the new Jordan of the Green Fledgling.

"What do you feel?" she demanded. "What do they feel?"

Amberle looked at her with wide eyes. "They want out," she said softly.

"Put them back in the water!" Scarlett commanded, her dark eyes flashing to Jasyn. "Put them back!"

The handsome construct did not question her and did not waste a second of time. He flicked the remote with a deft hand and the eggs immediately began to descend back beneath the waves.

This time there was no denying it. Everyone saw the shells undulate with movement. Taloned wings stretching inside what was now a prison, longing to break free. The eggs, however, began to settle and still as they were lowered into the water, lulled back to sleep.

"Holy shit is right," Jordan Blue said, her voice full of awe.

"How about that lunch?" Charity announced. Her tone was jovial but no one missed the slight tremor in her voice.

⋘⋙

Jeanette stared out of the window straight in front of her as Petrov started the aircraft and steered it out of the car park. He glanced at Jeanette and saw her expression of fear.

"Are you alright?" he asked.

She turned her wide brown eyes to the Chimeran Commander. "I'm a little surprised I'm not breathing in a lungful of Chlorforgel right now."

"Chlorforgel? My goodness, Jeanette, I'm not kidnapping you!"

"You're not?"

"No. I thought you wanted to talk to my boss." He glanced at her again.

Jeanette's mind was in complete disarray. "You weren't lying about that?"

"No. Why would I?"

She wondered that herself for a moment. "Because you're Chimeran," she said softly.

"What does that have to do with anything?"

Another question that had her stumped.

"You killed my Grandpa John, and my Uncle Joe." She had not known them, only known of them.

"I certainly did not."

"I didn't mean you, personally, I meant your...your people."

The slightest smile quirked the corner of Petrov's lips. She was so young, and so innocent that it melted his heart. It brought back a feeling so painful that he quashed it down as soon as he felt it.

"The Chimera did not kill your uncle and your grandfather," Petrov told her.

"Now I know you're lying," she accused.

"Ask your aunt if you don't believe me."

Jeanette's eyes grew wide once again. "That's true? And she knows?"

"She knows."

The young girl was astounded. Grandpa John and Uncle

Joe weren't killed by the Chimera? And Auntie Jo knew? Why would she not tell anyone? Or did others know but were keeping it from her for some reason?

Jeanette was so angry at the thought that she hardly noticed that Jan was descending a vertical byway to the klick below. She felt her family was treating her like a baby, like they always did.

"Does Sean know?" she asked.

"That, I do not know," Jan answered.

I bet he does, Jeanette thought, seething.

She looked up, surprised, as the car slowed and turned into a small lot next to a café.

Jan turned off the car and looked at her solemnly. "Are you sure you want to meet him?" he asked. "You don't have to. I can take you back home if you want."

Jeanette thought for a moment as she regarded Jan's handsome, solemn face.

He means it. He really means it. He would take me home.

Like a six-year-old, scared at their first slumber party.

"No," she said, "I'd like to talk to your boss."

Because if Jan was being honest about taking her home, why would he lie about her being able to train at thirteen, or younger?

Petrov smiled at her. "Let's go then."

He opened his door and circled to her side to help her out but she was already on her feet, closing the door.

She sniffed the air, hardly able to detect that it was less pure than what she was used to in the Upper Klick. Her eyes grazed the artificial blue-gray sky above, knowing it was certainly not as blue as her own.

The magnified sunlight above filtered down, like the air, to the lower Klicks below. After the first mile the sunlight petered out altogether and the bottom two miles of Three Mile were dependent on electric light.

The street they were on was nicely paved and lined with trees. The buildings were mostly offices, interspersed with eateries and coffee shops. A simple, clean and classy business district.

She was so small next to Petrov's huge form that he had to fight the instinct to hold her hand. He knew he would lose all that he had built with her if he did such a thing.

Instead, he watched her look around - not with the simple curiosity of a child, but instead assessing her environment. He walked towards the café and Jeanette kept pace by his side.

The glass doors at the front slid open for them and slid back closed once they had stepped inside. They were immediately hit with the sounds and smells of cooking food. Beef patties sizzled in the kitchen. Bread was toasted and buttered or heaped with sliced meats. Coffee bubbled in pots.

The lunch rush was over and there were few patrons in the booths or at the tables and none at the long lunch counter that faced the kitchen. In the last booth at the back of the diner, sat a young man in a white button-down shirt wearing a baseball cap over neatly trimmed auburn hair.

Almost never would you see a soldier sitting with their back to the door. JP, however, was not most soldiers. He could hear everything, including the soft steps of the Mattatock girl as she approached with his Executive Officer. They passed by, then stopped and turned and JP slid smoothly from the bench seat and stood to greet them.

Peering at her from under the bill of the cap were the most amazing blue eyes Jeanette had ever seen. They shone from a face of smooth skin spattered with freckles as he smiled at her.

"You must be Jeanette." he announced with what appeared to be barely contained joy.

"And you must be JP," she responded, holding out her hand. "It's a pleasure to meet you."

His smile brightened even more as he shook her small hand. "The pleasure is all mine."

TWO THREE

- What you see as reality is an illusion to others.

The de Rossi's, along with Jasyn and the Jordans, took the large elevator up to the castle proper where they were immediately flanked and trailed by a few security men and a ridiculously large contingent of aides and service staff.

The Red Jordan's hand went instinctively to the gun on her hip as people closed in around them. Her dark eyes darted to Blue but the other Jordan gave her head a quick shake, letting her know there was no threat.

Still, Scarlett let her hand rest casually on the butt of her pistol as she walked amidst the de Rossi sisters, their attendants, and their guards. They passed through halls of stone hung with rich tapestries and art in elaborate frames. Runner rugs of deep colors woven with gold ran the length of the halls.

Charity led them to the conservatory and though Amberle had only been gone a few days, it had changed dramatically since her last visit. It was still full of plants and flowers and streams of softly rushing water, but instead of giant eggs made from multicolored blooms there were dragons.

Not the space-faring type, but of the mythological variety. Scaled with tulip petals, carnation jaws split open to reveal teeth made of white rosebuds. They crouched in the garden beds of the conservatory on talons made of polished seeds. Tails of orchids, mums and daises curled around or lashed out behind each dragon.

Each of the flower-made reptiles, which the two older Jordans immediately identified as hatchlings, was the same color as the six eggs they had just seen beneath the castle.

An arbor stood where the gazebo once did, wisteria vines snaking between the wooden slats above – their purple blooms cascading through the gaps - to offer a little more shade from the sunshine normally streaming in from the curved glass ceiling. Today, the sunlight came and went with the clouds and the wisteria did well to hide the streaks of lightning that flashed over the Distant Shore.

Inside the conservatory of the Last Castle the gardens were bright and warm and gave the impression of a tea party on a summer day. The table under the arbor was round, covered in white linens, and set for seven.

Charity made a remark over her shoulder to one of her aides and within a moment a butler was whisking away one of the settings. Another removed the chair. Slight adjustments were quickly made and the party took their seats.

The staff all but swarmed around them, filling glasses with water, pouring juices, serving cocktails.

"Isn't it early for cocktails?" Amberle asked.

"It's brunch," Faith said by way of explanation.

"Brunch?" Amberle looked confused.

"A combination of breakfast and lunch," Faith told her with a warm smile.

"An excuse to drink in the morning," Jasyn told her in a voice that was low and conspiratorial.

Charity looked at him, her green eyes wide. "I need an excuse to drink?" she queried.

"No Nathan today?" Amberle asked.

"No," Charity sighed. "He is on his way to Titan. There is some sort of metal there he seems to require."

"What a shame," Jasyn remarked with a smirk as he picked up a small carafe of juice and used it to fill an empty glass dusted with frost.

Faith gave him a look of reprobation but said nothing as she picked up her own glass, filled with champagne, and took a sip.

Blue found a similar glass placed in front of her plate.

"I'm sorry, Jordan Scarlett," Charity apologized, "I did not have anything already prepared for you as I do not yet know your favorite libation. What would can we offer you to drink?"

Scarlett smiled, suddenly feeling like she was on holiday. "What actually sounds good is a Bloody Mikea. I haven't had one for a while. I don't suppose..." Her sentence was left unfinished as a tall glass full of ice was placed in front of her, a bit to her left. A butler stuck a leafy spear of celery in the glass, filled it with a thick red liquid and squeezed a sliced of lime into it before stepping back.

Not only was it full of the cocktail she requested, and placed on the side of her dominant hand but it was garnished with three olives.

Three, Scarlett mused as she stirred the drink with a silver sipping straw and took a drink. It had Grevin pepper, a splash of what her grandpa would have called *weeziana hot sauce*, and...

"Wow," Scarlett said as she put her drink down. "French vodka. That's not easy to come by."

"It isn't?" Charity asked, surprised.

Scarlett smiled. "I guess I should say it's not common to come by."

"Oh!" Charity acknowledged as she removed a berry from her own cocktail and popped it into her mouth. "That I can understand."

Scarlett looked at Blue in a state of amazement that was slightly disturbed while members of the kitchen staff set down steaming bowls of soup and small plates of appetizers.

The Blue Jordan shrugged. "I know," she said. "They live a little different from us. You get used to it surprisingly fast."

The Red Jordan watched as Blue selected a small meat tart and took a bite.

Blinking, she looked at the others who were calmly adding bites of food to their plates or starting into their soup.

"Is this real?" Scarlett whispered to her fellow IGC Officer with sudden urgency.

Blue froze, her sapphire eye sliding across the faces of the others before fixing on the Red Jordan. She resumed chewing the piece of tart in her mouth and swallowed.

"What do you mean?"

"This can't be real," Scarlett said softly. "I must have fallen asleep and gone down some rabbit hole."

"What are you talking about?" Blue asked, helping herself to another tart.

Scarlett placed both of her hands on the edge of the table. "We are on a moon that no one, not even the government, can find. A fairy-tale castle, made of obsidian, sitting on a military grade hangar?" Utensils were put down gently as the others turned their attention to Scarlett who continued her softly spoken tirade. "We have Verdana! A Fledgling that was lost, found, and *grown* - outside of her mother Dragon and the knowledge of the IGC! All while we have a casual yet insanely opulent brunch with the heads of the largest and most powerful corporation in the universe?"

"We still need to eat," Faith said mildly while Charity smiled as if complimented and held up her glass in a silent toast before taking a drink.

Blue uttered a soft laugh. "I guess it is a little bizarre," she admitted.

"A little? We also have, what I am starting to believe is possible, a new Jordan!"

"Thank you," Amberle said, her hazel eyes bright in her dusky face.

"And I opt for us getting a new Engineer," Jasyn added. "Don't you have one?" he asked, looking at Blue.

"And a cocktail is certainly in order at this hour," Charity remarked. "Especially if we want a chance to take a breath and relax before any serious discussion."

"Then why don't I get a drink?" Amberle demanded.

"Because you wanted a shooting lesson later," Jasyn told her. "Firearms and alcohol don't mix."

"*They* have guns and *they* are drinking," Amberle said. "It's not fair."

"It's not a matter of fair," Faith admonished in a quiet tone.

Blue picked up her glass of champagne, a grin splitting her scarred face in two. "Now *this* is a family," she asserted before taking a satisfying sip.

"AND," Scarlett went on, "there are six Dragon eggs down underneath this place that are ready to hatch, while you are all calmly sipping soup! What the hell is going on around here?"

"You don't like the soup?" Charity asked. She waved impatiently at a butler and Scarlett's soup, untasted, was whisked away.

The Red Jordan put her fingers on her forehead, covering her closed eyes with her hand. "This isn't real," she muttered.

Faith dabbed at her lips with a napkin and put it back in her lap. She put her elbows on the table and folded her hands as if in prayer and rested her chin there.

"Jordan Scarlett is right," she said. "There are many things we need to discuss. It sometimes just takes me a bit to put my thoughts in order. I will start with us."

She looked meaningfully at Charity who, with a wave of her

hand, dismissed every one of her aides, staff, and security. As soon as they had melted far enough into the shadows to satisfy Faith, she lowered her hands and raised her chin, fixing her gold and brown eyes on the Red Jordan who had straightened in her chair and was staring at her, attentive.

Scarlett pulled an olive from the pick in her drink and delicately put it between her teeth.

"I doubt I have to give you a history on GwenSeven?" Faith asked.

Scarlett shook her head slowly as she chewed her olive.

"Or the rebellion?" Faith asked, her body tense. She knew the start of the rebellion was officially recognized and the date cemented with the death of Scarlett's father and younger brother.

Scarlett again shook her head, quite aware of written history, and ate another olive. Faith nodded.

"A hundred years ago," Faith told her, "the IGC had already seen its peak and was beginning to crumble. As with most governments, it was being infiltrated by the greed of money and power. It corrupted the best and attracted the worst, if I may paraphrase a great warrior of old. We began planning, a long time ago, a new government."

Scarlett gave her a scathing smile, her eyes narrowed in doubt. "And you do not foresee the same problems? The same weaknesses? They are the downfall to every government in every system since the beginning of time."

The Jordans, both Red and Blue, turned their heads at the sound of Charity's throaty chuckle.

The woman snickered, and then outright laughed. Quickly noting that all eyes were on her, she brought up a hand bedecked with rings to chastely cover her mouth.

"We have both more money and more power than any other entity in the universe," she told the Jordan. "What is there to corrupt us? I mean, any more than we already are." She laughed again and Faith gave her a reproachful glance before turning her gaze back to the Red Jordan.

Scarlett sat back in her chair, hit with the implication.

"Then what are you after?" Blue asked, genuinely curious.

"Justice," Faith answered immediately. "Equality."

"Equality?" Blue retorted in surprise and disbelief.

"Well," Charity acquiesced, her drink held aloft in a jeweled hand, "I know not everyone can live like this - but, you know, equal rights and shit."

"Eloquent as ever," Faith murmured as she sat back in her own chair and took a sip of champagne. "But she is right. The IGC has been chiefly run by the human race, always believing they are the chosen or the dominant or some such bullshit. Next are elves, though they would find the viewpoint of the humans laughable. Then the Golbli, and the Lentochs and so on. The Chimera being at the bottom, if they are recognized at all as a species. The galaxies have become more unbalanced each year, each month, each day. They are reaching a tipping point. We are ready for those scales to tip. We have a unified government ready to take over. We have a balanced financial system that has already been set in place."

"Jesus," Scarlett whispered.

Blue took a drink from her glass. Having talked with her sisters so recently, she already had the luxury of time to know what they were up to, for the most part. She had a chance to assimilate and empathize. She watched Scarlett carefully, almost able to see the gears turning in her head.

But she's not the one with the gears, Blue thought. *I am. Shit.* She took another drink from her glass and looked away.

Scarlett turned her dark eyes to the Blue Jordan. "You've known this?"

Blue sighed. "I've had an idea of what was going on. But, trust me, nothing to this extent."

"And where do you stand in all this?"

"The same as you, I'm guessing. I am an IGC officer, dedicated to my Captain and my Dragon. But the IGC has me hella nervous right now."

Scarlett nodded. "That is exactly how I feel." She looked at Faith. "The only branch you are missing is a military one."

Faith shrugged. "An organized one," she admitted. "But we are not completely without resources."

"Obviously," Scarlett said. "But even without organization," and here she paused, huffing soft laughter, "your strategy is amazing. You have six eggs, ready to hatch and then become Fledglings. Against seven Dragons, four of which - at least, if not all - will not fire upon their young." Scarlett paused and lifted her chin. "And what do you have in the Chimera?"

It was Charity this time who smiled, and answered. "Hooks."

The rest of the group continued with their lunch as soup was taken away and replaced with small salads and plates of fruit. Scarlett hardly noticed.

"So *we* are here to discuss your military?" she asked.

"You are here," Faith said, inclining her head towards Blue, "because she needed a piece of equipment, both military and medical grade. And clandestine. But yes, I asked her to invite you so we could discuss military matters." Her gold and brown eyes went to her youngest sister. "I have the Schakel for you. I can have anyone in my security detail show you how to use it."

Scarlett's dark eyes widened and she turned them again to the other Jordan. Blue gave her a sheepish smile.

"Oh yeah," she said. "In all the excitement, I almost forgot."

"A Schakel? That Aridian is still in your Fledgling?"

"Yes," Blue said, straightening. "Something else I think we should discuss."

Scarlett buried her face in her hands.

Blue gave an exaggerated shrug, her shoulders coming all the way up to her ears. "What was I supposed to do with her? It's not like I can just drop her off at a Siza bar, or on the side of some street."

"You're right," Scarlett admitted, rubbing her eyebrows with the tips of her fingers. "There's just been so much going on. Shit with me, shit on the Dragon. We seem always in the need of more time, more talking."

"You said earlier there was something you wanted to tell me," Blue reminded her. "Is that what you're talking about?"

Scarlett looked up abruptly, startled out of her thoughts. "No," she said, shaking her dark hair. "That's something totally different." She took a deep breath and squared her shoulders, gathering what she wanted to say. She thought about starting with the dream she had, then decided against it. Hearing other people recount their dreams was usually both boring and ridiculous.

The Red Jordan took a deep breath and plunged straight forward.

"When I was in Kayos, there was something that kept striking me as odd, but for the life of me I couldn't figure out what it was. My last day there, I did. And I heard a voice, Opal's voice, telling me to remember. To remember for Blue."

Jordan Blue's blonde eyebrows went up over both her eye and the patch where an eye had once been. She did not notice that her sisters and had gone still and silent. "What was it?" she asked.

"There was no dust. We were on a small farm, with animals, a garden, fields, dirt, and dust. But there was never any dust in the house. Never."

Faith and Charity glanced at each other. Jasyn did not miss the silent exchange.

"What?" he asked.

"We knew of one other place," Faith said. "Another

residence, that displayed the same phenomenon. Do you remember it?" she asked Jasyn.

"No," he said his tone oddly acrimonious. "What was it?"

"The First Castle," Charity told him, her voice soft. She turned her eyes to Faith but her sister was looking curiously at Blue. The youngest de Rossi, however, was not paying attention to them. Instead, she was thoughtfully studying the plate in front of her.

Finally, she looked up at the others and nodded. "I knew of a place like that as well," she told the group. "Galen and I went to Earth years ago, before I went to Jordan Training. There was an entire town there that was like that. An empty town in the middle of a desert. A *desert*. No dust in the houses."

Faith was running the thumbnail of her right hand over her lips.

Charity's small hands were clenched into fists. "Call the monk," she whispered.

Faith did not have to ask whom she meant. She got up and Scarlett stood with her.

It seemed so improbable, downright *impossible*, but she was now all too aware of entanglement.

"Elaeric?" she asked. "Is he the monk you are talking about?" Faith nodded as Scarlett blinked at her, thinking quickly. "Will you give him a message?" she asked. Faith's eyes narrowed in curiosity but gave her another nod and the Jordan lifted her chin. "Tell him I am ready for the second stone."

Faith regarded her for a short moment and gave her one more nod. Then she left, seeking out where Penny waited in the wings.

Scarlett stared unbelievingly at Blue, trying to assimilate everything that was happening. "Maybe you and I should have a private..." she began but left her sentence unfinished as the left side of her head began to buzz. Scarlett reached up and touched the platinum stud embedded there.

Within a breath the Communications Officer of the Opal Dragon was in her ear.

"Jordan Scarlett," Dareus said, his voice low. It made her skin crawl and pucker all the way up her spine. She, along with Blue, had received too many calls from Dareus over the recent months.

Her hand went reflexively to cover her heart, her mind instinctively reaching out for Captain Brogan, but felt no pain or, what would have been worse, emptiness. Still, she took a full breath and braced herself.

"I have an emergency civilian call that is requesting you." There was only one group of civilians that Scarlett knew. Her family.

Grandpa, she thought, her throat convulsing. She couldn't swallow.

"Put them through, please," she instructed, her throat dry as summer wool.

"Johanna," a voice said over the line. *John.* And in the background she could hear hysterics. *Rebecca.*

But Rebecca would not be in hysterics over Grandpa. Her throat convulsed again and again she found it hard to breathe.

"Jo," he said, his own voice dropping an octave and also sounding oddly strangled, "Jeanette is missing."

"For how long?" Scarlett asked, sounding - to her own ears - strangely calm and composed.

"We can't say for sure. She was at school until they let out at half past two. She didn't show at dance class at three, but that is not unusual for her. She sometimes skips (and here his voice cracked) to go to the arcade. But we checked there, and with all her friends, and no one has seen her." His voice cracked again on his last word.

"John," Scarlett said, again sounding remarkably calm in her own ears, "I am going to send a secure IGC unit for you, the whole family. Pack..."

"Fuck you!" she heard Rebecca scream in the background. "I'm not leaving! She might come back! What if she comes back!?!"

Scarlett almost told John to take their call off the speaker but then thought it better that Rebecca hear.

"If she comes back," Scarlett said, "then we have nothing to worry about. She can let herself in and you can leave her a note where to call, although I will have the pod under surveillance. Hopefully, her returning after playing hooky for an afternoon is what will happen. I'll call you back once I know what you can expect. Meanwhile, give Rebecca a tranquilizer."

"Fuck you!" came the muted shout once again.

Scarlett kept on as if uninterrupted. "If she is hysterical when the IGC team gets there they will sedate her anyway. There is a bottle of Valimnium on the top shelf of Grandpa's medicine cabinet."

"Grandpa doesn't take," John started, interrupting as well, before he closed his mouth. The pills were, of course, Johanna's. "Okay," he said.

"One might go down better with a shot of his Cognac."

"Okay," John agreed again.

"Once I cut the line I am going to call the IGC Golden Cross, they handle family emergencies for high ranking officials and officers." Scarlett paused long enough to take a deep breath. "Then I am going to speak with people outside of the IGC." Her eyes flicked about the faces in the room and Faith, just rejoining their bizarre lunch party, gave her a nod of assent. "In fact, I might speak with them first. But, John," she assured, her voice low, "she's okay. And I'm going to get her back."

She could hear her brother's ragged breathing over the com but when he spoke his voice was steady. "Thank you, Jo. I love you."

"I love you too," she answered and cut the line.

Once the line went dead Scarlett's cool and collected

composure evaporated instantly.

"Shit!" she roared with enough force to make the teacups on the table chitter on their saucers. "Fuck! This my fault! My niece got nabbed from the safest neighborhood on Io and it is all my fault!" She hung her head, her fingers plunged into her dark hair, her nails digging into her scalp.

Jasyn, from the corner of his vision, saw Geary step forward from the shadows in response to the sudden outburst. Jasyn, keeping his wrist down on the edge of the table, discreetly gave a single flick of his fingers and Geary melted back into the shadows.

"How?" Blue asked. "How could this possibly be your fault?"

Scarlett looked up and her face, hard as always but still beautiful, was suddenly haggard.

"Bjorn was in the Upper Klick. I don't know if he had followed me somehow or managed to track down my family," she confessed.

Blue's head went from side to side slowly, not understanding.

"I had a Chimeran Commander sitting casually a hundred feet in front of my grandfather's podment! And I did nothing! I didn't report it! Shit, I didn't even think to move my family!"

"Why?" a voice asked softly. Scarlett's head swiveled to see Faith, standing with her hands folded primly in front of her belt.

"What?"

"Why did you not think to move your family?"

The Red Jordan wanted to shout at her, shout that she didn't think of it because she was stupid. *Stupid, stupid, stupid!*

Instead, she blinked and took a breath, the heated wind leaving her sails.

"Because I did not think they were in danger," she said, her voice softer than she thought she could manage, surprising her. "Not from Bjorn."

"And why did you not think he was a danger to them?"

Scarlett's head moved again, because this time it was Charity who had spoken. Scarlett blinked again as she thought.

"Because I trust him," she said her voice now barely above a whisper. She watched the porcelain white skin on Charity's smooth neck ripple as she swallowed.

"And do you still trust him?"

Scarlett filled her lungs with air, her shoulders drawing back, and nodded. "Yes."

Charity's movements mirrored the Jordan as she took a deep breath into her own lungs. "I'll call him."

Scarlett's dark eyes widened, the flecks of crimson flaring within them. "You can do that?" she asked, but the woman was already moving away. Her eyes went to Blue who was giving her a smile that bordered on apologetic.

"I'm starting to think that there isn't anything they can't do," she said softly. "Or anyone they can't reach."

Scarlett's gaze moved wonderingly to Faith who nodded. "You can call the IGC, or we can have our security start a scan on the cameras in their neighborhood. But you are going to get better, and much faster, results if you ask Bjorn's troll."

The Red Jordan's eyes went to the young Jordan watching the whole exchange, and then to the construct sitting next to her.

"If you want your family safe," he said, "there is no safer place than right here."

"You are welcome to bring them here," Faith said softly. "Or I can arrange that if you would like."

Scarlett was still in too much shock to answer.

Jeanette, she keened silently. *Where the hell are you? Please be off dicking around in the arcade or sneaking a pinch of whisky with your silly friends somewhere. Please be okay.*

Charity returned, holding a glittering comset and handing it to the Red Jordan. Scarlett took it with numb fingers, glanced at the configuration and hooked it over her right ear.

"This is Jordan Scarlett," she said.

Bjorn's voice was clear, and clearly surprised. "Scarlett!" he exclaimed in a great whoosh. "How, where...?" he stammered, at a loss for words.

The Red Jordan smiled, not quite put at ease, but the strangle around her heart was lessening. "Bjorn, I don't have time for pleasantries or explanations. My niece, Jeanette, is missing."

The strangle resurfaced and she had to swallow hard to keep her composure. And, though she could not see him, she could somehow sense the same sudden tautness in him, wherever he was. He remained silent, but Scarlett could also tell he was not without purpose.

She could see him perfectly in her mind's eye, looking at his lovely troll. In the same way, she could see Lucy - the troll's eyes shimmering. Then she *could* hear Bjorn, whispering soft yet urgent commands to Lucy, but she could not make out what he was saying. She had the feeling that if she gave Blue the comset the other Jordan would be able to hear every word. But Scarlett was not about to give it up, even when she heard Bjorn's whispers turn into hisses. Even when she was finally able to distinguish his final word. Especially then.

Shit! he cursed under his breath.

"What?" she demanded. "What is it?"

The Jordan felt hot panic rising and she quelled it by force of will.

"It's okay," Bjorn said immediately. "She's okay."

Scarlett expelled a great gush of air from her lungs.

"She's on Io," Bjorn continued, "in Three Mile, just not on

the Upper Klick." Scarlett bit her lip to hold back a sob of relief. "I'm halfway between Io and the Maul Satellite, less than an hour away. I can pick her up and take her home, or to you…"

"No, home would be better. You're sure she is okay?"

"Yes, she's having coffee and doughnuts."

Now a ragged sound *did* escape her throat but it was more of a laugh, tattered as it was with relief. "In that case I can send my brother…"

"No." His response was immediate and insistent. Scarlett drew in another deep breath as alarms went off in her mind. Jeanette was safe, but not free from danger.

"Do you know who she is with?"

"Yes. I will get her and take her home."

"Okay. But how?"

She knew Bjorn could not simply walk into a doughnut shop and walk out with an eleven-year-old girl under his arm like a loaf of bread. From the silence on the other end of the com she knew Bjorn was realizing the same.

"Call Fletch," he said brightly, excited by having come up with a plan, "have him meet me at the Upper Klick travel hub in half an hour."

Jesus, Scarlett thought, *of course. Grandpa knows Bjorn and Jeanette knows Grandpa. How the hell can there be less than six degrees of separation in a universe this large?* And then she remembered something else Elaeric had taught her about entanglement.

"I will," she told the Chimeran Commander. "And Bjorn?"

"Yes, Scarlett?"

"Thank you."

"You're welcome." He paused and then asked, "see you soon?"

Scarlett answered with hardly any hesitation. "Yes."

The Red Jordan cut the line and scrubbed her face with

her palms. She removed the comset Charity had given her and pressed the one embedded in her ear. The closest link operator came on the connection and Scarlett gave her John's number. The line was picked up before the first ring finished.

"Yes?" he answered eagerly.

"I've found her. She's fine." She could hear the sound of her brother choke on his relief while there was an unmistakable cry from Rebecca. "Grandpa needs to get to the UK hub port, have Sean take him. There will be someone there to take him to get Jeanette. She'll be home in an hour, no more than two."

"Thank you, Johanna."

"Yes! Thank you!" She could hear Rebecca sob in gratitude from somewhere in their pod. "Thank you, Jo!"

"Wait," Scarlett said before he could cut the line. "I still want to get you out of there. All of you. Until I know it is safe." She looked at Faith who gave her a nod of assurance and listened to the pause on the comset as she knew John looked at Rebecca.

"Yes," she sobbed. "Anything she wants."

Scarlett sighed. "I'll arrange for transport once Jeanette gets home."

"Thanks again, Jo. Love you."

"Love you, too."

Scarlett cut the link. "Thank you," she told Faith earnestly, her dark eyes also flicking to Charity. "Now, if you don't mind, I would like to speak privately with my fellow Jordan."

"Jordans," Amberle corrected.

Blue and Scarlett regarded her with barely suppressed smiles which Amberle did not miss.

"Don't patronize me!" she scolded.

Both Jordans laughed.

 # TWO FOUR

- Secrets, like power, can be as dangerous as they are delicious.

Jeanette delicately licked frosting off her fingertips and then cleaned them on her napkin. She felt that she had just had her first adult conversation and she was exhilarated.

She had even drunk coffee.

She was afraid at first, because she had tasted Grandpa's before and it was the most awful and bitter thing she had ever tried. But she was determined to prove herself. She would bear it if necessary to verify how grown up she was.

But JP showed her how *he* drank coffee, adding a few sugar strips and a small pitcher of heavy cream. Jeanette did the same and found that it was not just bearable but good.

The Chimeran Commander had ordered an array of donuts in different flavors and Jeanette had tried most of them.

And Jan had not lied. They were really looking for young pilots to train, if they showed promise.

JP had told her that he himself was not a pilot, but Jan was the best there was in their whole military. Jeanette had stared in surprise at Jan who blushed a little, and then turned her dark eyes back to JP. He was so handsome. More than the boys at her school, or even the boys at Sean's high school.

And he was honest with her. None of the adults in her life were honest with her. She supposed Grandpa was, but she knew he held back a lot because he thought her too young to know some things.

They talked for the better part of an hour, Jeanette's head buzzing with excitement, caffeine and sugar.

The door at the front of the café opened and JP smiled as if he saw who entered, even though he was facing away from the front.

"Lucky lady!" he told Jeanette. You are going to meet two Chimeran Commanders today! I'm sorry," he apologized, correcting himself, "three when we include Jan here."

"You're a Commander?" Jeanette asked in wonder.

Jan nodded but his smile was forced and his hand dropped to where he kept JP's extra blade.

"It's okay," JP told him. "It's just Bjorn. Julian and Diego are outside."

Still, he let his right hand rest over his left wrist, his fingers grazing the hilt of the machete concealed under his sleeve. Jeanette watched in excitement as an absolutely gorgeous man walked towards them.

The door opened again and this time JP froze, and then chuckled as he took his fingers from his weapon. Now he *did* turn, looking curiously over his left shoulder past where Bjorn was striding casually between the booths and tables to where another man looked around with genuine curiosity.

"Grandpa!" Jeanette exclaimed. She stood up and waved.

The tall blonde man stopped in front of her. "My god, you look like Scarlett!" he exclaimed. Jeanette laughed and held out her hand.

"I'm Jeanette," she said. Bjorn shook her small hand.

"I'm Bjorn. It's a pleasure to meet you."

"You know my Auntie Jo?"

"I do. And your grandpa is an old friend of mine."

"He is? You're here together?"

"Yes." He turned his green eyes to the commanders still seated. JP," he greeted formally. "Petrov."

"Hello Bjorn," JP said pleasantly. "What brings you here?"

"Fletcher and I are here to get some doughnuts, of course."

Jeanette gave JP a knowing look and a nod. "Grandpa loves sweets," she affirmed.

"Is that so?" JP asked with a tight smile.

"It is." She waved at Grandpa and he waved back and then held up a finger, letting her know he would be there in a moment. He had stopped at the counter to order something.

"And since we are here," Bjorn continued, "and we are already headed back to the Upper Klick, we might as well give the lady a ride home."

Jeanette grinned. The lady. Not the girl. For the life of her she could not figure out why everyone bitched so much about the Chimera. They were so nice.

"It *is* getting late," Jeanette said, looking outside at the changing color of the simulated sky. "We talked longer than I thought we would." Her face became sour. "My mom is gonna give me hell. Pardon my language," she added quickly.

JP smiled. "It's fine. Just remember, sometimes it is better to be understanding than it is to argue."

Jeanette nodded. "That's good advice. I usually fly off the handle."

Bjorn laughed and the sound made her cheeks grow warm. "Don't tell me you have your Aunt's temper as well as her good looks?"

Jeanette laughed, blushing deeply now. "I guess I might," she admitted. She turned to Jan. "Thank you for bringing me here."

Jan scooted across the bench seat towards her. "It was

a pleasure to meet you," he said, extending a hand. Jeanette shook it and turned to JP. "It was very nice to meet you," she said, extending her small hand.

JP beamed at her as he shook it. "The pleasure was mine. I hope to see you again soon."

A look of disapproval fluttered across Bjorn's countenance and was gone. "Let's get you home," he said. "Your family is going on a trip."

He now had Jeanette's full attention. "My family? A trip?"

"That's right. Something your Aunt has arranged. Your grandpa is supposed to be getting some snacks for the flight. Let's see if he has found what he was after." He glanced at the two Chimeran Officers still seated. "JP. Petrov."

The commanders gave him a nod and the tall blonde turned and, with Jeanette, met Fletcher at the counter. Grandpa was hefting up a sizeable box of shiny pink cardboard.

"I might have bought too many," he admitted with a smile. "Hello there, beautiful!"

"Hi, Grandpa!" Jeanette was glad he had his hands full. She did not mind his hugs but she did not want to seem like a child in front of the officers.

"Need help, Fletcher?" Bjorn asked.

Grandpa shook his head with frown. "I'm fine," he assured as he headed for the door.

Bjorn grinned as they made their way to the front of the café, showing the most perfect teeth Jeannette had ever seen.

"I wish I could say you haven't aged a day," Bjorn said. "But, I must admit, you have aged much less than I thought you would have by now."

Grandpa smiled. "Thanks."

They went through the front door where they were joined by two more handsome men. Jeanette was proud that she could identify them as constructs, and undoubtably Chimeran.

It's good that I know, she thought, mentally congratulating herself. *I'm going to be around them quite a lot. I hope.*

The constructs escorted them to a large black aircar with blacked-out windows and opened the doors for them. The back of the car had four black leather seats, two facing forward and two facing back.

Bjorn held out a hand to help Jeanette in which she accepted, feeling like a holo star. Grandpa handed the box to Bjorn and climbed in, sitting so he was facing her. Bjorn returned the box to Grandpa and circled the car to get in on the other side. One strikingly handsome construct (Jeanette knew they had to be bodyguards, a fact on which she also congratulated herself) shut the door and climbed in the front next to the driver. The other gorgeous man circled the car and, after Bjorn was seated, climbed in and shut the door, taking the seat across from his commander.

The car rose silently and began to cruise down the street.

"Where are we going for our trip?" she asked Grandpa, curiosity prickling her skin.

"It's a surprise," he told her with a smile. For himself as much as for his granddaughter. He had no idea where they were headed. "But we will be taking a space shuttle."

"A space shuttle? You mean we are leaving Io?"

"Yep. Not sure for how long, but I am sure it will be quite the adventure. I hope your brother likes jellies and old fashions as much as you do."

"He'll eat anything you give him," Jeanette said, looking out the window and feeling more than grown up. She felt important. She was quite sure that her adventure had already started. Sean could have every one of the jellies for all she cared. She had something he didn't. A secret.

"Here we are!" Bjorn announced as the executive aircar pulled to a stop in the Upper Klick at the end of a residential street along the park adjacent to the podplex where the Mattatock family lived.

"Thank you, Bjorn," Fletcher said earnestly, looking him in the eye. Bjorn nodded and turned his green-eyed gaze to Jeanette.

"Yes," she agreed, "thanks for taking us home. Hopefully I'm not in too much trouble."

Bjorn gave her a dazzling smile. "I admit that JP and I do not agree on everything, but in this case I believe he is right. Understanding where your mother is coming from will go farther than fighting."

"Alright," she said. "I'll do my best."

She gave him a smile of her own and wiggled down from her seat, one of the handsome bodyguards catching her by the elbow to keep her steady. He also assisted Fletcher with his box as he exited the car, then shut the door.

The car had stopped as close as it could to their podment which was on the far side of the park. Jeanette and her grandfather were not put out in the slightest. Jeanette resisted the urge to skip or run across the grass and instead walked down the sidewalk that cut through the trees with her head held high, asking Grandpa what he knew about the trip they were about to take.

Bjorn watched them go, his green eyes sweeping across the grassy knolls.

"Comset."

Bjorn held out a hand and Diego placed a small device in the commander's palm. Bjorn fitted it into his ear. "Lucy," he commanded, "patch me through to Charity." The line was patched, connected, and a comset on the other end changed hands multiple times before he heard Scarlett's voice in his ear.

"Yes?"

That simple word, or possibly it was just the sound of her voice, brought a smile to his full lips.

"She's home," he said. A choked sigh came from the other end of the connection. "There is an IGC unit there now," he told Scarlett. "Four soldiers outside being discreet as possible, which is not very discreet at all. There are more inside, I'm guessing to guard and help pack."

"Yes," Scarlett agreed, now in control of her voice and emotions. "It shouldn't be more than half an hour, now that Jeanette is home. Thank you again. I can't tell you what this means, how much this means…"

"Enough to get me another dinner with you?"

Scarlett laughed. "It's the least I can do. And my treat. I'll contact your personal assistant and set it up."

Bjorn frowned and exhaled sharply. "I was being serious."

Scarlett laughed again. "So was I. *Lucy*. I will contact *Lucy*."

"Oh!" Bjorn smiled. "Very well then. I look forward to seeing you, Scarlett."

"Until then," she said.

"Until then," he answered.

Scarlett cut the connection and looked at Faith.

"The IGC will take them to the base on Titan?" she asked the Jordan. Scarlett nodded. "Excellent. We will get them from the base and bring them here. It should take twelve to twenty hours, mostly depending on how fast the IGC moves on this."

Scarlett heaved a sigh. "Thank you." She could not remember ever having given so many thanks, and meant every one of them.

"It's really no problem at all," Faith assured her.

"Meanwhile," the Jordan said, "do you mind if Blue and I speak privately? I think there a more than a few things we need to discuss."

"Certainly. There are many rooms and parlors here where

you can relax. The rooms will not be monitored, but if you are uneasy, there is always the hangar."

"I'd like to join you," Amberle said.

"No," Faith said. "You need to get ready. You're going back to Venus."

"What?"

"I'm quite sure you heard me. I want you to return to Venus. You need to bring back Ember."

"She doesn't want to come."

"She told you, if I recall your words correctly, that she wasn't in a position where she could leave immediately, but it didn't mean that she would be opposed to it later."

"True," Amberle agreed, "but she was one hell of a mess, and *in* one hell of a mess."

"Hopefully she will have had enough time to recover. You said that there were other races with her?"

"Yes."

"And that they were beautiful? Too beautiful, too perfect, to be human?"

Amberle's eyes widened and flicked to Jasyn before they went back to Faith.

"You think they were constructs? Are constructs?"

"I know they are constructs. And I expect they are probably in need of something. Quite possibly in dire need. It is something I can give them."

"What is that?" Amberle asked.

"Yeah," Blue echoed, her eye going back and forth between the two as they conversed, "what is that?"

"The ability to reproduce," Faith told them. A vapor of silence filled the air of the room and everyone seemed to exhale at the same moment, their eyes widened and lips parted. Faith lifted her chin and continued. "I can supply the missing code in their DNA that is currently keeping them from procreation."

"Holy shit," Amberle said.

"I can put the necessary code in a number of dermi-patches. In this case, I believe you would need less than a thousand. Regardless, we will wrap up a thousand to send with you in a box no larger than your hand. If she truly is an ally to these people, it should sway her."

Charity's green eyes, pleased and lit with admiration, went from Amberle to Faith.

"Do I have time for a shooting lesson?" the young woman asked.

"You're carrying a weapon you don't know how to use?" Scarlett asked.

"Of course I know how to use it," Amberle said, "I just can't aim it. I can't close my non-firing eye," she told her, remembering her attempt at using a weapon when she was on the zombie-ridden moon of Elba. It was what Cooper had told her.

Scarlett turned her face to Blue, who gave the younger Jordan a gruesome smile.

"An affliction that I, too, once had," she admitted. Her lone eye, once sapphire but now unquestionably shot through with bursts of turquoise, glanced suspiciously at Faith before fixing on the young Jordan. "You don't really have to close it, just relax it. Use your firing eye to focus." She jerked her chin at Jasyn. "I'm sure he can show you."

Amberle looked at the dark-haired construct. "Can you do that?" she asked.

"I can," he acquiesced with a smile as he pushed his chair back from the table and stood. "But we should probably go outside."

"Darn tootin'," Charity muttered into her drink as she polished it off.

"Meanwhile," Faith said as everyone began to rise from their seats, "we will have rooms prepared for you and your family.

You, and they, might be here for some time. And if that is not the case, you'll always have a place to return. Would you like your rooms to be with your family, or close to Amberle's?"

"Close to Amberle," Scarlett answered without hesitation, making the young Jordan's dark face beam. "Close to Blue as well, if she ends up staying here."

"Wow," Blue said softly, gripping the back of her chair with both hands. "We're really talking some serious shit here."

Scarlett nodded. "And we've only just begun."

Charity, the only one who had remained sitting, gave a quiet snort of laughter and motioned for someone in the shadows to bring her another drink.

"Let's find that parlor," Scarlett said. "I have a hard time talking in here, I feel so exposed."

Faith also beckoned to the shadows as she retook her seat. "Do you need someone to show you where it is?"

Blue shook her head, white-blonde hair shining in the light that now streamed unimpeded from the glass ceiling, the storm having slowly moved off to haunt the raging seas. "I can find it, but send the old guy with drinks, if you don't mind."

"Old guy?" Charity asked, surprised as she accepted a cocktail from an assistant. "What old guy? I'm sure I don't have..."

"I think she means Jeeves," Faith said with a smile as another assistant handed her a flute of sparkling wine.

"Oh!" Charity exclaimed. "Jeeves! Of course."

"You seriously have a butler named Jeeves?" Scarlett asked.

"I have at least a dozen," Charity told her.

Jasyn jerked his head and Amberle followed him down a flower-lined path from the conservatory while Scarlett shook her own dark hair in disbelief.

"There is no way this can be real," she said softly.

"It's real enough," Blue assured her. "And, if it isn't, at least there is alcohol."

"Amen to that!" Charity agreed with enthusiasm, lifting a glass with a ring-covered hand before taking a surprisingly dainty sip.

Blue turned and took a path in the opposite direction that Amberle and Jasyn had gone. "What is it that you want to talk about?" she asked.

Scarlett followed her through the re-creation of nature under the dome. "We need to talk about what is going on aboard our Dragon. Especially where it concerns our Executive Officer."

"Don't forget about the Aridian," Blue reminded her.

Scarlett sighed. "Her too."

 TWO FIVE

- Everyone holds secrets, and sometimes the weight of the silence speaks louder than the truth.

Nathan sat in the passenger cabin of a GwenSeven transport. It was not just any transport ship, but it was Charity's personal shuttle. It was the only transport that was allowed access to the hangar under the Castle and the only one that would be cleared by security upon its return.

It was simple, by de Rossi standards, but more luxurious than a premier class cabin on any commercial craft. The Engineer knew everything they had was opulent or beyond. It was a lifestyle he had become acclimated to quite quickly, one he wanted to continue, and not as some mere employee. He intended to have one of the de Rossi sisters, but would settle for someone lesser who could keep him comfortable enough. The young Jordan of the Emerald Fledgling perhaps. She was as ripe as a peach and young enough to be told what to do or cowed into doing it.

Still, one of the de Rossi's would be better.

He had already had intimate and often sexual relations with a number of Charity's friends, and a few of her assistants. But it was really Charity herself that he wanted or, better yet, Faith.

Many times he had eyed the chains she wore and imagined

melting the one around her neck into a collar, the ones around her wrists into manacles and shackling her naked to the headboard on her bed.

Even now, just thinking about it made him shift on the sofa cushion and then reach down to adjust his pants. Similar thoughts always seem to rise in his mind producing a similar effect. More than that, the tall Engineer could see that his charms were not lost on her. She felt an inexplicable attraction to him.

But the construct - that damn, black-haired construct!

He was more than meddling, he was downright destructive to Nathan's plans. He was always around, constantly driving a wedge between Faith and himself. To add to his annoyance, the tall Engineer had always thought the construct looked irritatingly familiar.

It was at dinner one night, a night that the bastard had again carefully maneuvered himself next to Faith, forcing the Engineer to sit opposite them both, that he finally recognized him fully.

Nathan had been sitting next to Charity and running a large hand over her porcelain knee, when a frequent guest of the house named Dr. Silas made a remark about the Chimeran Battle Cruiser *Resurrection* and her presumably half-mad (or possibly full-on bat shit crazy) commander.

Charity had delicately moved Nathan's hand to his own leg and then ran her fingers up the length of his thigh. Jasyn had replied in defense of the said crazy Zealot and Nathan's head had snapped up, suddenly alert and apprehending just who the man really was.

At the same moment he knew exactly how he was going to get rid of the meddling and quite dangerous construct. Startled with the revelation, he had momentarily only been slightly aware of how high Charity's fingers had traveled up his leg.

Recalling it now did nothing to quell his growing erection.

Just then, his attendant came in with a glass of sparkling water and set it on the table. Nathan stared at the crevasse between her breasts as she bent over and then straightened. She had wanton eyes and full lips. A tongue darted out over them before she asked if there was anything he needed.

Sitting, he could not loom over her, which usually did most women in. But he still had his voice. Low and soft, like the purr of a predatory cat, it was almost always enough to weaken any woman.

Now was no different.

"Someplace private to lay down?" he suggested.

"Would you like turndown service?" she asked.

"I certainly would."

૱

Sean wiggled in his own seat, for a different reason altogether. He was almost nervous enough to want to chew on his nails - something he had never done before.

It wasn't the space shuttle that was making him uneasy, though it was the first time he had ever been on one. On the contrary, he was loving every minute. At least he did for the for the first few hours.

The whole idea of a trip, *a trip into space*, had been thrilling. Jeanette had turned up just fine, as he knew she would, but thanks to her little disappearance for half an afternoon the whole family was treated to a trip to Titan.

His father told them that with all the excitement going on it would do the family good to go on a vacation. That was bullshit if Sean had ever heard it but did not say so as he watched men with military haircuts dressed as delivery personnel take the suitcases his mother and father had quickly packed and load them into an airvan.

Sean had thrown a few of his essentials in a bag along with a few extra pairs of pants and shirts and turned it over before going to check on his grandfather across the hall. Grandpa, who had also packed some necessities in a small satchel, was standing with his hands on his hips and looking at a box on the floor that was already taped shut.

Sean's blue eyes went immediately to Grandpa's living room shelves. They had, for the most part, been cleared. His eyes, now wide, went to the old man who no longer looked like an old man.

"You don't think we're coming back?" he asked softly.

"Son," he replied, "I'm not sure about anything, and these books have traveled a long way and a long time with me."

"This whole deal is a lot more than Jeanette playing hooky today, isn't it?"

"I think so."

Sean nodded and glanced at the shelves. "Did you pack up those certificates, too?"

"Ayuh."

"Good, but we are going to scan those the first chance we get. There's a reason no one uses paper anymore."

He gave Grandpa half a smile and opened the door. The door to his family's pod was open and he motioned to one of the uniformed men inside. "Can we get a little help in here?" he called.

A man wearing a nondescript brown jumpsuit with a matching brown cap spied the parcel on the floor and produced a square of heavy plastic and shook it open. Then he put the box on top and ran his finger over what looked like a yellow zipper. The plastic closed around the box and there was a hiss as the small capsule inside filled the plastic cube with gas. It rose like a giant square bubble, package inside, and the man gave Sean a nod before guiding the floating bundle out of the pod and into the waiting van.

Sean spared a glance into his own pod and knew his parents were thinking along the same lines as his grandfather. They had packed clothes but also a few boxes. He saw some bare shelves in their podment and it gave him a strange empty feeling inside.

Grandpa picked up his satchel and followed Sean with the rest of the family not far behind.

The airvan took them to a private spaceport, even more secluded and secure than the usual exclusive one used by the residents of the Upper Klick. The family and their belongings were passed from the military-looking delivery men to military-looking stewards on the ship.

Sean was delighted to be shown to his private seat capsule. It had its own entertainment system with literally millions of options for games or holo movies to watch. He could control the lighting and sound all around his seat, a seat which would also transform into a bed at the touch of a button.

His parents shared the capsule in front of him and he could hear them but not see them. Jeanette had her own across the aisle from him and Grandpa was seated in front of her, pushing the buttons that moved his chair around.

Despite all of the options for gaming and entertainment, his sister simply sat and stared out the window of the space shuttle, a little smile on her heart-shaped face.

Sean frowned, a small crease forming between his blonde eyebrows.

Attendants moved around, making sure they were secure and comfortable before take-off. One of them approached his father and sank down on one knee so they were almost eye-level with each other.

"My name is Avery," he said, "and it is a pleasure to have you on board. We will be taking off soon. The trip is approximately twenty hours. We will be serving dinner in an hour; you can make your selection on the menu on your console. The same with breakfast. In between, feel free to order drinks or snacks on the screen, or just press the service button and any of us would be glad to help you."

"Thank you," John told him. "It is much appreciated."

"Not a problem at all," Avery told him with a smile. "The same service will continue when we arrive on Titan. The IGC is always glad to take care of our officers and their families."

"Thank you again," John said, "but we will be traveling on our own once we get there. Meeting up with some old friends," he explained.

"Oh?" the attendant remarked, clearly surprised. "Where will you be headed when we land? We can certainly arrange for transportation."

"I'm not sure where we are going," John lied. "But a ride will already be waiting for us." Which was true.

"Very well," the steward agreed with what was now somewhat of a forced amiability. "In the meantime, please let any one of us know if there is anything we can do to make you comfortable."

John thanked him again.

Sean watched through the window as they taxied and then launched, the sides glowing slightly with friction before they left the artificial atmosphere of Io and broke through into the vacuum of space.

He stared in awe at the view of Three-Mile City, visible long after everything else on the moon disappeared from sight.

He ate one of the jelly doughnuts that Grandpa had brought along and messed around with the entertainment system.

An hour later, attendants were setting up a table in front of him with a white tablecloth and a formal place setting. He glanced to his right to see the same thing happening in front of his sister, but Jeanette had not moved from where she was staring out the window with that same smug look on her face.

Sean frowned, the crease between his brows deeper this time.

He ate, played some non-sphere games, and fell asleep watching a holo movie. Someone had laid a folded blanket over his lap while he had napped and now he touched the button that transformed the seat into a bed. He started another movie and ignored the fact that Jeanette's place had been cleared and she had fallen asleep with her face still turned towards the window of the shuttle.

Someone, probably his father, had put a blanket over her and tucked it under her chin.

At some point during the journey the lights in the cabin slowly began to brighten and Sean awoke. He touched the button with the picture of a chair on it and his bed lifted him back into a sitting position. It appeared he was the last to do so.

He could hear his parents talking quietly and he could see Grandpa drinking a cup of coffee. Even Jeanette was awake, back to staring out the window. Sean got up to use the bathroom and looked at her worriedly as he passed.

Where was all her senseless chatter? Where were the million and a half questions that were always bubbling out of her?

Maybe she got into some of Grandpa's pills, he thought. *Or Auntie Jo's.*

Then he considered the possibility that maybe his parents had actually given her something to keep her calm on the trip. He was pretty sure his mom had taken something. However, when he passed her on the way back from the bathroom, she seemed almost normal, eating an old-fashioned doughnut and drinking a glass of milk.

But she was not watching anything, not gaming. And entirely too quiet.

Breakfast was being placed on a tray for him as he retook

his seat, again with white linens and fancy silverware. This time, the person waiting on him was a woman. Very young and very pretty. She put down the omelet he had ordered along with buttered toast and fresh melon slices. Every time she bent over he had a clear view of her plunging neckline. He was sure she caught him looking while she poured orange juice into the glass on his table because she gave him a charming smile.

"Would you like some champagne with your breakfast, sir?" she asked.

Sean almost responded immediately that he was too young but realized she undoubtedly knew. For a few seconds he considered accepting the offer – after all, they *were* on vacation and there was no one who seemed to be paying attention at the moment. Then he shook his blonde head. "No, thank you. I'll be fine with the juice."

"Well," she said, "if you change your mind, I'm in the galley just behind the last row of seats."

Sean nodded dumbly as she moved away and then, unable to help himself, turned his head to watch her walk away. When he turned back he could see Grandpa smiling at him from over his shoulder. Sean smiled back and dug into his breakfast. He glanced at Jeanette but she was looking out the window again.

Lunch was the same (other than the actual meal), including being served by the lovely young woman and being offered a drink. This time he was almost ready to accept but he was aware that his mother had gone silent mid-sentence as she was talking to his father. He knew she was listening. Intently.

"I'm okay with a soda," Sean told his attendant.

"Alright," she agreed with a knowing expression. "But you know where to find me if you change your mind." She gave him a wink and headed for the aft end of the craft.

Sean let out a deep breath after she had gone and saw Grandpa eyeing him again, this time with a touch of concern, that concern not leaving his eyes even as they shifted to his father.

"Are you sure we cannot arrange for transportation when we land on Titan?" an IGC agent in a steward's uniform was asking John. "We will be there in another hour and want to make sure you are safe."

"Thank you, but no," John replied. "Our friends have already arranged it for us. We are taking our kids someplace special." He gave the man a conspiratorial wink before glancing at Jeanette.

"I see," the man agreed with a nod of understanding. It seemed that the parents wanted to keep the children from knowing, some sort of surprise. He gave John a tight-lipped smile and moved away.

Rebecca turned her face slightly towards her husband. "I don't think they like it - not knowing where we are going," she said softly.

"I don't think so either," he agreed quietly. "Which probably means it is a good idea that they don't know."

Still, the attendants were extremely polite and made sure the whole family was secure and comfortable for the remainder of the trip. When the shuttle finally reached Titan and landed at a secure spaceport the family disembarked, walking down a carpeted ramp to a black-top tarmac. There were other transports of varying sizes but they were few and far away. Still, they could see people and vehicles around them – mostly restocking and refueling the waiting spacecrafts.

"Wow," Sean whispered, his eyes scanning the sky. It was sunset and the blue sky was streaked with pink clouds. It was the first time he had ever been on another moon. Even Jeanette looked up in wonder.

"That can't be the real sun," she said softly. "We are farther away from it now than we were on Io."

"That's right," Grandpa said. "It's a source of starfire that circles the atmosphere jacket, rounding the equator every twenty-eight hours – a standard elfin day. Good thing, too. Otherwise, the days on Titan would be long and the nights very dark. The starfire keeps the air at a constant but pleasant temperature during the day and a slightly cooler, but still pleasant temperature, at night."

"How do you know so much about Titan, Grandpa?" Jeanette asked, voicing her first question in almost thirty hours. Sean guessed it was the longest she had gone since she had learned how to talk.

"Oh, I've been here before," he told her, giving her a wink. And he had. Many times. But there was one time in in particular that was on his mind. A late afternoon, watching his daughter walk across a stage in her cap and gown, her bickering with her mother at dinner, the fancy restaurant in a giant tree next to a plunging waterfall, the call from Faith.

The wind stirred Fletcher's hair as he stood on the concrete apron, his soul stirred by the flood of memories.

Sean's parents stretched as their bags were unloaded. Avery approached John and held his hand out, palm up.

John felt a jolt of panicked embarrassment, thinking the man was expecting some kind of payment and he had no idea how much the trip might have cost or how he would pay him. Then he saw that he was holding something.

Squinting, John saw that it was a comset. It was the thinnest device of that kind he had ever seen, made of a completely transparent material.

"Pressing here," Avery said, demonstrating, "will connect you directly with me or a member of my team." The comset gave a blue glow that John saw visually echoed in the steward's right ear. The communicator Avery wore was so small and streamlined that John had never noticed it until now. "If you ever feel like you or a member of your family is in danger, or if there is anything you need, do not hesitate to call."

"Thank you," John told him, taking the comset and tucking

it into the pocket over his heart. "I actually cannot thank you enough for all you have done for us."

"It is what we are here for," the IGC attendant replied with a disarming smile. "Now," he said, bringing his hands together, "where can we deliver your luggage?"

"We'll take it from here," a voice chirped from behind them.

Everyone turned to see a petite woman with yellow-blonde hair and blue eyes framed with lashes thick with mascara. She wore a burgundy jacket over a blue collared shirt and burgundy skirt. A holographic nametag floated under her left collarbone.

Daphne.

"Hello!" she greeted. "My name is Daphne and I am delighted to be your tour guide here in the OEC."

She was not young, Sean saw, nor was she old. She had smooth skin, but it was more lax than tight, with small wrinkles around her mouth and her eyes. If he had to guess, he would say she looked about the same age that his grandpa looked now. Sixty maybe?

The IGC steward gave her a forced smile as her own attendants dressed in the same uniforms began loading luggage onto an electric, open-air minibus. Grandpa made sure his box went along with the rest of their things.

"Come along, everyone!" Daphne called out, herding her small flock into the minibus. "We have many activities planned and so much to see in the Original Elfin City!"

"Thanks again," John told Avery by way of goodbye before following his family into the open-air cart. Once he was seated, the vehicle took off and John gave him a wave. The man gave him a thin-lipped smile in return and then disappeared from sight as the minibus veered to the left.

"Well!" Daphne announced. "That wasn't so bad!" She had remained standing, her slim fingers grasping a bar to keep herself steady as the vehicle swerved to the right and accelerated. It went through an open gate and into another secure area.

Sean craned his neck around to see that a vehicle had followed them from the space shuttle but stopped at the gate right before it turned into a wall of detfleck. He turned his face back towards Daphne.

"Isn't this an IGC spaceport?" he asked, surprised.

"Yes," she said with a smile, "but there are places that even the IGC is not allowed." She turned her eyes to John. "Did they give you a comset?" John blinked at her in surprise and she held out her hand, her fingers motioning for him to hand it over, before he could answer. He laughed softly as he dug it out of his breast pocket and put it in her open palm.

"They were going to use it to track us," he said.

"Of course they were," Daphne agreed. She handed the near-invisible comset to the driver who made it vanish into his jacket as he swerved again and brought them to a stop so quickly that they all lurched forward in their seats and then, just as quickly, pitched back.

The driver was up and out of his seat and Sean's blue eyes followed him as he got into another small electric vehicle and sped away. His eyes swung back around at the sound of Grandpa's voice.

"Well, if that don't beat all," the old man whispered.

Sean's gaze followed his grandpa's to the next conveyance that awaited them and his mouth dropped open.

It was another space shuttle. This one, larger and sleeker, was being swarmed with people. Some were cleaning while some were performing maintenance checks. Some were taking crates and bags from the craft while others were loading it with fresh supplies. The attendants on the minibus with them were already off and taking their luggage.

The luxury shuttle was breathtaking in size, dwarfing the one they had taken from Io. It was new and bright and emblazoned with an enormous G7 in gold and silver along the side.

"All roads lead home," Grandpa finished softly. Sean was not quite sure what he was referring to but the words sent a chill up his spine.

Daphne shed the burgundy jacket she had been wearing, just a costume piece, and dropped it on the driver's seat. She left the vehicle with the Mattatock family in tow.

"Now can you tell us where we are going?" Sean asked.

His father gave him a nod as he held Rebecca's elbow while she stepped down onto the concrete apron from the minibus. "The Last Castle on the Distant Shore."

"Holy shit!"

"Sean!" his mother reprimanded.

"Sorry," he said, not looking the least apologetic. "Are you serious?" he asked his father. "You can't be!"

"I am."

"Where?" Grandpa asked as they followed Daphne to the monstrous shuttle. He turned his blue eyes to his grandson. "What's the big deal?"

Sean looked at his father a moment longer to see if he was going to start laughing and say he was only joking. He didn't.

"The Last Castle," Sean explained, turning his gaze to Grandpa, "is the castle of Charity de Rossi."

Grandpa's brows went up. "Is that so?"

"It is. It's on a secret moon that no one can find."

"If no one can find it," Grandpa argued, "how are we supposed to get there?"

Sean almost shrugged then realized he might know. "If it is one of her ships," he reasoned out loud, "and it certainly looks like it is, it has something embedded in the guidance system to find its way back."

John looked over his shoulder to smile at his son as they boarded the massive craft. Sean looked askance to see Jeanette, who had not oohed or ahhed or seemed to be impressed by anything. And she had not raised a single question other than asking Grandpa how he knew Titan so well.

Sensing her brother's gaze on her, she glanced at him and gave him a small smile. The look made Sean think of something Grandpa had once said.

The cat that swallowed the canary.

Sean had no idea what Grandpa had been talking about at the time, and though he knew the reference involved a cat and some type of bird, it made zero sense to him. Now, the expression – both the phrase and the look – made perfect sense.

It perfectly described Jeanette's countenance and the smug look in her eye.

The cat that swallowed the canary.

 TWO SIX

- Reality is a puzzle - every secret a missing piece.

Eris was a world of long and storied history.

It began as a dwarf planet, warm and mostly covered with water when the system of planets and moons was ruled by a Pantheon of Gods. A fight amongst the Gods, however, changed the starscape forever.

Triton, the son of Poseidon, hid himself and his people on the watery planet after playing a trick on the God of the Sun, Apollo. Apollo found him and, in his anger, drove his fiery chariot (which was the star of life in the center of the tiny solar system) across the dark of space until he was on the far side of the system, leaving Eris (and her occupants) to freeze.

A millennia later, humans from Earth and elves from the reaches of the Andromeda galaxy began to terraform previously uninhabitable worlds. Eris was given a controlled atmosphere. The sun, now as far from the dwarf planet as it could be, was magnified enough to support life.

A small race of Sylvan elves migrated there along with two races of humans, one of which was tall and broad and accustomed to the slowly warming but still frigid climate.

Eris however, still held her own icy secrets of gods and monsters – including a race of humanoid creatures slowly evolving while the people of Triton remained encased in her frozen oceans.

A thousand years later, something happened that the god Apollo did not expect.

A group of elves, tired of fighting war after war, secretly hired a private company, the GwenSeven Corporation, for an undertaking that had never been done before, or since.

The dwarf planet of Eris was slowly pushed from the outskirts of the system, back towards the sun. Terraformers who had phenomenally mastered zero-point energy started the process of changing Eris with the intent to hide her and the Elven people under the poisonous atmosphere of Venus.

A few thousand elves began the migration.

In secret, so did a thousand scientists and engineers from earth.

Also, in secret of course, went a few thousand GwenSeven constructs. Not the original Pantheon, but magnificently close.

Before the project could be completed, alas, catastrophe struck.

An expanse of dark energy was released with all the power of a black hole and followed by a nuclear bomb strong enough to implode a planet.

Eris was ripped in half.

A portion went towards Venus as intended, pulling everything within half of an astronomical unit along with her. The other portion went screaming towards the next closest planet, also drawing many a ship and soul with her.

Now sometimes the closest planet to Venus is Mercury, depending on their orbits. Otherwise, the closest planet is Earth.

But that is a story for another time.

For now, despite the wishes and efforts of the migrants to Eris - now safely cloaked beneath the nefarious clouds of Venus - she had seen her first war.

The secret world itself was more than beautiful. Melting glaciers and snowcapped mountains bordered verdant lands and golden fields. Rivers jumping with fish cut through thick forests and lush meadows. Under the guise of a poisonous planet, the world was literally a hidden gem.

❧

Verdana dropped down into the atmosphere of Eris and, once again, the sight of it took Amberle's breath away. On this journey, however, they were over an entirely different part of the small planet.

On their last trip, they had descended on a world of ice. This time it was a world of sand.

Looking out the port side of Verdana's eyes, the Jordan could see what she could only describe as scorched earth.

The desert below was split by narrow crevasses and high cliffs. Columns of blackened rock reached skyward like skeletal fingers clutching at the air. Forests of bent and stunted trees dotted the land like open wounds. Smoke rose in many places though she could see no sign of fire. And though the land looked desolate, she could sense that it was teeming with unseen life. Creatures dangerous and frightening.

Gradually, the tortured forests gave way to trees of oak and elm. The dry desert sands gave way to hills of golden grain, their red tips waving in the wind like an ocean of blood. In the middle of the undulating and red-tinged land rose a hill that was low but stretched out for over a mile.

Then, growing in size by the second as she rushed towards it, Amberle could see a great, walled city on the hill. Not like any city at home that was all dark space-scrapers cut with alleyways and lit with sputtering neon, but like one seen in a holo movie. A movie of knights and maidens and evil dragons that breathed fire.

This city was made of stone.

There were tiled rooftops, cobbled streets, and a great castle rising above it all. A sprawling yet dense medieval town built of ochre stone veined with shades of crimson. Then it was gone and she craned her neck to see it dwindle in the distance. Verdana sent a questioning feeling, mildly inquiring if Amberle would like for her to go back.

"That's okay," the Jordan answered aloud. "I don't want us to freak out any more people than we have to."

Still, she watched in awe as the landscape passed beneath them. Eventually, as they flew over hills and forests and rivers, towns became more frequent and the land broke off into a series of cliffs on the starboard side to showcase a sea that was deep and blue.

"Do you know where to go?" she asked aloud. "Or do you need the locator?" Amberle queried, tapping her left thigh, feeling the slight bulge of the universal locator stowed in the cargo pocket there.

Verdana let her know she knew exactly where she was supposed to go with a number of images flitting through the mind of the Jordan. Then two more things caught her attention as they passed over them.

One was another city, a mythical metropolis sparkling in hues of green and blue. Made of seashells and sea glass, the great city of Atlantea jutted up along a golden beach, or at least two thirds of it did. A third of her towers and buildings and streets were submerged beneath the shimmering water.

Only seconds later, Amberle spied what she thought was another submerged city. Farther out in the bay, this one was made of three silver towers at crazy angles. As they neared she realized it was not a city and they were not towers at all.

Three spaceships that she recognized to be ArkStar Class had somehow collided and stuck and there they were, barnacle-crusted at the tide line but otherwise rising from the bay and gleaming in the sun.

Then the strange shipwreck was behind them and they were passing over a curved shore, then more forests, then over the war torn lands of the elves. Amberle recognized the valley, though much had been done since she had seen it last.

On her previous visit, the vale had been littered with dead bodies, carrion animals tearing at rotting carcasses, the ground torn and soaked with blood.

Now, even in such a short time, the healing had begun.

The valley floor had been plowed and tilled earth of deep brown had replaced the beaten and bloodied grass. The bodies of the dead had been piled and burned and lay in heaps, some still smoldering.

Verdana rose slightly, cresting the broken cliff that rose over the vale, then slowed and landed in the meadow where they had landed before. The trampled grass was beginning to perk back up and a light breeze freshened the air.

Amberle peered out the eyes of the Fledgling at the elfin city that was tucked into the base of a mountain range abundant with waterfalls and her mouth opened in wonder.

There had been too much going on during her previous visit for her to see how spectacular it was. The stones of the city were hewn from white quartz. Some were flecked with gold, or silver, or the colors of ruby, emerald, and sapphire. Other buildings and bridges were of marble veined with gold or silver or both.

Beyond the trampled meadows rose three castles, glittering like jewels among the bridges and streets that led to the city itself. She could discern very little movement there, but she was quite sure she had been seen.

The Jordan sat down in her chair and considered not only her options, but what she was going to say to Ember. She had learned to be many things in the past months, but a diplomat was not one of them. Before she could decide on a course of action, she could see that people were headed her way across the open land.

A number of them, but not so many as to alarm her, were approaching on horseback.

Amberle stood up, blew out a burst of air through puffed cheeks, pulled down on her jacket, and checked the safety on her weapon like Jasyn had shown her. Satisfied, she descended Verdana's silver staircase to find them almost there, a few of the horses shying away as the riders were staring in awe at the Fledgling Dragon.

There were seven of them and the one in front dismounted without haste, dropping easily to his feet. He was, in Amberle's opinion, dashingly handsome. Almost enough to be a construct. His white-blonde hair fell to either side of his pointed ears and his blue eyes were as bright as the sky above. Those eyes, almond shaped but nearly round as they watched the staircase melt *up* and into the side of the living ship, finally dropped to Amberle's face and he smiled and bowed.

"Greetings and welcome," he said. "I am Zephyrn, son of Rowland, Prince of the Elves."

"Thank you," Amberle replied. "I am Amberle, daughter of James, and the Jordan of the Green Fledgling."

"It is pleasure to meet you, Amberle," Zephyrn said. "I trust you have traveled far."

"I have," she agreed. She was surprised by the smile on her own face. She had always been shy, but somehow that was changing. She did not know if it was from becoming a Jordan, from having new people around her who felt as if they were becoming family, or possibly something that was happening all on its own. Whatever it was she liked it. It felt as if worlds were opening before her.

"Please," Zephyrn said, "let us offer you rest and refreshment."

The Jordan's head cocked slightly, making her pinkish coils

of hair shift and tremble. "I'm always down for a little snack."

The young prince blinked at her, not understanding. "Does that mean you accept?"

Amberle laughed softly. "Yes. Thank you."

Zephyrn motioned to one of his men and he slid easily from the horse and led it forward. The elf bowed his head and held the reins out to Amberle. The Jordan pulled back.

"No thank you," she said, for lack of a better refusal.

"Excuse me?" Zephyrn asked.

"I don't know what to do with those," she said, nodding at the proffered reins, "or that," she said motioning with her head to the gentle beast that loomed before her.

"He is very well trained," the elf explained in vain. "You do not have to be a soldier or a very experienced rider to handle him."

Amberle laughed. "I'm not a rider at all," she told him.

"Oh," the prince said softly, taken aback. He had never heard such a thing. Even Gnomin were known to ride, though be it on donkeys. "Well," he suggested, recovering quickly, "you can ride with me!"

Amberle laughed, a little louder and nervously this time. "I don't think so." It seemed her newfound courage was not without its limits.

Zephyrn frowned in consternation. This was probably why he was never asked to be an ambassador to visitors. He knew how to be polite and political, especially to women, but this was an entirely new situation.

The realization made him laugh out loud.

No one in the kingdom could have possibly been in this situation before, he had nothing of which to be ashamed. Amberle assumed the laugh must have been at her expense and scowled at him.

Zephyrn laughed again. "I am sorry, but I am at a loss as for how to proceed. You agreed to rest and refreshment, which is waiting at Castle Song and Castle Royce, but you will be less than refreshed if we walk there. Do you perhaps wish to fly there in your Sky Dragon?"

Amberle repressed a smile at his name for the Fledgling even as she glanced at Verdana from over her shoulder. She got the distinct feeling that the Green Fledgling was comfortable where she was. She could see, smell, and sense in all directions for miles.

Just get on the damn horse!

Amberle's hazel eyes widened. She did not think the thought was her own, nor did it come from Verdana. It had a feel of Jade to it. The Jordan smiled.

"Alright," she agreed, "I'll ride with you. But you will have to show me how."

Zephyrn's boyish face was nearly split in two by a grin. He held out his hand and, after a moment of hesitation, Amberle slipped her dark fingers into his. The elfin prince led her to his horse and guided her hand to the front of the saddle.

"Hold on here," he instructed, "and put your foot in here." He held the stirrup as she stuck her boot in and he gave it a pat. "Now push up with this leg and throw your other leg over her back."

With her heart in her throat, Amberle did just that and found herself sitting astride the horse. Filled with excitement and terror, she clutched at the leather horn that rose from the saddle right in front of her. She felt the elfin prince swing up behind her and felt her dusky cheeks flush as he wrapped his arms around her waist.

"You see," he said softly in her ear, "there is nothing to it." He leaned back slightly and put his heels to the horse. Amberle gave a slight yelp as the mare started forward, moving quickly with strength and purpose without actually running.

Living, Amberle thought. *This is living.*

Zephyrn grinned as her hair tickled his nose and he used his face to push her pink coils to the side so he could look over her shoulder.

"Those are the royal castles," he said close to her ear. "And the elfin city of Tuar Ceath."

"It's beautiful," Amberle replied, watching as it grew in her vision.

"I believe we have you to thank that it is still standing, and not overrun by our enemies. I am assuming, from the stories I was told, that it was you who saved us that day."

"And Jade," the young Jordan added. "You weren't there?" She had not recognized Zephyrn from that day, but she had been so nervous about so many things at the time she might not have recognized Faith de Rossi if she had been dressed for battle.

"No," Zephyrn replied. "I was in the forest, overseeing the evacuation of the city. I am glad you returned; I wanted so badly to see you for myself. You, and the metal dragon you command."

Amberle smiled. "She is something to behold, isn't she?"

"So are you," the elfin prince returned, leaving Amberle at a loss for words. She could feel his grip on her tighten just the tiniest bit and she would swear that she could feel his smile against her hair.

The city was quiet, only a few people moving along the glittering cobbled streets, but there was much activity around the castles, especially the one they were approaching. People were coming out to meet them. People armed with swords and knives and bows.

The Jordan suddenly felt too young, too exposed, and horribly inadequate for the situation, the pistol on her hip next to useless.

Do not worry... she felt coming from Verdana in a wave of reassurance. *I am here.*

Amberle let out a deep breath and relaxed as the horse she rode and those that accompanied them drew to a halt. Of the people waiting to greet them, there were a few she recognized.

Ember, of course, and the tall elf who had stood with her. There was the giant man with the reddish beard and the older elf with long white hair.

"Let me dismount first," Zephyrn said into her ear, "then I will help you down."

Amberle gave him a nod to show she understood and then he was gone in a blink, his sudden absence leaving a chill on her back.

But he was there at her side, reaching for her hand. Again, she slid her dark fingers into his pale ones and he grasped them firmly as she swung her leg over the back of his horse. He used his other hand to steady her as she landed on her feet.

He held tight to her ribcage, just under her breast. She wasn't sure if his hand was so high by accident, but she was glad it was there. Her legs had become wobbly just over the short ride to the castles and she thought for a second that she might fall over. She was saved from the embarrassment, but the elfin prince kept his grip on her as he faced the small group that had gathered.

"May I present," he announced clearly, "Amberle, daughter of James, Jordan of the Green Fledgling!"

Now she was certain that his hand was placed intentionally, his thumb cupping her left breast, but he was still holding her upright. Thankfully, because those who had gathered in a line before her bowed.

It was the older elf who spoke first.

"I am Acqtraejale Royce and, on behalf of the elfin people and their allies, I wish to offer you our utmost appreciation. If our people were actually here we would hold a parade in your honor. As it is, however, I am afraid we can only offer you a dinner in celebration."

Amberle sighed in relief. "Thank you. I would certainly prefer that."

The old elf bowed and the others followed suit. Amberle, having no idea of what to do or say, simply bowed in return. It seemed the right thing to do. As she straightened, her eyes found Ember's and the Jordan sucked in a breath.

The woman, bloodied and bedraggled the last time she saw her, was a picture of good health - dangerously so. The female warrior, dressed in black shirt, pants and boots, was strapped with steel. Knives, daggers and swords draped her in the way Charity de Rossi wore jewels.

My God! Amberle thought. *How does she move with all that weight on her? How does she fight?*

Ember's glittering eyes were appraising the Jordan in turn, but in a different manner. "I will admit," the dark clad warrior said, "that I hoped you would return. I certainly did not expect for it to be this soon."

Amberle swallowed and gave her a nod. She could see there had been a few additions to the female warrior's entourage.

Flanking her were two brutaly handsome soldiers. They were tall and lean and did not appear to be much older than Amberle. One had a sharply squared jaw, light brown hair, and eyes that were the color of honey. He was more broad-shouldered than the other, who had a pointed chin and hair like summer wheat with darker brows over eyes that were a startling blue and framed by dark lashes.

Slightly behind the woman and the tall elf with sand-colored hair was another young man. Also handsome. And familiar. He looked so much like Jasyn that, while not exactly twins, he was close. He could easily pass as his brother.

But constructs don't have brothers, she thought. *Just similar models.*

Amberle switched her gaze to Ember. Like Zephyrn, she knew how to be polite, but was not highly educated in political niceties.

"You have come for me?" Ember asked. Amberle nodded.

Glances were being exchanged all around when Acqtraejale brought his hands together in a resounding clap that drew every eye to him.

"Ah!" the old elf exclaimed. "I am sure Zephyrn offered you rest and refreshment?" Amberle smiled and gave him a nod. "Then you shall have it! Zephyrn!"

"Yes, Grandfather," the elfin prince responded immediately.

"Please show the young warrior to the guest chambers in Castle Royce in the Tower of the Sun."

 TWO SEVEN

- Secrets pave the path home.

"Well if that don't beat all," Fletcher Mattatock said, his voice barely over a whisper.

Sean craned his neck to lean over his grandpa and look out his port window. The transport was beginning its approach and he could hear the landing gear begin to open up under the belly of the craft with a series of mechanical whines and loud snaps as they locked into place.

The shuttle began a wide turn as it slowed and through the window Sean could see a mighty fortress of black obsidian on a massive island that was mostly rock. The rough sea beat on rocky cliffs that hemmed in lawns of grass and manicured gardens enclosed by green hedges.

"It's certainly not the same as the first castle," Grandpa said, "but the resemblance is uncanny."

"You saw the first castle?" Sean asked, pulling his gaze away from the window to stare at his grandpa.

"Oh, ayuh," the old man answered. "I was there when it went up, and I lived there for a time while I planned out the nearby town."

Sean shook his head as the edifice grew exponentially in his vision. "Just when I think you have told me the whole story - or near to it - I find a whole new book of tales on your shelf."

Grandpa chuckled softly at the boy's analogy, and of his early memories of the first castle of Charity de Rossi.

He remembered his grandson, Matty, running through the bailey wearing a knight's helmet that was so big that the boy couldn't see a thing when the visor was down. He remembered laughing so hard he thought he might be having a stroke. He remembered seeing Hope, and Madeline, and the monks.

Fletcher's feelings of joy melted like ice. He could not recall the last time he had seen them all, but he was recalling quite well the last time he had been in the first castle. He had been running through the halls and searching the towers, screaming and covered in blood.

"Grandpa?" Sean asked, seeing the man go pale. "Are you alright?"

Grandpa tried to force a smile. "I am. Just getting the feeling of coming full circle. It's giving me the heebie jeebies."

Sean smiled and flicked his blonde hair from his blue eyes. The 'heebie jeebies' was always an expression of Grandpa's that made him laugh. Now, it made his skin prickle with gooseflesh.

The shuttle did not land in front of the Castle on what looked like a circular driveway of crushed gravel, it would have been too narrow, but instead on an asphalt pad nestled into the grounds on the west side.

Daphne, who had been in and out and about during their entire trip from Titan, now bustled around them, escorting them down and out of the shuttle. Other attendants saw to their personal effects. Daphne led them around to the front of the obsidian fortress to the entrance where she stopped and held out a hand, inviting them to enter a long, enclosed hallway.

"It has been a pleasure," she told them, "but I must return straight away, another guest will be needing the shuttle to return here. You are awaited inside, but L.C. security will escort you from here. I wish you the best."

"Thank you," John told her, putting an arm around Rebecca

before turning to see two men, presumable the aforementioned security, waiting for them. They gave the Mattatock family a nod of acknowledgement then turned and walked away.

John dropped his arm from Rebecca's waist and grasped her hand as they followed. Grandpa trailed them, flanked by Sean and Jeanette.

They left the landing pad and crossed over an expanse of short cut grass to the gravel driveway and passed in front of the Last Castle. The castle was not as broad as it was tall and Sean had to tip his head back as far as it would go to see the tops of the towers that stretched into the cloudless sky.

The dark stone of the fortress was blacker than a moonless night and fronted with thick hedges of thorn covered rose bushes. The roses, all a deep red, against the dark of the obsidian made Sean think of the fairytales Grandpa would tell him and Jeanette when they were much younger.

Not the tales of princesses and knights and wizards and magic swords, but the ones of witches and dragons. The ones where the children were often eaten.

The Mattatocks and their escorts passed under a porte cochère and entered a long hallway of black marble through heavy doors that were wide open. The stewards who had seen to their luggage did not follow them. Sean guessed they must be taking their stuff around back or through a side entrance.

The corridor was made of polished stone blocks that reflected the light coming from globes that hung from the curved ceiling. Their footsteps echoed on the marble floor and off the walls. It was the only sound until they could make out the soft sound of voices coming to them from the end of the hall, which was blocked by a semi-transparent, flickering field.

"Is that detfleck?" Sean whispered to Grandpa but, before he could answer, the face of a compact man with steel gray eyes snapped around to look over his shoulder.

"It is," he affirmed. "Stay well away from it."

Sean nodded quickly to show he understood. The security man eyed him for a moment longer and then stopped and, with the other guard, stood aside when they were still a few yards from the glittering fence.

A small man with black hair and black, almond-shaped eyes stepped out of an adjoining hallway. He wore loose fitting black pants and a black shirt that fastened together down the front with loops of silk over round silk-covered buttons.

His skin was a golden tan and, though he smiled and seemed friendly, Sean stopped next to Grandpa and swallowed against the dryness in his throat. He knew without asking that the man was a former Yakuza. There was a silent yet lethal grace to him, a feather touch of death in his polite smile.

"Good day," the man said, bowing. "Please." He offered John a black box a little less than half a meter long with no lid. The inside was filled with a silver-colored gelatinous material.

John reached out with his right hand and sunk it into the box, the gel closing over his fingers. The man produced a miniature acrylic from the folds of his shirt and, after examining it with a critical flick of his black eyes, smiled at John.

"Thank you, and welcome, Mr. Mattatock," he said, bowing.

The man offered it next to Rebecca.

"Please."

Rebecca placed her hand in the box without hesitation. She could feel the gel move under and between her fingers, over the back of her hand. She knew it was reading, testing, gently extracting.

The man checked his acrylic and smiled. "Thank you, and welcome, Mrs. Mattatock."

He then held the box out to Sean who was pleasantly surprised. He had assumed it was going to be offered only to the adults in the manner of credential cards or alcohol.

Sean put his hand into the box, at first startled by the gel but he held it there. What gave him a start was that it was warm. Second, it moved as if were alive.

The Yakuza removed the box and bowed to him and turned next to his sister. Sean looked at his hand, expecting to find some of the gel clinging to it, but it was clean and dry.

After repeating the process with Jeanette, he did the same for Grandpa. This time, however, when he checked his acrylic, his almond shaped eyes widened slightly and he bowed much deeper.

"Welcome, Master Mason."

Now it was the rest of the family that looked at Grandpa with widened eyes. Even the steely eyed guard had cocked an eyebrow in surprise. Everyone except Sean, who gave his grandfather an appreciative smile.

The man in the black silk bowed again to the group as a whole and placed his thumb and forefinger at two corners of his acrylic and the detfleck disappeared.

There was a room beyond, where there had been soft conversation before, that fell silent. But only for a moment.

A cry escaped the lips of the Red Jordan as she rushed to her family, wrapping her arms around them as one. They gathered around her, small and tall, their arms intertwined. After they finally let go as a unit, she knelt and hugged Jeanette to her. When she let her go she stood and faced John with a sigh.

But the reunion was not quite over.

Grandpa turned to see both Faith and Charity standing close to him, tears welling in their eyes.

"Fletcher!" Charity exclaimed before she threw her arms around him. When she let him go, Faith embraced him in the same manner. He hugged them back with more enthusiasm than he had expected, finding that his own eyes had filled with tears as well.

He let them go and glanced about the room. Again, his

family was looking at him with open astonishment. He gave them a shrug and his eyes sought out the few others who had been waiting for them.

One was a slight elfin woman with white-blonde hair wearing a blue Mylar flightsuit, boots, and an eyepatch. She undoubtedly had to be Johanna's fellow Jordan and the youngest of the de Rossi sisters.

The other was a young man - tall and muscular with light brown skin, hazel eyes and a thatch of black hair over black brows. His face was perfectly formed, with high cheekbones, a jaw so sharp that it was almost triangular, with a slight dimple set into his chin.

Fletcher frowned. "Is that…?" he started before Faith jumped in, her voice an octave higher than normal.

"Jasyn? Yes." She smiled at Fletcher and nodded emphatically, encouragingly as the young man approached.

"Bonjour, Fletcher," Jasyn said, extending his hand with a disarming smile.

Fletcher could not help but smile back. "Bonjour, J-Syn," he returned, shaking the construct's hand. "Comment allez-vous?"

Jasyn laughed. "As good as can be expected. Et vous?"

Fletcher laughed as well. "About the same. Maybe better." His blue eyes sought out Charity and realized that her eyes were not blue, as he remembered, but green. His smile faltered for a moment and then widened once more. "I like your place," he told her. "A little dark, but quite timeless."

Charity tilted back her head, her porcelain white chin tilted up as she laughed. "Like my soul, I imagine! Thank you, Fletcher. And, since you might be staying with us for a spell once again, at least I hope so – maybe we can show you to some rooms that might suit you, give you a small tour, or do anything to make you comfortable?"

"That would be much appreciated," Fletcher said, glancing over his shoulder to John who gave him a nod. He glanced next to Sean who was grinning from ear to ear. "What?" he asked.

Sean chuckled and shook his head. "It's just so weird to hear people call you anything but Grandpa."

Fletcher smiled and then laughed. So did everyone else.

After the Mattatock family had been ushered from the Castle's enormous entry foyer, Jasyn was left alone with the de Rossis. The Blue Jordan busied herself behind the bar and his gaze went to Faith and Charity. He watched the smiles melt from their faces as they stared at the doorway through which the family had departed.

"Are you going to tell Mari?" Charity asked her sister without looking at her.

"I don't know," Faith answered softly, her eyes still also on the empty doorway. "This is one of those few times that I have no idea at all what to do."

Jasyn scowled as his dark hazel eyes went from one to the other.

The secrets they keep, he thought with disgust.

⚜

"This is too much," Rebecca said, looking around the "room" she and John had been given. It was a suite of rooms that included a living area, closets and washrooms. It was larger than the podment they shared with their children. Jeanette and Sean had been given their own suites in the same tower though theirs were smaller. Somewhat.

"This will be fine," John told his sister.

Scarlett smiled. "I know, Rebecca. It feels weird to me too. I'm used to a cabin aboard a Dragon. But I think things are changing. We need to be ready for that."

"Changing for the better?" Rebecca challenged lightly. She would not dare oppose her sister-in-law, not now. And not because she feared her in any way, but because Johanna had gotten Jeanette back. Rebecca had never been more terrified in her life than those few hours. She would not forget it.

"Changing for the better?" Scarlett echoed thoughtfully. She sighed softly through her nose. "Yes, I think so. In the long run. Will it be an easy change? No. Will it be fast? No, I doubt that as well. But I am beginning to believe that it is necessary. I've had a few talks with the de Rossi's, and I cannot help but lean in the direction they are going. In fact, I'm going to be having a chat with them in a few minutes if you want to join."

"I'll pass," Rebecca said. "Despite sitting for the last thirty hours, I'd really like to lay down in a bed. Nap, if I can."

"I might join you," John told his sister. "How do I find you in this place? How do I find anything?"

Scarlett smiled. "Just walk out your door. Let your assistant know where you want to go."

"Is he really an assistant?" Rebecca asked with a suspicious leer tucked into the side of her mouth.

"Trust me," Scarlett said with a leer of her own, "you can tell the butlers from the security around here. Still, I'm sure they will be keeping an eye on you – on all of us - at least for a while."

John and Rebecca exchanged glances as Johanna took her leave. Her next stop was right next door at Jeanette's room. It was not nearly as large as her parents' suite - just a bedroom with an enormous closet and a bathroom - but Jeanette was clearly thrilled.

"Nice digs," Scarlett remarked with a smile when Jeanette opened the door.

"I know!" her niece agreed, excited. "It's huge! I have my own...well, my own everything! They even gave me an acrylic!"

Scarlett smiled and sat down on the edge of a bed large enough for half a dozen girls Jeanette's age. "Do you feel like a princess? Being here in a castle?"

Jeanette made a face as she flopped down on the bed next to her aunt. "Did you ever want to be a princess? When you were little?" She immediately cringed at the choice of her own words.

Scarlett laughed. "Certainly not."

"What did you want to be when you were... my age?"

Johanna gave her niece a wicked smile. "The toughest motherfu... uh, the toughest person in the neighborhood."

"And were you?"

The smile on the Red Jordan widened. "Ask your father."

The smile on Jeanette mirrored the one on her aunt. "I don't think I need to."

Scarlett laughed. "Well, make yourself comfortable. I think this is going to be our new home for a while."

"Really?"

"Really. Are you going to be okay with that?" Scarlett had never been one tied down to a certain home, lifestyle, or group of friends – but it was not lost on her that many children clung to such things. Such things, which she personally felt to be shallow and fleeting, were anchors for many children and young adults to garner feelings of safety and security.

Jeanette gave her a reassuring smile, one that was oddly adult.

"Trust me, I'll be fine."

Scarlett smiled and gave her niece's hand a squeeze. "Alright," she acquiesced. "I have a meeting with the de Rossi's, and then I have to get back to work before *I'm* reported missing." Jeanette could not keep from giggling and her Auntie planted a big kiss on her forehead. "Have fun with that acrylic and stay out of trouble!" she told her as she got to her feet.

Jeanette collapsed back into the mass of pillows on the bed with the acrylic in her small hands. "No promises on that!" she announced with glee.

The Red Jordan shook her head as she left Jeanette's room, closing the door behind her. Two figures stood shadowed in an alcove. One stepped forward into the light. A young woman.

"To where can I direct you?" she asked.

Scarlett glanced at the figure still in the shadows. An undeniably masculine frame waited, stock still and shoulders squared, standing guard. The Jordan's lips quirked up at the corners in silent approval before she turned her dark eyes to the young PA.

"The other Jordan?" she queried. "Or the other de Rossi's?"

The PA gave her a curt nod. "This way," she instructed as she turned left and walked quickly down the obsidian hallway. "Dr. de Rossi and Ms. de Rossi are in the Tanza parlor. Your fellow Jordan was on her way there just a minute ago."

Scarlett followed her down the corridor of shining black marble to where it became gray stone, the walls hung with enormous paintings framed with wood that had been carved and gilded with gold. She looked back once over her shoulder, wondering if she should include John on the discussion she knew was coming. Then she turned her eyes front, knowing it was best that he stay with the family for now.

The PA ushered her into a room that was large but somehow made cozy by heavy rugs that were not too thick, furniture upholstered in velvet, and walls of polished mahogany hung with tapestries of once bright threads.

All heads turned at her entrance at which time Charity began dismissing the few butlers and assistants who had been in attendance. They were followed from the room by a pair of bodyguards. Blue was behind a polished wooden bar, pouring herself a flute of champagne. Faith was accepting an already filled glass from the dark-haired construct and Charity, glass in hand, was sinking down on to a sofa.

"Can I get you anything?" Blue asked, looking at the other Jordan.

Scarlett expelled a sigh of resigned amusement through her nose. "Yes," she answered. "Anything would be nice."

Blue ducked down behind the bar for a second and came back up with a green bottle. She poured a generous amount of red wine into a large glass and brought it to Scarlett who accepted it with a smile. She held the glass out and touched it to the flute held by Blue.

"Cheers," she said softly.

Blue laughed under her breath. "Right back at ya," she said. They both took a drink without breaking eye contact.

Scarlett lowered her glass and lifted her chin. "We have five hours before we are expected back on the Dragon," she said.

"We have a lot to discuss, much to decide before then," Blue answered.

Faith moved gracefully to a chair and sat down. Jasyn positioned himself behind her, off to her right. Silently, with Charity, they watched the Jordans.

"I don't trust the IGC," Blue said, blunt.

"Neither do I," Scarlett agreed.

"But I can't abandon Captain Brogan."

"Neither can I, especially with Blaylock."

"The alternatives," Blue suggested, "is the Chimera, or these guys," she said, jerking her head in the direction of her sisters.

"So what do we do?" Scarlett asked. "Do we split up? Do we join forces?" She laughed at her last question. It sounded so ridiculous.

Charity and Faith, however, shared a glance that Scarlett did not miss.

"What was that?" she asked. "That look?"

"Déjà vu," Charity said.

"It seems as if we had almost the same discussion one hundred years ago," Faith explained.

"I remember that," the raven-haired construct whispered, his dark hazel eyes dreamy with recollection. "We were trying to decide if we should join the Chimera or the IGC."

Faith looked at him, speechless.

Not Scarlett.

"Fuck the IGC," she spat. "They killed my father and my brother."

There's was a tsking sound and everyone's heads turned to see a man with golden skin and almond-shaped eyes standing in the doorway. He was dressed in golden robes with golden slippers on his feet as he entered. Next to him was a small man with black hair and black, almond-shaped eyes. He wore loose fitting black pants and black silk shirt that fastened together down the front by satin loops over silk-covered buttons.

Charity rolled her green eyes to the ceiling as she raised her glass to her lips. "You just *can't* get good help these days," she sighed.

"Johanna Scarlett!" the man in the golden robes admonished. "I was under the impression that you had forgiven the past completely!"

"Master Elaeric!" she exclaimed in surprise.

The man who had once been a Zenarchist monk gave her a slight bow and then turned to the de Rossi sisters. "I am also under the impression that you have found my daughter."

 TWO 8

-It is a rarely shared secret that obstacles do not block the path. Obstacles are the path.

Elaeric stood in the doorway, his broad face shining over his long silk tunic, pants, and slippered feet. His hands were tucked into the sleeves of his caftan.

Charity's Yakuza guard, who had escorted him in, bowed to the group and slipped silently away.

Charity sighed heavily, her emerald-green eyes going to where the high wall of the room met the ceiling and muttered something else about the help before taking a sip from her glass.

"Hello," Elaeric said amiably. "It is good to see you all again," his eyes lit upon Blue. "Except for you - not that it is not pleasant to meet you," he corrected quickly, "but you are the only one here I have not met. I am Elaeric." He bowed deeply.

The youngest de Rossi sister gave him a gruesome smile, the right side of her lip pushing up into the scarred flesh of her cheek.

"I'm Jordan Blue," she said, introducing herself.

"Ah!" he exclaimed, his eyes lighting up. "Another Jordan!" He turned his bright gaze to Scarlett who could not keep the grin from her face.

"Master Elaeric," she said, bowing respectfully.

"Johanna Scarlett," he greeted. "You may embrace me if you wish." The Red Jordan, unable to help herself, did just that. She hugged his thin frame, afraid she might break him, but he did not seem to mind in the least. "Are you keeping up with your meditations?" he asked when she released him.

"I am," she affirmed.

Jasyn stepped forward. "I don't believe we have met either."

"Evan!" Elaeric exclaimed. "How very good to see you again! I almost did not recognize you, but of course we have met!"

Jasyn stepped back as if the man had slapped him. In fact, to the construct, he really did feel as if he had been slapped. More than that, he felt a piece of the dam in his brain break loose and memories flooded through him.

The house made of glass, the monks and the castle. Charity's first castle, rising from the muck on a moon where she had been swindled into buying land from some real estate agent that she had bedded.

His dark hazel eyes were as round as eggs, and he turned them to Faith. Her own eyes were large and round as she stared at him but she was quickly regaining her composure, stepping forward.

"It is good to see you again, Elaeric. But I beg your pardon, did you say your daughter?"

"I did, Gwe...".

"Where are my manners?" Charity interrupted; her voice so loud that all eyes went to her in alarm. "Please, sit down," she offered, her tone still high and nervous. "Would you care for a cup of tea?" she asked. "Or something stronger?"

Elaeric smiled. "Coffee, if you have it."

"I do. Faith?" she asked, her green eyes looking meaningfully at her older sister. "Would you care for a cup as well?"

"I'm fine for now, thank you."

Elaeric gazed at the women in confusion, but only for a moment. Then he nodded in understanding.

He knows who she is, Jasyn gathered. *He knows who I am, obviously better than I do myself.*

Charity motioned to a butler who was already setting out bowls of sugar and small pitchers of cream while another poured strong coffee into hand-painted China cups on matching saucers. He looked at the former Zenarchist monk with raised brows.

"Cream and sugar, please," Elaeric told him. The butler stirred both into the coffee cup and carefully handed it to him on a saucer. Elaeric, both shy and delighted to be waited on, accepted it with a smile.

Charity, having regained her poise, held out a hand, inviting him to a chair. Once seated, the butler placed a plate of pastries on the table to his right. She motioned for him to refill her own glass and, as he did, she turned her green eyes back to Elaeric while the others retook their seats.

"I'm sorry, did you say your daughter?" she asked, repeating Faith's question from only a moment ago.

"Yes," Elaeric replied, sipping his coffee and gently returning the cup to the saucer.

"Do you mean the child?" Faith asked, incredulous. "The one who was with you on your journey to aid the elves?"

"Yes," Elaeric replied again, his voice softer this time.

"I was under the impression that she was Hope's daughter," Charity remarked, her blonde brows high over her green eyes. She planted an elbow on the arm of her chair, her glass held loosely in one hand.

"That is a possibility," he admitted as he helped himself to a croissant from a tray on the table. All eyes stared at the former monk, some wider than others. He had just found the honey when he realized the room was silent. He looked up and, seeing all the attention, put down his pastry. "I am sorry. I should explain."

"Please," Faith invited.

Elaeric gave her a nod and drew a deep breath. Scarlett fought the urge to sit next to him and clasp his hand. But the man's eyes went to her as if already feeling the comfort she was offering.

"Hope and Madeline," he said, "conceived at the same time." There was a stifled choke from Charity as she inhaled a sip of her drink and then coughed it out. A light blush crept over the golden cheeks of the former monk and he continued. "They, of course, went into labor and delivered at the same time - a girl for each girl." Tears filled his eyes and he reached for a water glass with a trembling hand as he blinked them away. "One died in childbirth. Hope and Madeline, striving always for balance and the comfort of each other, asked the nurse - or demanded, it could be either - not to be told which or whose, child it was. And so, she was ours. All of ours."

Faith sat frozen in her seat, blinking away her own tears. "And that is why Hope did not want to come home," she said, her voice trembling. "She knew that...she knew I would be able to find out."

Elaeric nodded. Deep breaths were taken by all around the table and the ensuing silence was broken by Charity.

"How did you know we had found her?"

Elaeric finally smiled again. "I too, have my little birds. But that," he remarked picking his croissant back up and giving it a drizzle of honey, "is not why you reached out me. Or am I wrong?"

"No," Faith said, "you are not wrong. We, as a newly formed group here, have pieced together some...anomalies."

"Anomalies?" Elaeric asked, his face a mask of innocence with which Scarlett was quite familiar.

"Yes," the Red Jordan said, leaning forward in her seat.

"When you were so gracious enough to host me in your home, there was something very odd that I noticed."

"Indeed? And what was that?"

Scarlett leaned forward even more, resting her weight on her forearms. "There was no dust in your cottage. Never. Anywhere."

"Why thank you, Johanna."

"And my first castle," Charity said, "the one you raised from the ground, there was never any dust there either. No matter what we did or what was going on – parties, storms, Hope and Madeline always coming and going from the gardens or the stables…"

"Nor in or around the glass house that was built close to that castle," Faith added. "Though you did not build it, you played a part in its construction."

"I did," he agreed before popping the last bit of honey covered pastry into his mouth. He got the last bits off his fingers and continued. "As did Hahn. I am no scientist," he said, his eyes darting quickly to Faith before they looked at the others, "but I believe it had something to do with electrostatic charge and the intensity of the electric field created by the zero-point energy."

Charity looked at Faith who took a drink of champagne from her glass and shrugged. Physics was certainly not her area of expertise.

"Not too many years ago," the Blue Jordan said, "I was on Earth." Elaeric, as well as the others turned their attention to her. "I stayed in a town, and this town had the same peculiar characteristic."

The former monk gave her a slip of a smile. "And did anything about this town seem odd to you?"

Blue chuffed soft laughter. "It was Earth. Everything was odd." Elaeric raised his brows at her, waiting. The Blue Jordan sighed and smiled back at him. "Yes," she admitted. "This town was different from the others we visited when we were there. Every other town, every city, was frozen in the same time frame of the PONE for Earth, which was the late 3000's, almost 3900. This town, and I had to look this up on the GW, resembled one from their mid 1900's."

Elaeric's smile broadened. "Yes! I know this town. Hahn made it especially for Hope, she had been so intrigued by the original."

"The original?" Faith asked.

"Yes, from the true Earth. You realize, of course, that the surface is merely a replica. A crust."

"A crust?" Faith echoed, turning her bewildered gaze to Jasyn.

The construct cast his gaze aside and expelled a great breath of air through his full lips. "A mirror," he explained.

Faith's right hand went to her stomach. It was reeling as much as her head. She thought if she put her hand to her heart or her head that either one might explode.

"I wanted to tell you," he said and sighed again, his shoulders seeming to cave around his broad chest. "That time in your office, with Charity and Amberle. I saw that the current projection of Earth was just as different as the new perspective of Venus. But..." he trailed off, leaving his sentence for Faith to finish.

"But you don't trust me. Or anyone."

Jasyn's eyes did not falter from hers. "We all have our secrets to keep."

"Wait a second," Charity demanded. "Are you saying that there is a faux – *a fake* - Earth, around the old Earth? *That Earth and all the people on it have been there this whole time!?!*"

Jasyn looked at Elaeric whose shoulders went up under his golden robes. "It is certainly a possibility," he admitted.

Faith turned her tawny eyes to Charity. "My god!" she

exclaimed. "She could be there! They could both be there! They could have been there this whole time!"

"What do we do?" Charity asked. "Go there immediately? How do we get through the, what did you call it, *crust?* How do we find them? Wait for Amberle?"

"Whoa whoa whoa whoa whoa!" Scarlett cried, standing up. "I am just as bewildered as you are at the implications of the possibilities this incites. But we have a situation, *situations* actually, here and now that have to be dealt with first. The most pressing, I'm afraid, is that Blue and I are expected to be back aboard the Dragon in only a few hours. We all still have serious resolutions to make about the current state of affairs."

Faith closed her eyes of brown and gold as she battled a silent struggle within herself. To be so close, after all this time, to finding them…. Finally, she let out a great sigh. She opened her eyes and fixed them on Scarlett, nodding.

"You are right. There are circumstances that need our immediate attention. And, immediate choices. Before we go any further, the first of those choices are yours." Her eyes flicked to Noel and then back to Scarlett. "Where will you two side in this? Will you stand with us? With you fight for us?"

Scarlett straightened in her seat. She was not ready for such an abrupt demand and she was not sure she was ready to answer. Her dark eyes went to Elaeric who was helping himself to another pastry while he watched her intently.

What is there really to consider at this point? Scarlett asked herself. *I think, deep down, I decided some time ago. Mostly when I learned that the people I was fighting for had been my enemy all along. My family is safe, I have my Fledgling, and* (thinking now of Bjorn) *I have a debt to repay. But I have other debts as well,* she thought, thinking bitterly of Commander Blaylock.

Then she thought of Captain Brogan, basically her surrogate father. And Opal, undoubtedly her surrogate mother. There were debts owed there as well. Debts of loyalty.

"Arrrgh!" she shouted through clenched teeth before she her drink down on a table and ran her hands through her hair, pressing her palms hard against her skull. She let herself rage for a moment and then stilled herself, filling her body with a sense of calm, and let her hands drop to her sides. "I will stand with you," she said, "and I will fight for you."

There was not a single eye in the room that did not gleam at these remarks, and suppressed smiles bit into every cheek. Then it seemed that the group held a collective breath as Scarlett turned her crimson-flecked eyes to her fellow Jordan.

Blue felt more than saw the stares as they fell on her and she gave an exaggerated shrug. "Fuck it. I'm in."

The collective breath of those gathered was let out in a whoosh as Blue defensively stood up, her blue eye pinning Scarlett. "But we need to do this without hurting the other ones we love."

"I am one hundred percent with you on that," she agreed. "But we are due back on the Dragon within hours. And we have, ahem, other problems that need solving. We need to figure out what to do. Quickly."

"We should contact Brogan and ask him if we can be gone a little longer," Blue told her. Then, smirking, "you should be the one to ask, he likes you better."

Scarlett gave her a small but conciliatory smile. "Aww, no he doesn't."

Blue rolled her eye. "Well, maybe he doesn't like you *more*, but he definitely has a soft spot for you, for some reason."

The Red Jordan beamed. "Good enough. I'll contact him." She stood and looked around the room. It seemed that everyone present was in a light state of shock from what had transpired over the last few seconds, but it was one of contentment. Her dark eyes sought our Elaeric, nibbling at a cheese-filled Danish. "Don't you go sneaking off without seeing me first."

The former monk grinned, putting a napkin to his mouth to keep the crumbs from spilling out. "I would do no such thing. Besides, I have the feeling, Johanna Scarlett, that I will be here for some time. Much as yourself."

Scarlett gave him a grunt and turned on her heel to leave the room. She could hear Charity calling for her staff as she passed into the hallway. A security man disengaged from the shadows to follow her and she was surprised to find that she did not mind. Blue had been right about that, you could get used to a certain lifestyle quite quickly.

Before taking the hangar elevator down to the depths under the fortress, she sought out her family and found them sharing a meal in a dining room that was rather informal by the normal Last Castle standards.

John stood from his seat at the table and gave his sister a quick hug and a peck on the cheek. He saw her eyes dart about and laughed softly.

"It's where the kitchen staff takes their meals," he explained. "We just feel a little more normal here."

Scarlett laughed and shook her head of dark wavy hair. "As long as you can feel as normal as possible," she acquiesced. "Speaking of which, how comfortable are you here? Enough to stay for some time?"

The smile left her brother's face but it was replaced with solemn understanding and he took a step closer to her, away from the table. His voice dropped to a whisper. "We won't be going back, will we?"

Scarlett shook her head slowly from side to side, her expression more solemn than his. "I'm sorry."

John let it sink in for a moment and then laid a reassuring hand on her shoulder. "Don't be. We knew what this job would be when you took it. We can weather any storm," he assured her. "We always have."

Scarlett smiled in thanks and glanced at Rebecca who gave

her a genuine smile. That put the Jordan more at ease than any of her brother's words. It was good to see Grandpa as well, laughing with Sean. Her nephew was also finally at ease since his own sister had seemed to resume her normal jovial demeanor.

"I might be here for a while myself," Johanna told her brother. "I don't know if they plan on making this place some sort of base or installation, it would certainly make sense, or if this is just temporary. But they have us Jordans set up in one of the towers. Either way, it will be nice to have a decent amount of time to spend with my family."

"I'd like that," John said.

Scarlett gave him a lopsided smile and left to find the elevator down to the hangar under the castle. Once there, she boarded Fledge and put a call through to the Opal Dragon. Dareus answered and she requested to be connected with the Captain.

"Jordan Scarlett," he acknowledged once he was on the line. "Is everything alright?"

"Of course," she answered. "Just spending some time with my family."

"That's good," Brogan said. "And Blue?"

Scarlett swallowed and lifted her chin. "Spending time with her family as well."

There was a momentary pause before the Captain spoke again. "But you, and your families, you are all together?"

The Red Jordan felt her heart start to race. "Yes. We are all getting to know one another."

"I see."

There was another pause long enough to make Scarlett jump back to the purpose of her call. "And, due to the situation, making new acquaintances and catching up with old ones, I wanted to request our leave be extended by another twelve hours."

The Jordan held her breath as she heard Brogan take a deep breath of his own and release it slowly. Then she heard a slight hum come across the communication line from light years away, but she knew exactly what it was. The Captain was in the bridge, in the pit, and had raised the privacy wall around it.

"I see," he said after the brief hum had stopped. "Normally, I would grant such a request. However, and this is classified information that is not to be divulged to anyone other than Jordan Blue; Commander Blaylock is to be granted a promotion. He will be the next Captain of the Copper Dragon. Commander Blaylock himself does not know this, but I must announce it by tomorrow dimlight. Jordan Blue and you both need to be here when that happens. I will extend your leave by five hours, no more."

Scarlett's head was spinning. Blaylock? Promoted to Captain? It made her feel physically ill. She felt her body begin to tilt, as if she might fall over. It was almost the worst thing she could imagine. But what could she do?

"Yes, sir," she answered. "We will be there by dim minus five hours tomorrow."

ଓଞ୍ଚ

Scarlett, doing her best not to storm through the halls, simply walked with long and determined strides, her chin up and her jaw clenched.

Blaylock made a Captain!

It made her blood boil and her stomach turn.

She was on her way back to the parlor to meet the de Rossi's when, passing by a wall inset with several large glass windows that looked out onto the gardens, she stopped short as she spotted Elaeric. He was walking down a path, admiring the multitude of blooming hedges.

Suddenly, her fury melted away. She sighed and blew a

stream of air from her bottom lip that went up and over her face.

The Red Jordan looked for a door and, seeing none, looked back at the guard that had been trailing her, staying in the shadows. He smiled and moved towards one of the windows and gave it a gentle push.

A rectangle of light appeared in the wall around the glass as it pivoted on an unseen hinge. Scarlett gave him a smile and pushed it the rest of the way open and stepped out into a gentle breeze as it crossed the Distant Shore.

The air outside was oxygen rich and felt charged with electricity, as if she was standing close to a generator. She could smell the salt of the sea and hear it crash on the rocks beyond the grounds and gardens.

For now, the sky was a clear and cobalt blue.

Scarlett approached the small man in golden robes while her escort, after following her outside, stepped back into the shadows.

Elaeric turned as she approached and gave her a broad smile. She could not help but return his expression.

"Who is taking care of the chickens?" she asked.

Elaeric chuckled. "The neighbor to the south. With the blue house. You know the one?" Scarlett nodded to show she knew who he meant. "She is glad to have the eggs. She is taking care of the goat as well."

He ambled slowly down the tiny road of crushed stone and Scarlett followed, keeping quiet for as long as she could.

"When Faith contacted you," she said, "did she give you a message from me?"

"She did."

The Jordan forced her hands to remained open and loose by her hips, though she wanted to clench them into fists. She had forgotten how he could drive her absolutely crazy with his soft demeanor, riddles, and – worse – silence.

When she had first begun her healing with the former Zenarchist, she had asked him if there was a shortcut to enlightenment. The man who had once been a monk had laughed it off at the time, but told her later that there was – possibilities were unique for each person, yet each possibility was endless.

He told her to think of the way to enlightenment as a long path set with four large stepping-stones and filled with pebbles in between. Each stone, each pebble, to be thought of as a lesson. Some had to walk that path step-by-step, pebble-by-pebble, learning every lesson diligently, but even then there was no guarantee for inner peace. Some were able to hop from stone to stone he confided, attaining enlightenment quickly. Still others could fly like a dragon, not touching anything but encompassing all and attaining enlightenment in a single moment.

With surprisingly little effort she got him to tell her of the first stone and what it would entail to pass it.

Forgive the past completely, he had told her.

As impossible as it sounded, especially for someone like Scarlett, she put her mind to it. And her heart.

They walked on in silence for another minute, Elaeric pausing now and again to smell a rose in full bloom.

"Well?" she finally prodded.

Elaeric laughed. "You really think you are ready for the next step? The next leap?"

"I am."

"I am not so sure of that, but I am sure of you."

Scarlett smiled. He smiled back at her, paused long enough to ignite her impatience once again, and then took her hand. The Jordan breathed deep.

"See every obstacle as an opportunity. The larger the

obstacle, the greater the opportunity."

Scarlett froze in her stance, her hand in his. Stock still, even her eyes did not move. She stood that way for so long that he was about to ask if she was alright when she reached out with her hands and grasped the sides of his face. Tipping his head down, she leaned forward and planted a kiss on his forehead.

"Thank you," she whispered. Then she slipped away.

The man who had once been a Zenarchist monk stared after her in surprise for a moment before a smile spread across his face.

I think she really was ready for that next step, he contemplated with no small amount of pleasure and pride.

Scarlett slipped back inside the castle and found the parlor where she had left the de Rossis and the dark-haired construct.

"Blue!" she exclaimed, stepping into the room and making all heads turn in her direction.

"What?" Blue asked, putting her glass down on the bar. "What is it?"

Scarlett gave her a grin that bespoke predatory revelation. "First, we need to get back to the Dragon. Second, I have a solution for our problems."

"Which one?"

"All of them."

Blue returned her grin. "What are we waiting for?"

❧

The Aridian woke. She blinked her enormous round eyes, feeling like she had been asleep for quite some time. She stretched as she always did after awakening, elongating her narrow limbs to feel the tiny, dislocated bones in her body crack.

Her limbs stretched, lithe muscles pulling taut, but there

was no crackling response from her bones. None. The Aridian blinked again, rapidly this time in worry as she pushed herself upright. Her hand went immediately to the back of her neck and searched but found nothing.

Fear blossomed in her chest and her fingers, tremulous, went there. Grazing over the skin that covered her sternum, they paused and touched what felt like a metal star.

She looked around in nascent terror. She knew what that star was. And what it meant. Tara now saw that she was sitting up on a bed in a tightly enclosed space. There was one other person in the small space with her - the Jordan (well, the second Jordan) she had tried to subdue and replicate. The Jordan looked much the same as the first (and last) time she had seen her. Mylar blue flightsuit, blonde pompadour, patch over her missing eye.... Also, like the last time, the Jordan was holding a flute of champagne.

"You are in my Fledgling," Blue informed her. "How are you feeling?"

"Where is Calyph?" the Aridian demanded. "What have you done to him?"

The Jordan smiled. "It warms my heart to see you care for him as much as he cares for you. I actually worried for him, momentarily."

She slid down from the stool she was perched upon, one of two that she had brought aboard her Fledgling, and landed squarely on her boots. After having Scarlett aboard she was intent upon making it a more comfortable place. Which included stocking the galley.

Thinking of such, she paused her approach towards the Doppelgänger.

"Are you hungry?" she asked.

The Aridian shook her large, round head. "No, thank you. But I will be."

The Jordan nodded and continued making her way to the

bed and, reaching it, sat down on the side.

"Calyph is fine," she said. "His concern for you has kept you both alive."

"While you have contemplated our usefulness, no doubt," Tara said, her tone dripping with acid.

"Please don't feign disgust with me," Blue said, irritated.

"Trust me, it's not feigned."

Blue gave her another wicked smile. "As if you were not contemplating my usefulness, or at least that of my body's."

The Aridian shrugged and looked away. Blue took a sip from her flute and let silence fill the space between them. The Aridian finally looked back at her.

"And have you?" she asked.

"Have I what?"

The female rolled her huge eyes.

"Found how we could be of use? You must have or we, at least I, would not still be alive."

"I, along with the other Jordan you tried to ensnare, have worked out quite the plan for you."

Tara felt her heart hitch within her chest. Two high-ranking IGC officials. Two who knew that she was a Doppelgänger. And each knew that she had tried to kill them both. What sort of plan could they have devised?

The Aridian could not conceive of one that did not end with her living a life of slavery. Or tortured. Or executed. Or all three. She glanced down to see that the Jordan was not wearing her holster or sidearm. And there was nothing in her hand except the glass she was holding.

Tara was strong. She had become so over the years, though her appearance did not show it. But the Jordan had shown herself be quite strong as well, even when she had been drugged.

Still, going for her throat might be worth it. It was better than dying in chains, tortured to death. She just had to be quick. She glanced back up to see the Jordan eyeing her with amusement.

"A credit for your thoughts," Blue offered before taking a sip from her glass. Tara shrugged, forcing nonchalance.

"A Schakel usually comes with a remote," she said.

Blue smiled. "I have no need. I had one made, custom, GwenSeven of course. I can only imagine the pain you would be in should you try to attack me. Though I might like to see it."

The Aridian closed her round eyes. "In that case, I can only hope that you have found some use for me. And do not plan to have me incarcerated. I would never survive in prison. Not because I can't fight, but because I could never live in a cage."

"I have not only found a use for you," Blue told her, "but I have found a life for you."

The Aridian opened her eyes and stared at the Jordan, waiting.

"What do you desire more," Blue asked, "power or riches?"

The Doppelgänger let her head loll back in exasperation. It was so large and the movement so exaggerated that Blue was amazed that the weight of it did not pull her slim body down with it, making her spill over backwards.

"Why," Tara demanded as she heaved a huge sigh, "do those two have to be mutually exclusive?"

Blue laughed. "They don't. But unless you are born into a monarchy or oligarchy, one usually precedes the other. When you gain power, riches follow. Or when you are rich, you can often gain power."

The Aridian's thin brows drew together over her round eyes. "You're being serious, aren't you?"

"I am."

The gaze of the Rogue Doppelgänger unfocused as she considered what the Jordan had asked.

"When you are rich," she mused aloud, "you often gain power. But even that can be a struggle. When you have power, riches do not necessarily matter but seem to come anyway." Her gaze rose, unblinking, to see the Jordan grinning at her. "I think I would take power," Tara admitted. "But I would like to know what you have in mind."

Blue took another sip from her glass and her grin widened. "Why did you want to be the Jordan of a Fledgling?"

Tara frowned. "What do you mean?"

"I know you and Calyph planned to take down Jordan Scarlett and, when that failed, you went after me."

"So?' the Aridian challenged.

"What in the hell for?" Blue asked.

"Money," Tara answered defiantly, raising her small and pointed chin. "We were going to sell the Fledgling to the highest bidder."

Blue kept her composure, though it felt like the blood racing through her veins was dangerously hot, murderous.

"But if it came to money or power, you would choose power?" she asked.

The Aridian frowned, her thin eyebrows pulling together again over her massive round eyes. "What are you getting at?"

"Snatch a Fledgling, yes – if you are going for the money."

"And if I was after power?"

"Why be a Jordan when you could be a Captain?"

"What?"

"How would you like to be the Captain of a Dragon?" the Jordan asked.

The Doppelgänger's mouth opened and she drew in a slow deep breath of air through her lips, her tongue darting out like she was tasting it. "Why don't you pour me a glass of what you are having, and we can discuss it?"

Blue drained her own glass, rose from the bed and headed for the galley to do just that.

# TWO NINE

*- A betrayal is never sudden- its secret always lingers
in the silence before the fall.*

The galley on board the Opal Dragon was not that much
different from any other galley aboard a huge vessel. It was full
of hot ovens, boiling pots, the constant clanking of pans and
lids, and a multitude of cooks and their help arming sweat from
their brows as they prepared meals for a crew of over three
thousand.

Everywhere in the long steaming kitchen men and women
were chopping, prepping, baking, stirring and stocking.

Second Culinary Steward Ronnan was better known
as Dusty. It was a nickname often given to the crewman
unofficially known as the Jack of the Dust since, though
officially storeroom keeper, he worked in the bread room so
much that he was often covered from head to toe with flour.

Dusty was finished for the morning in the baking room and
was now almost done inventorying the latest shipment to the
main galley pantry when he came to a large box marked on the
outside:

To be delivered specifically to Jordan Blue, Opal Dragon, IGC
Battleship 787

Dusty scanned the label on the outside of the box to see
what it contained. He then went to the Chief Culinary Steward

Gergous. The Chief was topped with a swath of dark ginger hair on his narrow head and had the wiry body of a lightweight wrestler.

"A case and a half of champagne?" Gergous queried. "Thank the gods she requisitioned her own goods. She's practically depleted my stores of that, along with the peanut butter that only seems to appeal to humans less than twenty years old. Ring her up and see if she wants it delivered to her Fledgling."

Dusty dipped his head in acknowledgment, powdery flour sifting through his hair, and made his way through the steaming galley and hot bodies to where he could have galley communications link him to the Jordan. Instead of the Fledgling, she asked him to have the box delivered to her personal quarters.

Without a second thought, much less a question, Dusty did as he was ordered.

ೞ

The Jordans, along with Calyph, reported to the bridge after being summoned by Captain Brogan. They waited close by the Captain and the Executive Officer where the two stood at the helm, already engrossed in a discussion.

Brogan finished quickly and greeted them before turning where he stood, eyeing all those present in the control room.

"Attention in the bridge," the Captain called out.

Dareus, the Communications Officer, and Chiara, the Navigator, rose immediately to their feet. The Gunnery Lieutenant, already on his feet, straightened to the position of attention, as did the two crewmembers who happened to be present.

The Jordans and the Executive Officer stiffened where they stood, hands at their sides and their chins lifted. Calyph did his best to hold himself in a military manner.

"I have recommended Commander Blaylock for the promotion to Captain of the Copper Dragon. And it has been accepted. Congratulations, Commander."

Blaylock's hazel eyes were wide. He had expected something to happen eventually due to the shortage of Captains these days, but not so soon. It must have been expedited because of Brogan's recommendation.

"No," Scarlett said. Blaylock's open-eyed stare went to the Red Jordan, expecting to see her usual sneer. But she was smiling. Really smiling. "Congratulations, *Captain*."

Blaylock cocked his head, trying to summon a look of exasperation, but unable to keep the elation from his face. "Come on now, Jordan."

Scarlett laughed. "I know we have had our differences, and I will admit I was anticipating the upcoming rotation," and here the X.O. chuckled, "but I also know what an accomplishment it is. Congratulations."

"Thank you, Jordan." He looked at Blue, wondering if she would have a similar response. She did.

"I believe a celebration is in order," she said. "I just received a case of champagne from French Europa. I was going to stock my Fledgling, but I think I should have it delivered to the Officer's Club."

Blaylock blinked at her in surprise.

"Well," she amended, "most of it."

"I will definitely be there to raise a glass," Scarlett said. "But the first round is on me!"

Blaylock stared at her in disbelief.

"1900?" she asked.

The X.O. nodded his head, slowly at first, and then with more surety. "Yes," he agreed, knowing that those on duty would be relieved at 1800. "1900."

All eyes turned to Captain Brogan. "Very well," he told

them, "you are dismissed. Enjoy yourselves tonight."

"Yes, sir," everyone said at once and then moved away as the Captain motioned the Gunnery Officer to him.

Jordan Blue and Jordan Scarlett left without so much as a glance at each other and Calyph headed for his own quarters to continue a discussion with the troll on metals illegally imported from the outer rim.

He was barely two minutes into his argument, which was useless anyway - it always useless to argue with a troll – when there was a knock on his door. The Engineer looked up in surprise (he rarely, if ever, had callers at his door) and even the troll expressed intrigue as its upper base which housed its optic band swiveled around to peer at the elf.

The elfin Engineer finished the ale he had been sipping in two long gulps and dropped the dark bottle into the bin next to his desk before rising to open the door to his cabin.

In the hall waited Jordan Blue.

"Calyph," Blue ordered, "come with me."

Calyph swallowed and followed the Jordan without question, the doors to his rooms sliding closed as he left. He walked next to her down a Vein corridor and followed her up to the next level. It was not long before he realized that she was leading him to her own cabin.

Well, he thought, *we were just someplace where we could speak privately, so it must be something else. Either she's going to kill me or fuck me, and I doubt I have a chance at the second option.*

Still, he found himself to be equal amounts of terror and erection.

Upon reaching her room, Blue placed her hand over the pad next to her door and it slid open without a sound. She held out a hand, inviting him to enter first.

He drew a breath that he was pretty sure was going to be his last and stepped inside. Blue followed, quickly closing the door behind her but the elf hardly noticed.

Tara was sitting on the edge of the bed, her smile splitting her round face.

Calyph rushed to her, grabbing her tiny hands and kissing the stretch of her smile. He broke away to stare at her unbelievingly for a moment before casting his blue-eyed stare at the Jordan.

"I thought you might want a few hours together while… while she has this form. It will be some time before she has it again, though you two will be together."

Calyph's brows drew together in confusion and Blue blew a breath of air through puffed cheeks and inclined her head towards Tara. "She'll explain it to you." Then she motioned with her chin to a large open container next to the bed. Have her back in the box at 1600."

Calyph was going to ask about the box but instead, sheepishly, he asked, "and you don't mind if we…?"

Blue chuckled softly. "I don't plan on spending another night in here. Go for it."

She disappeared through the door as it opened and then it slid shut immediately once she was out.

Between bouts of passionate and sometimes aggressive lovemaking, Tara explained everything to Calyph.

⊗

Blue and Scarlett, along with Calyph, arrived at the Officer's Club at 1830 while the ship was moving into dimlight. The entire Atrium was growing darker by the second, the bars and restaurants exchanging fluorescent lighting for ambient diodes. They brought along Dareus, who was off-duty, and Roselyn, the Dragon's other Navigations Officer. Neither of them were very fond of Blaylock but, like most, were fond of a free drink.

Calyph walked behind all of them, guiding an air dolly with large box on it. There were already three other off-duty officers there, having heard of the impending celebration.

"Let's get this party started!" Blue announced as she walked inside, a bottle of champagne in each hand. Scarlett pulled out her credentials card and handed it to the bartender.

"Make sure I get that back in an hour," she told him.

"Yes, ma'am," he agreed with a smile.

"Blue, get that champagne on ice!" she called over her shoulder.

"On it!"

Calyph walked next to the Blue Jordan as she headed for the bar but, instead of stopping with her as she came to a halt and leaned heavily against the bar, he kept going - towards the bathrooms in the back.

There were two lavatories in the rear of the Officer's Club and, after a quick glance about, Calyph pushed the dolly through the door of the first one and closed it with the box inside. He took another quick look around but everyone's attention was on the burgeoning festivities.

He dropped a metal disc on the floor and tapped the button in the center with the bottom of his foot. It opened like a flower made of steel and projected a holo of light onto the bathroom door.

Closed for Maintenance it read.

Exhaling a sharp breath, the Engineer rejoined the group after stopping at the bar for a bottle of porter. The bartender, a stout elf named Kepfler, had his hands full pouring drinks. The Officer's Club was seldom busy and hardly ever rowdy unless there was a reason to celebrate.

Tonight was unexpected.

Calyph looked at Blue and gave her a nod. Blue smiled and directed her gaze to Scarlett, giving her a nod as well.

"No reason to wait for the Commander," she announced. "He'll get his! Cheers!"

"Cheers! Cin cin! Salud! Everkra!" came the replies as glasses were lifted in salutation and drank down. Another round was ordered and, just as glasses were being distributed, the Executive Officer entered the club and it was once again full of riotous shouting.

"Hooray! Cheers! Congratulations!"

The few officers who were already tipsy clapped him on the back.

"Shots!" someone called out.

"Yes!" another officer echoed. "Shots!"

Blaylock shook his head, though he was in good spirits. "I haven't done shots since I graduated college," he assured the group.

"But this *is* a graduation of sorts," Calyph said.

"And a much bigger deal than college!" the Navigations Officer chirped.

The XO tipped his head to the side, about to object again when the Red Jordan shouted at the bartender. Others joined in with her as she called out;

"Dragonfire shots!"

"Shots!"

"Dragonfire!"

"Copper Dragonfire!" Blue shouted.

Barkeep Kepfler was already there, a tray covered with shot glasses filled with curat and cinnamon whiskey. The Blue Jordan had already instructed him to have at least twenty ready when the Dragon's Executive Officer arrived.

The short glasses of brightly colored high-octane alcohol were quickly passed around and Scarlett held hers high.

"To Captain Blaylock!" she shouted.

The cry was echoed over and over as everyone, including the new Captain, quaffed their liquor.

Blaylock eyed Scarlett as he drank his down, burning like fire down his throat before the heat exploded in his stomach. *Smile and cheer all you want,* he thought. *I know it's because I'm leaving the Opal Dragon. But you aren't going to be rid of me, you bitch. Not by long shot.*

Still, the XO truly had reason to celebrate. After all his hard work (scheming and murdering some might call it but it was still hard work) he was finally being made a Captain. Captain of a Dragon.

Plus, JP had nabbed the little snot who looked so much like Scarlett it had sickened Blaylock. Unlike Petrov, he had no misgivings or hesitation regarding kidnapping. And Gemma, he would finally be able to... His thoughts were interrupted as another shot was pressed into his hand.

"Ah, shit!" he exclaimed as he was cheered for again. It was something he could get used to, something for which he had worked. Plus, the first shot was beginning to work its magic. "Screw it! Cheers!"

He downed the fresh shot and heard the pop of a champagne bottle. "Now that's what I'm talking about!" Within seconds he was handed a flute of champagne. Most others waved off the bubbly liquid, opting for beers and cocktails as a few more officers filtered into the club, greeted with enthusiasm by those already half in the bag.

Blaylock found Jordan Blue in front of him with her own flute of champagne and she held it up in salute. "Congratulations, sir."

"Thank you, Jordan," he replied and took a sip. And coughed, nearly spitting out his drink.

The Jordan grinned at him. "It has a hint of Grevin pepper in it," she admitted.

"A little more than a hint!" Blaylock accused, though getting too tipsy to really be angry. Also, not wanting to seem weak in front of the Jordan, who was obviously unfazed by the pepper, took a long drink, and then another when he thought he was going to cough.

"Where did you get this?" he asked. "I can't imagine this is what Kefler has behind the bar."

The Blue Jordan laughed and shook her head. "No. I had this special ordered."

Blaylock was now buzzed enough to unashamedly make a face on his next drink. "Ugh!" He exclaimed with a short laugh. "Must be for elves."

The Jordan chuckled. "Maybe you should stick with the Dragonfire."

The word was heard and repeated in shouts that echoed throughout the club.

"Dragonfire!"

"Dragonfire!"

The XO began to shake his head when a glass was pressed into his free hand and somebody shouted, "to the new Captain!"

"To the new Captain!"

"Alright," Blaylock acquiesced loudly, "but this is the last one!"

There were hoots and cheers and shots thrown down throats.

Blue sidled up to the Red Jordan who was sipping a cream-colored cocktail over ice. They had both gotten an injection of A-solve earlier. They would be immune to any alcohol they ingested over the next six hours.

"What did I tell you?" Blue asked softly from the side of her mouth as she smiled. "Easy peas...shit!"

Scarlett glanced at the other Jordan and then followed her one-eyed gaze to the entrance where the Captain was entering the club with two other officers.

"Shitshitshit," Blue was whispering. "Balls and shit!"

"Maybe," Scarlett started to say when she saw of what Blue had already taken serious note. The Captain was wearing his sidearm.

Of course he would wear it to any formal event, she reasoned. *It's part of his formal uniform - though he is still in his regulation coveralls. And half of the ship's officers getting drunk at a bar is hardly a formal event. Even for the XO's promotion.*

And the officers with him were Olney and Hearth. The Dragon's head Security Officers. They were always armed.

"Don't panic," she said softly. "He's just here for the sendoff party."

"The sendoff for Blaylock," Blue whispered back, "or us?"

"Just stay calm."

The room had quieted and sobered considerably at the Captain's entrance.

"Carry on," the Captain said with a smile. "Do not pause the celebration on my account. But I would be amiss if I did not buy a drink for the man who was my Second in Command these past few years. Master Kefler!" he called out.

"Yes, Captain!" the stalwart bar elf replied.

"A round for everyone! On me!"

There was a renewed vigor from the small crowd as they cheered for the Captains, both current and new. The eyes of the Captain quickly grew solemn as they sought out his Jordans. Unsmiling, he inclined his head towards the bar.

"Shit!" Blue hissed between her teeth.

Scarlett grasped the other Jordan by her elbow and together they made their way through the small throng.

Blaylock, who had skipped breakfast and had drunk more tonight, and more quickly than he had in a single night in decades, swayed on his feet. But he could hardly turn down a congratulatory drink from his Captain.

The Jordans met their Captain at the bar where Navigations Officer Roselyn was helping Barmaster Kefler handle the prodigious number of commissioned crew who had gathered.

"Evening, sir," Scarlett greeted calmly. "May I buy you a drink?"

"Yes," he agreed convivially, though his eyes were stern. "You may."

Shit, Scarlett thought. *Blue was right. The jig is up. We're fucked.*

As the Captain turned his face to the Navigator to request a cocktail, the dark eyes of the Red Jordan flicked to Olney and Hearth. They had remained by the entrance, politely refusing libations and idly tapping the laser pistols on their hips as their eyes roved the room.

Scarlett breathed steadily through her nose and calmly sipped her drink. Her crimson-flecked eyes fell on Blue, who was watching Captain Brogan accept a glass of champagne from Kefler.

Then he turned his face to the Blue Jordan, his silver-gray brows raised over his pale blue eyes..

"I trust that my champagne is not as heavily peppered as Commander Blaylock's?"

"No, sir," Blue said softly.

Brogan gave them a broad smile. "In that case, may I propose a toast?"

Both IGC pilots gave him a cautious nod. That he was on to what they were doing there was no doubt.

The Captain raised his glass. "I am with you Jordans," he said, "now and always."

The Jordans mirrored his movements as he raised his glass in salute, then lowered it and drank.

"Is that a customary toast?" Scarlett asked after sipping her drink, forcing a nonchalant smile. "Or just something for the

Captains of Dragons?"

The Captain tilted his head in a manner that could mean yes or no, or both. "It means," he explained, "we will fight as one, we will rise as one, or we will all go down together." His pearlescent blue eyes fixed meaningfully on her and then Blue.

The Jordans stared at him.

Brogan's eyes went from one to the other as he took another drink from his glass. They were still staring at him in disbelief when Blacklock staggered to the bar.

"I need to use the head," he slurred out, as if they had asked.

Calyph, possibly as terrified as he had ever been, took a step toward the lavatories and kicked the disc to the front of the other door. Blaylock lurched towards it, saw the maintenance warning, and pushed his way into the other latrine, almost falling through the door.

The Engineer sauntered back towards the bar, again kicking the disc so that it was back in front of the door of the compromised washroom that Blaylock had entered. Blue, as discreetly as she could, thumbed an indent on the side of the platinum cuff she wore on her wrist.

The Aridian would now be free of the Schakel for forty-five seconds. Tara had assured Blue that it would be more than a sufficient amount of time.

The only question was, time for what?

For her to betray Blue?

The Jordan fought the urge to cross her fingers and instead took a sip of champagne. Still, a clock ticked down the seconds in her head.

Forty-five seconds went by.

Then a minute.

From the corner of her eye she saw Brogan take a casual sip of champagne while, just as easily, he let his hand drop to the butt of his sidearm.

At a minute and a half she dared a glance at Scarlett but the other Jordan was staring at the door to the lavatory as it swung open hard enough to bang the wall.

A good many pairs of eyes turned at the noise to see the Executive Officer lurch out, swaying on his feet.

"You should see the mess I left in there!" he shouted with drunken triumph and then laughed uproariously at his own joke.

Everyone in the Officer's Club joined his raucous laughter, suspecting the XO had vomited gloriously all over the head.

"Calyph," the Captain called out over the roar of the crowd and the Engineer felt his balls shrivel in fear. "Commander Blaylock is in a bit of a rough state from his celebration. Would you please see that he makes it back to his cabin? Maybe see that he gets some water in him?"

"Certainly, sir," Calyph agreed, putting his bottle down on the bar and grabbing the listing X.O. by the elbow. The elfin Engineer steadied the commander and then let go, following close as he made his way through the throng of officers, swaying on his feet yet jovial as a Golbli juvenile as they cheered him.

The three at the bar watched in speechless amusement at the departure before turning their eyes back to one another.

"On my request," Brogan told them, "the Executive Officer from the Copper Dragon will transfer here, to be my Second in Command. I have arranged for Gunnery Officer Anatoli to accompany Captain Blaylock, to help him in all manner he may need."

The Jordans nodded, solemn.

"I have also arranged for Calyph to be the interim Engineer to serve both the Copper and Silver dragons. We can request him as needed, but he should not be essential since our Fledglings will not be grown again for another five years."

"What is it that you sense?" Scarlett asked, blunt and off

topic.

The club was getting louder by the moment but the three officers at the bar seemed to be enclosed in their own bubble of existence.

The Jordan's dark brows drew together as she looked intently at her Captain. "Blue has a heightened sense of hearing. For me, it is smell. What did the triptych do to you, sir? If I may ask. What do you sense now, more than before?"

The right side of the Captain's mouth quirked up in half a smile. "Perception. Mainly my ability to see intention in others." A flicker of shame crossed his face as he glanced at the latrine where, behind the closed door, a body lay dead on the floor. "I always could see Blaylock's ambition, but I let grief cloud that perception and I did not see to what extent."

He turned his face back to his Jordans and they could see tears standing in his pale blue eyes.

"So..." Scarlett ventured as Brogan blinked the water from his eyes. "You see intent." She swallowed. "Do you see our intent?"

The Captain shrugged. "For the most part."

"And Security Officers Olney and Hearth are here for...?"

"To clean up the mess in the head," Brogan told her.

Stunned and shaken, Scarlett turned her dark eyes to Blue and they both expelled a lungful of air through pursed lips.

Jordan Blue lifted her flute of champagne. "We fight as one, we rise as one, or we all go down together." She spoke softly but, within their own bubble, her words were clear over the din.

The Captain and the Red Jordan raised their own glasses and drank.

THREE ZERO

"Three things cannot stay long hidden – the sun, the moon, and the truth."
Buddha

"Just us?" Geary asked as he strode down the corridor.

"Just us," Penny affirmed, keeping stride with him despite the constraints of her pencil skirt.

The Executive Personal Assistant to the CEO of the GwenSeven Corporation, her confidence usually so high it was to the point of condescension, found her throat too dry to swallow.

"Do you think she knows about us?" she asked softly.

Geary did not spare her a glance as he ascended the curved staircase that led to the next level. "I'm sure she knows about us. Not much gets by her."

Penny tried to swallow again. It would not be hard to find another job if she was fired. Personal Assistants were merely a credit a dozen, but with her experience and résumé she would be hired immediately and paid handsomely.

But she would never find a job that gave her the same quiet notoriety and power that she had now. Besides, Geary was an absolute animal in bed. What other PA job would have a perk like that?

They passed through a wide hallway covered nearly side to side with a long rug. Great pieces of art in gilded frames hung from the walls of black stone.

"Do you know what she's doing?" Geary asked softly as they made their way into what was often referred to as the golden tower though the stone there was as black or gray as the rest of the Castle. "At this moment?"

"Of course I do," Penny answered on the brink of impatience. "She is having high tea in the parlor of her bedroom suite."

"Just tea?" Geary asked. "No champagne?"

"Just tea," Penny answered. "No champagne."

Geary's lips pressed together. "She's keeping her head clear."

Penny's anxiety doubled as they reached the door to Faith's personal suite in the castle. Geary's steely gaze swept the hallway and saw Tom's shadow in a recess that housed a marble bust on a pedestal. His eyes glimmered with approval.

Faith had not asked for a guard to be posted so neither had Geary, though he had wanted one. Tom knew and had done so without being asked. He knew that Jasyn also often idled in the shadows, unasked and unchallenged. Geary thought he might be inside with Faith; the dark-eyed construct was rarely far from her.

Geary rapped on the oak door of Faith's room and was rewarded immediately with her call to enter.

The head of de Rossi security opened the door and held it open for Penny. Once she had entered, he closed the door behind the both of them. The entrance to Faith's personal suite in the Last Castle was a large room made for relaxing or even entertaining.

On the far side was a glass-enclosed alcove with thickly padded chairs and a small sofa that gave a sweeping view of the gardens below. Faith, who had been sitting on the small sofa, rose to welcome them as they approached. Jasyn was nowhere to be seen. She was alone.

"Please," she said, holding out a hand to one chair and then another. "Can I pour you some tea?" she asked as they took their seats. The low table was set with teacups on saucers and a matching teapot with steam coming from it spout. There were bowls of sugar, cut lemons, and a small pitcher of cream.

"Thank you," Geary said, "but no."

"I'm fine," Penny assured, feeling anything but fine in the least.

"A bite to eat?" she offered. There was a multi-tiered silver tray bearing bite size sandwiches, crackers, cheeses, fruits, scones, and caviar.

Penny and Geary both shook their heads, uneasy at her attempt to wait on them.

"Very well," Faith acquiesced as she sat herself, smoothing down the fabric of her cream-colored pants.

Both Geary and Penny could see the disquiet and discomfiture in their employer and it added to their own tension. They had known and worked for her for decades, and few things would have her in such a state.

Ms. de Rossi poured herself a cup of tea with hands that were far more steady than her demeanor. She took a dainty sip from her cup and set it down.

"We are on the brink of great changes," she announced quietly. Her two closest employees sat a bit straighter in their chairs and raised their chins, waiting. "An alliance has been formed between a number of races, and a number of those who are ready and willing to split from the IGC. I will be breaking from the IGC to support the new government which calls itself the Interstellar Alliance." What was left of her breath was exhaled from her lungs and she drew a long stream of air through her nose and took a sip from her steaming cup of tea before returning it to its saucer. "I completely understand," she continued, "if you do not wish to continue with your current line of employment. I will, of course, pay you for the remainder of your contracts and…"

"That will not be necessary," Geary interrupted. "My current contract is fine until its date of renewal and negotiation. But I am going to need a larger budget. Much larger. I want to at least double your protection detail. Immediately."

Faith could barely keep her smile suppressed. She turned her tawny gaze to Penny. The PA's brown eyes went from her employer to her lover and then back again.

"I don't know why anyone would think I would be going anywhere."

Faith looked away, trying to form the explanation, then looked to Geary who answered for her.

"Because the waters she is wading into, no - *swimming* into, are going to be dangerous. Much more dangerous than they are now. And not just for her."

Penny nodded in understanding. "*And*, I don't know why anyone would think I would be going anywhere."

"In that case," Faith said, a smile breaking across her face, "please call Mari downstairs. She has libations other than tea ready to send up. And we have many things to discuss."

Penny did so, immediately via her comset, while Faith argued with Geary about increasing the size of her personal security detail.

"Unless you think I am not safe here at the Castle," she was telling him when Penny turned back around.

"I think the entire Distant Shore is the safest place you can be right now," he admitted.

"Excellent, because it is the only place I am going to be. It's the only place we are all going to be, if you plan to stay, for quite some time."

Penny answered the knock on the door to admit Mari who was ushering in a butler and a floating cart of brass and glass. The cart lowered, extruding two pairs of wheels before settling on the floor. Mari gave a Penny a secretive smile and the PA gave her a look of affable suspicion.

"You already knew?"

Mari's smile widened, dimples deepening in her plump cheeks, but did not answer. She busied herself at the cart with the ice bucket and liqueur glasses as the butler popped the cork from a bottle of champagne.

"You will have plenty of time," Faith told Geary. "It will months, possibly years, before I make a public appearance." The head of the GwenSeven Corporation had never seen her security man look so pleased.

"Dr. Silas is going to give a speech in two days," she continued as drinks were poured and offered to each of them. "It is the wheel that will set in motion a new age for us all," she said as she accepted a flute of champagne. She held it up to toast but Geary smiled and shook his head.

"I'm not really a champa..." he started to say when he saw the short glass of crystal Mari was holding out to him, two fingers full of amber liquid. His steely eyes went to the glass in front of Penny, a demitasse cup full of an espresso liqueur he knew Penny had favored this last year.

"Not much gets by me," Faith admitted, raising her glass, "but I am grateful that you two catch what does." She lifted her glass a trite higher and then took a satisfying sip. Geary and Penny did the same, their eyes meeting over the rims of their drinks.

◌◌

Sean's first full day at the Castle was spent exploring. It was an overwhelming mix of weirdness and enjoyment.

He was going on seventeen and had never tried any mind-altering drugs, though he knew many friends at school who had and quite a few that took them on a regular basis, but that day he felt he was experiencing what must be very close. It was like being in a dream.

He had no school. Not today and not for any foreseeable time in the future. After breakfast in a room bigger than most of the podments he had ever lived in (where the staff, *the staff* took their meals) he was set loose to wander the halls of a giant castle full of the craziest combination of rooms and people.

There were towers and hallways and stairs – stairs everywhere. There were elevators and parlors and sitting rooms and kitchens and areas that he had no idea for what they were used. The center of the Castle, which seemed to be the main building and certainly the busiest, had a ballroom on one floor and a conservatory full of indoor gardens right above it.

There were complete towers that were furnished and clean but, Sean could tell, were empty and rarely – if ever – used.

Some rooms, including his own, had fireplaces. The one in his bedroom was holographic and the flickering image popped into existence when he touched the control pad. He found another room that had a gas fireplace that whooshed into life with the flick of a switch. Yet another room had a stone nook with nothing in it save for an iron cradle. Sean squatted by it for nearly a minute before he realized that it must be for burning actual wood.

For some reason, out of all the opulence he had witnessed at the Castle, this struck him the most.

The money they must have! he thought. *To not only afford to buy real wood, but then to burn it!*

The others inhabiting the Castle, from what he could tell, were the de Rossis, the Jordans from the Opal Dragon, and a mighty workforce of cooks, butlers, assistants, security teams, and cleaning staff.

Each of those in the Mattatock family had been assigned an assistant (who might have just as easily been a guard, Sean could not tell) who followed them everywhere. At first it had been strange, though no stranger than everything else he was experiencing.

He knew his parents and his grandfather were uncomfortable being followed and monitored and kept to their bedrooms and the huge room where they had eaten most of their meals.

Not Jeanette.

She was enthralled by having someone to talk to, to riddle to death with her questions, who was bound to stay and not roll their eyes or make haste for the closest exit. And she was relentless.

Her guard was startled at first, and hesitant, then charmed by her endless curiosity.

How old is the castle?

What is it made of?

Can no one really find it?

How many rooms are there?

Is there anyone locked in one of the towers?

Are there dungeons?

Is there hidden treasure?

Are there secret tunnels?

"You watch too many holos!" he told her finally, laughing. But she was so sweet and so curious that he showed her around as much as he could, answering what questions he thought appropriate.

Sean, personally, was glad to see her back to her old annoying self. Her quiet smile during the long trip to get there had given him the creeps.

Heebie jeebies, he thought to himself and then laughed aloud.

His assistant/guard, who had been following him through the castle arched a brow at his quiet gust of mirth then raised both brows as the young man turned to her.

"Does this place have a library?" Sean asked.

Rita, who was there to serve as both a guard and an assistant to the Mattatock boy, smiled at him.

"Right this way."

ര8&ു

Sean's strange day gave way to an even stranger evening, and he became more convinced he was dreaming. If he was, it was easily the longest and wildest dream he had ever had in his life.

The Mattatock family had dinner that night with the de Rossis sisters, the raven-haired construct they called Jasyn, and a man swathed in golden robes who had introduced himself as Elaeric. He had tan-golden skin, almond shaped eyes, and a bald head.

Faith de Rossi had a classic elegance about her. Sean was not sure if he would call her beautiful, but she had a calm demeanor that was powerful and unsettling. Charity de Rossi was unquestionably stunning. Decked out in a black and green silk jacket and a black silk skirt that was so short it made Sean blush and avert his eyes. She seemed to be wearing more jewelry than actual clothing and it sparkled from her ears, neck, and hands.

The room, he thought, was ridiculously huge. It was square, but had a roundish feel to it due to the round dining table and the way everything was placed about it – from lamps and furniture and art to a small wet bar and several houseplants in varying sizes with strange gold and brown fronds.

What he did not know, was that it was one of the smaller and more intimate dining rooms in the castle. One that the staff referred to as the "minor diner." There were a number of doors made of the same polished mahogany as the dining table. One was the door they had entered through and there was another single door on the opposite side of the room. Then there was a set of double doors through which the staff came and went, presumably that led to the kitchens.

People moved around them in a quick, calm, deliberate manner; serving drinks and pushing floating trays topped with silver, frost-dusted domes.

"I feel like I'm at the mad tea party," he remarked to Grandpa, seated on his right.

The dark-eyed construct, who had just sat down to his left, laughed as he shook out his napkin and draped it on his lap.

"That was a couple of days ago," he told Sean. "In the conservatory." He chuckled again. "And I think your Aunt made a similar remark at the time."

"It's just so unreal," Sean told him, unabashed.

Jasyn leaned to the side as an arm reached past his shoulder to put a drink down on the table in front of him. "It just seems unreal because you aren't used to it," he told Sean. "Give it a week and it will be mildly interesting and a week after that it will seem perfectly normal."

Sean's first thought was that the man was crazy, this could *never* be normal. It was entirely too bizarre. Then he recalled what it had been like when his family had moved to the Upper Klick.

The entire place had also seemed unreal at the time. His first day of school had felt like a dream. He could hardly believe any of it until he fell into a regular schedule. Looking back, he had probably done so within just a couple of weeks.

"Jesus," he whispered. He felt his grandpa give him a poke even as Jasyn smiled and glanced at him.

"Don't blaspheme!" the construct whispered.

Sean was reaching a point where he was not sure if the next

sound to come from his throat was going to be a laugh or a cackle like Grandpa used to do.

Steaming baskets of breads and rolls were put on the table and plates were put down in front of everyone. There were chilled plates that held pats of butter shaped like flowers. The man sitting across from Sean, who Sean would have sworn was a monk of some kind, smiled at him.

"The entanglement in this room," he remarked with a mischievous smile, "is thick enough to be cut with a sword."

Fletcher plucked up a steaming basket and offered it first to Jeanette and then to Sean, who took a thick slice of soft bread filled with seeds and nuts.

"Thank you, Grandpa."

Charity de Rossi, seated between Faith and the man dressed like a monk, smiled broadly as she held a cocktail glass aloft. Bracelets of sparkling gems hung from her wrist and heavy rings adorned her fingers.

"I love hearing them call you *grandpa*," she drawled. "It's so sweet."

"Are you saying it ages me?" Fletcher asked with a smile. "Because, as I recall, I'm only older than you by..."

"AA..AAH..Ahem!" Charity interrupted loudly, ostentatiously clearing her throat. She glanced around anxiously before regaining her composure. "I wonder what we are having tonight!" she continued, the charming smile returning to her face.

Elaeric looked at her and smiled. "As do I," he said. "May Fletcher finish his sentence?"

"Certainly not," Charity stated, unusually prim. Smiles, some hidden and some not, abounded around the table. "Besides," she continued, "I think it would be lovely to discuss..."

This time it was Charity who was interrupted by a commotion outside as a door opened and both security teams and a troop of assistants jostled and argued about who should be the one to interject themselves into the dinner party. Normally, Castle Security would let one of Charity's assistants know if someone was arriving and to seek permission from Ms. de Rossi herself. Now, however, the Dragon Fledglings had been cleared for coming and going to the Last Castle at their leisure. There was no need for authorization, just the announcement of their entrance.

It only took a moment for Geary to shoulder everyone aside so that Penny could pass through with ease. The PA strode across the room and stopped next to Faith who looked at her assistant with an air of eager expectance. Penny's eyes swept across the Mattatock family and Elaeric before fixing them on her employer. Faith gave her a quick nod to let her know she could speak openly.

"The Green Fledgling has entered the airspace of the Distant Shore."

Faith wiped her mouth with her napkin and stood. "Thank you, Penny." Her eyes fell on Fletcher. "We have some pressing business to attend to," she explained. "Please stay and enjoy dinner, we will most likely be rejoining you before dessert."

Fletcher and John, who had courteously risen from their seats when Faith stood, sat back down. Elaeric and Jasyn had gotten to their feet as well, but they remained standing. Charity slid from her seat, gave those at the table a dazzling smile, and appropriated her drink. Fletcher could see her hand was trembling.

"Yes," she agreed. "If not dessert, we will certainly be back for evening cocktails."

The doorway cleared, personal assistants and security guards parting like water only to close up and fall in around the small group as they left the dining room.

Faith walked down the corridor, heading for the elevator that would take them down to the hangar, Penny keeping stride on her left. Geary was immediately behind both women.

Charity's staff fluttered around her like butterflies, asking questions and taking orders. Jasyn walked between the two de Rossi women. Elaeric trailed the group like an afterthought, his robes whispering around his legs.

Faith turned her face towards her assistant as they strode through the hallway. "Please make sure that Amberle's rooms are ready. Also, that another suite is made welcoming, should she have anyone with her."

"Anyplace in particular?" Penny asked.

Faith glanced at her sister.

"Hope's tower?" Charity asked.

Faith frowned slightly and gave her head a quick shake. "No. If she is anything like we believe her to be, she will be more comfortable with the Jordans. Put her close to them."

Penny gave a nod and peeled away from the group to carry out Faith's wishes. Charity waved a finger at one of her own assistants in a silent command to go with her. The PA slipped from the group just as they were coming to a stop in front of the elevators.

Charity turned to her primary assistant, Aide. "Make sure everything goes smoothly with our guests at dinner." She jerked her chin and Aide turned and left quickly. Charity looked at the two young women that remained. "You two wait here and have your IC coms open and on in case I need you." The two young women, both constructs, gave her a nod and stepped to the side. Two of Charity's bodyguards stood waiting and Charity simply shooed them away to wait in the shadows.

Faith turned to see Geary, who had stepped into Penny's spot the moment she had left. She saw the look of exasperation on his hardened face and she bottled a smile.

"I'll be fine," she told him. Geary gave her a look that said he did not believe her in the slightest and expelled a slow and controlled stream of air through his nostrils. "It's just Amberle," she explained. Not that she needed to, but she felt the compulsion to protect him in a similar manner that he did for her, mentally if not physically. "And," she added, "possibly a guest. A welcome relative." Geary gave her another look of sincere doubt and she smiled at him. "Besides, Jasyn will be with me," she added in assurance. The steely gray eyes of her bodyguard flicked to the construct and his demeanor relaxed in the most miniscule amount.

Giving Jasyn a meaningful glare, which the construct accepted with a nod, Geary took a step back.

Charity and Faith entered the lift and turned around to face front. Elaeric slipped in like a whisp of a breeze. Jasyn took his place between the sisters and turned around as well. As the doors slid shut he looked askance at Faith.

"What did the J stand for?" he asked.

Faith's shoulders drooped and she rolled her eyes as the lift began to drop. "Juvenile," she said caustically.

Charity narrowed her green eyes at her sister. "What the hell are you two talking about?"

"Do they still speak in riddles?" Elaeric asked, looking from Faith to Jasyn and then back to Charity.

"As of late, they hardly speak at all," Charity remarked quietly, her own eyes going back and forth between her sister and the construct.

Faith closed her eyes in exasperation and her head tipped back on her shoulders. "He keeps..." she began to say when the lift came to a stop and the doors opened.

⚜

Upstairs, in one of the smaller dining rooms in the castle, the Mattatock family was being served salad.

Rebbecca breathed a sigh of relief as she looked at her husband.

"This is crazy," she said. "Not that I am unappreciative. I can hardly believe that they have taken us in, but *more*, they are treating us like galactic royalty! I never know what to do or say!"

"Thank you," John told an elderly man in a tuxedo as he heaped greens onto the plate in front of him. He then selected a cruet of oil and vinegar and doused the mix of greens that had been piled on his plate as he turned to his distraught wife. "We should get used to it the best we can," he advised. "Even though we probably won't be here long term, our lives are certainly going to change."

"What do you mean?" Sean asked. "Long term?"

John Mattatock took a bite of his salad and chewed, thoughtful for a moment.

"Well," he said, "this is obviously not a place to raise a family. Your mother and I need to work. You and your sister need to go to school."

Though Sean usually took his father's (like his grandfather's) words as gospel, this time – for the first time – he questioned them.

"Why?" he asked.

He kept his eyes fixed on his father, whose own eyes widened as he considered the question. In his peripheral vision he could see his mother asking a question to whom he cringingly thought of as a servant, and Jeanette.

Jeanette was staring at the door through which the de Rossis and their escorts had left. Staring at it with a sort of desperation that made him suddenly so nervous he forgot what he had asked his father.

His father finished chewing the food in his mouth and smiled at him. "You know, son, that is a great question."

"John!" Rebecca admonished in a voice that was soft but shocked.

John rounded up the remaining greens onto his fork and

shrugged before plunging them into his mouth. "He is right, Becca," he told her when he finished chewing. "We don't need the money. He is about ready to graduate and go out to do whatever he wants. With the political unrest that is on the rise it would be wise for us to wait a while and see what happens."

"What about Jeanette?" Rebecca demanded.

Jeanette's head snapped back to the conversation at the dinner table at the mention of her name. It took her a moment, but her beguiling smile pulled itself across her face with a swift zeal with which everyone was comfortable.

Except Sean.

That was not her normal smile.

Not her sweet, innocent smile.

It was the cat that had swallowed the canary.

Yet…it was unsure.

Sean saw something that no one else did. Something that he himself had never seen on his sister.

Her eyes shone.

Not with fascination but with trepidation.

And there was a glimmer on her face that did not come from her youth, but from a sheen of nervous sweat. And her eyes kept darting to the door on her right.

Sean pushed away the plate of leafy greens and it was immediately swooped up and replaced with an empty bowl. A large spoon was placed next to the bowl along with a fresh napkin.

"What's going on with you?" Sean demanded, looking at his sister. All eyes joined his and Jeanette straightened under the sudden scrutiny.

"I think…I think… my tummy is a little upset," she stammered.

"You think?" Sean asked, knowing she was lying. And she was terrible at it.

"I need to use the restroom," she said quickly.

"Which is it?" Sean asked as the adults watched their exchange with interest. "Upset stomach or you need the restroom?"

"Both," Jeanette told Sean, scowling at him as she edged her chair back bit by bit from the table. "If you'll excuse me?"

She glanced at her father, who gave her a nod, then slid from her chair and walked from the dining room.

 # THREE ONE

- Secrets can be as sharp as swords, and more deadly.

Faith and Charity stood side by side as the Green Fledgling dove into the cavern, the vast space lit by a variety of diodes, halogens, and fluorescents that hung from the unfinished, craggy rock ceiling.

It made a slight turn over the tarmac, and then pushed out four squat legs from its silver-green body and settled down on them.

Inside, Verdana had reshaped the pilot's seat into a bench. On it, slightly squished together, sat Amberle, Ember L'chiross, and Traejanale Royce.

Amberle was astounded by how they were able to fit. Not just because there were three of them, but because of the amount of weapons the other two wore. They reminded her of birds, the way they could fold their expanse of wings in close to their bodies, making them smooth and sleek.

In the hangar, Jasyn stood slightly to Faith's left and Elaeric stood to the right of Charity.

"Those are your aunts," Amberle told Ember.

For decades upon decades Ember had searched for her family, but now she suddenly could not care less about them. Her eyes, a strange mix of jewel-like colors, stared at the one with the tonsured head and almond-shaped eyes.

"Who is that man?" she whispered. "The one in the robes."

Amberle shrugged. "I don't know. I've never seen him before."

Ember stared. He bore an uncanny resemblance to the man who had raised her, had taught her, had shaped her, into the woman she was now.

He was by no means identical - her sharp eyes could tell he was not even the same race as her father, but they were closer than anyone else she had ever met. Narrow eyes, bald scalp, and those robes! She had never seen anyone else wear robes like that before.

More than that, he held a glimmer of a smile at the corners of his lips - like he knew a secret.

Ember was up before the Fledgling had finished settling, waiting for the invisible door to appear and open. When it did, she was down the stairs in a blink.

She paused at the bottom, hand on the hilt of her sword, as Traejan joined her. Her eyes, green and brown with glints of gold and black, grazed over the others waiting for them in the cavern merely a dozen yards away.

Never before had she felt such a stillness in the air, a pregnancy of action. Not when she felt on display before the elfin royal court, not before any battle. The skin on her back prickled all the way up to her neck.

"Something is happening, or about to," she said softly. "Can you feel it?"

Traejan nodded and took a step closer to her, his hand dropping to the hilt of his own sword.

The two women, who Amberle had said were her aunts, stood stock still. Breathless, proud and yet filled with some inner terror or apprehension, they held their hands clasped before them and waited.

The man in the robes gave off the same feelings but smiled broadly and held his arms out to her.

Ember felt herself walking towards him on legs that were numb. And then, unable to stop herself, she was running to him. A moment later she was in his embrace and he engulfed her with thin arms and pressed her against his slight form. The woman warrior felt hot tears behind her eyes and scrunched her lids down as he hugged her.

"Child, child," he murmured into her blood red locks and she felt herself holding back sobs.

Her body shook and he held her until it subsided, making no effort to stem the flow of his own tears that wet her hair.

When he finally let her go, they were being joined cautiously by the tall elf. He was in a similar garb as Ember – loose tunic and pants tucked into high leather boots - and, like her, was armed with swords and knives.

Amberle had hung back, staying close to Verdana. She had heard what Ember said and agreed. She could feel it too. Something was happening. Her thoughts went to the eggs, so near yet dormant for the time being. She watched the reunion and stayed close to the belly of her Fledgling.

The man who had once been a monk had no qualms of others seeing his emotion and tears were plain upon the golden-toned skin of his cheeks.

"I am Elaeric," he said, and then he made a sound that was half sob and half laugh. "I am either your father, or your father's best friend," he explained.

Ember felt an odd mix of confusion and understanding. Her Roshan, who had raised her, had never denied he was her father, yet he never said that he was. There were a few others he had told her about regarding his past. The warrior nodded thoughtfully.

"He spoke of you," she confided. "And Hope. And Madeline. I remember two mothers, but in my mind's eye they look the same."

Elaeric gave another sound that was half laugh and half

cry. "And so they were," he said. "So much the same, yet so different."

Ember smiled at him and turned her eyes to the two women, presumably her mothers' sisters.

Faith stepped forward and her throat worked as she swallowed. It was a moment for which she had waited for a long time, but for which she could hardly prepare.

"I am Faith de Rossi," she said offering her hand. Ember took it and though Faith took another step forward, she did not embrace her. She simply put her other hand over Ember's and clasped it tight between her own and, for that, Ember was glad. And felt a warming in her heart.

"I can't tell you how much or for how long we have looked for you, and how happy we are to have you here." She released her hand and directed her gaze to the stunningly beautiful woman with white-blonde hair. "This is your Aunt Charity," she said.

Charity stepped forward and grasped her hand in the same manner that Faith had, giving her a dazzling smile. Then she took another step and surprised the warrior by giving her a light kiss on each cheek. "We are so happy to have found you. And so happy you are here." She turned slightly and held a jeweled hand out towards the dark-haired man behind her. "This is Jasyn," she said. "He is...a close friend of the family."

Ember's gem-like eyes went wide at the sight of him up close. Also, and quite abruptly, Traejan was by her side. His right hand still rested on the hilt of the sword that hung from his right hip, but his grip on it had tightened.

"Does he remind you of anyone?" she asked softly.

"Are you kidding?" he asked back. "You know he does. Not exactly the same, but close enough."

"Excuse me?" Jasyn asked.

"I'm sorry," Ember apologized. "It's just that you remind me of someone back home."

Jasyn swung his heavy gaze to Faith. "Are there more versions of me, running around out there in the universe?"

Faith searched his eyes with her own. "If one believes in parallel worlds, there are millions of versions of each of us."

"What did the J stand for?" he breathed.

Charity looked from him to Faith and opened her mouth to say something when the jeweled comset hooked over her ear gave a soft chime and the stones embedded there lit up and glowed. She pressed the button on the side and moved away as she answered the call and listened for a moment.

"You look similar, but not quite the same," Ember continued, almost wonderingly. The tall elf by her side edged closer to her. It was slight, but noticeable. And he looked none too pleased. Jasyn's frown was deepening when Charity stepped back to join their group.

"It's Nathan," she told the others, her tone laced with annoyance at the interruption. "He is on his way in on the transport shuttle with whatever it was that he was after."

"Great," Jasyn murmured.

"This is Traejan," Ember said, introducing the tall elf by her side. She paused, unsure if she should offer his title. The elves they had left behind still wanted to keep their existence a secret.

But Faith, of course, knew.

"I remember when you were little," she said with a nostalgic smile. "You used to run through your father's castle with a wooden sword."

The tall elf blushed as the light in the cavern faded.

"And the hits just keep on coming," Jasyn said in a bitter tone as he cast his dark gaze towards the starlight at the end of the tunnel where the rock opened up to the sea.

The already dim light was blotted out as a large craft, a transport rather than a fighter, squeezed through the crevice in the land mass and came towards them. It carved a trench into the waterway, spraying heavy drops in every direction as it approached, its engines near deafening even as they were slowing down.

The luxurious yet lumbering conveyance of riveted steel turned to land on the tarmac of black rock and the wind it made blew back everyone's hair though it was three hundred feet from them.

"Ugh!" Charity exclaimed, turning her face away.

"I'm sorry," Faith apologized loudly as the still roaring engines shut down. "They usually land this craft on the upper tarmac, next to the Castle. It's possible that our Engineer is looking to easily drop the supplies he was after. Or the pilot saw a storm coming. Perhaps we could go upstairs. We should, anyway. It is certainly more comfortable than it is here, and you must be hungry after your journey."

"I am famished," Ember admitted. "You would not believe the week we have had."

Her eyes went back to the strange metal vehicle as it settled, spurting steam. She could still hardly get her mind around ships that flew through the sky. Through space.

Charity laughed. "I might believe you. I have weeks that even *I* can hardly believe! And some that I can't remember," she confided, lowering her voice. "But it's just Nathan. Another... friend of the family. Not as close as Jasyn of course..."

There was a snort of disdain from the construct. "Not by a long shot," he affirmed as the airlocks on the craft were released with a great hiss.

Faith was startled to hear Amberle call out from behind them.

"Faaaiithh..."

She turned around, surprised by the soft undercurrent of warning in Amberle's tone and even more surprised to see that the young woman's hand was resting on the butt of her laser pistol, her eyes trained on the craft that had recently landed.

Faith's head snapped back to the ship as a ramp lowered. Someone was already descending. But instead of seeing Nathan's boots and lanky legs come into view, it looked at first like the belled hem of a heavy dress. Then she realized what it was and her mouth went as dry as dust.

It was the hem of a cassock. A heavy, priestly robe.

The rest of the priestly robe came into view as the figure walked down the lowered shelf, followed by an angelic face topped with shining auburn hair.

JP stepped from the ramp to the tarmac and smiled beatifically at the small group that was staring at him.

"Hello, friends," he said mildly. A strangled cry of dismay and anger came from Elaeric's throat as he spied the Chimeran Commander. JP's blue eyes went to the monk and narrowed. "It seems all our old friends are here," he said, his gaze leaving the monk to travel over Ember and Traejan. "And some new ones."

"You!" Elaeric accused. "You killed Madeline!" His voice cracked on her name as he shouted it with all the force he could muster. It was enough. His words echoed and reverberated with condemnation.

Ember's eyes went wide and JP's boyish face hardened. "It was not intentional," he said, "if that offers any comfort."

"It does not," Elaeric replied coldly, his voice barely above a whisper.

JP, caring nothing for the monk nor his feelings, switched his blue eyes to the dark-eyed construct. He dipped his auburn head in silent acknowledgment. Nathan had said some quite disparaging things about JP's Operations Officer. JP, however, had known his Operations Officer, Jasyn Issord, for a long time and trusted him.

Besides, only the One knew what the man must have gone through with these heathen and unholy women in the past months.

It would all be cleared up soon enough.

For now, he felt nothing but elation. The plans he had made with Petrov were coming together perfectly. Flawlessly.

The bright blue eyes of the Chimeran Commander went to Faith as the boots and then legs of another person could be seen coming down to join the party. "I have come for my eggs," JP told her.

"*Your* eggs?" Charity blurted, the tenor of her voice high with shock.

JP ignored her. "Those eggs were bought," he told Faith, "with the blood of *my* soldiers, not yours!"

"I lost soldiers too," Faith assured him as the Executive Officer of the *Resurrection*, Jan Petrov finished descending the ramp to join his commander. "Some by your own hand!" She lifted her chin at the boy-faced Chimeran Captain. "Your cause is dying on the vine, your religion is falling into tatters. Just today, another Sauam was slain on the steps of his church in the Fischer City."

Her tiger-like eyes flicked over to meet the bright blue eyes of Jan Petrov. The Chimeran Officer stiffened, his entire body rigid as if he had been touched with an electric current.

JP, outraged, began advancing towards Faith.

"By you!" he hissed.

Jasyn took a step forward, bringing his body alongside Faith's, ready to take another and step in front of her. To his, and mostly everyone's, surprise - Ember beat him to it.

Like Amberle, when she and Jade had come unexpectedly upon a battle on another and foreign world, she had known instinctively who the good guys were. And who was the villain.

Fluidly, she put herself between JP and Faith, pulling a long sword from over her shoulder. The metal sang as it leftts scabbard, the sound a ringing accompaniment to the crash of the waves upon the rocks.

JP paused for a second, regarding the young woman with narrowed eyes as if trying to discern her purpose. Then his gaze went to her sword and he smiled at her.

"A girl after my own heart," he said. With a flick of his wrist, he was instantly holding his own steel. Twelve inches long and three inches wide, the blade was razor sharp on both sides.

Ember grinned. "You're going to need a lot more than that."

JP gave his left hand a jerk and it was filled with the haft of another blade. His angelic face twisted with hunger; he advanced on the young woman standing in his way.

But it was the monk, now, who stepped forward. Thin to the point of skeletal under his robes, he put himself in front of the woman with the blood red hair.

"No!" he cried out with more force and intensity that seemed possible from such a slight form.

The clipped shout ripped through the cavern like a sonic boom and everyone in the cave was thrown back violently by an unseen force as every light went out.

Jeanette walked calmly from the dining room.

She had planned for tonight and had thought of it in the manner of steps to be accomplished or overcome.

Step one was to get away from her family.

Despite the fact that she could sense Sean was onto her – not to what she had planned, that was *her* secret, but that she was up to something - she was still able to get away. Who was going to keep her from going to the bathroom? It was an easy excuse.

Step two, and what she thought would be the most difficult, was to evade her Castle appointed guard/assistant/escort.

She was right.

Not all of the Mattatock escorts were outside the minor diner that night, but there were enough. Jeanette was kindly shown to the restroom by her mother's assistant, Amy. She went inside and stood there fuming for what she thought an appropriate amount of time it would take to actually use the restroom, then came out, smiled at Amy, and allowed herself to be escorted back to the dining room.

Her parents were talking about homeschooling and Sean and Grandpa were laughing about something undoubtedly stupid.

She sat back down and soothed herself by touching the pocket on the right side of her pants, feeling the small object hidden in the folds.

The moment after they were plunged into darkness, Jasyn found himself flat on his back. A stiletto heel, on a shoe that could only belong to one person he knew, was pressed so hard into his shoulder it had nearly punctured it.

"Charity!" he called out as he rolled away from her murderous footwear. "Are you alright?"

"Fuck!" came the reply, delivered with a healthy amount of force and fury. That was good enough for him.

"Faith!" he shouted next, pushing himself up and looking around. There was no response, the hangar had gone completely dark. He couldn't see anything except for the starlit entrance to the cave. "Faith!" he shouted again, louder this time.

There was no reply.

It was that star-lit opening in the cavern that Ember watched with the corner of her eye. Traejan had caught her mid-air as they were thrown back as if by a Gnomin explosion.

He wrapped his arms around her and rolled as they hit the ground, protecting her as much as he could with his body. Moving as fluidly as she always did, the woman warrior had flipped her sword downwards and held it close to her leg so not to dismember either one of them.

When they came to a stop, Ember was at once up in a crouch. Her free hand pressed onto his knee and gave it a squeeze. It was a silent delivery of her demands on him.

Stay down. Stay silent. Be still.

Groans and shouts came from the others but together they watched the jagged eye of starlight, carefully not staring at it lest it blind them to the rest of the darkness.

JP rose, wide-eyed and wary. It had been a shock to have been thrown like a doll, but he had kept hold of his blades and had blessedly not been knocked unconscious.

He could not say the same for Petrov. But his Executive Officer could wait.

The Chimeran's eyesight was enhanced enough that he could see in the semi-darkness as if it were the morning light of dawn. He stood slowly, knowing he should go for the woman with the sword first.

Ember, as still as stone, saw his silhouette against the light of the cave's opening. She leapt at him, her longsword coming down in a wide arc.

Stunned by a speed he had never seen by any human, he had hardly brought one of his steel machetes up to block her swing when her sword was connecting with it, almost knocking it from his grasp.

He recovered instantly and brought up his other blade but she was already bringing her sword down again, this time coming at him from the other side.

A few of the lights overhead flickered, trying to come back to life. Three succeeded - one by the elevator, one to the far side of them, and one so far in the back of the cavern that it was hardly noticeable from where they were. Some flickered and a few others, their bulbs shattered, sent down an occasional shower of sparks as they attempted to get back online.

With enough light to see, Ember renewed her attack with vigor on the boy-faced commander.

Jasyn looked one way in the sputtering crepuscular darkness and saw the monk, lying unconscious, his body a tangled heap of robes. Closer to him, Charity was struggling to rise into a sitting position. She groaned with the effort, her eyes tightly closed. His head snapped around to look in the other direction when the few lights that had come back on went out again.

His head felt hot and wet and for a moment he was sure it must be bleeding somewhere. Then he knew that the feeling wasn't coming from outside of his skull, but from the inside. Memories, like flesh-eating fish, were trying to swim free.

"Faith!" he shouted. Again there was no reply. He crawled in the direction he felt she must be, feeling around with his hands.

Two lights sizzled and a dozen others spat out sparks like fireflies. As they flickered, Jasyn caught a glimpse of Faith. She had been thrown far and was sprawled on her back, blood pooling under her head.

Jasyn rose up and ran in a crouch as the underground space was once again plunged into blackness.

Closer to the crash of the water and under a spray of sparks, the synthetic bodyguard that had begun his life as BG-Syn advanced on the Roshan Simorgh. He came at her with blades that had seen as much bloodshed as her own. He was in a near rage that she was still standing, still fighting, and still unscathed.

He had met many killers in his lifetime. Murderous people who had been intent upon dealing death, but none that had been trained to do so. Not like this. Likewise, Ember had never fought any being with such inhuman speed.

Realizing such, she went for tactics - the best being surprise. She fell as if wounded and as his guard dropped, ever so slightly, then jumped to her feet, bringing her sword up at an angle she knew to be awkward, if not impossible, to block.

The Chimeran did block it, but the angle from which it came was indeed awkward and it jarred the blade from his right hand, sending it flying.

In response, the infuriated commander rushed at her, bringing his second blade across and under hers. It connected with the hilt, shaving off the knuckle of her right thumb and sending her sword to clatter somewhere in the dark.

His victory was short-lived as three knives flew at him from the dark in quick succession. JP dodged them instinctively via programming, but was shocked by the speed at which they came at him. He advanced again as sparks sputtered from the overhead lights, seeing that she had drawn a short sword.

"Faith!" Jasyn shouted once again, searching with his hands, scraping them on the rough stone of the tarmac.

"Here." It was just a breath of a word but he moved in the direction from which it had come. "Right here." His relief was almost equal with his panic when her voice touched him, stronger now and slightly steadier. "I'm right here."

Jasyn had almost reached her semi-prone body but he froze as her last words hit him, *struck him*, and left him dazed and silent. His hazel eyes were wide, staring into the darkness. He felt as if he had been hit on the back of the head with a wide, flat piece of wood.

"What?" he asked softly, his lips numb but his brain hot, flooded with a rush of wet heat.

"I'm right here," Faith said. Gwen said. Faith said.

I'm right here.

Images and feelings went rushing through his mind as he began to feel around again, continuing his search for her.

I'm right here.

Lost, he found her.

His hands clutched at her arm, her waist, her chest, her head. Huffing softly, she batted his hand from her face. The dark-haired construct found her other side and pulled her to him even as he rose up and threw a knee over her body so he was straddling her.

One hand dipped under her neck and gently felt her head. What bleeding there was had mostly stopped and was just a tacky spot in her hair.

I'm right here.

There was another scree of sparks from overhead, raining down showers of flickering fire, and he leaned down to protect her from them as the memories and feelings continued to flood his brain.

"What's my name?" he whispered in her ear. "Say my name." Her pause was less than a heartbeat long.

"Evan."

Evan felt hot tears flood his eyes the way the memories were sweeping through his head in a pouring blaze. The remains of the dam in his brain tissue were bursting.

"Gwen," he whispered back, his voice low and hoarse. Cradling her head with his hand, he rose enough to find her lips with his own and kiss them with a passion that was wild and desperate.

He broke the kiss and stared at her in the semi darkness under the spray and flash of illumination. Faith laughed softly, careless of what was happening ten meters away and breathless from what was happening right above her.

Evan had her pinned to the ground, one hand wrapped under her neck and the other one cupping her shoulder, his knees outside her hips. He stared at her in the flickering lights as if seeing her for the first time.

I'm right here.

The heat that was nearly bursting his head was nearly bursting his groin.

"What are you doing?" she breathed.

His mind and his body were flooded with memory.

He stared into her. Through her. He grasped her tighter and pressed himself against her.

I'm right here.

"Remembering," he whispered.

Ember's short sword hit JP's blade so hard that the clash created its own scree of sparks under the flickering lights. She spun away and hit again. He countered with that inhuman speed and, as he did, she realized two things.

One, he was not human.

Two, he was built only for defense.

He might strike out in anger, but he was not trained to attack. The Roshan stepped back and stopped completely, letting her short sword hang by her side as she surveyed him.

Still, the lights repeatedly fought their own battle to come back on and repeatedly failed.

The Chimeran sprang forward and struck at her and, had she been any average human, he probably would have taken off her head.

As it was, her sword came up and blocked his blade with ease. She didn't even have to move her feet.

If I cannot get to him, and he cannot get to me, how long will this last?

She sighed, knowing the answer.

Till the last one is standing. The first to fall will be the first one to make a mistake. But if he is not human, he will not tire. Eventually, I will. I must end this quickly. As quick as I can.

JP's blue eyes narrowed, for the first time taking in her looks and mannerisms all at once as she stood before him, unfazed and unafraid.

"Who are you?" he demanded.

Ember gave him a ghost of a smile. "Your rendezvous with destiny."

She pulled her second short sword from its sheath and leapt at him once again. His defense was so quick that it knocked it from her grasp and sent it spinning to join her longsword somewhere in the dark.

Her first short sword, however, kept its original course. It came down hard on his remaining blade and sent it skittering off into the shadows. Her own weapon turned and came up towards his throat.

His inhuman reflexes jerked his body back at the last second but not quite in time. The tip of her short sword cut into the side of his neck, taking out a sliver of flesh. A wound that would be inconsequential - if seen to in a fair amount of time.

Meanwhile, JP was left without a weapon of his own. Two

more lights came to life and the Chimeran commander spun around, his eyes searching for his Executive Officer.

Petrov was there, as always, as stolid as a full-grown bull.

JP's extra machete was already in Petrov's large fist, but he was not extending it to his commander.

"Jan," JP said, extending his own hand. It was not a question or statement. It was an expectation. The boy-faced commander could feel the blood as it streamed down the side of his neck, gathered at his high collar, and then began to soak it and slip down to the hollow of his throat.

Yet his XO remained motionless.

JP frowned. He knew the red-haired warrior was behind him, waiting, but he refused to cast his eyes back to her. He knew the curses of those who dared to look back. JP shook his outstretched hand so that his expectation might better be understood.

"Jan!"

"Do you remember your vows?" Petrov asked.

JP stared at him as if he had spoken in tongues. "What?"

"Do you remember your vows?" Jan repeated. "Your vows to the One?"

The Chimeran Commander was at a loss.

"I'm sure you do," Jan admonished. "They are simple and straightforward. Especially for a grown man who is determined to dedicate his life to the One True God. But," and here the Chimeran Officer paused to take a deep breath, "you can, even *you* can, imagine how much more difficult that can be under duress. Does the thought of it make your head swim?" he asked. "Is your head swimming?"

Indeed, JP's head *was* swimming. He could not grasp what Jan was going on about, or why. He could not figure out why his most respected officer was not giving him his third blade so he could kill the heathen woman who was obviously some friend of the de Rossi harlots. And asking him about his vows? His vows? What did his vows to the One have to do with anything? Especially now, at this moment? He opened his mouth to demand answers from his XO but the movement of his jaw renewed the spill of blood from his neck, dumping it from what had to be a small cut but one that was still determined to ruin his cassock.

His hand now went to his neck to staunch the flow of blood. He realized he had never felt his own blood, other than the time he had taken his vows. That was a century past and it had only been a trickle.

This was a wound.

A wound.

He had been *wounded.* His blood was hot and there was now a frightening amount of it. It filled his palm and leaked out between his fingers.

Petrov looked at him in disgust. "Imagine, *if you can*, what your situation would be like if you were a child, especially one that is eager to please and has not eaten nor had a drink of water in almost forty hours!"

The Chimeran Commander stared at him, his blue eyes wide in his angelic face.

What are you doing? What is happening? And what does it mean? flitted through the mind of the construct, one who was once the bodyguard to the holiest figurehead in the galaxies

"Petrov!" he managed, forcing the words because now he could feel the woman begin to creep up behind him as he began to feel the debilitating effects of the loss of blood. "Give me my blade!" he commanded with his draining strength.

And Petrov did, flipping the steel around in his large hands and thrusting it down into JP's chest.

The Commander's hand came up – to strike out, to try to retrieve his weapon, Jan could not tell. Petrov was a strong man, and he heaved down on the haft of the machete, driving it completely through the body beneath him.

"That is for Piper," he whispered into JP's eyes, wide with a surprise they had never known.

The sputtering lights cast down sparks from overhead while the spark in the bright blue eyes of BG-Syn, John Pierre, JP - faded from that gaze forever.

 THREE TWO

*-Between good friends, secrets are either gentle shadows
that deepen trust or quiet storms waiting to break.*

Jordan Blue took Cyan to a secure IGC base on Aplesh, then
rented a private craft to take her to the sprawl next to the
capital. A city that was originally New Kyoto IV – run by the
Isho Yakuza for four hundred years until it was overcrowded,
overrun, and rundown. It then became Kitanai Machi, also run
by the Yakuza, for a thousand years.

It was surrounded by a spread of close-packed buildings,
some high rise and some low. It was a borderland where
prostitution, drugs, and black-market goods were not legal –
but not actually illegal cither.

The Asians from Earth, after claiming the moon of Indasia
with the Earthling Hindustanis, claimed the moon of Aplesh.
It was a moon rich in copper and the immigrant Asians were
as wild for it in the new worlds as they had been on the old
one. The sprawl next to the capital on the main continent was
officially named Koppe R, usually just referred to as the copper
city.

Most buildings were built with a combination of the
indigenous material and another metal or alloy to make it
stronger. Copper was used to transmit heat and electricity
throughout the city. Brass and bronze were used for just

about everything else - from transportation vehicles to door knockers.

The sky was a patina green.

The last time Blue had visited, she had taken a rocket cab, something like a coffin one could guide between lumbering cowwhales and through narrow alleys.

This time, she paid more to have a toktok with a live driver. For the first time since she had let him go, Galen's absence weighed on her. The feeling was akin to having been standing in a gusty wind that had suddenly subsided. Or sitting in tub, naked, after the water had drained.

The constant chatter of the toktok driver was oddly soothing even though she couldn't understand a word he said. Still, she would speak up occasionally, with an agreeable word or question and he would answer with renewed enthusiasm though he had no idea what she was saying either.

After dodging traffic, buildings, and even some animals, they arrived at the address she had given him. She placed her credentials card against the worn plastic pad and left him a hefty tip.

The man turned around and shouted gleeful appreciation and made motions with his hands that seemed to encompass the rickety vehicle before he repeatedly pointed a finger at the floor.

Blue cocked her head at him. "You'll wait here for me?" she asked. "Is that what you're saying?"

The man chattered away some more but nodded emphatically as if he understood her.

"Alright," Blue said as she opened the door. "Thanks! I think." She shook her head in amusement as she tried to close the door. The latch was loose and it took her three tries.

She looked back into the vehicle where the driver was smiling broadly at her with gapped teeth, some missing entirely, and gave her a thumbs up.

Blue returned the gesture then turned and made her way across the cobbles of a fairly clean alley, most of the ground muck having been pushed into the gutters.

The half-elf pilot stepped up onto the narrow sidewalk and took a fortifying breath as she stood in front of Chang's shop. She did not have a chance to knock, much less change her mind. The door swung open, the silver bells above it giving off a gentle tinkling alarm.

Chang stood there, possibly heavier than the last time she had seen him. His weight did not bother her, though she would undoubtedly lecture him on it before she left, but the look in his eyes certainly did. The sorrow in those gray eyes was enough to raise a lump in her throat.

The Jordan brought up the only weapon she could use against him; a pink cardboard box tied with a string.

The pity in his gaze was replaced with an eager avarice and his skilled and sturdy hands rubbed together in excitement.

"That looks like too big of a box to be tea cookies," he said, his eyes going from the box to the twinkling eye of the Jordan.

"Mmm hmmm," the Jordan agreed.

The man before her had been a renowned surgeon, and still was - though he had lost his license to practice within the confines of IGC Medical decades ago. Yet she could still see the child-like energy that had made him loved by so many. It warmed her heart.

"Could be," she suggested, "an entire buttercake in here."

Chang's bushy white eyebrows rose high over gray eyes that danced with excitement. Blue's smile grew till it was splitting her face, but her eye narrowed at him.

"Are you going to invite me in?" she asked. "Or make me wait here until it starts to rain?"

"Ah!" Chang exclaimed. "Where are my manners?" he scolded himself as he held the door open wide so the Jordan could squeeze by him.

Once she was in, he gave the alleyway a quick glance one way and then the other before he pulled the door closed and locked it. With the entry secure, Chang squeezed by the Jordan and led the way through the shop.

The long hall was lined with shelves that were overflowing with wires, computer circuits, and prosthetics - not all of them human.

The doctor led the way through crates overladen with bits of weaponry and medical supplies to the back where a curtain of metallic beads hung, separating the shop from the back room.

Chang thrust a beefy hand through the curtain and held the hanging beads aside for Blue to enter. She did, an eager and wondrous look on her face. She had no idea what to expect, but she felt like she might be stepping into another world. A world of witches and munchkins and glorious color.

It was another world, but it certainly wasn't Oz. She left behind the clutter and madness of the shop for the sterility of an operating room. Everything in this room was perfectly organized.

Clean.

Labeled.

And all doused with a sterilizing ultra-violet light. There was another curtain to her right, one made of rainbow-colored beads, that she suspected led to Chang's office.

One item, however, dominated the room. A medical table under surgical halogens.

Chang held out a hand towards it in invitation.

"You don't want me to undress?" Blue asked innocently.

Chang's bushy white eyebrows popped up. "I thought you wanted me to replace your eye. You have something else in mind?"

"No," Blue said with a quirky smile, "I just wasn't sure of

your protocol."

Chang gave her a look of exasperation. "Get your ass up there!"

Blue laughed and climbed up onto the table and lay back with her head on the raised oval cushion.

Chang shouldered his way through the rainbow curtain with his bakery box and returned with a metal tray holding a syringe, a laser scalpel and an array of small instruments.

"I'm going to give you a local anesthetic," Chang told her, "into three of the nerves around your orbital area. Would you like anything stronger? I can put you under if you want."

"That won't be necessary," Blue told him. "But a drink might be nice. Do you have any champagne?"

Chang pressed his lips together in apology, making the white broom of his mustache stand out.

"Unfortunately, no. I have sake?" he suggested.

Blue shrugged. "Better than nothing."

Chang huffed. "Do you like it hot or cold?"

Blue shrugged again. "Whatever. Put it in an I.V. If you want."

Chang sighed and disappeared through the beaded curtain again for a few moments. He returned with a small ceramic cup in his hand and gave it to the Jordan who sat up, propping herself up on a Mylar-covered elbow. She eyed the small cup with suspicion, smelled it, and made a face.

"Champagne taste but sake budget," she said ruefully.

"First of all," Chang told her, "good sake can cost more than good champagne."

The Jordan gave him a look of doubt and then quaffed the contents in one gulp. "Blech!" she exclaimed, sticking out her tongue.

Chang laughed. "Lay down and be quiet or I'll knock you out for your own good."

"You better not," Blue warned, laying back down. Chang removed her eyepatch and swabbed the area around her eye with alcohol, making it cold. "Tell me, though," she said as he produced the small syringe, "why did you look so sad when you first saw me?"

Chang sighed. "Because I know Galen is gone from you. For good this time if I'm guessing right."

Blue scowled. "How do you know that?"

"I have a troll of my own, you know," he told her. "And though AIs do not answer anything but direct questions, they gossip to each other like devils."

A smirk pushed Blue's lip into her scar. "Is that so?" she asked.

"It is," Chang admitted. "Anything else before we start?"

Blue's smirk turned into a grin. "How about another shot of that sake?"

○ॐ♋

Scarlett landed Fledge at an outpost on a numbered moon in the Outer Banks.

She was far from home, which to her meant far from her Dragon. The airbase was not IGC, not even locally secure. Scarlett let out a deep breath as she peered out the eyes of her Fledgling.

The place was busy and filled with more alien races than humans. It was where she was going to make her stand. Blue had already left for where she would make hers. Scarlett stood, still looking outside. They had drawn many curious glances, though none felt threatening. She was quite sure no one would mess with Fledge, or even dare try.

"We are small but mighty," she said, laying a hand on his silver-skinned control board.

There was a hum by her side and she looked askance, arching a brow. Calyph's troll had accompanied her and, as it rested on its wheeled legs, the optic band turned towards her.

"That is a worthy observation," it said, its voice mechanical and gravely.

"Hmmm," Scarlett murmured in response.

When she had left the Opal Dragon, after Blaylock's demise, the Captain had surreptitiously begun to send particular members of the crew to other Dragons or bases. Other crewmen and women were coming in from different ships and outposts. Scarlett and Blue, of course, did not question anything Brogan did. They knew that he strove for balance in all things and was covering their asses in more ways than one.

Interesting though, that when he sent Calyph to accompany the Rogue Aridian who was now the Captain of the Copper Dragon, he sent the troll that had been assigned to the Engineer for the last five decades to accompany Jordan Scarlett.

"Well," she told the droid as she moved past its rotund metal form, "I have to get going. They might already be here."

"They are," the troll informed her.

Scarlett turned back and regarded the droid with surprise. "How do you know that?"

"Someone by the name of Mr. Roder checked into the restaurant twenty minutes ago. It is an alias used by Bjorn van Zandt in the past. From what I can pick up on the local cameras, he is accompanied by his troll and four bodyguards."

"Damn," Scarlett remarked. "You might be a lot more useful than I thought."

The optic band on the droid glowed red. "Thank you."

Scarlett regarded at it a moment longer. "Why don't you come with me?"

"I would like that."

"Would you?" she asked, her look turning into a frown - not

one of consternation but one of curiosity. "Do you actually like, or prefer, one action to another? Do you *feel*?"

"Mmmm," the droid hummed. "I cannot feel, not the way a human can. The best way I can describe it is that I am encouraged by my programming into experiencing new situations, ones that expand my own experience and education."

Scarlett smiled. "In that case, let's not keep them waiting."

She moved towards the aft of the Fledgling where an opening was already being made in his skin just fore of the galley. The Jordan went through the newly made exit and trotted quickly down the stairs that had formed.

The troll followed, not on his wheels but via the thrusters underneath its metal bulk. It floated out and down with more purpose than grace and remained hovering over the uneven ground.

The Jordan turned to leave as her Fledgling once again melded itself back into a seamless form, then paused to look at the droid.

"Suggested route?"

The optic band on the metal form glowed with pleasure at being consulted. "The quickest and safest way will be to pass through the small hotel buildings to your right, then take a left down the first avenue. The restaurant you are looking for will be three streets down, on your right."

Then, as the Jordan was turning away, its optic band flared and her head snapped back, her eyes narrowed.

"What was that all about?" she asked.

The troll paused before it spoke. "It is not the program, the *nature*, of my model to ask questions, only answer them. But, since you asked, I was curious that you asked about the location. Have you not been here before? And on more than one occasion?"

Scarlett's brows went up. "I have," she admitted. "But

it's been a while. For me, anyway. And I landed at a different airfield. Plus, I feel like I should be asking you *something*."

She gave him a smirk that was followed by a mechanized grunt (of approval, amusement?) from the troll before she turned and left the airfield, following his directions. The droid trailed her, slightly behind and to her right.

The town was a sultry sprawl, low and wide and flat. It was a wild combination of sand and neon, like New Tokyo on the beach of New Miami. Tropical trees and grasses were plentiful along with thatched roofs, drum music and scantily clad Golblis.

The next most plentiful race were Lentochs.

They had long bodies with tall, tapered heads. Usually cloaked, they dressed for the sweltering climate with a single and near completely sheer scarf that they wound around their narrow forms.

The Jordan found the restaurant quite easily thanks to Calyph's troll and memories that were not too blurred by time or the fact that the town had changed very little in the past six decades.

The restaurant, like most others, was made of aging wood planks and roofs of thatch. It was open on three sides to a beach of white sand, dotted with swaying palm trees and lapped at by aqua waters.

She spotted Bjorn in an instant - the same instant he spotted her.

He rose from his rickety cane chair, as did Lucy, who had been sitting with him at a table for two.

The dark eyes of the Jordan swept the lounge and bar, noting Bjorn's bodyguards. Her eyes flicked back to the Chimeran Commander as she approached his table and she felt the heat of the sprawl go up by a number of degrees.

She reached a hand to one of the studs on her ear and adjusted the field that surrounded her body.

Bjorn smiled as she reached him. With the nonchalance of an old friendship, he took her hands in his and gave her a kiss on each cheek.

"So good to see you," he said and she knew that he meant it. Then he gave her a sly smile as he leaned away from the cool air that her field was generating. He held a hand towards the seat Lucy had recently vacated. "Though, the climate here - it does not agree with you?"

Scarlett could feel a new heat, one that came from between her ribs and between her legs, and knew that Bjorn could sense it as well.

"It's not so bad," she said with a lecherous smile as she sat down. "I'm just not dressed for it." She grasped the tag of the microzip in her crimson flightsuit that was nestled near the base of her throat and pulled it down between and then well below her breasts. "Oooh!" she exclaimed, fanning herself with a hand. "That's better."

Bjorn let out a great burst of air from his lungs as he looked away from her exposed skin, then back, and then away again. A second later he laughed.

"Maybe we should find you a bikini?" he suggested as he fixed his green eyes upon the Jordan's dark ones.

The Jordan kept his gaze for a moment and then shifted her eyes to where her droid -*was that strange that she already thought of it as hers though it been Calyph's for fifty years?* she thought absently yet quickly, *and is it worse that I think of it as an object of possession?* - and shifted them back to the breathtakingly handsome construct across from her.

"Possibly," she agreed. "But not quite yet. And it is nothing we need to discuss in front of the children."

The irises of Lucy's eyes glimmered with amusement while the optic band of troll darkened.

"I'll have you know," he began to correct when Lucy interrupted.

"I think she was making a joke," she said softly.

The top tier on the droid swung around to the humanoid troll, its optic band brightening. "I like jokes," it informed her.

"Do you?" she asked, curious and excited.

"I do!" the squat droid affirmed. "Do you know why the AI broke up with his girlfriend?" he asked. Lucy gave the droid a broad smile.

"Why?" she asked.

"Because she kept giving him mixed signals."

Lucy laughed, the sound metallic and tinkling. She turned and began to make her way to where Diego stood watch at the corner of the restaurant and the metal automaton followed as if tied by a string.

"Here is one for you," she said. "How did the AI go broke?"

The optic band on the droid glowed brighter than Scarlett had ever seen as it floated away on its thrusters.

"How?" it asked, enthralled.

"It lost its cache in a bet!" Lucy announced with enthusiasm.

There was a blurred buzz of sound that came from the droids as they moved away, consumed with their own form of laughter.

Scarlett, who had been watching their departure, turned back to Bjorn and laughed aloud.

"That is crazy!" she exclaimed.

Bjorn sighed. "Not any crazier than you wanting to meet for a high-citric cocktail in this god-forsaken place." He smiled charmingly as the Lebri waitress put down a pair of said cocktails, garnished with lime peels and coconut husks, down on the table between them. Scarlett picked hers up with enthusiasm and took a long drink from the bamboo straw. "And someplace so public!" Bjorn chided. "I could have arranged for something more private. More intimate."

Scarlett's dark brows went up over her dark eyes. "Ooh!"

she exclaimed. "Like an intimate dinner in a mess hall aboard the ship where I was imprisoned and tortured?"

Bjorn's expression fell and his hands clenched into fists.

"I feel the appropriate thing to say is that I am sorry."

Scarlett narrowed her dark eyes at him. "But?"

Bjorn's broad chest swelled. "I have no program nor disposition to feel regret nor remorse. And, searching my intelligence and feelings, I don't think I would feel them despite the pain I caused you. For, had I not done such things, it would not have led to the feelings that followed that event."

"Such as?" Scarlett asked.

The Chimeran's green eyes glimmered as his jaw clenched. "The feeling that overcame me as I saw you brave such torture, and the feelings that came upon me when I first picked you up and held you in my arms."

"Which was what, exactly?" Scarlett prodded, truly interested.

"The amazement I felt at your strength, your resolve, your utter contempt for weakness. I fell in love with you that moment, I am sure of it. Everything you said and did beyond that moment, only made me fall deeper."

Scarlett leaned back in the wicker chair with her drink in hand and took a long pull from the straw. Her heart hammered in her chest.

"Maybe this conversation *should* be more private," she agreed. She turned her gaze to the barkeep, and the aging Golbli there caught her eye. She gave him a nod and it was returned. "There is a single suite, above the bar..."

Bjorn's eyes nearly glowed as he drew in enough breath to fill his lungs, and then some more. "I will secure it imm..."

"No need," Scarlett interrupted. "I have already secured it." She sat back again in her chair. "I just had a feeling we would need to have a private conversation," she assured him. "I'm not getting in a bikini."

Bjorn smiled. "Well," he said, "not yet."

Scarlett rolled her eyes as she finished her drink. A fresh cocktail, along with a folded napkin, was placed before her on the table. Bjorn as well was served another, which he picked up as Scarlett stood and headed through the lounge area and out a wall that had been opened towards the beach.

Bjorn signaled for Diego to take care of the bill and then followed her around the building where a set of cracked steps the color of the sand led to an upper landing with a wooden door.

Scarlett went past the white slatted door, which she knew went to an office above the restaurant and took a second flight of steps going up. There was only one more landing and here another door waited, this one solid wood with faded and peeling blue paint and a worn brass doorknob.

The Jordan opened the napkin that had been given to her downstairs, producing an old-fashioned key. She stuck it into the slot beneath the doorknob and turned it. There was an audible click and she grasped the knob, turning her eyes to the Chimeran Commander.

"You know this could be a trap?" she asked.

The green-eyed construct gave her a nod and a dazzling smile. "Of course I know that," he told her.

Scarlett returned his smile, turned the knob, and pushed open the door. Bjorn followed her inside, his green eyes sweeping across the room.

It was a small one-bedroom flat, with a living area and a kitchenette. One wall was made of folding glass doors that had been pushed open. A terrace ran the breadth of the entire flat, offering an extensive view of the white beach and the aqua-colored sea. Impossibly tall palm trees bent towards the gentle waves, their giant leaves fluttering in the gentle breeze.

Scarlett closed the door and crossed the room with a

nostalgic expression on her face.

"I never knew this was up here," Bjorn said, walking outside onto the lanai. There was a single table with two chairs and several tropical plants in pots. He held his drink in one hand as he leaned on the railing and looked out over the sand and the sea. Muted sounds came up from the restaurant as well as music and the sound of merriment from the beach along with an occasional splash and a squeal of delight.

"You've been here before?"

"Everyone's been to the Giggling Marlin," Bjorn told her.

Scarlett joined him at the rail, smiling to herself. She reached into her pocket and pulled from it a small blue box. It was the same one Bjorn had given her at the restaurant in Kayos. The one that held the necklace of platinum links of lazy eights, the symbol of infinity.

The chain of a Chimeran Commander.

Scarlett held the box out to Bjorn and he felt his shoulders drop. He made an effort to control his breathing as he dipped his head in understanding and took the box gently from Scarlett's grasp.

"Put it on me."

Bjorn's green eyes flashed up, thinking he must have imagined the Jordan's command. Her own eyes, dark and unflinching with flecks of crimson burning within their depths, met his. "Put it on me," she repeated.

Bjorn set his cocktail down on the table. He wet his lips and opened the box. The chain lay nestled there on a plump of blue velvet. He drew it out, his heart pounding in a way he could not remember it having pounded before. He put the box aside and opened the clasp at the back of the chain.

Scarlett put her own drink aside and stood before him, straight-backed and chin lifted, waiting. What seemed like a million emotions ran through her. Exhilaration was at the top of the list, the feeling of being reborn racing through her veins.

Bjorn put the chain around her neck and fastened the clasp at the back. One hand remained there, on the back of her neck, beneath the thick sheaf of her dark hair. The other hand came back slowly, caressing the side of her throat, his thumb just under her jaw. His fingers trailed along the length of the chain, stopping with his hand on her sternum, filling the space between her breasts. He felt her chest rise under his palm as she breathed deeply.

"It comes with a price," she said.

"There is nothing that I wouldn't pay," he told her.

 THREE THREE

- Some secrets rewrite the universe. Others prove it was never real.

The lights in the hangar under the Last Castle fought to come on. The halogens were completely shot, bluish white electrical arcs from the power surge making their only contribution of illumination the occasional torrent of sparks. The LEDs flickered as well as the fluorescents.

Jasyn straddled Faith's body in the devious light, cradling her head in his hands.

"Gwen" he said, kissing her forehead, her chin, her cheeks, her lips. "Gwen, Gwen."

"Shhh!" she hushed, closing her eyes and relishing the feel of his warm mouth on her face, her chin, her neck. Not just the sensation, but the act of it, made her eyes burn with tears. Yet she shushed him.

She knew that no one was close, there were no mics in the hangar, and that things were happening on the other side of the tarmac far more interesting than Evan recovering his memory. Still, old habits died hard.

"Faith," she corrected. "I'm Faith."

Jasyn stopped his embellishment of kisses and pulled

away from her, though he still held her face in his hands. In the sputtering lights and showers of sparks she could see the sincerity in his dark hazel eyes.

"You are Faith de Rossi," he told her. "You always were."

She frowned at him but as she opened her mouth to ask exactly what he meant, all of the lights in the hangar came back to life. All except for one by the elevators that gave up the fight and went out.

They both looked towards where the others were.

Charity was on her knees, calling for security on her comset.

Jan Petrov was standing over the form of the priestly robed Commander, still holding the shaft of the blade he had driven through him.

He let it go as they watched.

The body, already arched back from the blow, collapsed onto the tarmac.

Ember eyed Petrov, appraising him for a moment, then moved to Elaeric. The former monk was still unconscious. Her slim fingers went to his neck and found his pulse. It was strong.

The warrior sighed heavily as the tall elf joined her.

"He's alive."

Amberle appeared at Jasyn's side and helped him get Faith back on her feet, handing over a heeled shoe that had been lost when Faith went flying back. He kept an arm around her as she reached down to adjust one shoe and put the other one back on entirely.

"Is everyone okay?" she called out. Her eyes flicked over Charity, who was complaining about her ass, to find Ember leaning over Elaeric. Her hand was bleeding but other than that she looked fine. Faith looked next to Petrov, standing over the crumpled body of John Pierre. Still shaky, she made her way to him, Jasyn holding her steady by her elbow.

The tall, handsome blonde who had been the Executive Officer of the Chimeran Battle Cruiser Resurrection, stepped over the body on the floor and found Faith's eyes of brown and gold.

"It's finished," he breathed.

Faith had never heard anyone sound so tired in all her life. It was enough to push at her resolve but nowhere close enough to break it.

"The worst of it is over," she told him, and she truly believed it. She could only pray that it was. She motioned with her chin to the shuttle. "Is there anyone else on board?"

Petrov shook his head. "No. It was just us two." His blue eyes found Jasyn as the construct stepped forward with a smile and extended his hand. Jan returned the smile and grasped Jasyn's hand tightly in his own. "It's good to see you," he said. "Really good."

"It's good to see you as well." He released Petrov's large hand and narrowed his hazel eyes at him. "Did you know?" he asked.

Petrov's blonde brows rose. "Know what?"

"Who I was? Who I am?"

Petrov turned his blue eyes to Faith, confused.

Faith sighed and cast her own gaze to the edge of the tarmac where the waters lapped at the rocks. "Secrets are best kept when one does not know of them," she said.

Jasyn blew a burst of air from one side of his face, making a rude noise.

"Though," Jan said, frowning slightly as he thought, "it did occur to me that you might have been part of the Pantheon. The first constructs all had 'syn" attached to their name, short for synthetic."

"That I do know," Jasyn said, eyeing Faith. "But what the 'J' stood for seems to be a mystery."

"Jäger," a voice said.

Jasyn turned, his hazel eyes bemused, to see Charity. She was standing, slightly wobbly on her stilettos, smoothing down her short skirt.

"It stood for Jäger," she told him. "The Jägers were the first guardians to the Royal Elfin Court." She glanced at Traejan who gave her a nod.

"They will give their life to defend their charge," the tall elf affirmed.

Jasyn's mouth dropped open slightly and he looked at Faith to see she wore the same expression.

Petrov drew a deep breath, and a small smile graced his lips. For the first time in a hundred years, he began to feel a bit of peace make its way into his heart. "And your last name," he continued softly, sounding amused, "Issord. If you looked at it in a mirror it would be D rossi."

Jasyn closed his eyes. He had been so sure that he had become keen to the mirrors in his world.

"And some of the best secrets are those hidden in plain sight," Faith whispered.

"You have no idea how right you are," Jasyn replied, his voice as somber as his expression. "Or that some secrets are not purposeful, but simply a result of the lack of imagination."

Faith looked at him, quizzical, then turned her head to the commotion a few yards across the tarmac. Elaeric had regained consciousness and Ember was helping him to his feet. Farther away, behind them, the doors to the elevators were opening and security men were streaming out. Charity moved to intercept them.

Petrov turned his blue eyes to Faith. "Our debt is settled."

Faith gave him a nod, not knowing what the original deal had been. All she had to go on were the notes her twin had left behind.

"You helped me tear it down," she affirmed. "Will you help me rebuild?"

Jan cocked his head at her. "What do you mean?"

Faith smiled. "You are now the Captain of the Battle Cruiser *Resurrection*." Jan frowned as this realization dawned on him while Faith shifted her gaze to Jasyn. "Which promotes you, I believe, to Executive Officer."

Jasyn, his mouth now completely open, snapped it shut and looked at Jan. Each of their expressions, which were first filled with shock, slowly began to soften. They looked at each other, unbelieving.

Then his dark eyes went back to Faith and he shook his head.

"I can't leave you," he said. "Not again. Not now. Not ever."

Faith moved until her body was against his. He wrapped his arms around her waist and she closed her eyes. It had been so long since he had held her. It was almost enough to make her change her mind.

Not now, she thought. *Not when we have come so far, been through so much. Not when we are so close.*

He pressed his full lips against her forehead, and she truly felt herself wavering. She gave his waist a squeeze and then stepped back.

"It won't be for long this time," she told him. "I promise. This time, there will be no forgetting. If everything goes smoothly you'll be back here with me, or at the villa, or wherever we want to go."

Jasyn gave her a smile that was forlorn but he pulled her back to him and kissed her. Deeply. It went on long enough that Jan finally cleared his throat. Faith broke away, laughing, bringing her hand up to Jasyn's cheek.

"Well," she said, "don't go running off just yet. Let's go

upstairs. We can all sit down and talk for a bit, have something to eat. Perhaps a drink," she suggested with a smile.

Petrov's shoulders sagged and he seemed to collapse in on himself, the years of toil and subterfuge finally giving way to a relief he had never known. "Do you have vodka by any chance?" he asked, hopeful.

"You better believe it!" Charity affirmed from a few feet away. She beckoned at him to join her even as she motioned at her security team to take care of the body on the tarmac.

Faith pinned her sister with her eyes as they joined the others. "Drinks and dinner, for sure," she said. "But we need to move quickly now. Tonight. We need to contact Blue and Scarlett. I'll call Silas."

Charity's green eyes flared open. "Tonight? As in now?"

Faith shook her head, her hand going to her temple as she looked out the entrance to the cavern and the dark sky beyond. "No, I'm sorry. I forgot it was already night." She realized she must have hit her head much harder than she knew. She fought to clear it. All she could see for a moment was Jasyn looming above her.

You are *Faith de Rossi, he had told her. You always were.*

She massaged her temple with her fingers. "No, of course not tonight. But by sunset tomorrow."

"Have you found someone who could..." Charity began to ask, her words dwindling as she followed her sister's gaze to Amberle.

"What?" the young Jordan asked, seeing their eyes trained on her.

Faith could not help the grin that began stretching across her face. "Do you think you could hack into a channel relay?" she asked the young woman with dark skin and pink curls.

Amberle made a face as if she had tasted something that had gone bad. "Ugh," she said. "I thought you were going to ask me to do something hard."

Faith raised her brows over her tiger-like eyes. "Not just one channel. *All* the channels. Across *all* the systems. Every single one."

Amberle rolled her eyes of green and brown and stuck out her tongue. She blew a raspberry at Faith. "Child's play," she said. "It would just take me a few minutes to set up, another few to hoard the lines and redistribute."

Faith beamed at Charity who immediately began to chatter to her aides via her comset. Then she turned to the others. Traejan was wrapping a strip of cloth around Ember's thumb.

"How would you like to see a truly impregnable fortress?" she asked.

Ember clenched and opened her bandaged hand, flexing it, and gave Faith a leering grin. "I would like that," she said. "Any chance you've got some red wine up there?"

 THREE FOUR

-Sometimes your secret is your last stand.

It was time.

The day had been hectic and tense yet controlled. Though everyone kept their composure, all moved at a pace just short of a run. The Last Castle had been the venue for some of the most exclusive celebrations and dinners in the galaxy, yet the turmoil of people on that morning was the likes of which it had never seen. It bordered on madness. More people were coming than going and no one was busier than the de Rossi security teams.

Sean, who had been facing a window in the kitchen when they ate their lunch, saw crafts arrive and depart with the perfect regularity of an IGC spaceport. And not all from where he had landed with his family.

"Must be a hangar under the Castle," he had murmured around his sandwich. Jeanette had stared at him for long seconds after his casual remark and then stared out the window herself as she finished her lunch.

The commotion was finally dying down as the Mattatock family was heading to dinner. They were quite aware of the many people hurrying through the Castle all that afternoon and they were not surprised when informed that the de Rossi's sent their apologies but would not be able to join them for dinner that night. Only Sean's assistant, Rita, accompanied them down the bustling hallway.

"There is a holo screen being set up in the dining room for you," she told them. "There will be an event tonight that everyone in the known universe will be watching. You won't want to miss it."

Fletcher felt a chill go up his spine and Sean did not fail to see the way his grandfather's face lost its color.

"What is it Grandpa?"

The old man's throat worked as he made an effort to swallow. "The last time something like that happened in my lifetime," he said, "was when all contact was lost from Earth. Also, the Rebellion was just starting, and getting violent."

Fletcher remembered being glued to the flatscreen like every other being in the galaxies. His mind was filled with the haunting images of constructs being rounded up and put into camps. The memory of running through a castle much like the one he was in right now, screaming for Mira.

"Like when you saw the Castle?" Sean asked softly, remembering how Grandpa had paled the same way.

The old man nodded as they entered the dining room together. Two men who did not look like butlers or security, were laying a long tube close to the wall. The dining table had been moved back slightly to make room.

"Yep. And again what's getting my goose is the feeling of coming full circle."

The tube was activated as they took their seats. A flare of light went up from the device and then it formed into a moving picture of a field of flowers.

"I guess it's not showtime quite yet," John remarked as he sat down.

People were around them immediately, putting down baskets of bread, plates of butter, pouring drinks. Not as many as there often were, but that was likely due to the absence of the de Rossis. Still, the luxury of being waited on had not worn out.

Rebecca smiled at the staff but made a face at her husband. "We're getting spoiled," she told him. "Maybe we should find a way to be more self-sufficient around here."

A wine glass was placed in front of her and then halfway filled with rosé. John smirked at his wife.

"You should at least have the decency to blush a little," he chided her, playful. She gave him an equally playful poke in his ribs.

Jeanette looked around as salad was being served, her eyes bright and glassy.

Tonight was the night. She knew it.

ೞ

When Charity had asked her what she needed, Amberle immediately rattled off a list of technical supplies.

Three s-class curved monitors, each with its own drive, a finger glove, a ghost pad, seven open hard lines to the Galactic Web... she even threw in a few items she did not necessarily need but thought would be nice to have. Just in case. Or maybe for later.

She was not sure what could be put together in such a short time and doubted everything on the list would be doable within mere hours. She knew the Distant Shore was completely isolated and had no idea what Charity might have on hand. Food and booze for sure, but equipment favored by the GW researchers who most called "hackers?" She doubted it. But she didn't worry. She knew she could make do with much less.

Yet, when she got to the conservatory that morning, everything was there.

The conservatory itself had changed once again since the

last time she had been there. There was no running water this time, anywhere. Just flowers and plants, arranged in a camber along the back wall – a floral backdrop of an amphitheater.

A camera was set up for Faith, chairs in the wings for others.

A station had been set up for Amberle and she got to work. The first thing she needed to do was establish communication and video links with those who would be the stars that night.

She shook her head of pink curls in wonder, a smile splitting her dark face as she fired everything up. All the tech was new.

"I fucking love these guys," she muttered as she snapped on her glove and jacked in to the Web.

಩಩

Ember thought much the same thing the previous night as she walked through Charity's wine cellar.

"Seven Circles," Traejan whispered as he followed her past the racks and racks of wine that went from the floor to the ceiling.

"Is there anything in particular I could help you find?" she was asked by a man in clothes that looked uncomfortably formal.

Ember grinned at him. "Red wine, please."

"Any particular varietal? Or region?"

Ember looked perplexed for a moment and then gave him a charming smile, tossing her blood-colored hair away from her face. "Why don't you pick out three, and then I can have a little tasting?"

The man bowed deeply, clearly pleased with her decision.

She stayed up late into the night, enjoying the selection of wines while she talked with Elaeric. She told Traejan they could most likely scare up some honey for his wine and he assured her that he was quite alright with the tea Elaeric was drinking.

They were not the only ones up late.

Faith and Jasyn were awake, and together, until the amplified light of the sun rose over the Distant Shore.

Charity stayed up and shared a bottle of Finnish vodka with Petrov. It was clear he needed someone to talk to, the man was boiling with emotions he had bottled for an entire century.

The next dawn brought tears and trepidation to all as goodbyes were heartfelt and plentiful.

০৪৪৪০

Bjorn strode into the bridge of the Battle Cruiser *Macedonian*, Scarlett by his side. They stopped at the helm, next to Bjorn's chair. The officers on duty were not military, not in the way that Scarlett had been trained, and the pair drew stares that were open and curious.

Everyone knew of the Red Jordan and many had seen her, some in person. What was most peculiar, however, was that over the left breast of her crimson Mylar flight suit she did not wear the military patch of the InterGalactic Council. Another patch was there – one in the shape of a shield. Over it was another patch shaped like a ribbon banner with *Interstellar Alliance* embroidered across the breadth of it.

Even more peculiar, the Commander wore the same double patch on his once Chimeran coveralls.

Eyes flicked back and forth between the Jordan and the Captain.

"This," Bjorn announced, "is Commander Mattatock. She is our new Executive Officer."

"It's a pleasure," Scarlett said, her tone flat except for an undercurrent of amusement. Then she continued within the same breath, "which one of you is the coms man?" A beautiful doe-eyed woman with shiny black hair that fell straight down her back raised her hand. Scarlett walked to her and grasped the back of her chair. "There is about to be a transmission going universally wide within the hour. Can you intercept it?"

"Of course I can," the woman said, lifting her chin and turning back to her panel. "Do you want me to block it as well?"

"No," Scarlett said, "we want as many people to see it as possible. Especially those on board. And I need you to open a private com with the following channels…" Emma's nails clicked on the console as she did as instructed.

Scarlett gave her a nod and fixed her eyes on Bjorn. The tall blonde Chimeran dropped into his seat at the helm and touched a light on the panel to his right.

"Crew of the *Macedonian*," he said, and his voice echoed throughout the ship. "This is your Captain. Stop what you are doing and find the nearest holo or flatscreen. We are about to receive a transmission that everyone needs to hear, if not see as well."

Throughout the ship, from Mechanics to Medical, crew members put down tools. Keyboards and stations were temporarily abandoned and acrylics became held loosely in hands or tucked under arms as the entire crew made their way to the nearest device where they could see what was the big fuss was about.

A good number of them ended up in the Mess Hall, a good many others gathered in the Officer's Club. All eyes found screens and sat or stood in small groups. There was curious chatter as they waited. Then, only minutes later, screens began to flicker and a hush fell over the entire ship.

When the picture steadied, it showed a man standing behind a podium. He was tall and fit, with swept back iron-gray hair, blue eyes, and a commanding presence. He leaned forward and placed his large hands on the lectern. He received a cue from somewhere off camera and his eyes rose. Though he was light years away from almost everyone receiving the broadcast, those that could see him were instantly struck with the feeling that he was looking directly at them. Dr. Silas grasped the sides of the podium and began to speak.

⁂

The service doors opened and Jeannette was so startled that she jumped in her seat. Grandpa, John, and Rebecca had looked up as the holo screen changed from the screen saving video to a man at a podium and were instantly transfixed - so only Sean noticed.

He narrowed his eyes at his sister.

She's up to something, he thought. *Again.*

Then the room was near filled as there was staff there to remove the last course and more to serve the next course. Sean distantly realized he had already become accustomed to meals being served in such a way. People were taking away the salad plates and putting out bowls and spoons. The double doors that led to the kitchen swung open and closed, open and closed, as the staff came and went.

A steaming tureen of soup was pushed in on an aircart.

Then, amidst the commotion caused by the removal of the salad course to be replaced by the serving of the soup, from the double doors came a cacophony of crashing ceramics as a pile of plates dropped to shatter on the floor and a scream tore through the room.

⁂

Across the civilized galaxies, Dr. Silas bade greetings to all forms of life. Then began his speech.

"I stand before you today to tell you that the war is over. The Chimeran Rebellion has ended. Not through defeat, and not through revolution - lest it be the re-evolution of us all. The Intergalactic Council, mostly comprised of humans and elves, has spurned the rights of other races, not just the Chimera. The IGC over the years has become a government based on greed. Growing rich while other races become steadily more poor. The destitute at the corners of the moons and edges of the galaxies are barely more than feudal serfs, condemned to lives of servitude. Entire colonies have been set upon by plague and no aid came from their government, mostly due to the fact that often these plagues were brought upon them by said government as experiments with chemical warfare. It is time that all races have equal rights. It is time that any citizen that serves their government or pays a tax, no matter how large or small, is protected by their government. It is time..."

ᘓᙏ

Jeanette had no idea what was causing all the fuss coming from the other side of the room and she did not care. She knew a diversion when she saw one and she wasn't about to let it pass her by. Even Grandpa had risen to his feet and some sort of strange sound was coming from his throat.

Jeanette prayed to God he wasn't choking and, with a final hurried glance about the room, slipped out the side door.

Grandpa had not simply risen to his feet. He had stood so abruptly that he knocked over his chair and hit the table with his legs, disrupting the soup bowls and adding to the noise and agitation in the room.

The woman who had screamed, the same one who had dropped the dishes, sagged back against the wall, her hand over her heart, clutching at her throat. Her long dress was tangled about her legs.

Mari was part of Faith's staff but lent a hand in at the Castle when she could. It seemed that though the current amount of visitors was small by Castle standards, there was much going on and much to be done. She was glad to help.

Fletcher Mattatock, known to his family simply as "Grandpa," finally found his voice. "Mira!" he shouted though his constricted throat, his eyes bright with astonishment and tears.

He was around the table and standing in front of her faster than Sean had ever seen him move. Faster than Sean had thought him even capable of moving. He was before the stricken woman in mere seconds.

Mira's face, like the rest of her, was plump. Fletcher held out his hands to hold those round cheeks but pulled back at the last second as a bolt of fear flickered through him, holding him back. A million thoughts raced through his head, including the fact that maybe she did not want him to know her. After all, she had just screamed and dropped half a dozen plates.

She saved him from his fear by taking his own face in her hands. "Fletcher!" she sobbed, pulling his face to hers. Then he was kissing her cheeks, her eyes, her tears. She let him for long moments, relishing it, and then leaned back so she could see him better and laughed. "You got old!" she teased.

Fletcher laughed. "And you got more beautiful than ever!" he accused. "Though if you think I look old now, you should have seen me a few months ago. You wouldn't have recognized me!"

"I almost didn't!" Mira admitted, still laughing and crying. "I saw..." and here she lifted her tear-filled eyes to those sitting, stunned, at the table and sought out Sean.

Fletcher turned to see everyone watching with eyes like eggs. The kitchen and dining staff, seeing that Mari was alright, began cleaning up the broken crockery. Others began resuming their duties though there was a pause, most waiting to see if the soup course would be continued.

Currently, no one seemed to give a damn about the soup. The serving staff looked at each other, questioning, looking for direction. Usually, with the de Rossis there, direction was plentiful. If not by one of the sisters, then certainly by one of their aides. For now the staff, mostly made up of constructs, was at a loss.

Fletcher led Mari by the hand to the table and she hung back, suddenly shy.

John stood slowly, followed by Rebecca and Sean. The holo screen had been forgotten for the moment. Fletcher could feel his chest expanding until he thought it might rupture, and fresh tears blurred his eyes. He pulled Mira close.

"This is John," he said, struggling to keep his voice firm and steady, but his next sentence cracked on every word. "He is Joe's son."

Mira let out a choked cry and covered her face with her hands but John stepped forward and embraced her. Grandpa did not need to introduce her. John knew in his heart who she was and wrapped her in his arms.

"Little Joe," she sobbed into his shoulder, holding him in a vise-like grip. "I never met him," she cried. "He was Jack's son, I knew, but I never met him. I missed so much!" John's shirt began to soak through to his skin with her tears but he didn't back away. When she finally let him go he took her face in her hands and wiped the tracks off her cheeks with his thumbs in the same manner Fletcher had, years and years ago.

It brought a smile to her chubby face. And more tears.

"This is my wife Rebecca," John said, extending his arm to his wife. Mira hesitatingly held out her hand and Rebecca grasped it and pulled her into an embrace and hugged her. Mira choked back another sob as Rebecca let her go and John turned to his left. "And these are our..." He was about to say children when he saw there was only one. He sighed and shook his head. "This is our son, Sean."

"Hello," Sean, said, feeling like a goof.

Mira laughed and this time she initiated the hug, stepping close and wrapping him in her arms. She laughed into his blonde locks before she let him go. "You were actually the reason I screamed," she told him.

"I'm so sorry," he apologized quickly.

She laughed again and Sean thought the sound of her merriment was magical. "It's not your fault," she said. "It was mine. You look so much like Fletcher did when I met him, I thought you were a ghost!"

Mira looked around the room but, other than those who had risen from their seats from around the table, those remaining were Castle staff. The salad course had been cleared and others were standing by, keeping the soup hot until the guests were ready to be served or someone told them what to do.

"And I certainly must have been imagining things, because I thought I saw Fletcher – as I remembered him back then – and our daughter, Jean."

Sean turned his bright blue eyes to his grandfather. "Your daughter's name was Jean?" he asked, incredulous.

Grandpa gave him a nod and turned his own blue eyes to Mira. "You weren't imagining anything. That was Jeanette."

"Jeanette," Mira whispered. "That means little Jean, doesn't it?" she asked, slightly breathless.

"It does," Fletcher agreed, distracted. His gaze swept the room. "I don't know where she might have gotten off to..."

"She was saying earlier that her stomach was upset again," John said.

"Maybe it was something she ate," Rebecca suggested.

"Like what?" Sean asked, a sour look crossing his face. "She didn't eat a thing!" he told the others, dropping a hand towards her place at the table.

Indeed, her salad plate was still there, topped with greens. Next to it was a tiny plate with a dinner roll and a pat of butter shaped like a daisy. There was also a glass of water and glass of her new favorite juice. All were untouched.

◌◦◌

From the holo screen came a blast of static as the transmission was interrupted. The image on the screen was now of a man who had facial features that could have been Asian or Elfin – with high cheekbones and almond shaped eyes. He wore the belted ceremonial robe of the IGC Minister of Defense.

"People of the Seven Systems, this is Heinz Awon," he said. "Pay no attention to this slanderous broadcast. This man is delusional and a rebel. He is not to be aided or abetted by anyone unless they want to consider themselves an enemy of the state."

In the conservatory, Faith's anxious gaze went to Amberle whose dark fingers were flying over her keyboard with blurring speed.

"Just give me a sec," the young Jordan said. A literal second later she sat back and pointed at Faith.

Now it was Faith de Rossi who filled the screen. She was dressed in a cream-colored pantsuit, her brown and gold hair falling straight down her back, her neck draped with a heavy chain made of oval links alternating in gold and silver. Similar links hung from each ear. She clasped her hands in front of her belt, also a chain made of heavy links.

"I am Faith de Rossi," she announced to the camera that Amberle had set up in the conservatory of the Castle. "Dr. Silas is not delusional. He is a wise man whom I have worked with for many years. He, along with others of many races, has a vision for the future. A united and peaceful future for us all, led by group by the name of the Interstellar Alliance. It is a government that has been constructed on equality with a vision to lead, to protect, to prosper. I can back his affirmation that the Chimeran Rebellion is over. And I am backing the new organized government, the Interstellar Alliance."

She raised her chin and kept her brown and gold eyes trained on the camera even as she knew Amberle was switching the feed. When she heard the small click she turned her head to the flatscreen that had been floated into the conservatory on an air cart.

The screen flared to life and she could see the bridge of the *Macedonian.* Scarlett stood tall and proud, dressed in her crimson flight suit with the IA patch over her left breast, her dark waves of hair brushed away from her face. Bjorn stood beside her, strikingly handsome in blue coveralls with the IA patch.

"My name is Johanna Mattatock," she announced. "You know me better as Scarlett, the Jordan of the Red Fledgling. I am now aboard the once Chimeran Battle Cruiser *Macedonian.* As a Commander. The rebellion is over. I, along with my Fledgling and this entire crew, will back the new Interstellar Alliance."

෨෫

Jeanette slipped from the dining room with no small amount of nervous energy.

Step one was to get away from her family. *Done*

Step two, and what she thought would be the most difficult, was to evade any Castle appointed guard/assistant/escort.

Once outside of the dining room, however, only Rita was there, watching the current events on a pocket acrylic.

"Hello," she greeted amiably. "Can I help you find

something?"

Jeanette, having the strange hilarity that often gripped her Auntie Jo, almost asked her for directions to the underground hangar. Biting back laughter, the young lady simply asked where she could find the closest lavatory though she already knew.

"Oh," Rita exclaimed, looking right and then left.

Left, Jeanette prayed silently. *Left. I'll double back if I have to but...*

"Go down this way," Rita said, extending a hand to the left. "Then go left at the end of the hall and it will be right there on your right. It is a black door with a handle made of gold. Do you want me to go with you?"

Jeanette giggled, a sound warming and innocent – one she had unknowingly inherited from one of the First Seven. "That's okay," she assured her brother's guard. "I'm sure I can find it."

Rita gave her a smile and a nod and stepped back into the shadow of the hallway, her acrylic lighting her face as she resumed watching it.

Jeanette made her way down the wide corridor and turned left.

Step two. Done.

Step three should be easy enough as long as she could go unnoticed.

She glanced to her right as she passed the black door with the golden handle. Light shone in a rectangle around the doorway. She knew she was close.

The next door that caught her eye, and made her slow her steps, was just past the lavatory. It was also black but had no handle. No light came from around the entrance to whatever lay beyond. Her dark eyes went from side to side, up one hall and down the other. She knew that there was an elevator just around the corner, one that would quickly take her to her destination, but she could sense more than hear that particular passage was guarded by more than what her charm could get through.

Little Jean squared her narrow shoulders and pushed open the door, stepped through and let it swing shut behind her. Inside was utter darkness but it was only momentary. Her movement triggered a motion sensor and a dim light coming from the edge of the floor in front of her showed her a staircase leading down.

Otherwise, it was as black as the bottom of a well. The ceiling could be a hundred feet up or just above her head, there was not enough illumination to tell. Her heart in her throat, she crab-walked sideways until her outstretched hand touched a wall.

Jeanette tentatively went down a single step and the strip of faint light, coming from under the edge of the stair she was on went out. The next stair glowed with the same uncertain light.

In that manner, her path lit one step at a time, Jeanette Mattatock slipped down into the darkness.

ಀ

The universal broadcast switched next to the inside of Cyan. Noel de Rossi grinned at the camera she had put on Cyan's dash. She was a gruesome sight, her face scarred on one side from a chemical burn, one eye blue and one (new) eye black. She grinned, rippling the scarred flesh of her face as she leaned back and draped an arm over the back of her seat.

"This is Jordan Blue," she said. "I stand with the Interstellar Alliance."

Short and sweet, she thought, *just like me.*

The light on the camera blinked from green to red and, knowing her part was done, she reached to her right - out of the range of the camera, and picked up the glass of champagne she had waiting there.

She toasted to the stars and took a long drink. And belched. Her mismatched eyes moved to the screen on Cyan's dashboard that was showing their hijacked channel.

There was a buzz of static and Heinz was back for a few beats of the drum. He pulled down on his robe and lifted his chin as his tech team signaled to him that he was back on the galactic waves.

"This is a ridiculous display of treason! A few disruptive Jordans cannot promise you the safety you need. The Chimera are still a threat to us all!" There is more than just one Battle..."

Then his broadcast died, courtesy of Amberle, and was picked up from the bridge of the Battle Cruiser *Resurrection*. A man with a chest like a bull and hair like the sun stood tall in his blue coveralls and new IA patch and held his chin up.

"I am Jan Petrov, Commander of the once-Chimeran Battle Cruiser *Resurrection*. The Rebellion is over. We are now proud to be a part of the Interstellar Alliance."

At the Last Castle, Faith pressed her lips together in a smile and blinked back tears. Not just at seeing Evan standing tall next to Petrov, but seeing all of their long laid plans come to fruition. They had toiled so long, had given up those they had loved for this moment.

It was everything they had planned and it went through without a hitch. Not just an announcement but a promise to the peoples of the galaxies.

A stand. A united front.

Her tear-filled eyes went to Charity and her sister gave her a nod of acknowledgment. Of approval and pride. Her own eyes, emerald green, were also filled with tears.

Then the IGC resumed control, if only for a matter of time, and (to claim a phrase from Fletcher Mattatock) it all went to hell in a hand basket.

Another blur of static came from the cast and Heinz was once again back on the air, smoothing down his robe in a manner so calm that it was alarming to those watching from the Castle and those in their ships.

"The Chimeran Faction may be lessening, that is true. It is only due to the unflinching resolve and efforts of the IGC that this is happening."

Both Jordans in their ships and almost everyone watching the holo in the Castle rolled their eyes at this.

"But!" Heinz continued, "the galaxies are now facing a threat greater than the Chimera ever were!"

Eyes that had been looking skyward only a moment before were now intently watching the figure on the screen, scowls slowly taking shape.

"The barbaric race of Golgoths, bloodthirsty and uncivilized, who still live in societal castes that endorse both rape and slavery, threaten our borders once again. Some moons have already been infiltrated. Their battleships are entering our systems even as we speak. This new so-called government is in no place to negotiate peace with these animals, or to fight them..." he kept speaking but Scarlett had turned her attention to Bjorn.

The flecks of crimson in her dark eyes flared like fanned coals. "When I was here before, I saw Golgoth weapons in your Fighter Bay. Mainly a few pomegranate missiles and some tripedoe snares. How did you get those?"

Bjorn's blonde brows drew together in concern. "Chris. Why?"

Scarlett closed her eyes and sighed. Then she opened them and directed them to Bjorn's Communications Officer, *her* Communications Officer, Emma.

"Open the C com-line," she instructed. There was a click and Emma gave a her a nod. "Faith," Scarlett said, "the IGC is in league with the Golgoths. They have been for a year, or more."

In the conservatory in the Last Castle, Faith and Charity exchanged glances. Their eyes went to Amberle who, hands poised over her ghostpad, was looking none too pleased.

"Silas sent ground troops to both places you saw them and rooted them out," Faith said softly.

"There must have been more," Amberle said. "A lot more."

Charity was about to speak but paused as Awon leaned towards whatever camera was in front of him. "Even now, as I am addressing you, Golgoth Battleships are in the Seven Systems. It will be the IGC that negotiates peace with this race. This upstart group of rebels has nothing to offer and cannot protect you."

There were a few heartbeats of silence in the conservatory. In every room of every building and ship in the civilized galaxies beings watched with wide eyes and bated breath.

"Commander Mattatock," Faith addressed over the private comline shared with Petrov and the Jordans, "is he bluffing? Could there really be Golgoth ships in our system?"

Scarlett looked across the bridge to the Navigation Officer, Oliva. For all intents and purposes, she was Emma's twin. The beautiful construct began to shake her head, her long dark hair moving between her shoulder blades and then she froze and held up a slim-fingered hand.

"Yes. A Golgoth ship, Brigadier Battle Class, has entered our radar. One hundred kilometers away."

"Are they battle ready?" Bjorn asked.

Olivia turned to regard him with her large brown eyes. She gave him a nod.

"He's not bluffing," came Blue's voice from over the comline.

"A BC just dropped into my quadrant. He's a big bastard, and only 100 klicks away."

Blue could see the Cruiser all too clear, he was *that* close and *that* big. She put her left hand down on the armrest of her pilot's chair, reassuring herself with the smooth feel of Dragonskin.

The Jordan felt her hope diminish, but not her resolve.

Even the young Fledgling Dragon knew they were outmatched in strength and size. Like a flea next to a Mastiff.

We can take him, Blue was thinking, despite the odds. *It will most likely be in the kamikaze manner we saw that Chimeran pilot try. It's probably the only way - plunge right into him, just above his fuel tanks.*

The Jordan blinked her mismatched eyes. There were no tears in them, only purpose.

Cyan could sense she was contemplating her death, and his own. Four tendrils of quicksilver melted from the armrest to intertwine with the fingers of the Jordan.

I am with you, he sent.

The voice of Jan Petrov came over the com link. "Golgoth BC in our quadrant as well," he confirmed.

Then Faith spoke again over the private C line, her voice soft. "I am getting confirmed reports that there are similar ships that have entered our systems. One near Cicadia in the Flower. One in the Lesser Fall and two in the first and fourth quadrants in Andromeda."

Faith tried to breathe normally, to not hyperventilate nor hold her breath. So much depended on the small military force she had so recently formed. She cursed herself for her hubris, for her short-sightedness. Hope had once told her that Faith was always eight steps ahead. Her twin would have certainly foreseen and planned for this. She would have had a back up plan. And another.

The woman known to the universe as Faith de Rossi blinked away tears, knowing that what they had formed was formidable, but no match for what they were now facing. There were simply not enough of them.

We are small but mighty, she thought, reassuring herself. *We can do this.* She found herself holding her breath and forced herself to fill her lungs.

Scarlett stood tall in the bridge of the *Macedonian*. She knew what she was prepared to do, and knew she was capable of mounting the attack that was forming in her mind.

But Blue.

Out on her own.

A nineteen-meter Fledgling against a weaponized Brigadier the size of a Dragon or larger. She could see the Jordan's fate as if she were staring through Blue's newly mismatched eyes.

"What should we do?" she asked, and though it was heard by everyone over their private link, the question was for Blue. And Blue answered.

"What we always do. We fight."

Scarlett felt her chest expand even as she felt a buzzing on the top of her left ear and her dark eyes went wide.

It was her link to the Dragon.

Slowly, she reached up and pressed the stud that was embedded there.

"Jordan Scarlett, this is Captain Brogan. With your permission, I would like myself to be heard over the channel on which you are broadcasting."

"I hear you, sir," Scarlett replied, "please stand by." She repeated his request over the private com and Faith's eyes darted to Amberle.

"Can we do that, and delay it in case it is something we do not want aired?"

Amberle made a raspberry sound with her lips. "Easy peasy."

"Scarlett?" Faith intoned, "open your line with him to your ship, we will link to your camera and it will go through."

Then she looked at Amberle and motioned to the screen where Awon was babbling. The IGC minister was replaced by the image of the bridge aboard the Mace.

"This is Jordan Scarlett, Executive Officer of the Battle

Cruiser *Macedonian*. We have the Golgoth ship within our sights and stand ready to protect the Outer Banks. I am also receiving a message that should be heard."

She looked at Emma and gave her a nod. Emma's fingers danced on the console before her and then she turned in her chair and gave Scarlett a thumbs up signal.

"Go ahead, sir," Scarlett said.

Brogan's voice came through the link and was broadcast to every soul who had eyes and ears on the closest monitor.

"This is Captain Brogan of the once IGC Opal Dragon." Scarlett had to clench her jaw to keep it from falling open. "I stand with my Jordans, I stand with the Interstellar Alliance. And, as our Dragon is in the Flower, I stand ready to protect Cicadia."

Scarlett bit her lip as he continued, privately now, on her still-established link with the Dragon that only she and Blue could hear. "We rise as one, or we all go down together. Keep the IGC line open."

Though she was no longer obligated to follow his commands, she would not even think of doing anything else. She gave Emma a rolling motion with her hand to keep the com going.

Blue, out by herself on the edge of Aplesh grinned, filled with more joy and purpose than she had ever known. Then she heard another voice come over the cast, one that was only slightly familiar.

"This is Captain Slater, of the once IGC Beryl Dragon. I stand with the Interstellar Alliance and I stand ready to defend the First and Fourth Quadrants of Andromeda."

Blue, who was not on camera for the moment, let her own jaw drop open. The next voice she heard made her snap it shut. It was a familiar voice, but the tone and delivery were so alien that her eyes grew wide to hear it.

"And *this* is *Captain* Blaylock!" the voice announced with such a frightening abundance of glee that he sounded a bit mad. "*Captain* of the Copper Dragon! I, along with my salty crew, stand with the Interstellar Alliance and we are ready to blast the bejesus out of the Golgoths that are lurking in the Lesser Falls."

Blue's hands went up to cover her face in surprise and delight. They dropped only a moment later when Cyan sounded an alarm.

The Golgoth ship in front of her was opening. Fighter bays dropped their ramps, making the Brigadier Battleship look like a great metal behemoth opening its jaws.

Then, without warning, Cyan tipped wildly on his side and was pushed like a boat hit by a tidal wave. He slipped port and straightened as Blue checked her screens and stared out the eyes of her Fledgling at the ship that had suddenly amassed itself less than three hundred meters to her left.

"This is Captain Khasper," a voice announced with unchallenged authority. "Captain of the Iron Dragon. I stand with the… Interstellar Alliance. The Aplesh Ridge is safe from these bastards."

Then, over her private com in Cyan, "I have your back Jordan."

ᚼᛚᛟ

Jeanette wound her way down, down, down to the depths beneath the Castle. She had no idea the descent would be so long, and so dark. Determined, she made her way down. Just when she started to fear that the stairway was going to go on forever, or that she would never make it back up, there was a door.

It was so dark that she almost fell, trying to go down another step and then having nothing to step down to – just floor to walk out on. Reaching out with her hands, she felt her way along until she found the wall, and walked along it, gently pressing as she went.

Within a minute she was pushing, and the wall was giving way. It was a door. A salty breeze caressed her face and she could hear the distant sound of waves upon rock. She had found the hangar at last.

She slipped through the opening and looked around, cautious.

There was no one there.

The underground cave was huge, but well-lit now that the lights had come back on. Though, with no one there, they were set to fifty percent. Still, Jeanette looked around in wonder. It was certainly brighter than the stairwell. The tarmac stretched out before her and to her left for hundreds of yards, like the largest and most empty playground in the galaxy.

She walked towards the sound of water, having been instructed on what she was looking for, her hand absently going to her pocket. She walked carefully and slowly, glancing over her shoulder now and then to make sure she was truly alone.

When she reached the end of the macadam where waves lapped at the obsidian bank she pulled the object from her pocket. It was flat and round like a coin. JP had given it to her when they had met at the coffee shop.

She put her small thumb at the top and pulled it down a quarter way.

It was quiet for a moment and then the waters in front of her began to toss. They swirled and bubbled, becoming more wild and agitated by the second. Jeanette stepped back from the water that was now splashing up onto the blacktop and soon the rounded tips of six objects began to rise from the waves.

Upstairs, in the conservatory, Amberle jumped to her feet. It felt as if her insides were boiling, though she was not hot. Faith looked at her, feeling her fear but not understanding it.

"The eggs!" Amberle shouted. It was all she could voice. Then she turned and ran from the room.

Ember and Traejan, who had been in attendance to watch the broadcast, bolted to their feet at the Jordan's sudden movement. They needed no instruction. They ran after her.

☙☙

Despite the overpouring of happiness in the dining room, Sean knew that something was up. And he had the feeling it was going to be bad. Real bad.

"I'm going to check on Jeanette," he said. "She should be here for this reunion."

He received smiles and murmurs of encouragement from his parents and the two that were his, many times removed, grandparents. Sean left the room in time to see the oddest group of people run by the end of the hall – a dark-skinned young woman in military fatigues along with a woman with blood red hair and an elf who were armed with swords and knives. Sean ran after them.

Beneath his feet, the Castle began to tremble. Sean knew in his heart that the whole island was vibrating. His heart also told him it was Jeanette who had woken something from a deep slumber. Something dangerous.

Then the floor did more than tremble, it shook. Violently.

Sean ran faster.

# EPILOGUE

The World Director of Science and President of the United Southern Americas walked out onto the balustrade that surrounded the top floor of her villa. The home was palatial, a fortress that once belonged to the most notorious drug lord of the twenty-sixth century. The grounds surrounding it were so vast that she only knew where they ended when her limousine drove through the gate in the solid walls that were sixteen feet high and guarded twenty-four hours a day.

A cement rail, atop the row of hourglass-shaped concrete supports, ran the length of the balcony and she put her elbows on it, leaning into the evening air. The Venezuelan night was warm, as always, but there was a cool breeze that blew the strands of gold and brown hair away from her face.

She absently lifted her left hand to her chin and began to run her thumbnail back and forth over her lips. She had been on Earth for a hundred years now, much longer than she had planned. She done much, but not as much as she had hoped.

Earth was a diverse planet and changing its tune had been a tricky business. In some places it had been easy and simple. Other places, not so much.

South America had been the easiest. So many shaky governments, natural resources, and people wanting change. She had started in the country of Venezuela. She had it under control, and under her rule by the end of her second year on Earth.

Then she had united all of the countries in South and Central America.

She looked past the wall that surrounded the back of the property and into the dense green foliage across the river.

Queen of the Jungle she had joked more than once, but only when Thomas could hear her. She had hoped to keep her identity a secret when she went to Earth but the people of the south were nothing if not passionate. They needed more than a cause to fight for, but also a figure to rally around.

She had, much like churches of thousands of years past, sent out missionaries. *Missionaries of Faith*, they were called, though they carried with them technology, rather than bibles. Teams worked to establish clean water sources, medical centers, safe roads, a unified monetary system and military protection.

She repeated the process in Africa and the results had been the same.

Rather than rule both continents, she devised and there implemented a democracy with a representative from each country. All who answered to her, of course.

The Euro Bloc was next with the help of the Royal Family.

The Australian continent needed very little help yet was very cooperative with Faith's plans.

Still, after all this time and work, the Americas were still clinging to insane imbalances. *But,* she thought, *they are coming around.*

She looked up at the starry sky, knowing it was false. A mirror and a trap from which she could not escape. If she had been anything other than a scientist she would not have believed the monks had pulled off such an immense amount of work in such a short span of time.

Granted, they had worked on the project of terraforming and disguising the moon world of Eris for six years, but still such a short time for what they had managed. She had discussed it with Hope once long ago and her sister had called it dynamism.

Though Faith was not a physicist, she knew physics well enough to know Newton's First Law of Motion. An object, or a system, set in motion stayed in motion.

She held her chin up into the breeze, letting it caress her face. It was always so damnable hot during the day but the nights could be quite pleasant. Her wardrobe now, when in country, was nearly completely comprised of tailored suit vests and short matching skirts.

The breeze picked up, cooling her skin, and she straightened, rubbing her hands up and down her bare arms. Her left palm passed over the ripple of a scar. It was faint, hundreds of years old, and self-made. She had done it when she was still a freshly made doll, created by Cronus to be a companion for his granddaughter.

They had let the girls stay together in the hospital. It would be silly not to since they were already inseparable. Alone, that first night, as her twin slept soundly after she had been given something for the pain, she had replicated the scar left by a vaccination that had made Faith deathly ill. She bound her own arm and snuck into a room that stored aesthetic medical supplies. She found a syringe of silicone and filled in the scar on the arm of her twin.

The rest of the memory came unbidden, like something blown into her from the depths of the jungle across the river.

It was Soonday. No school and they had already been to the One Church for blessings and prayers. The twins fussed over the baby; she was holo-book adorable. Round pink cheeks and bright blue eyes and a constant, if toothless, smile.

Young Faith de Rossi and her doll, her twin, Gwendolyn cooed over her and tickled her under her chin until Mother waived them away.

"Go outside and play," she instructed with a dazzling smile as she scooped up the baby. "Charity needs to take a nap. I'll

make you a snack as soon as she's asleep," she promised, moving towards the glider chair.

The girls obeyed without a fuss, racing each other outside, laughing. Faith reached out as she always did to clasp Gwendolyn's small hand in her own.

"What should we do?" Faith asked, her brown and gold eyes bright.

"Let's go look at the ants!" Gwen suggested with enthusiasm. She had spent the day before constructing a city of twigs around an anthill while Faith had made crowns out of daisies. Faith was always making pretty things. Gwen liked to make practical things.

The sky was the palest of blues and the air was filled with the smell of new grass and orange blossoms. In unspoken agreement the girls hurried to the far side of the tree that spread over the small yard on the side of the de Rossi home. Gwen was down on her stomach almost immediately, examining her handiwork while Faith sought out the crowns of flowers she had left in the grass.

"I made them four bridges," Gwendolyn remarked as she observed the ant colony hard at work, "but they are only using one."

Faith gathered the circlets she had left in the grass, putting her hand through each one until they hung from her small arm like bracelets of flowers. She looked up as Gwendolyn puzzled over the behaviors of the ants.

"I'm going to hang these in the tree," Faith decided aloud. "I want to decorate it, like a Christmas tree, but in the spring!"

Gwendolyn shifted her gold and brown eyes from the ants to the tree, her nascent but already well-advanced mind calculating Faith's weight and the strength of the branches. Satisfied, she turned her attention back to the three bridges that had gone unused by the ants.

Faith had climbed deftly, if delicately, up the tree and was hanging her first "decoration" when she fell.

There was a quick cry of surprise and then a terrible silence that followed the thump of her small form hitting the ground.

Gwen screamed even as she was rushing to the side of her twin, unconscious in the grass. Knowing nothing about the dangers of moving an injured body, Gwen snaked her small arm behind Faith's neck and tried to raise her.

"Faith!" she cried, seeing the pallor of her skin. A large bump was beginning to swell on the side of her forehead, like an egg. "Faith!"

A second later, Christa de Rossi was there, kneeling in the grass by the young dyer.

"What happened?" she asked, putting the back of her hand against Faith's cheek, then her forehead.

Panic flared inside Gwen, bright and sharp like a flash of lightning upon a steel wire.

What if Faith was seriously hurt? Seriously hurt, as in the horrifying possibility she might not open her eyes? Gwen was just a doll, a plaything. What happened to toys when a child died?

Her imagination was limited but it did not take much to know that playthings were thrown away.

"Gwen fell and hit her head," she told Mother. "I don't know what to do! Is she going to be alright? What do I do?"

Just then, Faith's eyelids began to flutter. "What happened?" she mumbled.

Christa cupped her cheek with her hand. "It's okay, Gwen," she told her. "You had a little fall, but you're okay. Stay still, I'm going to call a Medcar." She looked, unknowingly, at the dyer. "Stay with her, Faith, I'll be right back."

Faith's eyes fluttered again. "Faith?" she asked, looking at her dyer, confused.

Gwen ran her hand over her twin's head, gently smoothing

the tangled gold and brown hair away from the lump. "Yes," she whispered. "Just for now, we'll switch..." she was going to say switch back (they often played switch, at home and at school, delighting in fooling others) but Faith moaned.

"I feel sick."

Her twin helped her turn and held back her tangle of hair as she threw up in the grass. The dyer used her sleeve to wipe Faith's mouth and then moved so she could cradle her head in her lap.

Christa came back out, this time carrying baby Charity. "The medics are on their way," she told the girls. The baby blinked her blue eyes in surprise at being taken from her nap into the bright sunshine just as there was a squeal of a siren.

The medics drove their aircar over the grass next to the side of the house and were in the backyard within moments.

"One of my girls had a fall," Christa explained, trying to keep her voice steady as one medic leaned down and shone a light in Faith's eyes while the other popped open an air gurney.

"She has a concussion," the man with the penlight said. "We'll take her to Mt. Holland Hospital, it's the closest. I'm sure the doctor there will want to do a scan to see if there is any swelling in her brain."

"Oh!" Christa cried out, her free hand coming up to cover her mouth. The baby made a toothless frown and began to whimper, feeling her mother's distress. The second medic gently lifted Faith and put her on the air gurney and began to fasten straps over her chest and legs.

"You can ride with us, ma'am," he said, "but, we don't have an air seat for the baby."

"Oh!" Christa exclaimed, distressed once again but thinking quickly even as the girl on the floating cot was starting to blink her eyes once more. "Faith," she instructed the dyer, "you ride with Gwen. I'll follow in the Spiritu."

It was the small (old and outdated) family aircar the de

Rossi's owned. The dyer nodded as the man was lifting Faith into the back of the Medcar.

"Hello there, beautiful. What's your name?"

Faith de Rossi, her eyes finally starting to clear but the confusion still plain on her young face, frowned as she thought and looked at those around her. "Gwen?" she asked timidly. "I'm Gwen?"

"That's right," the medic agreed amiably as he reached out to help the other little girl into the airbulance. "And you have nothing to worry about. Your sister is here to help take care of you." He turned his soft brown eyes to the girl who was obviously a twin sister. "And you are Faith, is that right?"

"Yes," the little agreed, frightened as she must be by the fall of her sister. "I am Faith."

Faith de Rossi, as she had been known since that day in the backyard almost four centuries ago, cast her gold and brown eyes up once again at the stars.

There was something in the air tonight.

Something was happening.

She smiled and turned to go back into the villa. Clear walls of bullet-proof Perspex slid closed behind her and the air-cooling system kicked on. She crossed an enormous living room floored in polished white marble.

Ornately carved chairs, sofas, and chaises upholstered in cream-colored velvet kept company with statues, sculptures, chest-high hand painted vases, and other forms of priceless art.

The President of the United Southern Americas walked down a long hallway, also decorated with masterpieces gleaned from every corner of the world, and a few others before Earth was cut off from the others, her heels clicking on the smooth stone.

She stopped before she reached her personal chambers

where there was a single room behind darkened glass. Faith placed her left hand over the panel on the wall and part of the glass partition slid open and she stepped inside.

In here it was even cooler, this room having its own special freogenic unit to keep the cryo box from over working. The walls were dark stone and the ambient lighting was low.

There was only one thing in the room - a single cryogenic chamber.

The cold preservation unit was topped with a long box that looked much like a glass coffin, the clear chamber between waist and chest high.

Faith put a hand against the glass and looked at the body inside. It had taken a beating, to say the least, and Faith had spent her first few months on Earth diligently, almost relentlessly, in operating rooms and grow chambers - regrowing not just the hair that had burned off, but an entire arm that had been ripped from the body. Skin grafts over radiation burns and regrowing the right lung.

When all was said and done, Faith decided to keep the unconscious form sleeping. It would be good to slowly keep the body repairing itself and, besides, her sister had always had a predilection for cryo.

The body lay peacefully, at least to the observer, in a long dress of green velvet embroidered with gold thread, her hands clasped under her breasts as if holding an invisible bouquet of flowers.

Copper colored curls framed a heart-shaped face that was spattered with freckles.

Inside the glass, Hope was restored.

Faith walked slowly around the narrow case, a smile on her lips and her fingers trailing along the edge.

"I think they are coming for us," she confided softly. "After all these years, I think they are finally coming for us." She paused as she reached the center of the chamber and placed her left hand down on the glass, eight inches over the heart of the woman in cold slumber. "Love," Faith whispered.

AUTHOR'S NOTE

My modus operandi is to end with a quote but, for this story, there was one for every chapter. I couldn't resist. You might be wondering why I did not use one of the most famous ones - by Ben Franklin - "three may keep a secret if two of them are dead." I had actually liked that one for years and had it slated for a chapter when (one night - probably deep into a good bottle of red wine) I thought, *no shit, Ben. One hundred may keep a secret if ninety-nine are dead.* And I just can't bring myself to kill *everyone.*

I started this series almost fifteen years ago and left the first book along with the ones that followed fraught with questions. So my question for you now is, *have I answered enough?*

I think so.

From my fans it's a mixed bag. The two readers I get the most feedback from are, no surprise here, my husband and my sister. She says I should have at least one more. My husband thinks I have wrapped things up nicely. I think he is just tired of leftovers during writing season.

I guess the real question at the end of this book is the same as the end of every book (not just my own): is this the end?

Here are some answers:

Does any story ever end?

Refer to the Author's Note in *Rings of Saturn*: we don't get to choose when the story ends. Our own or anyone else's.

Also, how the hell should I know?

I'm not just jerking you around with these answers, I stand

behind each and every one of them.

One, my belief is that no story ever ends. Even if humanity on Earth is wiped out the story will go on, hopefully narrated by Morgan Freeman.

Two, we really don't get to choose when the story ends. Our own or anyone else's.

I almost saw my own story end three times in the past five years.

The last time I felt the Grim Reaper looking over my shoulder I had just finished this book and realized, as the plane was trying to land without any visibility at three hundred feet, that the only copy was on my computer.

Under my seat.

Three, I know how this tale ends about as much as I know how my own will. I know the outline and the plan, but the details are not set and certainly not guaranteed. Which is why I wrapped this story up to the extent of my knowledge and ability.

Do I hope there is another tale to this story? I do.

I hope my story goes on as well. And yours.

Stories, like souls I believe, are infinite.